# There Will Be a Highway There

**Dave Kyger**

WESTBOW
PRESS
A DIVISION OF THOMAS NELSON

WestBow Press books may be ordered through booksellers or by contacting:

WestBow Press
A Division of Thomas Nelson
1663 Liberty Drive
Bloomington, IN 47403
www.westbowpress.com
1-(866) 928-1240

ISBN: 978-1-4497-1593-9 (sc)
ISBN: 978-1-4497-1594-6 (dj)
ISBN: 978-1-4497-1592-2 (e)

Library of Congress Control Number: 2011930222

Printed in the United States of America

WestBow Press rev. date: 5/20/2011

# Foreword

Pieces of the characters you will meet in this story have floated in and out of my head like butterflies mixed with jagged clouds for as long as I can remember. It feels good to tie them up in print so I can let them live together on these pages. Maybe my daydreams and nightmares won't be so cluttered now.

Cambridge Town and Cambridge County do not exist anywhere except in my imagination. None of the characters exist but pieces of them may have. None of the circumstances that take place in this saga ever occurred, but they could have. Fighting, loving life, hunting and politics are a way of life for us Virginians and great sources of entertainment and speculation. I hope you enjoy the tale!

I would like to sincerely thank the following:

K.B. Getz for the use of his photo on the cover; Chris Bolgiano, who gave me the right encouragement at the start; Cameron Nickels, who entered the game in the 9th inning and opened my eyes; my wife, Pirjo Nylander, who introduced me to Finland with its beauty, intrigue, and powerful people; Vernon and Kelley Hughes, for the use of their inspirational song 'Trust Jesus'; Jane Smootz, who gave me needed encouragement and suggestions; my father, William Kyger, a fine story-teller; Earl Ritchie and Raymond Phillips, who gave me a mental tour of Alaska; and Uncle Bud Neff, who stormed the gates of hell during the Normandy invasion. I would like to give a special thanks to my friend and colleague Larry Barnett who was a great policeman and fought a heroic battle of his own against cancer. Larry's great faith in God and his interaction with the early chapters of this book was the finest inspiration to me. Most of all, thanks to my Father in Heaven who makes all things possible.

# Part 1
# The Launching Pad

# Chapter 1

September 1994

His huge hands wrapped around the rail in front of the electronically opened doors, and he felt the warm air from inside brush over his face. His legs ached, his shoulders hurt, and his size seventeen feet felt like they had been beaten by a baseball bat. His gut hung over his belt like a sandbag that gravity and time had pulled from a retaining wall. The walk he had taken stretched longer than he had planned, and John was tired and worn out. He was wondering if he could make it into the cafeteria. Seventy-one years of dragging a six-foot-seven, 316-pound body over the hills of western Virginia and half of Europe during World War II, and then the Korean War, had not done much for the condition of his knees and hips. But his grandson Davy had promised that if John walked every day to build his strength up, then he would take him to the Mountain Top Reunion the first weekend of October. Davy was true-blue loyal and John's only remaining hope in life.

The Mountain Top Reunion had been held every year for close to one hundred years. All the neighbors, cousins, and offspring of the families that had settled and tamed the Shenandoah Mountain highlands would get together over an old-fashioned community picnic at Ben Dean's cabin on top of Lost Mountain. There would be tons of food, a pickin' session by all the bluegrass musicians, horseshoe contests, and the inevitable brown jug making its rounds, smuggled in behind the women's backs. Even better than the reunion, Davy had promised him that if he would take care of himself and get in shape, Davy would come and take him deer hunting up at the home place when the season opened in November. That was plenty of incentive to give John hope of getting out of this place he secretly called "Jesus' Launching Pad," if just for a little while.

With a pull on the rail and a roll of his head, John made it through the first set of doors and sat down on the small bench in the vestibule beside the ash tray and plastic leafed plants. There was strictly no smoking allowed in the building and very few of the residents smoked at all, but the ones who did used this area to do so. The doors shut, and he sat alone for a few minutes getting himself together before going into the lobby of the Brethren Home where he had lived for the last two years since Fern had died. He watched as a couple of moths and a dobsonfly crawled and fluttered around the bright glow of the fluorescent light along the outside porch ceiling, seeking reprieve from the certainty of the coming coolness of the late September twilight. His legs started getting stiff and his back hurt.

Two old women walked toward the door. The electronic beam caught their movement and the doors jumped open. He could hear the clanking of silverware and sounds of supper being served. The odor of cafeteria-fare meatloaf wafted to him as one of the ladies said, "John, you better get in there! You'll miss supper." He shifted in his seat and turned away from them with a grunt. He didn't like those two. Their compliments sounded too much like sarcasms to him. No wonder their husbands were long dead and probably glad to be gone from two old bats like that. The one named Sarah said with a sneer, "John, your zipper is down."

John got up, towering over the two women, nodded to them, and shuffled through the door toward supper and zipped his pants up as quickly as he could. The black girls that worked in the dining room were more to his liking. They weren't so quick to point out irritating things and liked to joke with him. He grabbed a tray and went down the line. "How you doin', Mr. John?" bucktoothed Mary asked. One side of her nametag sagged down on her ample breast, and John hoped the little round clip that was supposed to hold the back side of the peg in place had fallen down her bra rather than into the mashed potatoes and meatloaf gravy she was ladling out. Her upper lip rode out over her front tooth as it stretched her big mouth into a smile. John replied, winking, "If I was twenty years younger I would take you out and show you how I'm doing."

"You too big for me, Mr. John. Way too big. Big man like you cost too much fo' me to keep."

"I got money, woman," he bantered. "Don't need nobody keeping me. Load that tray up so I don't have to come back for seconds before I sit down.

Bucktoothed Mary piled the tray up and John grabbed four wheat rolls and six patties of butter. He reached for more, but Mary smacked his knuckles with her serving spoon: "What good it do fo' you to go walkin' if you just gonna load your plate wif all that food?"

John grunted and took off with his tray. If there was anything that made him rile up it was somebody getting on him for eating too much. All his life he had been in the habit of eating very little for a couple of days and then gorging himself to the point of danger when the notion hit. In here, they wanted you eating regular and not too much at a time. Tonight he could have eaten the whole pan of meatloaf, chased it with the other pan of mashed potatoes and then drunk the rest of that gravy if they would let him. He had put on many eating exhibitions for the heck of it over his time. Mostly to show off. One evening not long after Fern died, he was downtown, and sat down at the counter of a little hot-dog joint owned by a Greek guy. John had joked to the waitress, "I'm so hungry I could eat thirty of those little hot dogs." The Greek spoke up and said, "You eat thirty dogs, I pay for them. You don't make thirty, you pay for them, big man."

John asked the girl to start fixing those dogs five at a time and not to spare the chili. He also told her to set a six-pack of warm Dr. Pepper up there to wash them down. Cold ones made his head hurt. John polished off the thirty hot dogs in twenty-two minutes as the Greek sweat bullets, not believing what he was seeing. The most anybody had ever eaten there in twenty-six years of truck drivers and college students from the local university had been nineteen by a 300-pound football player. That guy had walked out the door and promptly lost them on the sidewalk. John horsed the thirty hotdogs down with no trouble, and as the last one disappeared he told the girl, "That was pretty good. Fix me a couple more." The irate Greek went off and started cussing, yelling, "You got your damn hot dogs! Get the hell out of here!"

John stood up and rumbled, "Don't give me any crap. I didn't throw out the challenge, you did!" Storming out the front door, he walked down the street to another little grill and ordered two more hot dogs. He carried them back to the Greek's greasy joint and beat on the front window. When he was sure everybody was looking at him, especially the Greek, he shoved both hot dogs in his mouth and swallowed them. Sticking his head back in the door he yelled at the waitress, "What time is it, Honey?"

She looked up at the clock over the counter and said, "Twenty to six."

"I gotta run. Sorry to leave good company so early but my wife has supper ready at six every evening, and she'll be mad if I'm late!"

The Greek threw his dishrag at the window and John left smiling. He walked down the street in the gathering darkness, but his smile wilted as it hit him again with the impact he had felt under mortar attack in Germany: Fern was not at home, and no supper was waiting; she was cold in the ground. That happened three years ago, and not long after that his grandson Davy talked him into selling the house and moving into "Jesus' Launching Pad."

John sat alone at the first table he came to and cleaned up his plate. He ate it all in about four minutes and looked up to see Mary putting the trays in the refrigerator. John wondered what it would be like to live with the bucktoothed black woman. Probably pretty nice. She is an honest person and friendly. When she takes her clothes off tonight, maybe she will find that little clip she lost from her name tag. He chuckled to himself.

Back in his room he sat down in his recliner. Flipping on the TV, Andy Griffith and Goober were at a dance with Helen and Thelma Lou, who had a date with Gomer. Goober was doing his "Judy, Judy, Judy" impersonation of Cary Grant. A public service announcement came on and the local Sheriff, who had gotten elected for the most part because of his looks and family money, was telling all the senior citizens how to avoid credit card fraud. "Must be election year again," he thought. Every four years senior citizens and Special Olympics became popular for little jerks like this Sheriff who was smiling at him from the TV screen in what amounted to a free political advertisement. The old women in the Launching Pad thought the Sheriff was just great, but John knew a fake when he saw one. He cut down the volume and picked up a <u>Virginia Wildlife</u> magazine that Davy had left for him to look at. Davy was the only one out of the whole bunch that gave a damn about him. John's son, John Jr., was still up in Alaska fooling around, trying to make a living with a bulldozer. Davy's mother had pretty much raised the boy alone until she and John Jr. had divorced in the late '70s. For a couple of years, all of them were better off for it. Then one day right out of the blue, she had left a note for Davy and said she wouldn't be back. She added that she was sorry. Davy had come to live with John and Fern. He never did get mad at either one of his parents, and it always was a wonder to John Sr. that Davy turned out so good. John Jr. would make a lot of money working long hours with his bulldozer and then lose it all on some off-the-wall venture. He always seemed to keep the bills paid for Judy and little Davy, though. Until she had left too. John Sr. always blamed Vietnam for the way his son lived and acted. He seldom called and never wrote except at Christmas. Davy, on the other hand, was true blue -- wouldn't let him down or anyone else down, for that matter. He was a steadfast young man, and John Sr. was proud of him. He had taught Davy to cut and lay stone, and until John had retired after Fern died they had run a masonry business and were never short of work. Made good money too. Davy had a couple of part-time boys working with him now, and John missed going to work. Missed it bad. Work had been his sole purpose in life and now he had none.

Leafing through the Virginia Wildlife magazine he came to an article about deer management and the problems of deer in the cities eating people's shrubbery and causing wrecks. They ought to run all the Yanks off who moved down here from up north and just let people shoot the bothersome deer, John thought. That would solve a lot of problems. John's neighbor in the next room was a retired probation and parole officer from New Jersey and he was a first-class jerk. He always liked to make fun of John's size and make smart comments in front of other people at John's expense. His name was Rennick and he had overheard Davy tell John he would take him hunting with him. Rennick had told everybody, "That boy is not going to drag Big John along with him hunting. The old man is just dreaming! Besides, he couldn't shoot a deer in somebody's backyard eating up bird feeders and flower gardens, much less go to the mountains with those boys. Too fat and old!"

John had told him to mind his own business and to shut up or he would kick his skinny Yankee butt out of the building. Rennick laughed. He was one of those guys that didn't like men bigger than himself and knew exactly how to get under their skin and just how far to push them. Sooner or later, John would show him.

But soon he fell asleep in the chair as the faint sounds of Andy Griffith's whistling theme song played homage to another day.

About 2 A.M. he woke up and had to go to the bathroom. That was a nightly occurrence now and sometimes twice a night. He had a hard time getting back to sleep and kept a book by the bed to read just for such times. Exceptional vision had always blessed him, but now he had trouble reading without the use of some reading glasses he had bought at the Dollar Store. *Essays by Mark Twain* was one of his favorites, and he could start anywhere and begin reading with interest. Tonight Twain was going on and on with a letter to God from the "Accounting Angel."

Putting the book down, John prayed, and tried asking forgiveness for his many sins. With a shudder he wondered how he would fare in front of Saint Peter when he went on down that road soon. It was hard to stay on the subject when praying. With best intentions at attempts to give thanks and talk to God, invariably his mind would drift to things like bucktoothed Mary right when he was struggling to make a point with the Lord. When his mind would stray from his prayer he would snap back to attention with a feeling of guilt. He truly wondered if Satan was the one who made his mind wander so. John had tried to talk to Fern about these things, but she just gave him the look that meant she thought he was crazy sometimes. And she was right. At least the talk with God comforted him to the point that he was able to doze off again around three o'clock and escape the demons of war memories and lifelong shortcomings.

John's doctor came by to see him the next morning. Dr. Malone walked into his room and caught John sitting in his underwear on the edge of the bed. His gut hung over his lap so that he looked like he was nude, even when he had his shorts on. Malone said, "Doesn't look much like you lost any weight in here, John."

"No, and I don't care to either. I like to eat and it's one of the very few things I still like to do and am good at. Comes easy to me, kind of like breathing. I may commit suicide by eating some day. Just start eating and not stop until I blow up."

"Yeah, I hear you. Still need to get some of that weight off," the doctor said. "You must be taking your medicine every day. I haven't had any complaints on your behavior and that's a good thing." John had dealt with some obsessive-compulsive problems for most of his later adult life, after he retired from the service and "went off the deep end" as Fern had put it a couple of times. The doctors called it battle fatigue or war shock. One time he ended up naked on Main Street and climbed a telephone pole up about twenty feet. He didn't remember much about it except what people had told him and all the splinters he had to have taken out of the insides of his legs and arms. Some of them still bothered him and would need to be dug out occasionally. Then there was the time he made love to Fern and lost track of things. If Ben Dean hadn't stopped by and heard her sobbing and calling for help, his weight would have smothered her. She was so embarrassed. Some people had called him a pervert when he was younger. His physical appetite and his sexual appetite were always constant companions and had caused him problems here and there. He had been with hundreds of women in France, Germany, Korea, and elsewhere.

"You can bet I don't need to be told to take my head medicine," he told his physician. "I don't want to end up at Western State Hospital again. Those people up there are crazy! They tried to put a straightjacket on me and the only thing that kept them from doing it was they didn't have one big enough to fit around my gut. And you want me to quit eating and slim down so they can hogtie me the next time? I don't think so! I got claustrophobia anyways, and that place scares the Beetlejuice out of me."

The doctor chuckled and said, "John, you have been one of the most interesting patients I've had over the years and I have to tell you something. I won't be coming around making these visits anymore after the first of the year. I'm going to retire. Beth and I are going to move to Florida."

John stood up, stretched tall, and shook the short doctor's hand. He thanked him for all his help over the years and sincerely told him he would miss him.

After Dr. Malone left, John sat down in his recliner and flipped on the TV. A little Irish runt game show host was acting like he could still have a chance with the brain-dead blonde he was playing slap and tickle with. John got to thinking about the Doc and his wife going to Florida and suddenly tears ran down his long cheeks and slid into the folds of his chin.

John thought eating himself to death might not be so bad. If he did, he would make a point of doing it at the Greek's greasy spoon. Overdose on hot dogs and Dr. Peppers. Ha! He turned the TV to ESPN to catch the review of the Braves' play-off game. Then he thought about Davy, and, with a smile, he couldn't wait until Sunday. Going to the Mountain Top Reunion! By golly, that was something to look forward to!

# Chapter 2

Unexpectedly on Saturday morning about ten thirty Davy came rolling into the Brethren Home and told John to get a clean flannel shirt on with his coveralls. He said they were going to leave right then to go to Ben Dean's cabin to get the pig and the goat roasted for tomorrow's picnic. John was so excited that he rolled up out of his recliner and knocked over the magazine rack next to his chair. Davy patiently picked the magazines up and put them back in the righted rack, laughing at how his grandfather was acting like a kid.

"Calm down, Grampa! I didn't mean to excite you so much," the young man said as he watched his giant grandfather digging for clothes. "Grab your old guitar and lets go!"

"I thought I was going to have to work this evening at the football game helping the Ruritans direct traffic, but Tex Campbell said he wouldn't need me and I'm glad he didn't. I'd much rather go up on the mountain this evening. My wife said she'll come up tomorrow, so we can have the night with the boys and help with the barbecue. Ben called and said to get you and come up this afternoon to help him get the fire pit going. There's plenty of bunks and blankets, so we'll just stay up there tonight and come back tomorrow night after the reunion. You do want to go, don't you, Grampa?"

"Sure, sure," John replied as he jerked a blue and gray plaid flannel shirt out of his drawer slamming it shut with a pair of socks hanging halfway out. "You better bet I wanna go! Who else is coming?"

"I think the Judge and McNally are coming. The Trumbo twins might come but they'll probably go to the race in Charlotte if the guy from the parts store calls with extra tickets. Ben'll be there, and I think Leroy and Jake will probably come and bring their music. Ben's been wanting to limber up his fiddle. Said he ain't played enough to keep the cobwebs out and needs to knock the rust off of Grampappy Nimrods old fiddle. I got two new cans of Copenhagen in my pocket and a case of beer already on ice in the cooler. Don't forget to bring your medicine along and your guitar."

John was hooking up the shoulder straps on his coveralls and heading out the door and hadn't even tied his shoes. He turned back and fumbled in his medicine cabinet, pouring pills into an empty bottle from three different prescription bottles. When he was done he shoved the bottle in the pocket on the chest of his coveralls and zipped it shut, heading for the door as he jammed his favorite Virginia Tech hat down on his head. He reached in the corner and grabbed has old beat-up Gibson Southern Jumbo that looked like a toy in his hands. His old Army buddy Svenson got hard up and sold him the guitar for thirty dollars when they were back in the States fresh from Germany. John had dragged that guitar with him all over the world while pulling his twenty in the Army. It showed all the abuse. Svenson had tried a hundred times to buy it back but John wouldn't sell it back to him. Davy laughed out loud. It made him feel good to see the old man so obviously surprised and motivated.

One Sunday last spring Davy had come to the Brethren Home to visit, and it alarmed him to see his grandfather lying in bed, looking so gray and old and hopeless. *Pitiful* and hopeless, he thought. Just like the old man had given up was how it appeared to him. It had been a spur of the moment notion Davy had come up with, the idea of telling the old giant that he'd take him up on the mountain to the reunion and then maybe take him hunting—but only on the condition John would get some exercise. He had had no idea it would motivate the old man so much. His color was better now, and he'd obviously been walking. Davy wished his own father could be there to go along, but he was somewhere in Alaska, fooling around like always. As they headed out through the lobby, heads turned to stare but John was oblivious. His strides were four feet long, and Davy had to hustle to keep up, nodding to the ladies as they hustled past.

John didn't like riding in Davy's little truck and just barely fit in it, but they finally made it up all the switchbacks to the top of the mountain.

Then it was over the long dusty road that rambled along the top of the ridges to Ben's farm. There were lots of blueberries along the road and John kept wanting to pick some. Davy stopped at a good wide spot and let him go at it. John soon had purple fingers and a tongue to match. The berries were large and sun-ripened. Finally, as John waded into the briars like an old bear trying to fatten up for winter by eating handful after handful of the succulent blueberries, Davy had to threaten to leave him. Back to the truck at last, John said he would just as soon ride standing on the back of the truck, holding onto the cab. Davy dropped the tailgate and after three heaves John made it up on the back grinning like a boy.

They made a curious sight as they arrived at the sturdy log cabin after about an hour's ride. Sitting on the porch swing, Ben was sawing on his fiddle, his gray beard nearly covering the bottom half of the old reddish-brown instrument. It had been passed to him from his Uncle Nimrod Dean, legendary throughout the mountains as an old-time fiddler and liquor maker. The fiddle was priceless and so was the sound that vibrated off the strings. Ben was playing an old reel Nimrod himself had composed and passed down with the instrument that he called "Hopping Crow." When Davy pulled the little truck into the yard, with John standing up in the back with blueberry stains all over his face, making his chin look like he had clown makeup on, Ben quit playing and started laughing raucously.

"What in the world are you hauling on the back of your truck, Davy boy?" Ben asked. "I didn't know you had a permit to haul horse manure!"

John lumbered off the small truck and was smiling from ear to ear as he strode up to the porch carrying his guitar. Ben had built the cabin himself with the help of the Judge, Mac, John, and Davy. He had poured a cement slab forty by twenty and cut poplar trees, rolling them into place with his big red Massey Ferguson tractor and its front-end loader. John, Davy, and all of the crew helped, and it became a project they worked on for over a year as they notched the logs and chinked them up with cement and gravel. They laid a gigantic fireplace out of mountain stone on the west end of the building. The entire one-room log and stone building with cement floor and a loft was a refuge to all of them. Bunk beds lined the back wall and the loft had several mattresses on the floor. It would sleep twenty people during hunting season or when they had big events like the reunion.

Ben was always glad to see them. He walked over to John and shook his berry-stained hand. Ben, being a musician and a good one, always marveled at the unbelievable size of his cousin John's hands and was always scared John would get carried away and crush his own small hands while shaking, thus ending his fiddling. Ben couldn't fathom how John's giant fingers could move so quickly over the neck of the guitar. John could run the chords like Jimmy Martin. When Ben shook hands with John he took as slight a grip as possible. On the other hand, John thought Ben shook hands like a sissy.

Davy and John got the wheelbarrow and went to the woodpile next to the edge of the woods and started hauling cured hickory chunks down to the fire pit not far from the well pump. When they got it stacked up just right, Ben came down, squirted lighter fluid on the wood, and lit it with a kitchen match. Stepping back from the sudden inferno he said, "We gonna need a bunch of coals for the pig the Judge and McNally is bringing. He said it's gonna weigh about 280 pounds dressed so we need to get it started around midnight. The goat we won't put on until about daylight."

The fire gradually caught up after the initial blaze and they had a satisfactory fire in no time. John took a five-gallon bucket and pumped water into it, soaking the ground all around the fire pit. Ben and John sat on the porch while Davy kept watch on the fire. The afternoon grew cooler and the crickets were singing their farewell song on the early September evening. A few mares-tail clouds spiraled out over the mountain as the shadows crept toward them from the ridgeline to the west where a couple of sweet-gum trees were showing their early brilliant red.

Ben, an old widower, was interested in John's life at the Brethren Home. He had married as a young man. His wife and the baby boy had died in childbirth on a rainy Easter Sunday only a year after he had married. The fiddle absorbed his sorrow and consumed his life, blocking the pain as he searched to find order and meaning in his misery. He could scarcely talk to anyone for weeks at a time while working at the apple-packing shed during the day and pouring his soul out through the strings of his violin at night. Neighbors would hear the forlorn notes of his instrument coming from the graveyard where his darlings slept.

Over time he crept back into the world of the living and after a few years he surprised everyone when he bought 200 acres on top of the mountain from old Nimrod's brother Justin who was ninety-two years old at the time. Ben would drive up there on weekends and camp by himself in the back of his old pick-up truck. He got himself a tractor with a front-end loader. Then he bought a six-foot Bush Hog mower and cleaned up the fields. The next project was to build up the stone walls and split rail fences. Mac asked him why he was fixing up the fences, pointing out he didn't have any stock on the place to keep in. Ben said it made him feel good to reestablish some boundaries.

Eventually he became the best fiddler anyone had ever heard and his mountain farm was the only place he wanted to live. He finally presented the idea to McNally and John about building the cabin and actually living up there. McNally helped Ben with the financing and John supervised the building.

Many guitar and banjo players had sought Ben out and tried their hand at playing with him, but his style was different since he played alone for so long. Two brothers from the Dry River Valley west of Harrisonburg, Leroy and Jake Nichols who played the guitar and banjo, had started coming around and they were able to understand and adjust to Ben's rhythms and tunings. The product of their musical experimentations, along with John's driving guitar, blended so well that some people thought it sounded like the music had sprung from the soil of the mountains they stood upon. Natural and unadulterated with life blood flowing through it mingled with spirits from the past and blended like smoke rising on a moonlit night. Heavily influenced by Reno and Smiley from down around Lynchburg and the Stanley Brothers from southwest Virginia, the trio played together twice a week and eventually developed their own unique sounds. "True mountain music from the hills" is what McNally called it. Ben liked to call McNally "that sneakin' Philadelphia lawyer" and he told Jake and Leroy, "Watch him boys! He'll record us when we ain't lookin' and sell the record to them crooks in Nashville for a million dollars!" Ben would belly-laugh and give Mac a slap on the back. McNally had in truth thought of doing just that. He was a slick one. A local upright bass player named Charlie Cooper and a mandolin player from Franklin, West Virginia, just a young boy named Frankie Judy, would join them on occasion and all of them were supposed to come tomorrow to play for the picnic. Leroy and Jake were coming tonight and Ben was looking forward to having some music. The evening was perfect for it.

John heard a truck coming and a blue Chevrolet pickup pulled into the yard with a cloud of dust trailing behind. It was Judge Crawford and McNally. The Judge was riding shotgun and clearly on his way to getting plastered. His face was red and his eyes looked like he had taken them out and rolled them in mud.

McNally backed the truck over to the fire pit, and backed up way too far. Ben, John, and Davy all started yelling and screaming for him to pull up. McNally looked at them through his rear view mirror like they were crazy, not understanding what was going on. The rear end of his truck was parked over glowing hickory coals. Davy jerked the driver's door open and in one motion pulled Mac out from behind the wheel, jumped in, and started the truck. He gunned it forward as the smell of burning rubber and black smoke poured out from under the back of the truck. John had grabbed the bucket of water that he had wisely left by the pump and doused it up under the back of the truck as steam and more black smoke billowed out. The Judge sat stupefied on the passenger side and all at once yelled in his booming voice, "Order in the Court! Where is my bailiff?"

McNally all of a sudden realized what he had done and started whooping and yelling about saving the pig in the back of the truck. "For Heaven's sake! Don't let my pig burn up!"

Davy knelt down, looked up under the truck, and said, "You dumb ass, McNally! You 'bout to burn your spare tire off." That's when John threw the second bucket of water up under the truck from the other side, soaking Davy and raising another cloud of smoke. Davy rose up and looked at John across the back of the smoking truck, holding his dripping arms out from his sides, and yelled, "Grampap, you done soaked my ass!"

Jake and Leroy pulled in and parked their old Dodge Ramcharger, and then jumped out running over with concerned looks on their faces. Ben just shook his head and said, "I swear, boys. I swear. You all get that spit set up and get that hog roasting over something besides burning rubber." Turning to the Judge who was fumbling with his seatbelt and couldn't quite manage to get it unbuckled, Ben said, "Judge, let's get you over on the porch so you can kind of preside over all these idiotic schemes these boys is generating."

The Judge went with Ben holding him steady by the elbow. "I never wear my damned seatbelt in my own car," the Judge lamented. "I think the laws concerning wearing them are unconstitutional! I have never convicted anyone who's been charged for not wearing their seatbelts! I refuse to! I never wear the damn things in my wife's car when I ride with her. But when I ride with that damned McNally, I have to wear it to keep my courage up. He can't drive worth a shit! Many of the poor bastards I convict of drunk driving were driving better drunk than McNally does when he is stone sober. I need to write a letter to the Commissioner of the Department of Motor Vehicles and request he looks into McNally's road worthiness. He is a hazard and a threat to public safety! Why, he nearly ruined my pig I've

15

been fattening for the last six months in anticipation of this event!" The Judge was inclined to ramble in his instructions to the jury.

McNally was inspecting the underside of his $40,000 pickup and came out from under it wiping his hands on his pants. He yelled at Ben, "Take that old pompous loudmouth over to the porch and stick his pacifier in his mouth."

The Judge looked over his shoulder as Ben led him by the arm toward the rocking chair on the porch and glared back at him snarling, "I'll throw your ass in jail for contempt, Counselor!"

Jake looked at Leroy and whispered, "The Judge sure didn't act like that when he found me guilty of not having a county decal on my truck last month." Leroy was nodding his head, putting his false teeth in his shirt pocket with one hand and digging in his pants for his snuff can with the other.

Davy said, "You all come help me and Grampap get this hog on the spit."

Jake and Leroy helped Davy and John get the hog skewered on the roasting spit and hoisted it with no little effort into place above the glowing coals. The spit had been made by the Trumbo twins two years earlier out of some stainless steel pieces they had commandeered from a commercial ice maker they had helped to dismantle somewhere. It was a work of art and made the job simple if someone stayed sober enough to keep turning it and raking back the coals or adding some more wood at the right time.

The hog was as big as it could possibly be and still fit on the contraption. It would take all night to roast it right without burning it. Getting it to the perfection the women required would be mostly up to Davy. Steadfast young Davy. The one all of them relied upon to keep everything working. John dearly loved to help with anything over the open fire. In years past they had all helped Ben out in the spring when he tapped the sugar maple trees, collecting in buckets the dripping sap, capturing the condensed essence of early spring into glass jars. Ben had two large cast-iron kettles in which they would boil the sugar water down into smoky flavored syrup. Then they would strain it through cheese cloth and funnel it into quart jars to divide it up and take home. Boiling the sap out over an open fire gave it a flavor not achieved by the large evaporators in antiseptic conditions. Plus it afforded the excuse and pleasures associated with gathering on a cold spring night in the snow to stand around an open fire and sip George Dickel remembering old times, young women, and fine bear dogs. At the end of deer season they would gather here and bring the shoulders, neck roasts, and scrap meat from the deer they had killed. They would cut the meat off the bones and grind it into hamburger consistency. The Judge prided himself in mixing in just the right spices and ingredients. When he deemed it perfect he would authorize the rest of the crew to stuff the meat into cloth tubes to be boiled in the large kettles making huge sticks of bologna. Recently there was a young Mennonite boy who had opened a business at his farm down in the valley, making the bologna commercially, and he got most of their business now. They hadn't made bologna for several years even though John liked the Judge's mix better than the stuff the Mennonite boy made.

Ben called Jake and Leroy over to the porch and they got their instruments out of their cases and began the ritual of tuning up. Another pick-up truck arrived and Charlie Cooper got out with his signature pork-pie hat, smoking a Hav-a-Tampa cigarillo. Charlie had a tattoo of a topless hula girl on his forearm, which the young boys all marveled at and his wife hated. The Judy boy got out of the passenger side with his mandolin case, self-consciously looking around like a young deer searching for a place to run to. Charlie nodded to everyone and went around to the back of his truck and pulled out his huge old Kay bass fiddle. All the musicians milled around the porch like a pack of dogs recently reacquainted and needing a few minutes to sniff one another.

John stayed over at the fire pit with Davy. They turned the pig every once in a while and Davy opened up a brand new can of Copenhagen snuff. The silver lid required the expert sliding of a thumbnail around the perimeter between the shiny metal lid and the waxy cardboard that makes up the box with its familiar black paper wrapping. It didn't want to open smoothly so John pulled out his Old Timer pocketknife and handed it to his grandson. Davy took the knife and slid it around the can before popping the top off. He gave the knife back to John and then he expertly took the index and middle finger along with the thumb of his right hand and gouged out a three-fingered dip. Sliding it between the gum and lip, he made a good imitation of an African Ubangi warrior inserting a lip-stretching ring.

John looked at him in disgust, wondering why anyone would want to put that strong smelly stuff into his mouth. The smell alone was enough to gag a normal man. John had not ever been a chewer. He started smoking cigarettes mainly out of boredom and social pressure during his time in the army. Fern had really disliked it and had always asked him to go out on the porch to smoke. He kept a gallon can with the top cut out of it half full of sand on the back porch step just to snuff his butts out in. John wished he had a cigarette now.

Then the music started when Ben yelled out his trademark, "Give me a D chord, Leroy!"

The music made the porch come alive and the melody of "The Old Spinning Wheel in the Parlor" came bouncing off the strings of the instruments and floated among the grape vines in the grape arbor, where the last yellow jackets of fall were congregating, staggering around drunk on the last few sweet, sticky, fermented grapes left hanging. The Judge was rocking on the porch swing beside McNally with his head leaning against the chain as he listened to the music.

A few more locals rolled in and made their way to the porch and then over to say hello at the pit. The sun had sunk and the sky was a purple wonderland with Mars glowing in the southwest. It would be a beautiful night and no sign of bad weather for the whole weekend. John was getting hungry. Davy went to the back of his truck and unloaded his cooler. He got John to cut a couple of sticks and Davy broke out a couple of packs of hot dogs. The two started roasting the Ball Park hot dogs on their sticks. Somebody on the porch smelled the hot dogs and half the crowd moved over to the pit. John said to Davy, "Pulling out a pack of hot dogs around here's like pulling a hundred-dollar bill out of your wallet in a whorehouse!"

"You ought to know about that, John!" Ben answered. "I'd like to have half the money you spent in them places!"

Ben put down his fiddle and shuffled around in the cabinets in the kitchen of the cabin and turned up a half-empty ketchup bottle with dried black stuff around the spout. He magically produced a yellow bottle of French's mustard from a high cabinet. Ben had an old cable spool turned on its side close to the pit that served as a fine picnic table. Hot dogs and beer were consumed in short order.

Davy had brought plenty. It was a great time and John enjoyed it immensely. The rest of the evening the musicians played all the old songs and did them well. Ben sawed his soul out through the fiddle. Leroy sang John's favorite song, "Hemlocks and Primroses," and Charlie's bass reverberated through the hills like the drumming of a ruffed grouse. The Judge sobered up enough to proclaim Dr. Ralph Stanley and Curly Ray Cline "the best that has ever been." A brown jug made its rounds and the pig slowly roasted until everyone finally drifted into the bunks lining the back wall of Ben's cabin. Some of them crawled into the backs of pick-up trucks and pulled the topper doors shut. Quiet settled on the mountain. Davy and John stayed with the pig, turning it with the care of undertakers at a presidential funeral.

As Orion slowly stalked the sky Davy got two old wool army surplus blankets out and wrapped one around his mammoth grandfather's shoulders. Davy said, "I wonder what Dad is doing tonight."

"Ain't no telling, sonny boy. Probably hunting grizzly or caribou. He's doin' what he was made to do. He ain't fit for living around people too close and that includes you and me. It always was a wonder to me he ever allowed your mother to love him or to marry him, much less father a fine son like you. I never could talk to that boy. He's a true loner."

"Well, I sure do miss him sometimes. Miss Mom too. At least I hear from Dad every once in a while. I don't never hear from Mom. Grampap, I want you to know something," the young man said as he turned his face away to the sky. "I love you."

John coughed and turned his head the other way. "Well, I reckon I love you too, and I want to thank you for bringing me up here. I just wish we could all live here on this mountain together and just stay up here. I get so damn tired of people in general and all their scheming and idiotic ideas. There's got to be a simpler way of living than the way life has evolved in this country. Every time I get to the top of the ridge, up there at the lookout where you can see for fifty miles north and south, before you drop down in the hollow to this cabin, I want to jump out of the truck, drop my drawers, bend over and turn my backside to everything and everybody down in that valley."

Davy chuckled and said, "You're a crazy old man sometimes. You should have never left this mountain, Grampap! By the way, I got a call from Aunt Mary Alice this week."

"What'd that old bat want? She already hauled off all the things worth having that my mother and father owned!"

"Grampap, that was clean back in the 1950s that she took them iron skillets. Can't you ever forget about a couple old wore out frying pans? She's your only sister. Can't you just forgive her and make up?"

"Hell no! She knows what she done was wrong and I don't have no use for her ever since! Now let's drop it. It's much too pretty of a night to be bringing her hard head up in conversation!" the old man thundered.

They sat silently while both were lost in his own thoughts. Mary Alice was John's only sibling. Their mother had taken sick with the flu, developed pneumonia, and died when John was ten years old. Mary Alice was eight and had to take over the cooking and cleaning in their ramshackle mountain cabin. Their father died in the woods two years later when a dead treetop broke loose and fell down on him while he and John were working with a crosscut saw. One minute he had been sawing like a mad man and the next the butt end of a hundred pound limb fell fifty feet and nearly took his head off. The twelve year old boy had stared in horror at his bleeding father's body and then run two miles to the neighbors for help.

After his funeral they were taken off the mountain to live with their uncle and aunt who had no children and lived on the edge of Cambridge Township. When John returned from Germany his uncle and aunt had already passed away, their possessions auctioned off and property sold. His sister Mary Alice had taken the money and left for Norfolk where she had bought herself a nice house. John didn't begrudge her of the money. It had fallen on her to look after them in their last days while he was gone to the war. What had torn him up was that Mary Alice had taken along their mother's old set of cast-iron skillets, which John had always made clear would be his. He confronted his sister with his claim and she told him they were hers and he could forget having them because she used them every day. Enraged, he cursed her terribly, and she threw a phone book at him as he left, slamming her screen door.

That was the last time they spoke. Almost fifty years ago. Hating each other over a set of practically worthless iron skillets. Lately, she had been sending out olive branches via Davy, realizing the end of their lives were drawing near. She had never married and had no children. Fern had tried many times to get him to call her or to send her a card at Christmas or on her birthday. He would not budge on his feelings about the matter and it had kept them apart for half a century.

Later that night the Judge came out and joined them and John went into the cabin and took his place in bed. McNally came out about two o'clock and relieved Davy who wrapped up in his coat and blanket and slept like a log over on some soft grass by the side of the cabin. Orion slowly marched across the sky toward the west. Several spectacular shooting stars streaked across the star-studded void but the Judge and McNally missed seeing them as the two men stared into the fire, passing the small bottle back and forth as they remembered wars and whores and friends long dead.

# Chapter 3

At daylight a blue Plymouth van pulled in and a Middle Eastern-looking man stepped out and stretched. The Judge and McNally came around the cabin staggering with frowning faces. The Judge took a little shooter from a flask and McNally went over to the white pines growing at the upper edge of the yard and unceremoniously opened his fly and urinated. The Judge looked at him in disgust and shook his head. Turning to the Arab he said, "My good friend Aziz! If you would please overlook the pissing lawyer I would appreciate it. Do you have the guest of honor with you?"

Aziz smiled and answered, "Yes, sir, Your Honor. I picked him up at George's farm this morning." He walked to the side cargo door, reached in and pulled a brown and white goat out by grabbing a horn and holding onto a rope he had tied around its neck. The goat bleated and jumped but Aziz held on effortlessly, dragging the captive animal over to a fence where he tied him. The goat immediately started eating the grass around the fence that Ben had missed with his weed eater. John came out the door and yelled at Aziz, "Hey, you little terrorist. You got a bomb wrapped around your belly?"

Aziz laughed and picked back, "Maybe I could recruit you to become a martyr. With a gut like yours and as big as you are, you could smuggle a nuclear bomb up your fat ass into any Jewish wedding."

John snorted. He had only been half joking about his suspicions of Aziz and didn't really trust him. McNally liked him though and had started bringing him up to the cabin as his guest. John thought McNally, being one of those damn liberals, favored himself a cosmopolitan sort.

Aziz had worked at a local medical clinic until he packed up and moved to Alexandria to be close to some of his brothers. He still came up to all the yearly gatherings. He did not eat pork so he started bringing a goat or a lamb to the picnic. At first nobody ate much of it, but once folks tried it many actually liked it, especially the goat. Aziz shook hands all around and said, "It is a large goat and we must get it roasting if it is to be done by midday."

He went to the front seat of his van and took a wicked-looking knife out of a wooden box and started sharpening it vigorously on a stone. When he was satisfied, he walked over to the goat, untied it, and led it up on the little rise above the yard. The Judge went with him and held the rope. John went back to his pig roasting and McNally went with him, saying something about he was too hung over to take part in the murder of a helpless goat. Aziz got the goat where he wanted him on top of the little knoll behind the cabin and stroked its head to calm him. He turned it toward the east, looking into the golden-orange rising sun. A pair of jets ten minutes out of Dulles were leaving long contrails high in the crystalline sky above the sun like snails on a giant azure sidewalk. Aziz mumbled a prayer and quickly, professionally, and lethally drew the knife under the goat's throat. He held the goat with an iron hand. It was over quickly. The Judge held its legs apart on one side after they had rolled the goat on its back. Aziz knew what he was doing and had the goat dressed and eviscerated, lying on its own hide clean as if it had been prepared in a Chicago butcher shop.

The Judge looked at Aziz who was wiping his blade on a paper towel he had pulled out of his back pocket. "You are extremely efficient with that blade, Aziz. Where did you learn to clean up a goat like that?"

"Growing up in my land it was almost a daily job of mine. I have butchered hundreds of goats and lambs. Later on as a medical student I worked for the courts imposing sentences on offenders," the handsome Palestinian said in a matter of fact way as he finished cleaning his blade.

"What does working for the courts have to do with handling a knife?" the Judge inquired.

"Punishment is vastly different in my country and my hometown. If you are caught stealing and the evidence is overwhelming, the Judge may order your hand to be removed." He bounced a quick glance at the Judge and smiled.

"You telling me you did that, son? Cut prisoners hands off upon orders of the court?" the wide-eyed Judge asked.

"Many times, Your Honor. Many times."

"Didn't they fight like hell to keep their hands? My God, man. These boys around here would never allow the taking of their hand without a fight!"

Aziz put the knife away and looked the Judge in the eye. "Most of the time the prisoner was in shock and, believe it or not, would almost offer his hand to the knife. If you hit the joint properly it is off in less than a blink of the eye. The time they had to be watched closely was when I took the arm with the bleeding wrist and dip it in boiling olive oil to cauterize it to keep them from bleeding to death. That is when they need some assistance to remain under control. It was not bad. I got paid well. A sharp knife goes through a wrist with almost no pressure if you hit the joint correctly. Just like when I took the forelegs off this goat."

The Judge reflected. "I bet you didn't have many repeat offenders."

"Not many, Your Honor. Now if you will help me take this food to the pit, sir. We must get him cooking."

"I wish you would cut the head off the greasy thing. It upsets the women to see those eyes looking at them while he is cooking," the Judge said with an annoyed look on his hungover face.

"With all respect, sir, I like the meat from the head the best," the Palestinian stated.

"Let's get him roasting then," the Judge said.

Davy came around the cabin to help them and Aziz asked him to get rid of the hide and guts. As the Judge and Aziz took the carcass to the fire Davy fetched an empty feed sack from the woodshed, loaded the hide and the mess into the sack, and took it over the hill to the top of the ridge. He wanted to carry it far enough away from camp to keep the flies out in the woods when his sharp eyes spied a black and yellow timber rattler curled up next to a rock along the path. Davy put the sack down carefully and picked up a stick. The snake never moved until his back was broken with a swift stroke of the stick. Davy whacked him another good one behind the head just to make sure and then held its diamond-shaped head down with the stick until he could get his pocketknife out to cut off the business end. The rattlers rattled and the headless body of the snake coiled around itself in its death dance. He wiped the knife off on the sack and carried the goat remains a little farther before dumping it out on the ground. The possums and ravens will take care of recycling that mess in short order, he thought. He went back to the snake, picked it up by the tail, and slid it into the sack. When he got to the fire John looked at him quizzically when he carried the sack up. Davy dumped the snake out on the ground and John stepped back surprised until he saw the head was cut off.

"Holy smoke, boy, where in the world did you find that thing?" he asked astounded.

"Back over the hill when I went to get rid of Aziz's gut pile. Killed him with a stick. He's a nice one ain't he? Thirteen rattles and a button. Glad I killed him before all them kids get here and get to running around."

Aziz and the Judge were coming from the cabin with Styrofoam cups full of steaming coffee. McNally was right behind them. When they saw the snake they all impulsively recoiled until McNally saw the chance to show off. "Davy brought me my lunch but one lawyer eating another is probably not going to be acceptable to the ladies at the picnic."

"That snake would have probably surpassed you in the morals department before young Davy severed his head. Probably had more intelligence too!" the Judge opined.

Davy picked up the snake and said, "Shucks, McNally, if you want to eat it I'll skin it for you. I want the skin anyway. It will roast real easy. I ate one at Boy Scout Camp one time for a cooking merit badge. It tastes kind'a like fish."

McNally volunteered, "Skin him then. I think I'll eat him for breakfast. This mountain air and all the drama involved in murdering a goat and a snake all in one morning has spurred my appetite."

John asked, "You ain't a gonna eat that damn snake, are you McNally. Are you?"

"Sure I am. Go on and skin him Davy. Take the hide and wrap it around a two-by-four. It will stick right to it and dry there."

"How do you know so much about serpents?" Aziz asked.

"It's a lawyer thing. Takes one to know one and all that." McNally joked.

Davy went to the shed and got a hammer and a nail. He nailed the head end to the top of the post. He asked Aziz if he could use his good knife but Aziz absolutely refused. Davy took out his Old Timer and cut the snake down the middle of his belly from the throat to the tail. He trimmed out the neck and took hold of it, and by pulling down the snake slid right out of its skin. McNally brought a four foot two-by -four over and held it while Davy took the snake skin and stretched it on the board lengthwise. Then he hung the skin on the board up on the rafters of the shed to dry. Returning to the snake carcass he cut the intestines and organs out of it.

McNally took it over to the fire pit and placed it on the wire frame of the spit and it started sizzling immediately.

The judge shook his head. "Look there, John. Looks like some of that stuff you ate in Korea, doesn't it?"

"Some of the rest of the boys ate snake but I ain't got hungry enough yet for that!" the old warrior answered. "Ain't saying I wouldn't though."

"Allah will strike you dead, you infidels! Eating such unclean food!" the Palestinian muttered.

The eyeballs of the goat were bulging out and glaring in an unblinking, grotesque look. "At least that damn snake is not looking at us like your goat is," the Judge said as he spat into the fire, making a fizzling sound.

"If you dislike those eyes why don't you eat one, Your Honor?" Aziz dared the Judge. The Judge reached over into a pan that Davy had barbeque sauce in. He retrieved a spoon from it and gouged out the goat's left eyeball which popped right out in the spoon. The Judge looked around at everyone and said, "How much will you give me if I eat this eyeball?"

McNally couldn't resist. "I'll give you this one-hundred-dollar bill!" he said as he whipped it out of his wallet. The Judge smiled, tilted back his head, and swallowed the eyeball like it was a hardboiled egg. Then he snatched the hundred out of McNally's hand and stuck it in his pocket.

Davy almost threw up. McNally just shook his head and Aziz took off walking rapidly toward the field. John said, "If you are gonna eat that snake, McNally, you better turn it. It's gettin' right crispy on that side."

McNally couldn't handle it that the Judge had his hundred-dollar-bill and pouted about it all morning. He did eat some of the snake as did Davy, Jake, and Leroy.

Ben came out with a meat thermometer and decided the pig was done. The one-eyed goat was coming along fine and the Judge declined eating the other eyeball. The musicians were playing on the porch again. The morning was cool and clear and they couldn't have ordered a more perfect day.

They took the pig off and put him on a table made of three smooth oak planks set on top of sawbucks. They picked the pig clean and pulled all the pork, putting it in large tin serving platters. It was cooked perfectly and everybody was picking at choice morsels and chewing on bones and toasted pork skin. John got a large chunk of the skin and fat that came off the front of a ham and went over under the pines and enjoyed every bit of it, and then he came back for more.

He was having a good time. The women and various old neighbors and cousins arrived and soon there were over 200 people, all somehow connected to this piece of mountain high in the Alleghenies. Even Speedy Spencer who ran the local beer joint and had been with John, the Judge, and McNally on the beach of Normandy on D-day had closed his place for the afternoon and was there. They were the only ones remaining from the local boys who had survived that day. Davy took a picture of them together and everybody agreed what a remarkable thing it was that all of them had lived to be over seventy years old with such good health. John wished the day would never end and if it had to, why couldn't he just walk up a staircase into the mountains and clouds to the west and wave good-bye to them all? Simply let it be over with on a nice note. He turned and looked at the tables and all the food and thought better of it. He would like to eat first.

There were tables stretched for fifty feet bearing every kind of good thing grown in gardens—green beans, squash of several different colors and varieties, creamed corn, and butter beans—and homemade cakes, pies, and deserts. Homemade bread in the slice and rolls and a big bowl of real cow butter made in the churn. Apple butter, jams, and jellies. Even Aziz's goat tasted very good. Jake and Leroy argued for an hour whether it tasted more like deer or elk.

After everyone had stuffed themselves properly the musicians took over and the women found warm sunny spots in their lawn chairs to gossip and yell, "Don't you kids go in them woods. Did you see the rattler Davy killed this morning? Where there is one there is bound to be its mate close by!" The kids hardly slowed down and soon were in the pasture field playing a pick-up touch football game. Some of them sang along with the musicians and everyone stopped to sing along when Aunt Mary Alice, John's sister who surprised everybody by showing up, insisted that Jake and Leroy sing John Denver's "Country Roads," a song everybody loved but none of the musicians liked to attempt. They sang all the old bluegrass standards and some not so well known.

John drank the whole scene into his soul. It was home. It was family. It was his whole life wrapped into one afternoon. He missed Fern terribly, and when Ben played "Jerusalem's Ridge" it moved him to tears. He leaned his guitar against the split rail fence beside Nimrods old rifle Ben had propped there for everyone to see. John took off around the cabin by himself to hide his wet eyes. When he returned he got another paper plate and cleaned out the last of the mashed potatoes and sauerkraut along with another big hunk of fat meat from the hog.

The day ended like all days of this kind. Soon. Too soon. At dusk John wished again for a ladder or stairway to appear so he could walk up to the sunset, but it didn't come.

Davy hardly talked on the way home and John suddenly realized Davy's wife Lizzy hadn't come to the picnic. He decided not to say anything about it.

Walking back to his room at the home a large pain hit him in the belly and he said his thank-you and good-night quickly to Davy, just in time to make it to his toilet.

It surprised him when he realized he felt comforted to be back in his room again. John went to sleep with the words of A.P. Carter's old song "Will You Miss Me When I'm Gone?" floating over and over in his head.

Perhaps you'll plant some flowers
On my cold unworthy grave.
Come and sit alone beside me
While the roses nod and sway.

John floated off to sleep. He dreamed of his mother and barefoot children playing tag in the moonlight, running and chasing one another with cold toes in damp grass.

# Chapter 4

One afternoon John walked into the lobby, or the common area as Resident Director Bowman called it, and everybody stopped talking. Obviously Rennick had been talking about him. John just looked down at the much smaller man and stared at him. One of the women said, "John, Rennick says your grandson told you he's taking you deer hunting like he took you to the picnic. Is that right?"

"That's right," John replied. "He's going to come get me and take me up on the big mountain where my wife and I was borned and we gonna hunt all day."

Rennick laughed a little and shook his head.

John asked him, "You got a problem with something, Rennick?"

"For one thing, I don't think that boy will come to take you, and secondly, I don't think the deer would be in much danger if you stomped after them. You couldn't sneak up on a drink of water as big as you are!" Rennick sneered, looking from side to side as he sought to enlist compatriots in his sport of attempting to discredit the big man in front of the covey of women.

Surprisingly quick and almost gracefully, John spun on his heel, took one step toward Rennick, and grabbed the back of his neck with his huge hand. The room got quiet as the smile on Rennick's pink face sickened. He drew his shoulders in together, straightened his arms out at his sides and tilted his head back like a kitten being carried by its mother when it was too big to be carried that way. John said loudly so everybody could hear, "You know, I don't give a *damn* about friendship but I do care about things like respect." His hand on Rennick's neck had the same effect a dog has on another dog when he gets his mouth on his competitor's neck in an argument over pecking order. Rennick froze in terror and moved not a muscle. "I won't put up with bad manners or insults. Particularly from a little Yankee jerk like you."

John let Rennick go and headed toward his room. Rennick wasn't saying anything, praying nobody noticed he had wet his pants. One of the blue-hairs who was standing there with her eyes bugged out and mouth open turned on him and said, "You deserved every bit of that, you little agitator!" Rennick was suspected of cheating at bridge with the ladies and they were looking for another excuse to hate him.

The days passed in a blur as the leaves on the sugar maples in the front yard turned yellow and gold with red streaks in them. John got a talking to by the resident director, Donald Bowman, about the incident with Rennick. Of course, Rennick had done his best to get the police involved, claiming John had nearly broken his neck. Bowman had done some talking to defuse Rennick. He didn't need to have anything of a violent nature on the agenda at the next board meeting, much less in the news. It was the women who really saved John by turning on Rennick, magnifying and exaggerating his provocation almost to the point where John looked like a victim. When John survived the inquisition by Bowman it was the opinion of everyone involved John was justified in his *straightening out the little Yankee.*

Whenever he walked down the hall the residents spoke to him and watched as he headed out for his afternoon walks. John enjoyed the respect but made sure he appeared aloof to their attentions.

The Sunday evening before the opening day of deer season Davy came in with John's insulated farm boots and his blaze-orange coveralls, his hunting coat, and blaze-orange toboggan. Everybody in the place knew he was there and it was exciting for most of them to talk about John going out on a hunt.

As John walked Davy to the door several of the ladies watched him as if they were queens bidding their favorite knight to do their will on the crusades.

"Grampa, you get to sleep and get some rest. I'll be here around four o'clock to pick you up. We're gonna stop at Speedy's for breakfast before we go up the mountain. I have your Winchester 30-30 ready and your lunch packed so you don't have to worry about nothing. Tim and

Tom're going to meet us at Speedy's and they'll follow us up to the home place because they don't know how to get there."

John made it an issue to demand the right to pay for the breakfast and then he did something he had never done before. He put his massive arm around his grandson's shoulders and gave him a hug while thanking him. As John closed the door to his room he saw pink-faced Rennick looking across the lobby at him. John shot him the bird with his huge middle finger and shuffled into his room.

# Chapter 5

Davy pulled into the parking lot at five minutes before four and slid out the door of his Nissan pickup, boots crunching on the gravels. The light was on in his grandfather's room so that was a good sign. Walking down the hall, he noticed one of the doors was open and he could see in the room. A skeletal-looking old man lying on his back, nose pointed toward the ceiling with his mouth open, was snoring. Davy knocked on John's door and heard him grunt, "Come in." Davy slid in the door and John was in the bathroom.

"We gotta go, Grampap. You about ready?"

"Been trying to be," John mumbled. "Done tied myself in a knot but no luck. Hate to get caught short in the woods."

Davy chuckled and said, "Let's get going. The Trumbo boys will have conniptions if we're late."

John hauled himself into the bedroom and pulled on his coveralls. Davy helped him get his straps up over his shoulders right. John sat down on the side of his bed and struggled to pull on his boots. Using maximum effort to get around his gut left John winded. Davy knelt down and said, "Here, let me help you a little, or we'll never get going." Davy tied John's shoes for him and when he stood up he handed his Grandfather his coat from the hook on the back of the door and smiling said, "Let's go hunting, Grampap!"

When they headed down the hall toward the big exit sign, door after door opened as old women in hairnets and bathrobes from Wal-Mart peeked out to witness the beginning of John's quest. As they passed the front desk Maybelle leaned out of her door and whispered, "Good luck, John! Get a big one for us." Then she turned and walked to Rennick's door, kicked it with her foot, and said, "Lost your bet, you old Yankee fool."

When they got to the truck Davy realized they had a slight problem. John just barely fit in the front seat of his little truck with his coveralls and coat on. The bucket seats that wrapped almost around anyone else didn't handle but about three quarters of his grandfather. Finally managing to get the door shut, he made no attempt at getting a seatbelt around him.

Sliding into the driver's seat, Davy said, "When we get to the Trumbos' place you can ride with Tim. He has a full-sized Dodge truck and you'll fit in that one better. John's head was against the ceiling and his knees were against the dashboard. He looked out of the corner of his eye at Davy and asked, "I think I growed since the picnic. You got my gun and shells?"

"Sure do. Behind the seat but I can't quite get to them now," the young man answered.

"Let's get up the road then."

"We're going over to the Trumbos' trailer up at the Skunktown Trailer Park and meet them there."

Tim and Tom Trumbo were flaming redheaded twins, identical and inseparable. They were twenty-five years old and top mechanics for a local trucking company. Neither had graduated from high school, mostly because they couldn't get past twelfth-grade English and meet the state's requirements for graduation. By all accounts they were happy-go-lucky Southern boys and just didn't give a damn. Theirs was a world revolving around hunting, fishing, and fixing anything broken. Artists with their hands. For their work they chose Craftsman, DeWalt, and Master Mechanic. For their play: Remington, Winchester, Chrysler products, and anything from Cabela's catalog.

Davy pulled into the back of the brown and white mobile home at 4:15 A.M. and noticed Tom's truck was already warming up with ghostly clouds of exhaust rising from the tailpipe. The aluminum dog box on the back of the truck fit behind the tool box next to the cab. They were ready at a minute's notice to run a bear or overhaul a transmission. Davy blew the horn and the brothers rolled out of the door, rambling down the sagging back steps covered with frost.

"'Bout time you showed up!" Tim joked. "It's almost lunchtime. Darn, Mr. John, you look like a big largemouth in a Japanese sardine can. Hey, Tom, look here. We got little David hauling around Goliath in a Japanese sardine can."

"Yeah, Tim, can Grampap ride with you? This ain't working out so good. I done forgot how big a man he is with all his hunting clothes on. I was hoping Grampap could ride in your bigger truck."

Davy opened the passenger door and had to help John get his right foot past the door post and out on the ground. The old man slid his legs and butt out and the rest of him followed.

Tom chuckled. "Sure, Mr. John. Come ride in a real truck. Skinny butt Tim can suffer in that little Nissan with Davy."

Tim responded with a vulgar insult as he loaded up his lower lip with his first dip of Copenhagen snuff of the day. John got in the Dodge and even though it was still tight it was much better. Tom looked over at Davy as they got in their trucks and yelled, "See y'all at Speedy's for breakfast."

Tom punched some buttons on the radio and a Ralph Stanley CD started playing. Ralph was singing a song about killing his girlfriend down in a willow garden and Jack Cook was harmonizing real keen. John liked the music and didn't mind it being loud because he couldn't hear so well ever since the mortar went off right behind him in Korea. He thought about that a lot.

He was assigned to a demolition squad and his unit had spent most of the night sneaking a mile past enemy lines. Their mission required them to blow up a bridge that would cut off a retreat route the North Koreans would have to use when the American boys launched a major offensive. John had served four years in World War II and then stayed in long enough to get a dose of Gone-ta-Korea too, pulled his twenty, and retired. He had seen the roughest of the rough many times. An old man from Cambridge named Mr. Bass had gotten his ass cheeks shot off by German machine guns in WWI and couldn't sit down ever again. The boys in town called him No-Ass Bass behind his back. Even after John had seen the worst possible maiming and grinding of human bodies in Germany in WWII, that was still the one thing he feared the most. Getting his ass cheeks shot off scared him worse than dying. That morning in Korea they had set their charges on the bridge and the captain told them, "When we blow this thing it's every man for himself getting back across the line. Run straight down the hollow as fast and as far as you can. The bad boys gonna be some kind of pissed!"

At daylight they blew the bridge to splinters and took off running hard as they could. About a hundred yards down the trail the North Korean boys got over their shock and opened up with machine guns and mortars.

John felt a huge concussion behind him and something hit him in the seat of his pants so hard it knocked him down. It stung like bees and John panicked, certain his ass cheeks were blown off. He was going to be just as bad off as old No-Ass Bass. He laid still for what seemed an eternity with all hell breaking loose around him. Finally, he forced his hand back there and felt nothing but wet and slime. His worst fears had been realized. It took every bit of his will power to bring his fingers in front of his face. Expecting to see gore and blood he saw wet red clay. The damned mortar had gone off and blown a big chunk of red clay up against his ass so hard it had numbed him.

He jumped up and could have beaten Jesse Owens down that hollow, passing every man in the unit. His eardrums were damaged but his ass cheeks survived.

It seemed strange to him how stuff like that would pop into his mind at most any time when he hadn't thought about it in months, maybe years. It was like all of that had happened to someone else and it was all a terrible dream.

John pulled his twenty then worked as a stone mason twenty-five more and done all right. He liked fooling with rocks and putting random things in order. Kind of like Ben with his fences. Today was looking up. He was going hunting! For one day at least he had escaped Jesus' Launching Pad. Dr. Ralph and Curley were playing "Hard Times" and John was happy. Ralph's banjo was ripping and Ricky Lee was wearing out the guitar! John made a mental note to get Ben and his band to play that one for him at the cabin sometime.

# Chapter 6

Speedy's Service was a unique place and seventy-one year-old Speedy Spencer was a unique man. His store was perched on a bank of the Hawthorne River where it had cut through the first mountain in the Appalachian Chain. The whole place was made out of cinderblock and cement and it had withstood several floods that would have closed down lesser determined people. Speedy and his family lived in the basement and the store was upstairs on a level with the road. His wife and two girls helped him tend store when the girls weren't off at college. When the floods cut through Powell Gap it raced through with a vengeance and Speedy had been cleaned out twice in the fifty years he had been there, since getting his leg shot off at Normandy. After living through the war, a little high water wasn't nothing much to get excited about and he had used it to his political and financial advantage without losing his mind or abusing alcohol.

The Army Corp of Engineers had wanted for years to build a dam in "The Gap" and flood Powell's Valley all the way to the foot of the big Shenandoah Mountain so they could run a pipe line of good water to northern Virginia. The real-estate developers wanted it too. A 210-square-mile lake would create a lot of development. If Speedy hadn't been the head of the VFW and the son of the father of the local Democratic Party in the area and personal friends with Mr. Byrd himself, the dam would have been a done deal years earlier. Soon as he was gone he knew they would probably have their way. His daughters would move away and sell the place. Until then, he would just sit there, sell his guns and beer and enjoy looking up at the sheer rock cliffs above him and down at the water rushing below with the traffic buzzing past.

In one way he was like the Trumbo boys. He didn't give a damn either. People would stop in the store from D.C. every once in a while and be amazed that folks were being served beer with guns for sale hanging from the ceiling. Only place in the state where you could do that. Drink a beer, buy a gun, and get a side order of chili beans. Some of the anti-gun people at the university had tried to put him out of business but the local courts and politicians had pretty much told them to back off and leave him alone.

Hunting season was a boon for Speedy's business and he opened early at three thirty in the morning. He was also a game-checking station and knew he would be open until midnight serving all the hunters dragging their deer in to be checked. The next two weeks would decide if his year would be a good one or not. If the weather was good, he would do more business during the two-week deer season than he would in any other two months put together. If the weather was bad it was even better because a lot of the hunters spent bad days shooting pool and sipping suds. Speedy was open for business on time and a few orange-clad nimrods were shuffling in just as the three-gallon coffee pot was ready. His wife, Nell, twenty years younger, came treading up the steps. God had been kind to him to let this woman into his life and give him two daughters when he was in his late forties. When he saw her tired eyes he loved her for being so dependable. Speedy said to her, "Davy Dean is bringing Big John in and paid me to have this order ready at four thirty."

He handed her the ticket and she said, "John ain't changed none. What're we going to do with all that food if they don't show up?"

Speedy replied, "Sell it to somebody else, of course. He done paid for it so we ain't out of nothin' even if he don't show up and we got to throw it to the hogs."

She looked at the list. Davy had ordered the largest skillet she had full of fried taters and onions. Two dozen fried eggs over easy and a gallon of sausage gravy. She could see Big John had not changed any since he had been in last. Nell got at it right away. The girls had already peeled the potatoes. She took a large pot of chili beans that had been sitting on the stove over night and noticed there was at least a gallon left. She would clean that later when she got the chance. Speedy was serving coffee to Fred Hinkle and his boys as she noticed it wasn't quite four o'clock yet.

Nell yelled out to Speedy, "Turn on the radio. We need some music back here!"

Davy and Tim pulled off the narrow highway and into the lot at Speedy's in tandem and John's eyes were wide open. He hadn't been there in a while and this was like the best thing that could happen to him. No kid at Christmas was ever more full of anticipation and eagerness. He said, "Now I'm gonna pay for the breakfast and I don't want to hear any different from you boys."

Tom Trumbo chortled. "You got enough money to pay for what you gonna eat, Mr. John?"

Davy chimed in, "You all are way behind me. I ordered and paid for all of us last evening and Nell is supposed to have it ready just about now," he said as he looked at his watch. Four thirty on the nose. John pulled out a twenty-dollar bill and stuck it in Davy's shirt pocket. For a second he looked at his grandfather and started to make an issue of it, and then he realized how important it was for his grandfather to buy the breakfast. Davy held the door open and John went in first, walking tall.

# Chapter 7

John walked past the Coke chest and Nell yelled from the kitchen, "Hide the girls, Speedy! John is here with that good-lookin grandson of his. Lord, Lord, here comes Tim and Tom the terrible twins!"

Nell knew everybody's name and could remember it even if she had only met them once years ago. It made people feel good and they would stop in and buy a pack of cigarettes or a six-pack just to feel connected and known. She was always so cheerful and friendly. Her personality and work ethic was largely responsible for making Speedy rich.

Tim said, "Don't hide them daughters from me. I ain't done nothing except dream about them every night since they was in the beauty contest at the Allegheny County Fair."

"You don't have to worry about them girls. They're both on academic scholarships down at the College of William and Mary in Williamsburg. That means they are smart enough not to marry local!" Nell fired back. "Even with a good-lookin pair of cowboys like you two. Course that don't mean they might not let you kiss 'em when I ain't lookin'!"

Speedy came out of the back carrying a suitcase-pack of Dr. Peppers and started stocking a cooler when he noticed John sitting with his back to him. He came over and patted John on the shoulder as Nell loaded Davy's order onto the big table in the corner. She gave John a hug and a smooch on his cheek.

"Good to see you out with the boys, John. Been missing you at the VFW meetings," Speedy said.

John was looking over the table and breathing heavy through his nose, sucking every bit of the aroma in. His mouth was watering as he answered, "Yeah, Speedy, there ain't many of us boys left, is it."

Speedy turned on his prosthetic leg and said, "No it ain't. You boys excuse me. I got work to do. Enjoy your breakfast."

As they dived into their food the usual small talk and chatter erupted about where they were going to hunt and who had seen huge bucks in different people's fields at night. Before the other three were half finished John cleaned up his share, which was about half of everything. He started looking around and spotted the pot of chili on the corner of the stove when Nell came out of the kitchen. John reached back there and grabbed the handle.

"This leftovers?" he asked Nell.

"Left over from last night just for you. You clean it out so I don't have to and you can have it all for two dollars," she replied.

John took a jar of mayonnaise off the counter and dumped about two cupfuls into the chili pot and stirred it up. Then he poured about half a can of grated Parmesan cheese on top and stirred it up some more. With a long-handled spoon he attacked the pot like a hungry bear after a honey tree. Even Davy who was used to his ways shook his head. Some guy at another table who had been watching said, "Where you guys hunting? I sure as hell don't want to be downwind." That brought a laugh from everybody and a roar when John said to him, "If you gonna leave that toast to waste on your plate pass it over here!" He was having a good time.

When the four well fed hunters exited the restaurant a wind had picked up and was blowing out of the west through the gap. Davy glanced up at the sky and saw jagged edged clouds ripping across the starlit blackness in the pre-dawn hour of five A.M. Hopping in the truck Davy pulled out onto the highway leading the way because the Trumbo boys had never been to his Grandmother's home place before. It was remote even for such a back woods area. As soon as John got in the truck he felt the pain hit him.

"Boy, I gotta stop to find the toilet."

Tim said, "You gonna have to hold it cause I don't know where I'm going and Davy is hell bent for leather."

The ride up the mountain was at a fast pace and fortunately John was able to hold himself. As soon as the truck stopped he was out, throwing his coat one way and pulling at his coveralls as he staggered for a pine thicket. Walking back to the truck John got mad, the Trumbo boys were bent over laughing at him. "That's okay! Some day you little redheaded pricks are gonna get old too!"

"Getting old don't have as much to do with it as eating like a hog does, Mr. John!" Tom said with a smirk.

Davy changed the subject and told the twins where he wanted them to hunt and gave them direction to meet back at the truck around noon. They all had their lunches packed in the trucks. John wanted to walk over to the old orchard and watch the locust tree crossing. It wasn't more than a couple of hundred yards from where the trucks were parked and Davy told him if he had any troubles or got tired he could come back to the truck and blow the horn if he needed them.

The Trumbo boys took off with their rifles slung over their backs and Tom had one of those climbing tree stands on a backpack. John was mad at him for laughing and told him he hoped he fell out of his little stand he was carrying and busted his neck. The redheaded duo walked off into the dark giggling, and one of them said to the other, "Sounded like a Hereford bull dropping a pile from six feet high."

Davy got John's rifle out from behind the seat and loaded the magazine for him. It was a Winchester 30-30 lever action the old man had bought on leave back in 1956 and it looked like a toy in the hands of the old giant. Davy knew his grandfather was crazy at times and many people, including his father, had warned him not to take him hunting. John Jr. had said, "Putting a gun in the hands of that old man is just asking for trouble." Davy loved his grandfather and was a more tolerant and patient fellow than his father who scarcely acknowledged that John Sr. was still alive. Handing John a little flashlight, Davy said, "Now, Grampap, don't you let me down by doing something you shouldn't. Here is your lunch in this bag and there is three sandwiches and a bag of chips. You get hungry before we get back, go ahead and eat. There is Cokes in the Playmate cooler on the back and you know where the old spring is. I'm gonna be over the ridge about a half mile, over to where the cow pens was."

"Darn good place," John said. "Killed many a buck coming down off that oak flat there headed to the creek bottom." John flicked on his flashlight and pointed it at the ground to a nearly dry mud puddle. "Look there, boy. That's a spike buck's track there."

"Now how you know that's a spike buck track rather than a four-pointer?" Davy laughed.

"Just know, that's how!" John said. "Now don't you get to making fun of me. I been around this old world a long time and …"

"Don't get excited, Grampap. It's time to get on stand. It's getting light over in the east," the boy answered. "One thing I forgot, Grampap. You got a knife with you?"

John pulled his folding Old Hickory lock blade out of his pocket and shook it at Davy and started telling him how many hundred deer it had skinned. Davy patted his grandfather on the shoulder and said with gentle authority, "Grampap, listen to me." John stopped and looked at the young man. "Make sure of your target, be careful, and have fun. That's why we came. Now see you around lunch time."

With that he wheeled around on his heel and took off toward the cow pens at a brisk walk. John thought that if he hadn't done anything else right in this messed-up world, he would leave behind a fine young grandson.

He started walking to the northeast along the familiar path that led to the old home. He knew the trail well enough from having walked it a million times. The mountain air was crisp and smelled clean and sweet. The stars were bright in the ink-black sky. As he looked up he found the Big Dipper and then his eyes traveled over the outside of the cup to the North Star. He turned his head to his left shoulder and saw Orion, just hanging there, hunting the night skies forever. John thought that when he died he would ask God if he could go up there and hunt with Orion. Thinking those kinds of thoughts made him feel good.

The rifle felt good in his hands. Strolling along the path, he was once again glad he had been walking every day and he felt good all over except for his feet which always hurt. That came from wearing hand-me-down shoes when he was a kid during the Depression. Of course, he had also worn burlap underwear that had galled his crotch to no end.

The sky was starting to lighten up a good bit and a red streak of cloud turned the eastern horizon into a purple and orange glow out over the Blue Ridge sixty miles away. John could pick out the gap where his father had been raised and ultimately run off by the government when they stole the land up there to make the Skyline Drive. This land he was walking on now had been in his wife's family for 200 years. She had been the only survivor of the estate and she had left it all to Davy. John, Jr. was mad as hell when he found out. Good thing she had skipped over John Jr., but Lord, how that had pissed him off. He would have just sold it and gone to Las Vegas with the money or done something equally wasteful. Davy would keep it and know its value. Taxes was getting more and more on it all the time and Davy had been smart to get Buddy Mongold to rent it for grazing.

Mongold had chicken houses and hauled chicken litter on a big spreader truck to fertilize the fields of the ridge tops and the lower flats. Mongold kept the fences up and posted the place too. The rent paid Davy enough to settle the taxes and pay the insurance on the place.

The gurgling of the spring let him know he was almost in the old yard. The rock foundation to the house was still standing there as mute testimony to all the years of a family scratching out a living on the mountaintop. Thirty years back lightning had hit a walnut tree beside the old frame house, bounced over and hit the west wall. The pine logs had burned to the ground. What was left of the tin roof was nearly all rusted to pieces now and Virginia Creeper and rattler snakes had a den in the cool root cellar underneath in the summer.

John stood listening to the spring whispering to him and memories flooded his mind.

# Chapter 8

The spring bubbled out of the ground inside the springhouse where the butter and milk had been kept. John stayed there for a few minutes, listening to its music which seemed to whisper to him, "It's all gone, it's all gone, it's all gone." He reached his cupped hand into a little pool and sipped the pure water. The next handful he splashed over his face and the wet cold was shocking.

Everything runs in cycles forever, he thought. In the early first light he could see the outline of Fern's mother's flower garden. The last time he had brought Fern up here had been on an April morning and she had been so happy to see the daffodils were still coming up. She had cleaned the leaves out of the old garden and found iris bulbs shooting their spears out of the cold clay again and it had thrilled her. John had helped her dig a few of the bulbs and wrapped them in some newspaper he had in his truck. She had planted them in the garden at home in Cambridge where they flourished and bloomed every year since, but now that was sold and gone too. He wondered if the new owners liked them. Thoughts of Fern washed over him like stepping into a cold shower or the dull ache of a broken rib. John missed her so much.

Something moved in the semi-darkness and it snapped him out of his reverie. A deer was running at a slow trot from over the hill, silhouetted against the morning sky. It was an old doe. She stopped and looked over her shoulder and then continued toward the orchard. Likely she had winded the Trumbo boys as they went across the sod to their stands. Just then John saw motion behind her and there he came trailing her with his nose to the ground like a dog. He was a good buck with a high rack.

John brought the Winchester to his cheek, thumbed the hammer back, and found the front shoulder with the front sight. Squeezing the trigger, the gun went *click* with a sound that may as well have been a cannon shot. The buck spooked and wheeled back the way he had come from. John levered the rifle in anger, realizing he had forgotten to do so and had tried to fire an empty chamber. The buck stopped at the crest of the ridge and looked back toward the path the doe had taken. Despite himself he experienced a little buck fever then and as he snapped off a rushed shot he knew he had pulled it. The buck took off back over the sods. John cussed himself. He pulled another shell out of his pocket and slid it into the slot on the side of the rifle and felt the spring compress under it. His hands were shaking and his ears were ringing from the shot. He was cursing himself for missing in such a careless manner. His anxiety reached paramount levels a few minutes later when he heard a rifle boom over in the direction the buck had run, right where the redheaded twins had gone. John felt an intense sting of jealousy knowing he had run the buck right to them. "I hope they missed!" he said to himself. He would have to listen to their bragging and needling him that he had missed. How could a man who had killed so many Germans and Koreans and been through so much in his life get so excited over shooting a damn deer? It had always thrilled him and always would. But now the thrill had been replaced by the anxiety of failure.

John turned and, feeling dejected, walked the remaining short distance to the old apple trees. One of the trees had split and half of it was lying on the ground but still putting out apples. Fern always got apples off that tree to make pies. She and her old pappy had planted this orchard sixty years ago. Now it made a perfect bench to sit on and he could see the whole mountainside from that vantage point.

He made himself comfortable as the first rays of sun found him. No more deer came through that morning but he did see a flock of turkeys feed down the hollow to the west. He sighted his gun at them until one of them saw him and made a *putt-putt* alarm cluck and they all ran around the ridge out of sight. The morning was warm in the sunshine where he sat and after a while John lay down on the grass with his head propped against the apple tree. A smile touched his face as he wondered what that little jerk Rennick was doing. Soon John was snoring.

When he awoke the sun was behind him and he looked at his watch. It was already one fifteen. John was hungry and decided he would walk back to the truck to eat his lunch. Then he remembered missing the buck and the probability that the Trumbo boys would be back at the truck bragging. He went anyway, stopping at the spring to drink his fill. The old foundation to the house looked small and dirty in the stark rays of afternoon daylight. A chipmunk ran over a charred log and disappeared into the wreckage. He could see the remains of an iron bed headboard rusting in silence. The middle of it was like a valentine heart. He remembered sleeping on that bed and making love to Fern on it. Ashes to ashes, rust to rust.

When John approached the vehicles he saw no one. He looked in the beds of the trucks, no deer. He reached into Davy's truck and got his lunch bag. Walking to the back of the truck he dropped the tailgate for a seat. The Playmate cooler was hard to open but finally he got a can of Coke out and tore open the potato chips. The sandwiches were good and so were the chips and John polished them off quickly.

He sat on the tailgate and waited. After about half an hour John got bored and began wondering what else was in the trucks he could eat. Looking in Davy's lunch bag he thought that Davy wouldn't mind if he ate one of his sandwiches so he did. Snooping through the Trumbo boys' lunch boxes he took a granola bar out of the one and a hardboiled egg out of the other. Probably won't even miss them, John thought. As the afternoon wore on and he kept eating he suddenly came to the realization that all the lunch bags were empty. John rationalized the situation. "They weren't here at lunch time so they'll be ready to eat supper. I probably saved them the trouble of throwing that stuff away."

Around four o'clock he saw them coming. Davy was with them and they were dragging a big deer. John stood up and looked. They appeared worn out and he could hear the Trumbo boys running their mouths. He could see it was a wall hanger of a buck and had a big, high rack like the one he had shot at.

Tom Trumbo yelled at John, "Thanks for running him over to me this morning. You didn't miss him by much! He has a bullet crease across his brisket."

"I knew I hit that buck!" John lied.

He made up a good story about the buck running across the hill at top speed and how he never had much of a shot at him. He didn't mention firing on the empty chamber and spooking him. Davy asked John if he had seen anything else and John lied again, saying he had been hunting hard all day but never saw any more deer. He didn't tell them he had slept for five hours.

"I did see a whole flock of turkeys and I could have shot all of them if the season was in."

Tim Trumbo piped in, "We had to track that buck close to two miles. Tom gut-shot the bastard and it kept going down, down, down. We didn't catch up to him until about lunch time. We done dragged the hair off his one side. We could see traffic on Mitchell Knob Road we was down there so far."

John could see the exit hole a few inches in front of the hip joint. He walked over to the deer and lifted the rack by the right horn. Ten points with perfect brow tines and at least twenty-two inches on the inside. The rough base of the horns had cedar sap where he had been rubbing them and his neck was swollen up with the rut. Across the brisket a clean furrow in the hair with just a little of the hide cut was testimony to John's shot and his envy and disappointment was intense. Two inches higher and the deer would have dropped in his tracks. His jealousy made his hands shake.

John couldn't resist saying to the boy what every man who kills a big buck has to listen to: "If you would have let that one go another year he would have really been a good buck!"

"I suppose that is why you just grazed him instead of killing him, huh, John? You was leaving him for seed for another year?" Tom laughed.

John could feel his face getting hot. Tim Trumbo exclaimed, "I'm so doggone hungry, my belly button is rubbing against my backbone. I could eat the hams off of a hobby horse. We had to drag that deer up through laurel brush most of the way. Where's my lunch?" He was holding up an empty black lunch box and looking at it incredulously. Tom grabbed for his and opened it to find empty sandwich baggies and a banana peel with a granola wrapper wadded up in it. They were both looking at John. Tim muttered, "I ain't believing this crap."

Davy pulled his empty lunch bag out of his truck and started in on his grandfather. "I can't believe you done this, Grampap! Damn it, I just can't believe you done et all our lunches."

Tom Trumbo said disgustedly, "Hell, let's take him back down Mitchell Knob and let him eat the gut pile."

John could feel himself wanting to fall into a hole. He walked over and crawled into the Dodge truck and said, "Let's go home. I want you to take me home. Now!"

The buck was loaded onto the pickup and as the sun set in the west John and the hungry brigade headed down the mountain. There was not much talk in the Trumbo truck and John began getting more depressed the farther down the mountain they went. He had been so sure he would be able to tell everybody at the home how he got a big one, and to come that close and miss.... It was a long ride down off the mountain with each turn in the road adding to his melancholy. To top it all, clouds had moved in and a fog was settling in the valley as they pulled into Speedy's checking station.

John stayed in the truck as the inevitable crowd developed around the tailgate as hero Tom removed his tag from the deer's ear where he had shoved it. John sat motionless, looking out the window as they dragged the buck off the truck and onto the scales. He heard somebody say it weighed 188 pounds. Finally Tom crawled in the truck eating a Slim Jim and drinking a Dr. Pepper. He folded the check card into the little pocket on the sun visor. He didn't speak and neither did John all the way back to the Trumbo boys' trailer.

# Chapter 9

When they got to the trailer Tom backed the truck up under the limbs of an ancient walnut tree and set the parking brake. Davy and Tim pulled in behind them as John unfolded out of the truck. Tim jumped onto the back of Tom's truck and Tom handed him a four-foot locust stick sharpened on each end and about as big around as John's wrist. Tim cut the back legs at the joint and expertly slid the sharp ends into place through the tendons in the hock. Tom handed Tim a come-along that hooked to a chain looped over a strong limb of the walnut tree and the buck was cranked and hoisted off the truck bed safely hung in the tree out of reach of any of the assorted house cats, possums, and mutts that roamed the nearby area.

John squirmed into his grandson's truck without speaking to the Trumbos. Davy talked to them for a couple of minutes and John heard him saying he was sorry his grandfather had eaten their lunches. Then Davy crawled into the driver's seat and fired up the engine. The dash lights illuminated his face and as they pulled out onto the highway he said, "Well, Grampap, it was a good day." He looked over at the giant old man stuffed into the seat. "I'm sorry you didn't get nothing."

As they rode toward the Brethren Home, the closer they got the more John straightened up. When they pulled into the parking lot he opened his door before they were at a full stop and it surprised Davy how nimbly John got out. Davy had to hurry to catch up with him, and as they went in the door John was stretched to the fullest extent of his considerable height and striding like a twenty-year-old. The lobby was full of the residents and he walked through them like the emperor of Rome walking into the

Senate. Expectation was on their faces. Rennick was sitting in the corner where he read *The New York Times.* One of the old blue-hairs asked, "Did you get one, John?"

John strode on with his shoulders back and confidence in his gait. Each room he passed someone asked the same question or a variation like, "Have any luck, John?"

Davy was feeling like the gun-bearer in an old Tarzan movie, escorting the rich Great White Hunter to his camp. When they reached John's room he pulled off his hat and threw it on the bed and sat down in his recliner. There was a crowd at the door waiting in expectation. Even bucktoothed Mary was there from the kitchen and she was the one who finally asked, "Well, did you get a buck, Mr. John?"

John leaned forward in his chair and said in a booming voice, "I didn't get one, but I knocked a hell of a big one down! Now I'm tired and need some rest. You all get out of here."

Everybody was left wanting more details and Davy slipped into the bathroom closing the door holding back a laugh. His grandfather might be an old man going into his second childhood but he was hard to keep down long. Davy pulled the old hunter's boots off and put them in the closet, gave him a pat on the shoulder, and told him loud so everybody could hear, "I'll go back and look some more tomorrow morning. That hollow where he run is awful thick. I know you got him, Grampap. There's no doubt about that! It's just that I ain't as good of a tracker as you was when you was young or I'd a found him. I'm mighty sorry I let you down. I don't know how in the world you ever hit him that far off and running like you did," the young man lied. "I'll try to get off one day next week if you promise to show me some more good spots."

"Okay, sonny. Glad to help you out. Don't lose no sleep over not being able to find him for me, I think a mountain lion may have stole him!" John said with a big grateful wink at his grandson.

There will never be another one like him, Davy thought as he smiled at the ladies as he walked down the hall to the exit sign. History really is written by the survivors, he thought.

And the bull shooters !

# Chapter 10

December 10, 1994

Things settled down for John after hunting season ended. Davy had taken him out again on doe day and John had killed a spike buck in the field right after daylight. Davy was able to back the truck right up to it and help him field-dress the animal. John's Old Hickory lock blade was blooded again. Davy hauled the deer to the Mennonite boy back of Clifton Forge who processed wild game at his farm. John had it all made into deer bologna except for the tenderloins, which he had butter-flied. He gave them to Davy with half of the bologna sticks. The rest of it he kept in his refrigerator in his room. Rennick sunk further into disrespect with the population at the Launching Pad. Bucktoothed Mary asked the agitator every chance she got if John had given him a piece of his deer bologna because she knew he loved that kind of food.

John heard the old spinsters talking one evening and one of them had even said, "You know, John is a handsome old brute in a rugged sort of way." John didn't give them the time of day. Any conversations he had at the Launching Pad were pretty much limited to Mary in the cafeteria and not much else. She was a real person, not fake old shells like the rest of them.

Christmas was coming and the first days of December wore on in a blur for John. He was still taking his walks and was going out twice a day now. He got Davy to bring him his cane he kept in his rental storage building. There were all kinds of things he had kept when he sold the house and the rental storage space deal had worked well even though it was expensive. At least he had a place with his own things somewhere besides the Launching Pad. John made the cane himself some years ago by cutting off a young locust tree he found growing out of the riverbank while fishing. It had grown straight out of the bank and then in its quest for sunlight made a ninety-degree turn upward. John hacked at it for half an hour with his pocketknife before he could take it with him to the truck. In his shop he trimmed it, sanded it and put a rubber tip on the end so it wouldn't scratch the floor or slip so much. Then he put four coats of varnish on it and set it aside. It made a splendid addition to his walks. In the mornings he would walk up toward the college to the north-west and keep the sun behind him. Looking into the sun always irritated him, especially when driving. Of course he couldn't drive now. Didn't even have a truck anymore and he missed it. That little jerk, Rennick, had a big new Oldsmobile and still drove all over the place although John couldn't imagine where he had to go that was so important. He overheard Rennick tell one of the ladies he bought the brand new car just because he wanted it and the money he spent was just that much less his kids would fight over when the little Yank was gone. It still angered him that Doc Malone told him he thought it was a good idea for him to turn in his driving license to DMV. Made him feel less than a man although he conceded he really wasn't a good driver any more.

As John walked he would find things on the sidewalk to prod with the cane. Once he found a quarter and another time he found a set of keys in front of the library. He took the keys to the librarian who thanked him and said she would post them on the lost and found on the bulletin board. The quarter he had stuck in his pocket and kept it there. It was one of those 1963 Kennedy-head quarters, solid silver!

In the evenings he would walk to the southeast, keeping the sun behind him as best he could. That route took him past the Southern Baptist church and John noticed there always seemed to be a lot of activity around that place. He had seldom set foot in a church since his horrific experiences fighting in one in Germany. John wished he could go back and take Fern to church just one time. He would jump at the chance now. He looked at the doorway with a huge pang of regret that made him twitch all over because he could hear her begging him to go with her and how ugly he had been to her so many times. It didn't seem important then. But now....

He remembered the fit he had thrown when she had come home with a pin oak sapling in the trunk of her car. She wanted to plant it over at the

Brethren Church next to the new playground. "Kids' Castle," that's what she had called it. Fern didn't think the children had enough shade and she wanted to plant a tree next to the chain link fence. "Don't you think it will be a nice place for the children to play years from now when it gets so big and shady? When we're gone maybe our spirits will linger here in a cool cheerful spot." He remembered his response all too well: "When I am gone I won't give a damn about no kids playing or their shady spots either. Probably wish I had the shade in Hell where any damn spirit I have will probably be sent!" He could tell he had hurt her bad with that one, but he couldn't help himself. She had just put the shovel and a watering can in the back of her old Buick and started down the driveway. John watched her go, felt guilty, and then got in his truck and followed her.

When he got to the church playground she was trying to dig a hole in the hard, sun-baked ground. He walked up and took the shovel from her and started digging. All of a sudden he flew into a fit of rage and started cursing the ground and digging like a wild man. Fern picked up her little watering jug and walked off toward the hand pump on the other side of the church to get water and get away from him. Finally John was embarrassed with himself and settled into the task. One thing was for sure: that spot could stand some shade. It reminded him of digging foxholes in France. Of course, Germans were shooting at him then so the benefits of digging were more apparent.

He looked over his shoulder and saw Fern talking to three little kids. They had a red wagon and were hauling her water for her. John got the tree out of the trunk of the car and put the root ball in the hole and figured it was deep enough.

It had been thirty years ago and the last time John had been past the church the tree was at least thirty feet tall and the playground had some good shade from that pin oak. A dozen kids were playing and laughing under it that day. If only Fern could see it now maybe she would forgive him and laugh it off.

John turned into the sinking sun and headed back toward the Launching Pad. He wished he had been kinder to her. Why had he needed to give her so much hell sometimes? Suddenly, he looked up and saw Rennick in his car, trying to drive into the blinding sun with his hand up in front of his face. The Oldsmobile ran right through a red light and got T-boned by a cement truck. The truck kept going ahead like a bumblebee flying through a mosquito. The sickening *thump* and the parts flying off the Oldsmobile were horrendous. John made it up to the car and looked in. Rennick was slumped over the wheel and an air bag was all over the place and covered in broken glass. John took his cane and broke the rest of the driver's side window out and then tossed his cane over toward a pile of leaves someone had raked up next to the sidewalk. He could see Rennick's arms were badly broken and he had a gash on his head. People were coming out of nowhere and a goofy-looking kid with hoops and earrings in his lips was screaming into a cell phone, telling the 911 dispatcher where they were at. John had been in so much war and hell during his days that he could look at situations like this objectively. The cement truck driver was freaking out and started pounding John on the shoulder with both of his hands, screaming for him to do something. John reached inside the Oldsmobile and cut off the ignition but the motor kept on running. He could smell gas. All of a sudden smoke came creeping out from under the hood and a lazy flame popped out of the grill. John said, "We got to get him out of the car or he's gonna burn."

The cement truck driver was acting like a fool, squawking like a chicken and jumping around John's back like a rat terrier barking at a tomcat. John had enough of him and backhanded him across the lips knocking him back and away from the wreck. "Look, you damn idiot. It wasn't your fault so quit acting like a woman and help me!" The cement truck driver calmed down but then started screaming, "You hit me, you son of a bitch! Oh, God! It's burning, it's burning and it's going to explode!"

John knew the truck driver was right even if he was an idiot. The seatbelt was holding Rennick down and John couldn't reach the release on it. Reaching in his pocket he pulled out his Old Hickory knife and cut the strap. He grabbed Rennick under the arms and pulled him out the window as if the man was a rag doll. John held him in his arms like a baby and carried him across the yard of a brick house on the corner, safely away from the now fully burning Oldsmobile.

They were right in front of a big porch and John looked up to catch a glimpse of a tall, fat woman behind the screen door staring at them with her hand over her mouth. She had something in her hands as she ducked back into the house. John sat down on the steps of the porch. He laid Rennick down gently, and then took off his own coat which was more than large enough to cover the injured, unconscious man. John knew a thing or two about shock.

Rennick seemed to regain consciousness and John stroked his head and told him, "It's a good thing your head is so hard, you little Yankee prick, or you would be dead. Just relax. Unfortunately, you ain't gonna die unless you are broke up inside and your ribs are punching holes in your lungs. I don't think that happened, Rennick. Do you hear me, Rennick? Now you're gonna be okay so don't try to move. I can hear the help coming now."

Rennick murmured, "Oh, f#^%!" and seemed to pass out for a few seconds. He came to and sputtered something unintelligible.

John sat down on the ground and took Rennick's head in his lap and wiped the blood off his forehead with his sleeve. "Just take it easy, dickhead. Stay with me now. Stay with me! Don't you pass out on me! When you get better I'll give you a whole stick of my deer bologna if you listen to me. I know you like it." He held the little man's head in his giant hands like he was a baby in swaddling clothes and stroked his brow.

# Chapter 11

The rescue squad came screeching to a halt at a safe distance from the burning car. The cement truck driver ran over to them holding his face while pointing to where John was holding Rennick. An unmarked Sheriff's car rolled up and turned on lights and siren. It was that pretty boy Sheriff himself that got out of the car. As he shut the door of the unmarked Ford Crown Vic he glanced around to see if anyone was looking and tossed something into the pile of leaves on the ground beside the sidewalk. He was shaking his head, looking at the burning wreck with a disgusted look, and then he went to his trunk and started digging for something.

He came out with a red fire extinguisher and went over to the fire and tried to spray it. The fire extinguisher didn't work. He shook it and fooled around with the lever on top of it and was visibly frustrated. The look on the Sheriff's face made John think the high Sheriff smelled a pile of manure that he thought somebody else should be smelling. The cement truck driver ran over to the Sheriff, still holding his face, and then pointed to John. John started feeling like maybe these people were going to determine he had done something wrong.

A fire truck came clanging in and at last people were there who looked like they wanted to be. Those boys rolled off the truck and had the fire out in a few seconds, putting up a perimeter of yellow and black tape around the car at a safe distance. Two of the squad members came at a trot carrying first-aid kits to where John was holding Rennick at the bottom of the porch steps. They started checking Rennick out. A black-haired woman who had EMT written on her hat examined John. She checked his pulse and blood pressure and then put air splints on Rennick's arms. A horse collar went around his neck before they eased him onto a stretcher. The girl wrote down John's name and phone number and then gave him his coat back. She told John he had done a superb job and had probably saved Rennick's life. As the squad zoomed away with Rennick on board John made it up to his feet.

The tall, lean prissy Sheriff sauntered over to him like a rooster with a tomato stake up his back side. He stumbled a little as he came through the grass. John was putting his coat back on when the Sheriff said in an insolent tone, "So, what do you know about what happened here? Are you some kind of a nut? Pulling that man out of the car and smacking that cement truck driver in the mouth? You been pretty busy, old man." John could smell liquor on his breath and realized the man was fairly drunk.

John sat back down on the step and didn't answer right away. He just looked up into the sky like he hadn't heard anything and that only served to anger the Sheriff more. As the Sheriff looked around, making sure no one else was listening, he snarled again at the giant, "Which are you, old man? A hero or a dumb ass?"

John couldn't believe what he was hearing. He was a little confused and rapidly getting mad. Nothing he had done deserved this pretty boy fart with a badge to be talking to him like he was. John could see his reflection in the Sheriff's sunglasses and looking the Sheriff in the eye he said, "Why don't you go ride your bicycle or play with them Special Olympics kids in front of a camera. Go do something you do well, boy. You sure as hell don't know nothing about an emergency."

The Sheriff whipped out his handcuffs, grabbed John by the left wrist and tried to cuff him. "Okay, smart ass old man, you're under arrest for assaulting that truck driver!"

"You can't arrest me for that. You wasn't even here!" John yelled but the Sheriff was struggling with the cuffs, trying to get them on the old man's humongous wrists.

Without thinking about any of the consequences, and like a medieval log on a pendulum used to batter castle doors down, John's right forearm swung forward and his huge fist struck the high Sheriff fully on the nose, breaking his sunglasses into his face. The man literally flew ten feet backward and landed on his back. John was surprised almost as much as the cement truck driver who was walking up behind the Sheriff. It had been like hitting a scarecrow full of straw. The cement truck driver took off running, screaming, "He killed the Sheriff! He killed the Sheriff! If he killed one he'll kill another!"

John just sat there and felt the knuckles in his right hand starting to hurt. The one in his middle finger felt like it was broken. The Sheriff was stirring and John saw him draw his pistol. As he sat up it was obvious his nose was broken and bleeding like a stuck hog. The hole in the end of the gun barrel pointing at John looked as big as a Campbell's Soup can with the top cut out and it was shaking furiously. The Sheriff was trying to tell John he was under arrest but it sounded like a growling dog. His two front teeth were broken off at the gums and he had bitten his tongue in two. John just stared at him, unblinking, and said, "Go ahead and shoot me, asshole. Put me out of my misery. Do me a favor and be a real hero on the news tonight!"

John put his hands up in the air as another deputy and a town patrolman in a blue uniform pulled up. They jumped out of their cars and came running with their guns out too. The town man in blue took one look at the Sheriff and said, "Holy shit, Mark! Did you get kicked by a horse?"

John realized then that the Sheriff was really messed up and he was in serious trouble. The town cop told him he was under arrest for maliciously wounding the Sheriff. And John asked the deputy, "Is that a felony charge?"

The deputy drew his gun and aimed it at John. "You damn right it's a felony!"

They tried unsuccessfully to get a set of handcuffs on him but couldn't, and it wasn't because he was resisting, just the fact his wrists were too big. The town cop pulled out something he called flex cuffs made out of white plastic and took the Sheriff's cocked gun away from him. They couldn't pull John's hands together behind his back so they tied his wrists together in front as the meat wagon took off with Rennick. Another squad vehicle arrived and more squad members working with the Sheriff while glaring at John. Apparently the girls in the squad liked the Sheriff. "He won't be too pretty for a while with that big nose of his busted all over his face," John snarled. "His problem is he needs to learn some manners and stay out of the liquor bottle."

The town cop took John over to his car and tried to get him to get into the cage in the back seat. Finally John just kind of stuck his backside in the door and slid himself in backward across to the other side and they shut the door with him sitting sideways in the back like a dog in one of those car pens.

He had been arrested a couple of times before when he had gone nuts, and once in the military when he had gotten in a fight outside the EM Club, so he was familiar with the process. As they were driving away John saw the Sheriff being put in the wagon on a stretcher. The town cop said, "Mister, I hope you realize how much deep crap you are in. You probably gonna be charged with attempting to kill the Sheriff. His face is messed up bad? Why did you hit him?"

"He's a disrespectful little prick and shouldn't be a lawman if he don't want to do the job. Besides that, I think he's about half drunk!" John blurted out. "He talked to me like I'm a dog. Ain't he the same man that does those stupid commercials about how senior citizens can protect themselves from con men? Ain't he the one does those bike commercials in those queer-looking pants"

The town cop smiled a little and said that he was. Then he said, "He won't be doing no commercials for a while the way you messed his face up. He bit the hell out of his tongue and lost a couple of teeth. Gonna take him a good while and the help of a dentist and a doctor to get his face back on the TV."

John thought he saw the makings of a smile at the corner of the cop's face so he asked the obvious. "You taking me to jail?"

"We gotta go to the jail and to the magistrate's office. Then you either post bail or go to jail or get sent before the district court judge for a bond hearing. You have a lawyer?"

"Yeah, I got a friend who is a lawyer. You know McNally?" John asked.

The town cop looked back at him in the mirror. "You mean McNally Sr.?"

"Yeah, me, him, Judge Crawford and Speedy Spencer got off a boat together one time a long time ago."

"Oh, yeah? Where'd you go with them?" The town cop asked doubtfully, rather surprised.

John asked quietly, "You ain't from around here, are you son?"

"No, sir, I'm a Lantz from Moorefield. My daddy was Buck Lantz. Ran the Fresh Dock at the chicken plant. I been on the force for two years and before that I helped him on the docks. I am curious? Where'd you go on a boat with such distinguished company as Judge Crawford and Mr. McNally."

John started not to answer but then said, "A little vacation spot called Omaha Beach in a place called Normandy back in the early '40s when we was young."

Officer Lantz glanced quickly back at the big man in his rearview mirror. It had started to rain and Lantz turned on his wipers and headlights.

"I pulled six in the Marines and spent a while in Iraq a couple of years ago," Lantz offered. John just nodded.

"You know a little bit about hell then too, don't you?" John said quietly.

The radio was tuned to a local country music station. They were playing an old song by Roger Miller.

Ya can't roller skate in a buffalo herd
Ya can't roller skate in a buffalo herd
Ya can't roller skate in a buffalo herd
But you can be happy if you've a mind to.

It was getting dark when they pulled up to the big white jail house. Officer Lantz called the dispatcher on the radio and told them to open the gates. A big double garage door flew open and they pulled into the bay. Once the car was inside, the doors rolled shut behind them and four big jailers in brown deputy Sheriff uniforms came rolling out of the door. They looked to John like they were ready to get with it. He supposed they were also wanting to lay their hands on the man that put their Sheriff in the Emergency Room!

# Chapter 12

The three-time elected Commonwealth's Attorney was walking along the sidewalk from the courthouse to his car with a worried look on his face. He was carrying a large briefcase in one hand and trying not to drop a stuffed file folder packed under his other arm while attempting to get a cigarette lit at the same time. One of the young deputies driving down the street saw him and tooted his horn, darting his car into the curb close to him. He rolled down his passenger window with one of those looks on his face that said, *Wait till you hear this!*

"Mr. Grimes, did you hear about the Sheriff?" the deputy asked excitedly.

"No, what is going on with him?" he asked with a sinking feeling. He could tell by experience the story he was about to hear was going to generate more work for him. The CA was exhausted from carrying a monstrous caseload with very little help and only wanted to get home, kick his feet up, and have a stiff drink. He had had his butt kicked in court today. He was afraid he had won the case but lost the war with a local drug dealer whose attorney had spent far too many hours sparring back and forth concerning a case that was, in the CA's mind, all too clear. He had presented a flawless prosecution and a jury found the toad guilty after a two-day trial. During the sentencing phase of the trial the CA had thought for sure this man would pull at least ten years for selling a pound of crack cocaine to an undercover member of the drug task force. The jury had come back with a ridiculous sentence of three years with two years suspended. This guy could do a year in jail standing on his head whistling

"Dixie." It was no more than just the price of doing business for him. War on drugs? Where in the hell was there a war on drugs? Not here in the good old US of A. These bastards were getting away with anything they wanted while the CA kept having all these Oprah fans sitting on juries that had watched too many episodes of Judge Judy and CNN. He looked at the young, clean-cut deputy with the fresh-scrubbed *I'm gonna change the world with my ticket book* look on his face. All I need is to have another mess heaped on me, he thought.

"Some old man slugged the Sheriff in the face and busted him up good!" the young man offered enthusiastically.

"Where did *that* happen?" asked the incredulous prosecutor.

"The Sheriff rolled up on a wreck up on the north side and this old man who is supposed to be some kind of a giant went off on him and put him in the hospital. They say he's really messed up. Sheriff had to draw down on him and almost shot the old SOB when some of the city boys rolled in."

"Since when did the Sheriff start working wrecks again? Doesn't he have other things to do?" the prosecutor asked.

"Guess he just rolled up on it himself. Cement truck T-boned another old man in an Oldsmobile that they say ran a red light. I didn't even know Sheriff Watson was out today. Must have come back from the Sheriffs convention early," the deputy speculated.

"Who's working the assault, the city or the county?" Grimes asked.

"The chief wanted to work it but Major Thompson went to the hospital to see the Sheriff and he has Investigator Wilkins handling it. Major called the chief and told him it's by the Sheriff's direct orders and the chief ain't gonna buck him too much. You know that."

"Thanks for the info," Grimes said as he brushed off the young man and continued toward his car. It was obvious the rookie would like to talk for more time than Grimes was interested in spending.

Grimes' mind was working at warp speed. If this was the old World War II hero John Dean, the stone mason, who had slugged the Sheriff then his old crony McNally would represent him. McNally, as head of the Democrat Party in Cambridge County, would be his adversary in the upcoming vacancy in the state senate race either as a candidate or campaign manager. Grimes and the Republicans could score a huge political victory over McNally with a solid win in a likely high-profile case that was bound to draw media attention never seen before. More than likely it would be covered by the Richmond papers and TV too. Such a case, handled to his advantage, would be a political godsend!

Grimes got to his car and called Wilkins on his cell phone. Wilkins told him he had gone to the hospital and Major Thompson gave him a written statement he had taken directly from the Sheriff, which the Sheriff had signed. Wilkins was meeting the city unit that had taken the suspect to the jail. The man who had hit him was a John Dean who was a resident at the Brethren Home. He had smacked the cement truck driver in the mouth too. Grimes asked him how bad off the Sheriff was and Wilkins told him the injuries the Sheriff had sustained were serious enough that he was going to need a good bit of surgery. He was missing his upper two front teeth and had broken bones in his face. Wilkins told the prosecutor a man involved in the wreck was in intensive care and might not make it. Grimes whistled to himself and thought a minute, and then shook his head, marveling at how quickly the simplest things can turn to crap.

"What does the Sheriff's statement say?" the prosecutor inquired.

The investigator pulled out the legal pad Thompson had given him and summarized it to the CA. "Pretty much says the cement truck driver told him this guy had backhanded him when he was trying to help the man trapped in the Oldsmobile. Then the Dean man pulled the victim out himself and carried him over to the steps of a house there on the corner. When the Sheriff questioned him about assaulting the truck driver the man slugged him in the face with no warning. Sheriff says in his report that he was barely able to hold the man off at gunpoint until help arrived."

"Sounds pretty cut and dried to me," Grimes mumbled as if he were thinking about something else. Then with the manner of a high school football coach sending a play in with a substitute running back he ordered, "You go down and hook up with the City officer who took him in and see the magistrate. Charge this guy with one felony charge of malicious wounding of a police officer and then charge him with assault and battery for swatting that truck driver. Give the warrants to the city officer that brought him in. Let him serve the warrants on him so the chief can get a piece of the pie in the news this evening. I'm going to hang this old bastard by the balls! When you get him charged I want you to interview everybody concerned and get me a report by tomorrow. We'll get him certified in the preliminary hearing on these charges and then we may indict him on everything we can throw at him in circuit court," the cagey old prosecutor directed.

"Yes, sir!" Wilkins answered as Grimes hung up and then smiled. Wilkins had received the call from Major Thompson and met him at the emergency room. Thompson had been in to see the Sheriff and told Wilkins he was worried about this one. The doctor had smelled liquor on the Sheriff. They had checked him out and the doc had told Thompson they couldn't operate right away because the Sheriff's blood/alcohol content was too high: his BAC was .07. Legally drunk was .08.

Thompson tilted his head back and looked down his long nose, glaring with those bushy eyebrows and steely gray eyes of his, and told Wilkins he had told the doctor to keep his mouth shut. Thompson was an intimidator and his inference was clear. Wilkins didn't think he would put that in his report to share with the Commonwealth's Attorney. He knew the Sheriff was drinking a lot these days and had women problems, but he was the elected Sheriff! Who was going to challenge him on those issues?

Wilkins felt a rush of adrenalin knowing if he played his cards right and handled this investigation to his and the Sheriff's advantage he might move up the ladder a notch or two. Thompson was playing Pontius Pilate, washing his hands of this one by sending it to Caiaphas. Thompson was slick all right. Probably going to be the next Sheriff some day and he was handing it off to Wilkins, betting that Wilkins could handle it, but knowing also he could blame any failures on the investigator if something about the alcohol came out later. Well, Wilkins thought, old Caiaphas may just have a trick or two up his own sleeve. If I can pull this one off I just might move ahead of Thompson in the department power rating. That was the way the Sheriff's office worked under Sheriff Mark Watson. Stick a knife in your buddy's back, put your foot on it, and climb on up! Shine the right shoes and keep all the right secrets. It was time for him to rise, and he was ready to play the game.

At the jail Wilkins met Officer Lantz and filled him in on what CA Grimes had advised him to do. Lantz explained the chief had called the jail and told him it would be the Sheriff's office's case and to expect a Sheriff's department investigator to show up. Wilkins looked over at the huge old man sitting in the chair in front of booking. Lantz nodded confirming he was the one who had done the Sheriff in. Wilkins said, "Hell I know him. Isn't that the old Dean man who used to lay stone? Davy Dean's grand-daddy?"

Lantz said he didn't know anything about that but the old man hadn't given him any trouble. "There is one thing he keeps on insisting. Says the Sheriff gave him a bunch of crap and talked to him bad and tried to make an illegal arrest on him. Says the Sheriff is drunk. Is he?"

"That's a bunch of bull, Lantz. That old man has been in and out of the nut house a couple of times. The Sheriff doesn't drink on the job. That old man is crazy sometimes. You get everything he said to you and all you saw down there in your report for me by the end of your shift, even if you got to stay late, okay?"

"Aren't you going to talk to him?" Lantz responded.

"No, I think your statements are more than enough and he is definitely in custody now. I don't want to upset him," Wilkins answered. He did not want to get the old man stirred up and talking the drunk stuff in front of any more people than he had to. They would ask him why he didn't try to talk to the old fool but he could slip that punch by saying he wanted the old man to talk to his attorney first. Juries would like that. He had would appear to have been respectful of the old man's rights.

"I'll go ahead and see the magistrate and stroke him with what Grimes directed and bring you the warrants to serve. Get me copies of the warrants with copies of the fingerprints too. I'll handle it from there," the investigator requested.

"Yes, sir," the officer answered. Wilkins turned and headed out to the magistrate's office. Things were coming together nicely, he thought.

# Chapter 13

Her name was Mary Ann Bartley and the kids in the neighborhood called her Spider-Woman behind her back. Not because she enjoyed any superhero status but rather because she reminded them of one of those giant brown spiders a person might find around the dog's bowl in September. Mary Ann lived alone most of the time in the house on the corner. She had bought the rundown house with the latest installment of money her father had left her when he died six years earlier. He had wisely left the money in an account which paid her $100,000 in a lump sum every two years. Her attorney had told her she could live a hundred lifetimes and not use up her daddy's money at that rate. The loyal attorney had gotten his fingers into the old man's money too. The old man had been wise, though, and the latest was the third check she had deposited to an empty bank account. She would have blown all those lifetimes of money in one year if she had access to it and her father had known that.

The old house and a worthless college degree in sociology from Old Dominion University were all she had to show for herself thus far in life. Mary Ann's problem was not that she was dumb. Her problem was that she was too smart. Book smart with no common sense mixed with a lot of good intentions was her personal recipe for disaster and unhappiness. Her weight embarrassed her so she wore loose-fitting dresses down to her ankles, Mama Cass style. Her legs had not been shaved in years and there were open sores on them that bothered her greatly and made her worry. They didn't make her worry enough to go to the doctor, though. She didn't trust doctors. Mary Ann also had an annoying nervous thing going with her eyes. Whenever she talked to anyone and tried to look them in the eye her eyelids would flutter uncontrollably. When she chased the local brats out of her yard she did indeed resemble a big fat brown spider wielding a broom.

Before moving to the house on the corner she had lived in a trailer park on a small lot. A Mexican boyfriend she had once thought so exotic had abused and left her. She was sure he loved her dearly and was going to marry her until one day in June he just up and quit his job at the turkey processing plant and took off in the new Chevrolet pick-up she had bought for him. His name was Enrique Herrerra and one of his friends, Placido Lopez, finally explained to her Enrique had taken her truck to Aguas Calientes in Mexico to be with his wife and six kids. He said Enrique would probably stay there for a couple of years until the money he had saved working in the USA ran out. Of course Mary Ann was heartbroken. She hadn't even known he was married, so in her sorrow she got terribly drunk with Placido that night and woke up with a roaring hangover, naked in bed with him and two other guys he worked with on the cleanup crew at the turkey processing plant. She didn't even know their names and was so horrified at what she had done that she physically threw them out into the gravel parking lot. Then she threw their empty Budweiser bottles at them until they scampered into nearby trailers. Mary Ann immediately sold her trailer for half what it was worth to a Cuban man who had cash and then she went house shopping. The house on the corner in town suited her perfectly so she bought it and then, out of desperation, got Placido and his friends to help her move. They were only too happy to help, for a hundred dollars apiece.

Spider-Woman lived in the house alone and seldom went anywhere except to the grocery store and the video store. The things she enjoyed most were watching TV, bird watching, and exploring her new computer. She could do all of it from her recliner with her remote controls and the computer desk right next to it. A large bird bath in the backyard and four bird feeders were set up outside her back window. Cardinals, blue jays, sparrows, and starlings galore feasted there every day. Mary Ann had bought the most expensive camcorder money could buy to film her birds when the light was just right and had a machine that could copy VCR tapes of birds. She mailed them to her people all over the world whose names and addresses she found in magazines. That is what she had just finished doing when she heard the loud *thump* outside in the intersection when the cement truck collided with the side of Rennick's Oldsmobile.

She got up out of her chair and walked to the door with her camcorder and caught all of it on tape. She filmed the giant old man as he tossed his cane into the leaves along the sidewalk. She watched in fascination through the telescoping viewer on her camcorder as he backhanded the truck driver and took the much smaller man out of the car. A thrill ran through her as he carried the victim away from the burning wreck right toward her into the safety of her yard. She saw him look up at her as he tended to the wounded, crumpled man and wrapped him in his own coat. She knew right away a film of this unexpected drama would impress her friends. Spider-Woman was very glad she had just put in a new cassette and had fully charged batteries.

When the police car pulled in and the Sheriff himself got out of the car it was too good to be true; she zoomed right in on him and his tight little buns. She had long been fascinated with Sheriff Mark Watson and his Hollywood good looks. Of course, he wasn't wearing those spandex bicycle shorts he always wore in those safety commercials on TV, but that was too much to hope for, being cold weather and all. She watched him look around to see if anyone was looking and saw him throw a small brown bottle into a pile of leaves where the giant's cane was still lying. All of it she caught in detail for posterity on her film. Then the cement truck driver started yelling at the heroic Sheriff as he was frustrated with a fire extinguisher he could not get to work. The flames accelerated. She shivered with the epic efforts he made and her heart soared. The fire trucks got there and they rapidly hosed down the car and put the flames out.

Panning back to the drama in her yard as the rescue squad arrived, she captured all the action there and then, as the victim was carried away by the squad members, the Sheriff approached the giant. No one noticed her as she stood in the shadows of the door but she could see and hear all that passed between the two men through the lens of her camera now focused perfectly through a hole in the screen door. She could hear all that her microphone was recording in absolute clarity. It shocked her at first and then broke her heart to hear the Sheriff talk to the rescuing giant in such a belittling, insulting way after all he had done! Mary Ann absolutely could not believe her ears. Later, she would put the VCR tape into her machine and listen to it over and over, getting more furious each time she watched the drama in defense of the old man. And when he struck out, lashing at the insolent, sarcastic lawman, she almost dropped the camera and cheered. She zoomed in on the broken, bleeding face of the Sheriff, held her breath, and retreated farther into her hallway as he drew his gun and aimed it at the old man. The damn coward! She caught it all in the utmost detail and told no one. She nearly cried when they arrested the giant and led him away.

After everyone had left and the smashed, burned Oldsmobile was hauled away on a rollback, she put on her jacket and walked over to the place where the wrecked car had come to rest. She went to the pile of leaves and picked up the cane the giant had tossed there. Then with the toe of her boot she kicked around in the leaves until she found the brown bottle she was looking for. So the Sheriff likes to nip on Southern Comfort, she thought. What a sissy! Real men drink bourbon. She slipped the bottle into her pocket and walked back to the house. As she walked she twirled the cane in her fingers, wondering what was happening to the wonderful giant.

She decided to make a copy of the tape and then she watched it over and over again on her big-screen color TV thinking the guys that filmed that *Cops* show would love to see this! Maybe not though. They weren't in the business of showing the cop being a jerk and then being bested by an old man!

# Chapter 14

John thought he was going to be beaten by the Sheriff's men who looked like a pack of dogs ready to run a mean bull, but Officer Lantz rolled his window down and said, "Everything's cool fellows. He's calm."

One of the jailors bent down and looked in the window and said, "Hell, it's an old man! I thought we was going to have a badass to deal with and it's an old man!"

Officer Lantz got out and put his gun and his knife in a lock box along with his extra bullet magazines. He told the deputies he wasn't having any trouble with his arrest. "Mr. Dean is fine and I recommend nobody makes fun of him or gives him any crap. He is an old-timer and he has been through more hell than all of you guys put together in service to our country so treat him with respect."

He opened the back door and they had a hard time scooting John out of the back of the car, but finally he got his feet out on the floor. Lantz offered his hand to John who took it and pulled himself up to a standing position. The jailors instinctively backed up a half step and looked up at the ancient giant. John could see a little fear in their eyes. One of them whistled through his teeth and said, "No wonder the Sheriff is in the emergency room if that fist hit him in the face." He marveled at the size of the grizzled old hands that had laid so many men low and so many stones on the wall. The same hands that now were bound together with a puny piece of plastic band.

A glass plate door opened up and they all walked into a little room with another glass door on the other side. When the door shut behind them it made a heavy metallic *thunk* sound when the big electronic pins shot into place. The other door opened and John could see through the hall where there was a large complex of desks with a glassed-in room in the center with a girl running a switchboard. She was monitoring several TV screens and a huge control panel like she was one of those people he had seen on TV that mixed music in a Nashville studio.

The door clanged shut behind them and Officer Lantz got a pair of wire cutters from one of the jail deputies who was busy behind the desk entering data on the computer. Lantz then cut off the flex cuffs and John was able to rub his hands together and check out the swollen finger on his right hand. It was going to be sore enough but he didn't think it was broken. They took him to a table and asked him to put everything in his pockets on the table. It wasn't much: wallet, keys, handkerchief, and some change and an Old Hickory lock-blade knife. The jailer picked up the knife and shook it at Lantz, nonverbally chastising him for not taking it from the suspect in the field. John noticed Officer Lantz blush a little.

Then John had to take his shoes and belt off. His pants started to fall off without his belt on and he protested, but Officer Lantz stepped in and said they had to do the same thing with everyone who comes in. The deputy put on a pair of thin plastic gloves and told John to put his hands up on the wall. The deputy was thorough and patted him down well. He picked up John's shoes and after carefully inspecting them gave them back to him. They had John sign a receipt saying he had $228.34 in cash and listed his other belongings. Officer Lantz made sure John's pocketknife was in the ziplock bag with the other stuff.

"That Kennedy head quarter better not be swapped when I get my stuff back! That one is solid silver," John said. The jailer gave him a sideways glance and didn't respond.

He started filling out a lot of papers and was talking to the dispatcher behind the desk who was looking at John's Virginia Identity Card. Lantz left and said he was going to talk to the magistrate and would be right back. The other deputies asked John to have a seat. After they verified all his information on the computer John was forced to sit there for about a half hour. He saw Officer Lantz talking to a guy in a coat and tie, obviously talking about him. They must have talked for five minutes and then the guy in the suit left and went down the hall. He looked like he was all business. After a while he came back and gave Officer Lantz some green papers and they shook hands and he left again. Finally Officer Lantz came back with the green papers in his hand and said, "Let's go talk to the magistrate, Mr. Dean."

They walked around the large curved desk and John said, "Where's Captain Kirk? This place looks like the inside of that there spaceship on the *Star Trek* show." Officer Lantz laughed and said he thought so too. Down the hall on the right there was a small room with a metal bench in it and another glass window with a little fellow that looked like an accountant sitting on a swivel chair behind a desk with a computer screen in front of him. John figured he was all business too, like the guy in the suit, and he was right.

Officer Lantz indicated to John where to sit down on the bench and he said, "Mr. Dean, this is Magistrate Butcher. Mr. Butcher, this is Mr. John Dean." Officer Lantz went to writing on the green papers and John noticed there was a yellow one too. When he finished he tore off a copy of the green one and turned to John, handing him a copy, and said, "Mr. Dean, this is a warrant for your arrest. It says that on this date you did unlawfully and feloniously commit assault and battery on a police officer, committing malicious wounding. It is a class four felony." He tore off a copy of the yellow one and said, "The second one is a class one misdemeanor for committing an assault and battery on the cement truck driver, a Mr. Barry Zetty. Now answer any questions Magistrate Butcher has for you, please."

Magistrate Butcher had been one of the brightest members of his high school class. He had run a very successful jewelry store for thirty years. He had never married and the years of long nights spent alone had inspired him to answer an advertisement ten years prior for the job of night magistrate. Mostly because it offered him state employee benefits with full health insurance. Nighttime at the magistrate's office was either a long nap in the old green recliner or the surreal world of dealing with the gripes and sorrows of a rural community. He was well versed in the Code of Virginia and how it relates to maintaining a level of respectability. His greatest joy was slipping out behind the jail every night around midnight, if he could find a lull in the flow of business, to feed the local stray cats that roamed the alley behind the jail and adjacent railroad tracks. Magistrate Butcher was a kind, compassionate, and understanding man. At the same time had no problem sending people to the jail cells upstairs. He was perfectly suited for the job.

"Mr. Dean, you have been charged with two very serious charges, of which if you are convicted will put you in jail for up to twenty years. You have been charged with maliciously wounding the Sheriff of Cambridge County, Mr. Mark Watson. And, Mr. Dean, you have been charged with assaulting another man, a Mr. Barry Zetty. The Sheriff is in the hospital now. Do you understand these charges?

"Yes, sir, I do. And I have one question," John said.

"What is that, Mr. Dean?" the little fellow asked.

"Is anybody going to arrest the Sheriff for driving drunk? I believe he was drunk and I saw him drive into the wreck. Plus he tried to make an illegal arrest on me."

"Well, now, Mr. Dean, that is all I need to hear. Sheriff Watson is a well-respected man and I take offense in your obvious lack of remorse for your actions." He looked at the paperwork on his desk and said, "A man born in 1924 ought not be slugging the Sheriff in the face." He scribbled on a piece of paper, shoved it through to Officer Lantz, and said, "Give this committal to the jailer. Mr. Dean can go before the Judge tomorrow morning. I am not giving him any bond and District Court closed forty-five minutes ago."

John looked Magistrate Butcher in the eyes through the bulletproof glass and said, "Wouldn't expect nothing more from a little chigger like you."

Magistrate Butcher pulled the curtains over the window and headed out to feed the cats an early supper, muttering about impertinent old fools with no common sense.

Officer Lantz led John out of the small antiseptic room and said, "Man, you don't care about much, do you? You got the right to two phone calls if you want them."

John said he would just wait until tomorrow to talk to somebody. The only person he wanted to talk to anyway was Davy and he would just get upset and give him hell about being in jail.

John asked, "They got any supper around this place. I am starved."

Officer Lantz said, "We can check with the jailers. I think they serve supper around six. Supper at six and breakfast at six. They got pretty good food here."

Lantz took John around to the jailers who took the paperwork from him. They led John into another room, took mug shots from the front and side, and took his fingerprints. The jailer complained it was like trying to fingerprint King Kong. Once they got all that done they took John into a room and had him take his clothes off. They put all his clothes and shoes into a big paper bag, wrote his name on it, and threw it in a big closet. They gave him jail clothes which was a blaze orange jumpsuit.

Another jailer took him up to the jail nurse who took his blood pressure and temperature and asked him his medical history. She checked out John's hand and determined it was not broken but was sprained and bruised. Then she told John she would take care of getting his medicine together in the morning. Once she was relatively sure he was not going to die on her and not going to give the rest of the population anything worse than a cold they took John to an elevator and headed up. John asked them if they had any cells where he could be alone and the jailer told him they didn't.

Once off the elevator they walked down a hall to a closet where they gave him a flimsy mattress, some sheets, a pillow, and a blanket. The jailor talked on the little radio speaker that ran from his hip up to his shoulder on a spiral phone cord: "Central control, open 3-B-224." A door opened up and John could see half a dozen men standing in a semi-circle around a TV set mounted on the wall. One of them, a scrawny white boy, looked at John and laughing, said, "Would you look at that! They done brought in the Abominable Grampa!"

# Chapter 15

John walked into the common area and dragged his mattress and blankets to the only unoccupied cell, ignoring the young smart ass. There were about a dozen inmates in this pod and all of them except the little redneck were rough-looking Mexican types. One of the Hispanics, who appeared to be their leader, said in a heavy accent, "Where you think you going, old man? I run this cell block and you go where I say."

John just kept on going and threw his mattress on the bottom bunk. He turned to face the man and said, "Son, I am in here because I broke the nose of the Sheriff of this county and busted a couple of his teeth out when he pissed me off and disrespected me. He is in the hospital and probably going to have his sinuses rerouted so he can breathe through his ass. I don't want no trouble with you or nobody else in here. Just show me where I am supposed to sleep and get on with it."

John put his hand on his big stomach and pointing to the little redneck said, "I had one just like you for breakfast this morning, peckerhead, with some hot sauce. If I was your grampa, which I'm positive I ain't, I would have beat your daddy's ass for making you."

The Mexican leader stepped forward and pointed a finger at John. "It was on the news somebody whacked the Sheriff hard at a wreck today. If you are the man that did it then you are under my protection. I despise that Sheriff who is nothing but a goat molester girly-man." He turned to the rest of the inmates in the block and said, "Este hombre es mi tio ahora. Es un amigo mio y Ustedes necessitan dar todo su respecto a El."

He turned back to John and said, "You are now the same as my uncle and I have told them to respect you."

"Well thank you very much there, Pancho Villa, my little newfound nephew. Are they going to serve us any tacos or enchiladas or whatever you and your merry men eat? I'm starved."

"Don't call me Pancho Villa. My name is Horatio," the young man stated.

Supper turned out to be far from Central American fare: turkey loaf with mashed potatoes and gravy with two slices of Wonder Bread. It was actually pretty good and the trustees who served it under the jailers' supervision gave John a tray with an extra big portion. John suddenly missed Buck-toothed Mary and with a start realized he must be the talk of the Launching Pad this evening. He wondered if they had seen him on the evening news. Then for the first time he thought about his room and his belongings. They would probably kick him out of the home. He went in and lay down on the bottom bunk. His hand hurt and his shoulder ached. The mattress was covered with a plastic material and only about three inches thick. Within a few minutes he was asleep.

Horatio came into the cell and looked down at him. Man, he's one big, tough old Gringo, he thought. What would have made him hit the Sheriff in the face? He don't look too crazy and he talks all right. Horatio threw an extra blanket on John and went out to a game of spades that had started on the table after the trustees came by for the food trays. John was snoring.

John woke up twice during the night and used the urinal both times. The second time he had trouble going back to sleep and wished he had something to read. The jailers in the floor control room could see into all five cell blocks on the floor and he could see them move every once in a while. One looked like a blonde girl and the other was a little bald-headed guy with a pencil mustache.

John wondered how Rennick was doing. Then he wondered how the Sheriff was feeling. Looking around the cell he chuckled to himself. Wouldn't it be something if he died in this hole? Would the county have to bury him? Fern must be the most embarrassed angel in heaven. Somehow, all of a sudden, it struck him as funny and a deep laugh erupted from his belly.

Horatio was asleep on the other bed in the cell and woke up. He didn't move but watched John carefully out of the corner of his eyes. This man is really different, he thought. Over seventy years old and waking up laughing, locked up in a cell, in the middle of the night." Horatio was impressed. This old man has *cojones!* He watched as John stretched and rolled over on his side facing the wall and Horatio thought for a minute the old fool was playing with himself. Then he saw John was rubbing his knuckles. Horatio smiled. The macho Sheriff-man must have knocked the hell out of this man's fist with his face. At least John had quit snoring. Horatio rolled over and fell asleep thinking of how he could take advantage of John's presence in their little not-so-controlled world.

The trustees came around at 6:00 A.M. with breakfast: powdered scrambled eggs with grits and toast washed down by coffee. Not bad, John thought! He took a shower and looked his hand over good. It hurt like a toothache. His thoughts turned to the Sheriff and how he must be feeling. Maybe he would learn to be more respectful.

The inmates were all standing in their semi-circle watching the Cartoon Channel on the TV screen. Most of them had their hands down the front of their pants in their favorite posture. One of the jailers called in and wanted John to come over by the intercom. He told John to get ready to be taken over to District Court at eight thirty. How you were supposed to get ready was a mystery to John. What was he supposed to do? Have a manicure and get the Mexicans to cut his hair? Put on his Sunday suit and shine his shoes?

Finally at eight fifteen two jailers came over to the door and John could see them talk on the little microphones on their shoulders. Those little microphones had long twisted telephone-type cords that ran down to a walkie-talkie on their belts. John thought it would be easy to wrap that cord around their neck. Not a good thing to be wearing among desperate people. He wondered if that same girl was down there again today in the Central Control booth looking at him through her TV monitor. He absentmindedly checked his fly to see if his zipper was open. It was. He felt relieved he had caught it. That would be impressive, walking into court with his underwear showing through an open fly. The door slid open and John stepped out. They patted him down again and put shackles on his ankles. Then they put a big leather belt around his waist that buckled in the back. It had a bullring sized metal loop in the front. They had found an oversized pair of handcuffs that they slipped through the loop in the front. The bigger of the two jailers took his handcuff key, turned it around and punched the little holes on the edge of the cuffs to double lock them so they wouldn't clamp down on his wrists too tightly and pinch him.

The brown-uniformed deputies took him down to a lobby on the second floor where two other deputies were waiting with four sour-looking prisoners all bound and trussed up in the same way John was. One of them looked familiar and John kept looking at him until he recognized him as the little guy that cut the grass at the Launching Pad. His eyes got big in recognition when he looked at John but he didn't say anything. A tattoo of a dagger and a rose on his left forearm looked new and the rose part looked red and inflamed. "Long way from trimming the bushes at the old folks home, ain't you, boy?" John said to him, and one of the jailers jumped right on him saying, "There will be *no* talking on the way there or on the way back!"

A tall skinny black kid with a scraggly Afro, whose eyes looked like a deer ready to bolt, started cussing the head jailer, calling him a "honky police scumbag." He had a wild set of eyes and John could tell he was three-fourths crazy. One of the other deputies was irritated and said to the jailer, "Steve, why are you always saying something dumb to make them go off. I wish you'd learn to ignore stupidity. Let's just get them to court without no problems."

John could see the deputy really didn't like working with this Steve the jailer any more than he liked being with the inmates.

Steve said, "If we don't get going Judge Crawford is going to put all of us in jail for contempt so let's move it."

The black kid was muttering and cussing under his breath, glaring at Steve all the way down to a hallway that turned right and then to a roofed-in walkway that led over to the court building. The sun shone through the Plexiglas roof and white clouds floated overhead as the prisoners did their best to walk with the stunted, shuffling, short steps the shackles allowed them. They got to the end of the hall and went through another door that the girl in central control had to open for them. Finally, they were herded trough a narrow little room equipped with an old wooden desk and a barred cell on each side, and then through a door and into the courtroom.

Jailer Steve made a big show to guide them to the front row of benches. John thought Steve would have made a good SS man for Hitler.

There were probably a hundred people in the courtroom. Once they were seated John looked up at Judge Crawford, his old friend, who was up on an elevated bench facing them. The Judge's eyes widened slightly but that was all the recognition he allowed. There was a low wall about three feet high and a pair of saloon-type swinging doors that separated the seating area from the business end in front of the Judge. Right dead in front of the Judge was a booth for whoever was testifying to sit in. On each side of the booth there was a big desk. On the right hand desk the Commonwealth's Attorney sat with a stack of files and a pitcher of water with some Dixie cups next to it. He was a tall fellow wearing an old-time bow tie. John could see a huge ring on his finger that must have weighed half a pound. It sparkled green. On the other side sat a defense attorney next to a short fat guy wearing white pants and a Hawaiian shirt with red and blue flowers. The defendant looked really upset. The defense attorney was studying a book and rubbing his temple with the eraser of a pencil.

Judge Crawford coughed and then rumbled, "Well, Mr. Helsley, can you please advise the court why your client can't comply with the terms of his bond?"

"Your Honor, my client has been under a large amount of duress due to the psychological pressure he has been under with his family and...."

The Judge interrupted. "And what guarantee can you give me, Mr. Helsley, and how can this court be rest assured your client will be at work or at home as the terms of his probation dictate and not down at the swimming pool attempting to talk to the lifeguard again? I order him remanded to jail. Bailiff, take this man back to the holding cell," the Judge barked.

"Your Honor, please reconsider...." the defense attorney pleaded as the bailiff with a stern look jerked the little Hawaiian-shirted fellow to his feet and cuffed him behind his back in one swift move that let everyone know he was in control of this courtroom.

The Judge said, "Mr. Helsley, you can ask for another bond hearing on Monday when I will be playing golf if it doesn't rain. You can try your luck with another Judge who may not have listened to your client's pitiful excuses as many times as I have." Turning to the second bailiff the Judge said, "I will take a very short recess to make a phone call." He stood up and strode toward the corner door without once looking at John. The bailiff boomed in a loud voice, "All rise!" and everyone in the room stood up as the deputies took the fellow in the Hawaiian shirt out the door the prisoners had just entered through. Before the door shut John could see the bailiff shove his newest prisoner into the cell on the right and watched him slam the old door shut, locking it with his huge key.

The crazy black guy twisted in his seat and looked back into the audience and said to a weird-looking white girl with orange and green hair and a safety pin stuck through her lower lip, "Looks like I'm screwed for good, Baby. That Judge be in a *bad* mood."

It was by no mistake that the bailiffs required all the attending police officers who were there to testify be seated directly behind the prisoners on the second row. One of them was a big impressive young black man who had "U.S. Marines" written all over him. He looked at Crazyeyes and said, "You turn around again and I will bust your nappy head. You mind your manners now." Crazyeyes glared at him for ten seconds and couldn't match his stare so he turned around and faced forward with a scowl, muttering something barely intelligible about homeboys trying to act like whitey. The ex-jarhead meant business and looked at Crazyeyes with contempt. It was clear he would love to drum a long solo on Crazyeyes' head.

John just looked at his own knuckles and tried not to hear anything. This wasn't what he had expected. This definitely didn't fit the Perry Mason profile or even Judge Judy for that matter. John felt really tired and very old as he wondered who Judge Crawford was calling on the phone.

The lawyers were moving around and talking to one another and one of them opened up one of those new laptop computers and was studying it like it was the Dead Sea Scroll. Another one had a little thing in his hands and kept punching at it with his thumbs. Crazyeyes noticed it and said to him, "What game you playing, man?" The lawyer said without looking up, "Tetris." John started getting really depressed.

After a few minutes the Judge's door flew open and the bailiff yelled, "All rise!" Everybody made an effort to stand up and sit down. Once the Judge got settled behind his desk he shuffled his papers and looked at the Commonwealth's Attorney. "What do you have next?"

The side door in the courtroom opened and a very old, very distinguished attorney came in walking with a cane. The Judge looked over at him and smiled. "Well, well, Mr. McNally, what brings you slumming to our humble court this morning?"

"I have come to the legal aid of my friend, Mr. Dean," he drawled, "who I am sure you recognize, sitting there trussed up like a Thanksgiving turkey. The ladies miss him greatly at the retirement home and his absence has caused such a fuss they have dispatched me to come to assist him in any way I can and fetch him back to them." McNally nodded to John.

Crazyeyes leaned over to John and whispered, "Man, you got the alpha-dog attorney. See if you can get him appointed to represent me."

The marine cop in the second row grabbed Crazyeyes by the back of his jumpsuit and pulled him up straight, glaring at the back of his head. John just looked at the floor.

McNally asked the Judge, "Your Honor, may I have a moment or two in private with my client prior to the court addressing his issues here this morning?"

The Judge nodded to the bailiff and pointed to a room on the side of the courtroom. The bailiff helped John up off the bench and escorted him into the room. McNally followed. Inside the room there was an old desk with a telephone and a legal notepad lying on top of it. A small holding cell with a chair lined the back of the room. The bailiff locked John in the holding cell as McNally laid his briefcase and cane on top of the table and sat down in the chair. Smiling at the bailiff, McNally thanked him and the bailiff left the room, shutting the door behind him.

McNally looked John in the eyes and asked, "Old friend, what in the hell have you gotten yourself into this time?"

# Chapter 16

As they sat on their chairs facing each other across the old table held together with chewing gum pasted underneath bearing carvings on it from hearing days long ago, McNally looked his old comrade in the eyes. With the bedside manner of a country physician the senior attorney asked, "John, are you all right?"

John looked at him and leaned back in his chair. Emitting a long sigh of resignation, he almost whispered, "Sure, Mac, you know I'm gonna be all right."

"We don't have much time here before Crawford calls us back into the courtroom. In a nutshell, John, we have some major problems to overcome. The Sheriff had surgery putting his sinuses back together and his dentist did a couple of procedures trying to get his front teeth back in his head correctly. I know you had to have a reason for doing what you did, but we will talk about that later in detail. Right now, old friend, I have to tell you the Brethren Home's head honcho, Mr. Bowman, called my office and said they would not accept you back there under any circumstances. He mentioned another incident last fall where you grabbed someone by the back of the neck that he counseled you about?"

"Yeah, it was the same man I pulled out of the burning car, that guy from New Jersey, that Rennick guy. I should have let him burn. Then I wouldn't be in this fix. As for that show-off bicycle-riding drunk they elected Sheriff around here, well Mac, he got to breathing his liquored-up breath on me, calling me everything but a white man! I won't tolerate that kind of crap and you know it! Crawford knows it! And now that

81

Sheriff knows it." John was getting worked up and McNally recognized a dormant volcano was about to erupt inside John. "Hell, I'd do it again in the same circumstances, and as far as that mushroom that calls himself a man, that Bowman idiot, I don't want to live there! I got a good jail cell with television, food, a bunch of Mexicans that love me, and a warm place to take a crap! What else do I need at my age? I've served my purpose in this hellish world!"

"John! John! John! Listen to me! I'll take care of all of it, believe me. I owe you my very own life! For heaven's sake, man, the Judge and Speedy Spencer do too. None of us would have made it off the beach that day if not for you. I will give you the best of my experience, education, and political connections if you will just listen to me. I need you to take some deep breaths now and calm down!" McNally ordered in his most assertive voice. "If you want to stay in the jail for now that answers a lot of questions for me today. It will get Crawford's ass off the hook too. He sure doesn't want to have to make that decision now if he can avoid it. He will absolutely be relieved to not have to grant you bail, at any figure. You know he would do it but they would crucify him in the newspaper. The Sheriff is pretty popular even if he is a Romeo inebriant of sorts."

"Can't Crawford just hear this case today and make a decision? Hell, I want to stay in jail. I'll tell him that. Don't nobody else want to take care of me and I might be crazy but I can recognize my own inability to take care of myself. That's why I gave up my driver's license. But little jerk Rennick kept his, ran a damn red light, and got all broken up! That's the problem with most of those people in the Launching Pad. They got one foot on a banana peel and the other one on a grease spot and still think they're gonna live forever. Just fooling themselves while jerks like Bowman keep charging everybody $2,500 a month. Man, I ain't afraid to go on down the road. I'm looking forward to it!" He started to boil up again.

McNally looked confused and asked, "What is a Launching Pad?"

John laughed and answered, "That's what I call the Brethren Home. 'Jesus' Launching Pad.' Isn't that what the place is? They're all waiting to blast off to walk the streets paved with gold. You and the Judge and Speedy better start making your reservations. Ha! My room is open. Better book it, Mac, before twenty more old farts from New Jersey cut you out of it soaking their feet where the taxes is cheaper."

McNally leaned forward smiling and put his hand on John's massive shoulders, "Let's go out here like men and get this little deal over with this morning. We been through a lot worse mornings, haven't we? Crawford can't decide this case. He can only certify it to the grand jury. Let's go out and expedite things a little and get you back to your cell. Say you got some Mexican pals over there?"

"Yeah, their leader done made me his uncle or something because he was glad I smacked the Sheriff," John said with a chuckle.

As they went back into the courtroom a ruckus broke out and every one of the lawmen present was wrestling with Crazyeyes who was struggling mightily. They finally got him under control and dragged him out the other side of the courtroom. The black Marine Deputy had a bloody nose and was wiping it with a handkerchief that wouldn't be used again.

"Mr. Dean, I'm shocked and appalled to see you in your predicament," the grizzled old judge growled at him. "Mr. McNally, what great light of illumination can you cast on this situation?"

"Judge, Mr. Dean wishes no bail at this time and will be quite content to reside in the jail until such time we can schedule a preliminary hearing," McNally answered, fixing his left thumb under his suspender strap beside his shirt pocket.

"Very well, then. The defendant Mr. Dean is remanded into the custody of the Sheriff even though I understand the Sheriff is somewhat indisposed at the moment. Do you have any further matters to take up here this morning, Counselor?" Judge Crawford looked like a matador who had just let a bull with big horns slide through his cape to exit the arena without having to use his sword on him.

"No sir, Your Honor. Thank you, sir."

As the bailiffs led John away, McNally leaned forward to the Judge and whispered, "See you at the country club at six for a little shooter."

The jailers took their prisoners back to their cells. As the door opened up and clanged shut behind him, John felt like someone had thrown a glass of cold water in his face. This really was home now. He straightened up as tall as he could muster and strode into the cell block. Walking over to Horatio who was playing solitaire at a table with his back to him, John patted him on the shoulders and said, "Uncle John is back from court. You like to play straight gin, my favorite Mexican nephew?"

"I would rather drink straight gin, Tio Juan!" he answered with a smile. "Join me in a game."

Not much different from an army barracks, John thought, as he sat down across from Horatio. I can deal with this. Screw that Bowman guy and all those fools out there.

Thanksgiving came and went and then it was Christmas Eve. Davy went to the jail and visited John. John said it was just another day in jail except that the guy he shared a cell with, Horatio, was moody and upset he couldn't be back in Mexico with his parents. John filled Davy in on the circumstances of his "situation" as he called it. Mac waived preliminary hearing and John had been indicted by the Grand Jury on both counts. Mac was trying to decide if a jury trial or a bench trial was the best route for John to take.

It was really sad to leave him there that afternoon, but Davy honestly thought his grandfather was doing okay. He just wished the trial date would come and be over with. But they hadn't even set a date yet.

Davy hadn't heard anything from his mother until Christmas Eve. She called Davy and asked if his grandfather was still in jail. Davy told her, "Merry Christmas, Mom. You know I could use a little help from you sometime. Maybe a letter or something to let me know how you are."

She said she didn't have much time because she was so busy with her new business running a pick-up-and-lay-down service for some wildcat oil drillers in Oklahoma. She told Davy it involved supplying pipe to the oil rigs and paid big money if the wells came in. She was interested in hearing about what was going on with his grandfather and hoped Davy had a Merry Christmas and then she was gone.

Davy looked at the phone and wondered what screws were loose in his mother's head. Lizzy just shrugged when he tried to talk to her. She was reading another of her Sandra Brown novels. She lifted her head from the book long enough to say, "You and your whole family must have been dropped on your heads."

On New Year's Eve he took her to a Tom Hanks movie called *Forrest Gump*. It was a great movie and that night he went to sleep thinking about what the floating feather meant in the beginning and the end of the movie. He tried to get a kiss and a little more from Lizzy at midnight when they watched the ball drop in Times Square on the little thirteen-inch TV he kept on his dresser. She gave him a quick smooch and rolled over, turning her back to him. He drifted off to sleep wondering what he had done or not done for her and how his grandfather was doing in jail.

The last thing he thought before drifting off was, *God is great, God is good, and women are damn crazy creatures!*

# Chapter 17

McNally had settled on a jury trial for John and had interviewed the witnesses the prosecution listed in its case against him. He interviewed rescue personnel and took his own pictures of the accident scene. One day he spent two hours going over and over the details with John until he felt he understood the whole unfortunate ordeal from his client's perspective. Rennick remembered most of the details from the time John cut his seatbelt and pulled him out of the car. McNally stroked his ego and befriended the little man who sported a neck brace and upper body cast even though Mac shared John's sentiment that the Yankee was an impertinent jerk. His testimony would be crucial in building the defense Mac had in mind and it would be easy to get a local jury to feel sorry for the man if coached properly. If the prosecution wasn't careful with this witness it could blow up on them if his obnoxious character came out. The concrete truck driver would be relatively easy to discredit on cross-examination. On top of a conviction for domestic violence on his ex-wife he had a reckless driving charge the previous year for running a red light, which the Judge had reduced to improper driving. McNally found Zetty to be an emotional, somewhat effeminate ball of nerves.

One thing that puzzled McNally was John's emphatic position about the inebriated condition of the Sheriff. Everyone knew the Sheriff to be a young pompous ass, but the idea that he may have a drinking problem and the assertion by John that he had been condescending and terribly offensive to an old man who had just been through a very emotional and physically stressful situation was going to be hard to sell to a jury. If only there was a witness to what had triggered John to do the unbelievable and punch the high Sheriff in the mouth. Somehow he had to make the jury sympathetic to a physically imposing monster like John, while the Sheriff was going to sit there in court looking like a war orphan with swelling still visible in his face. When Mac thought about that scenario he seriously turned to thoughts of pleading no contest to all charges and go the insanity route, but he knew that was not an option. John's ego would never allow that to happen. Even though Mac thought he may be able to pull it off with John's prior history of mental depression and the fact he was on medication, his client, John, felt he had been wronged and acted in a justifiable manner. In his day, in the Southern mountains, a man who confronted you face to face and disrespected you was due an immediate physical response. McNally had a Great Uncle Lawrence who had died in a pistol duel shortly after the Civil War. That argument had supposedly arisen from insults erupting after a dispute during a cock fighting match. It was the way things were done in the South. John had only acted in a way his whole being and character dictated, the only way he knew how, the only way his honor could bear.

What Mac was looking for was a way to prove the Sheriff had acted in a way whereby a man of John's nature would strongly perceive that the Sheriff had crossed boundaries established by society and local historical upbringing, thereby eliciting sympathy in the jurors' minds. First he had to get John in the mood and frame of mind to fight this battle. That would be his biggest challenge.

The whole process was moving along quickly now since the holiday season was over and John had been formally indicted by the grand jury and arraigned by the circuit court. McNally had convinced him not to worry about it even though John seemed to take it hard. John made it clear to McNally he expected to be convicted of hitting the Sheriff. All he wanted was for people to understand why he did it and believe what he had to say about the unacceptable treatment the Sheriff had given him that day. Judge Crawford had been vastly relieved when the case was certified to the grand jury, knowing he would not have to preside over any more of the motions that could be attached to this sordid affair. He held John in a special place in his heart and it disturbed him to no end the predicament he had gotten himself into. The Judge was drinking entirely too much at night and friends who knew him could see it in his face and behavior.

Davy rented another storage unit and went to the Brethren Home and picked up all of his grandfather's belongings. A lot of the women asked nosy questions but he was as respectful as he could be with them. He went to visit John at the jail and it absolutely broke his heart to see his grandfather in there. It was an embarrassing ordeal for both of them. He had set up a canteen account for John at the jail and made sure an adequate amount of money would be available for the extras he would need. John was grateful but it truly hurt him to see the anguish he was causing his grandson. Davy told him he had called his father, John Jr., and left a message for him to call him as soon as possible but that had been almost a week ago now and he hadn't heard from him yet. What upset Davy most was his grandfather had told him he expected to die in that jail.

"I wish you and I could live up at the cabin with Ben!" the old man had said with a true look of longing and sadness. "I think I have just lived my life so long I've moved into another world that don't understand me and people my age."

"Aw, Grampap, there's still lots of good times ahead. Mac'll get it straightened out and then we'll get things back to normal," the young man half-heartedly answered.

"You seem to forget, Davy boy, whose belongings you hauled this week and put in a locker. I can't go back there. There ain't too many places what will take somebody like me," John responded. "It really is a nice place and I was lucky they took me in the first place. But I don't fit there. It ain't the way I can live. For some of those folks in there it's the only solution and a comfortable one. But for me it weren't."

"Well, you can come live with me then. We could move the stuff out of the extra room and move you in there, Grampap! We could make it work!"

With a smile the old man shook his head and said, "You know better than that! Your wife Lizzy is so proper and all. The first time I missed the pot in the bathroom she would go through the ceiling. She's a good girl but I know my moving in there wouldn't be fair to you and her. I'm like an old farm dog that is fine in the barn but not in the house. Like I said a while ago, I wish we could all live up on the mountain. When I was a kid that's the way things was. Everybody expected to live with old people and there was enough to do just surviving on the farm with chores for everybody's help to be needed, but things ain't that way now. That's why places like the Brethren Home are popping up everywhere."

"Yeah, well, me an Lizzy ain't exactly been having a bed of roses spread on the blankets these days. She's getting real different acting. Didn't you notice she never showed up for the picnic?" Davy cautiously blurted out.

John looked puzzled as he thought, "Well, I never give it no thought with all the other things going on and all. I never thought about it, Davy. Where was she at?"

Davy was visibly nervous and it was obvious to John something was dreadfully wrong, "Said she wasn't feeling good and stayed home but I know that was a lie. I changed the oil in her car on that Thursday night and wrote the mileage down on the little sticker you put in the window. I got in there on Monday morning to warm the car up for her in the morning and get the frost off the windows and she had put damn near a hundred and fifty miles on it that weekend."

"Did you ask her about it, son?" the old man asked.

"No, because I've asked her before where she been burning the road up and...."

"You think she been cheating on you, Davy?" John asked wide-eyed with eyebrows raised.

Davy hung his head and shook it side to side and scooted back from the glass window that separated them in the visiting booth. "You got enough to worry about without worrying about me. I didn't want to tell you, damn it!" he said through tears in his blue eyes. "I'm gonna be all right. Hell, Grampap, I don't *think* she's been cheating. I know so! Three days ago, right after New Year's Day, she told me she was going shopping after work and wouldn't be home until late. I hid Tim Trumbo's dog tracking collar in the trunk of her car and me and Tim tracked that thing right to the EconoLodge over in Wytheville. We set up on the hill and took pictures of her coming out of the room through the spotting scope with that digital camera in it that Tom Trumbo bought out of the Gander Mountain Catalog to take to Montana hunting. Got her just clear as a bell. Kissing Kurt Morris, a boy that works on the same shift with her at the bottle factory. Tim was taking the pictures and I was watching through the binoculars. Got pictures of them coming out of room 33 and kissing beside of her car. He looked all around but didn't see us. They'd been there in that room for over three hours." Davy wiped the stifled tears from his face with his sleeve.

"I'm sure sorry, boy! What're you gonna do?"

"I wanted to go down there right then and whip that Morris boy's ass but Tim dragged me back to the truck. He said somebody would die if I went down there and he was probably right. The Morris clan is all quick with a knife and I was about wild and crazy enough to do something stupid. I had my Smith & Wesson .38 in my pocket. Tim done a good thing stopping me until I calmed down a little bit. I confronted her when we got home. I had bought a little tape recorder and had it turned on in my pocket. I got it all on tape what she said. I knew to do that from watching one of those TV shows about private investigators. She admitted it, Grampap! I asked her why she done it and you know what she told me? She told me she done it because I am so boring and predictable! Boring and predictable! Then she said she needs a man who can challenge her!" he whispered as he looked away off into space. "It nearly killed me. The next day she had her brother come over with his truck and took the table and chairs her grandmamma gave her and all her clothes and just walked out and left me after nine years just cool as a cucumber. All I could do was to sit on the couch and watch her. She yelled at me as she left and said, "You ain't man enough to even get mad, are you?" I just let her walk away, Grampap. I couldn't even make my legs move. I guess she's right. All I did was sit there and cry like a damn baby."

"You listen to me, Davy Dean. You listen to me good!" the old man snarled. "You're too good for a woman that would do a low-down thing like that. Shame on her! When I was young you could have killed both of them and not had a thing done to you. It would have been right by the law. You're lucky she's gone and you don't have a couple of kids by her. You thank God for that! Now, you're one of the best people I ever known on this earth and that is a fact. You will survive this, but right now you have every right to feel blue. Do you have a lawyer?"

Davy shook his head and wiped his eyes again gathering himself somewhat. "I been thinking about taking the tape and the pictures to McNally and talking to him about it, but it's so damn embarrassing, I just dread it. She's already moved in with the Morris boy in his trailer up on the big mountain next to the Gathright Dam Road and says she don't want nothin' else, so what's the point? I been real careful with our money. Our house ain't big, but we don't owe much on it. She has her checking account and I got mine. There ain't no savings to amount to anything. I worked so hard at getting the house paid for. The vehicles are in both of our names. I guess I need to talk to somebody. So you see, Grampap, if you get out you can come live with me if you can stand a loser for a grandson." When Davy got that out he teared up again and looked away.

"You get this through your hard Dean skull, son. It ain't your fault!" the old man shouted. "You're a fine young man!"

The jailer working the visiting shift put his <u>People Magazine</u> down and glared at them and said to knock off the yelling or he would cut their visit short. Davy hung his head and John, not in the mood to listen to any crap from the jailer, glared back at him. Leaning into the window and putting his mouth close to the little speaker hole he said, "Son, I am going to get out of here and we'll figure out something! I love you, sonny boy!"

"I love you too, Grampap," was all he could get out as he got up and walked out turning his head so the jailer couldn't see his tear streaked face.

Just what it was they were going to figure out was unclear to both of them, but they both were keenly aware they were the only real family either one of them had. John sat in the booth looking at the empty glass window until the jailer came over and asked him to go back to the holding cell. When John walked away his walk was different from when he came: It had purpose.

# Chapter 18

Judge Crawford was tired. At seventy years old he was the oldest sitting judge in the Commonwealth of Virginia and he had had a long day. His wife, Anna, was gone to Williamsburg with some of her friends from the Presbyterian Church. They'd both been christened, baptized, and married in that church. A year after he had come home from the war he had courted her and led her to the altar. She had been engaged to a bomber pilot, Ashby Dice. He had asked her to marry him just before he left for the army. One year later he was shot down and killed on a raid early in the war in Germany. The Judge took her every year to Arlington to place flowers on Ashby's grave on the anniversary of his death. Ashby had been two years his senior and the Judge had respected and liked him in school. Anna was a good and cheerful companion and had supported him well through his long career. As a judge's wife she had excelled socially and spiritually. Two strong children had come to them: a son who was now a high school principal in western Maryland with two boys of his own at Virginia Military Institute and a daughter who was an advertising executive living in Washington, D.C.

This evening he was almost glad to be alone. Anna tended to question his drinking more than he liked these days so he sneaked his evening drink on the back deck while reading the local newspaper. He enjoyed looking over his long yard that led up to the woods that separated his estate from the country club golf course. It was an unusually warm evening and the afternoon sun felt good on his old bones. He looked out at his golf cart wintering in the shed next to a path through the woods that led right up to the lodge.

At his age, his mind had remained remarkably clear and his conservative Southern Democrat disposition had privately caused him to rebel and jump parties and vote for George H. W. Bush in the last election. How in the world can anyone with good conscience vote for a pusillanimous draft-dodging pot smoker, who didn't inhale of course, like Bill Clinton? There are lunatic Muslim terrorists running around the earth with a Russian A-bomb in one hand and a Koran in the other reciting verses about their duty to kill all the infidels in the world! And they almost knocked the World Trade Center down with their bombs in the basement! "We're in a sad state of affairs as a political party when we can't put up a better candidate than a Bill Clinton," the Judge said out loud as he beat his hand on the table.

The Judge suspected McNally privately agreed with him even though he was the long-time chairman of the local Democratic Party. Politics disturbed the Judge these days as did reading the newspaper and watching the news. How had everything changed so much since the hippies took over in the '70s? Crawford had traveled with his son to California to visit his wife's brother. The conduct of the young people on the streets of Los Angeles made him think the jet had landed on another planet. He wondered why he had gone to war against Hitler and the Japs. Neither of those cultures would ever have allowed such a disorganized bunch of soft-looking Mexicans and blacks with their baggy pants falling down, speaking their Spanglish and Ebonics or whatever that mumbling was they called language. And all those pasty-looking white kids with fishing lures stuck through their lips, noses, and nipples. Nazis, Japs, and Commies would never let this happen! Rainbow painted hairy idiots running around on skateboards with their cracks showing. What the hell has happened? At least there isn't so much of it in our hometown yet.

It made him tired to think about it. He viewed the social experiments of Lyndon Johnson's "Great Society" as being the ruination of many of the more promising young black men and lower-class white kids he had known from the early years after the war. This nation of people had lost all understanding of what the forefathers had gone through. Why, in Virginia, the first lesson learned was, *If you don't work, you don't eat!* Captain John Smith, now there was a man of substance. Where was his type now? Gone, gone, gone. Many times the Judge had strapping young men hauled in front of him in his court because they wouldn't support the children they had fathered or pay their bills. Totally capable of working hard all day long at legitimate enterprise but knowing all too well they didn't have to. He could throw them in jail and see them laugh at him as they were led off to ninety days of vacation playing cards, watching color television, and eating up the state's free food in an air-conditioned setting while the mothers of their babies deposited money in their jail canteen accounts that paid for Hostess Twinkies and cigarettes.

The whole damn place was screwed up and he blamed himself and the very party he had supported for aligning themselves with the liberal bastards who had tainted everything he had worked for. It all made him tired, so tired. They had made a damn religion out of the Constitution!

As he took a deep swill from his glass he wondered how his old friend John was getting along in the jail. It actually made him smile a little in sadness to think of how John would blend socially with the inmate population. For all of his life John had been like a force of nature as powerful as the turning of the seasons, as unpredictable as the weather but solid and certain as the mountains. He remembered clearly the first time he had seen him. He and McNally were little boys playing in the dusty October streets of Cambridge in front of the harness shop when a mountain man with a long weathered beard and his son wearing rough Depression-era clothes made mostly of burlap from feed sacks came pulling a cart loaded with ear corn into the town to sell at the Saturday market. The boy walking behind the wagon and leading a black pig on a rope was the biggest, strongest, toughest-looking kid he had ever seen. Always reckless, McNally had thrown a rock at the pig and the mountain man had stopped in his tracks and yelled at him, "Don't you be hittin' my pig with no rock, boy!" McNally had laughed and made a face at him. The mountain man turned and said to his son, "John, you gonna let somebody do that to yer pig? Ye got my approval to give that boy a whipping if'n he hits yer pig again." McNally, being the natural-born smart ass, winged another rock at the pig, striking it on the snout which caused it to back up squealing and bucking. John calmly walked up and tied his rope to the wheel of his father's cart and started walking toward McNally. Crawford, being smarter and more cautious, had slid back away, separating himself from Mac's lunacy as he slipped into Mrs. McCormick's boxwood bushes that lined the street.

"You can't catch me, you hillbilly!" McNally shouted and turned to run. Before he took ten steps the larger mountain boy had not only caught him but had pushed him down face-first in the dirt. John had grabbed

McNally by the ear and said, "My pappy says I am to whup you. Reckon you gonna hit my pig again if'n I turn you loose?" John took McNally's face and rubbed it in the dirt with the ease of a man holding a rag doll. McNally couldn't believe the intense strength the boy had in his hands and he nearly passed out when John kicked him in the butt and said, "Believe I done give him a lesson, Pappy. He won't bother our pig no more, will you, boy? I don't want to have to shame you no more. I don't even know you." The Judge thought what the mountain boy had done and said were the damnedest things he had ever seen and heard. He had reduced Mac to a pile of horse manure and had managed to do it almost humbly.

The mountain man spat a brown stream of tobacco juice into the dust a foot in front of McNally's red hair. He was still sobbing in the dirt. John untied his pig and checked to see if the rock had made its snout bleed. The pig squealed again but John was satisfied it was okay. The man shook his head and picked up his cart handles, taking off with the slow steady walk of a beast of burden toward the market. McNally had jumped up and wiped the tears, snot, and mud off his face and followed the pig. The future Judge yelled, "Are you crazy! Where're you going?"

McNally growled over his shoulders, "I'm gonna make him my friend," he said as he pointed to John. "I sure don't want him as my enemy!" McNally was always smart in his alliances and it had served him well. He had no pride, which was a great survival trait for a defense attorney. Defeat only made him smarter and craftier the next time. He knew how to survive.

That's how the three of them had initially become friends. John's father died the next year from a tree limb falling on him while trying to shake a coon out of a tree that he and John were in the process of felling with a crosscut saw. John and his sister had started coming to school in town when their aunt and uncle took them in. Speedy Spencer had often joined them in their baseball and football games and they had many adventures. The four of them had been good for each other and John was the greatest beneficiary. The Judge and McNally had helped him in school and their homes had been open to him, introducing him to whole new cultures and mannerisms. They all found him to be bright, if not aloof and moody at times. Days, months, and then whole years had drifted by. Then all of a sudden they were all seventeen. Hitler and the Japs were on their minds and all they could think about. All four of them had left on the same bus and were in the same outfit. Amazing times. Afraid? No way! They were going to Germany to kick Hitler's ass. They were the generation twice removed from the gray-clad boys of Manassas and Stonewall Jackson. Some things never change in the South.

The Judge relaxed on his porch drinking a glass of his favorite, George Dickel Bourbon. He wondered if the United States could still produce men like himself and his comrades. He doubted it. Too many freeloaders were involved today. But you never know, he mused. All the cur-dog descendants of criminals and misfits that make up what we call Americans will surprise you when somebody beats a drum and waves a flag. It was a pet theory of the Judge's that what was wrong with America now was the loss of its saving grace, its wild frontier. It had been conquered. There was no frontier for the adventurous, the crazy, or the criminal looking for opportunity or a place to hide, to disappear in. No place for them all to run away to or to beat themselves against to toughen themselves and sharpen their wits, to weed out the lazy, the perverts, or the unlucky. Australians understood what the Judge thought. Their country was much the same. Adversity led to excellence or extinction. The tracks of gravy trains led to garbage bins.

What to do for John was a great concern for him. It was such a shame Fern had gone first. John was so lost without her. The Judge loved the man but was afraid of him too. He just couldn't quit being John, could he? The Judge was certain of one thing. That young Sheriff had done something way out of line for John to have done what he did. He had never seen John Dean back down but he had never seen him provoke anyone or hit a man for no good reason. As matter of fact John never showed emotion in a fight and the Judge had seen him in many a barroom brawl. Everything was cold and factual for him. Striking out at another man was no more or less to John than knowing he had to split a chord of wood before he stacked it. If the man had been born twenty years later he would have been the greatest football lineman that has ever played the game. His strength and agility were legendary as was his courage. He was like a great dancing, deliberate bear. No, the Sheriff did something that provoked him and John had done what he always had done in his life when confronted with a problem: beat it into submission. What a shame. Was this great man, a decorated American veteran and war hero, going to die alone in jail? The thought made him shudder. The Judge noticed his glass was nearly empty. He wanted another.

He finished his last sip of brown courage and stood up to go in the house. With the smoky wild taste of fine bourbon on his lips he took a step toward the back door. A blood clot that had dislodged from somewhere deep in his veins clogged up an artery in his head, totally blocking the flow of his life blood. The sudden strong stroke shut his vision down immediately and he fell sideways over the cast-iron bird bath.

He was dead before he hit the ground, feeling no pain whatsoever with only the mild sensation of floating off into the cloudless heavens he had sought all his life.

When she found him the next afternoon, Anna's first thought was that he had a smile on his face.

# Chapter 19

It had been an unusually warm couple of days in January. The phone rang at the McNally residence as Mac had just come in the door from bowling with some of his Lion's Club friends. He had taken thirty dollars in the afternoon's bets from the bums too and that always made him happy. Helen, his wife, wasn't home yet and he didn't think he would reach the phone in time. Having taken his shoes off at the door, in his haste he stubbed his toe on the leg of the coffee table as he reached for the cordless phone on the lamp table. It was Anna Crawford and she was sobbing. She had done all right until she heard Mac answer the phone in his old familiar way and her emotions got the best of her.

Mac finally made out that something was dreadfully wrong so he told her to just hang on, he would be there in a few minutes. He jumped in his pickup and drove insanely fast over to the Judge's residence and was there within five minutes. Anna met him at the door and fell into his arms crying. She took him by the hand and led him to the back porch where he saw the Judge lying on the concrete tiles. He had been dead for twenty-four hours and the blood had settled down, making him look like his face was full of grape juice. Mac instinctively walked into the dining room and pulled the tablecloth off the oak table that had graced so many happy meals. He covered the Judge with the tablecloth and took Anna by the hands.

"I'm going to take care of you and help you through this, Sweetheart. Now, Anna, have you called the police yet?" he asked in his best bedside manner as he stroked her hand in his.

"No, you're the only person I have called. I just got home and found him," she answered as she accepted the handkerchief he offered to wipe away the tears from her face. Mac looked at her and couldn't help but to wonder where all the lines in her still beautiful face had come from. It startled him to think, *My God, she's an old woman!*

He snapped out of his reverie and leading her to the sofa he said, "Come on in here and sit with me on the couch and I'll make the call." He dialed the police department number that was on the little blaze-orange sticker that the Judge had stuck on the cover of the phone book. It also had the poison control hotline number and the animal control number on it. He told the dispatcher to send an officer to 11244 Greenwood Lane for an unattended death and to make sure they didn't come in with sirens on and to absolutely not put it over the radio for every person with a scanner to hear. The emergency was long past.

Then he sat with her, holding her hands as she poured out her heart with the sudden guilt she was experiencing at having been gone with the girls when it had happened and how maybe if she had been there she could have saved him. She chastised herself for not calling Mac the night before to have him check on him when he didn't answer the phone. She had tried to call home twice from the motel in Williamsburg where she had spent the night with the girls. He had been drinking more than usual and she knew that. He had been falling into a deep sleep in his recliner every evening. His hearing had deteriorated to the point where the phone would not waken him so she had just assumed he had fallen asleep early like usual with the television blaring on ESPN.

Mac assured her she was not to blame and the tears ran down his cheeks too. He heard a car pull into the driveway and heard a door slam so he got up and met the officer at the door. It was Officer Lantz, who had arrested John at the wreck. Mac took him back to where the Judge was lying. Lantz said he would need to call in an investigator because it had been an unattended death and Mac agreed. Officer Lantz went in and explained the situation to Anna and asked if she had any prearranged agreements with a particular funeral home. She started sobbing again and McNally sat down, putting his arm around her. She looked at Mac and said, "We never talked about that. He has said many times he wants to be cremated but I can't bear the thought of him burning!"

Poor Anna's wellspring of tears really burst out then. McNally told Officer Lantz to go ahead and call Sullivan's Funeral Home and Anna nodded in agreement. Mac told her they could work those details out later with Mr. Sullivan.

Officer Lantz called his dispatcher on the phone to get an investigator on the way. Then he asked permission to call the local funeral home for her. McNally called his wife, Helen, who had a new cell phone and let her know the circumstances and where he had gone. She had been off grocery shopping when he had gotten home and received the call from Anna. She was upset but like all good Presbyterian women immediately started planning who to call and how she could take care of her dear friend Anna.

Officer Lantz got nervous standing around in this high-class house and felt uncomfortable around grief so he went out, like the loyal public servant that he was, and sat with the body of the departed Judge mostly because he didn't know what else to do until the investigator got there. He didn't want anything to happen to the death scene until someone else could take responsibility. Looking at the Judge's shrouded body, Lantz scanned the area all around him to make sure he didn't miss anything. A Judge made a lot of enemies in a lifetime of settling squabbles and sending people to jail, not to mention fining the hell out of them when they deserved it. Lantz thought that a Judge probably had to be a better sport than a policeman about being called bad names and worse when he made his living pissing off at least half of the people he talked to every day. Officer Lantz could tell the Judge had been dead for a while by looking at the purple fingers on his hand with the worn gold wedding band cutting into the ring finger. Death is not ever flattering, Lantz thought. The dead Iraqis he had dealt with as a Marine in the Desert Storm campaign were all sickening. He had even helped a number of them to get dead. He heard the front doorbell ring and it snapped him back to the present as he went to let the on-call investigator in.

Detective Ritchie was all business and had already called to alert the medical examiner. The ME, as they called him, had given him the authority to move the body to examine it for any wounds or signs of foul play. Ritchie spoke briefly to Mrs. Crawford and offered her his condolences. He and Lantz then went out on the porch as Helen McNally arrived. Mac was infinitely relieved when she took charge. She was at her best in these situations and a much stronger and more loyal woman than Mac had ever deserved. Helen swooped Anna up in her arms and took her into the formal living room away from all the dreadful business on the porch. The funeral director, Mr. Sullivan himself, arrived and retired to the front room with the women. He made his presence known to them and then went to check on the situation on the back porch. Detective Ritchie said hello to him and asked him to wait inside until he and Officer Lantz were done. As soon as he disappeared back into the house Ritchie, who was kneeling beside the Judge, looked up at Lantz and asked, "Did you see him look at you from head to toe?"

"Yeah, I did. What's that all about?" Officer Lantz responded.

"He was measuring you for a box. He does that to everybody when he looks at them. Frankie Jones, one of our deputies, used to work for him and he said all them morticians pride themselves in knowing what size boxes everybody in town would take. Then when they get you hauled in they don't have to swap you around from box to box so much." The old investigator spoke without even cracking a smile.

"Really?" the young officer said with a shiver.

Detective Ritchie donned the usual plastic gloves and a mask and asked Officer Lantz to do the same. Lantz only had gloves on him and went to his car to get his mask. Ritchie removed the tablecloth and busied himself with taking pictures of the body from all angles. Once Lantz got back he helped Ritchie to open the Judge's clothes and rolled him around into the necessary positions until they had looked him over from head to toe. Satisfied with that examination, the investigator took a swab sample from the judge's mouth and put the glass he had been drinking from into an evidence bag.

McNally was standing in the doorway and said, "You won't find anything in there but George Dickel Bourbon. Probably won't be a drop of water unless some ice melted in it."

"I'm sure you're right but I have to do the job," the meticulous investigator stated.

"That's why I have so seldom defeated any of your cases in court, Mr. Ritchie. You do good work. That is a fact and you leave few stones unturned or unexamined. I respect that," the old lawyer complimented.

Ritchie asked to use the home phone and called the medical examiner who heard him out and issued the order to have the body taken to the hospital. He wanted to do a careful exam of the body himself, taking into account the distinguished person they were dealing with. Mac walked over to the Judge who was lying on his back and kneeling down with his fingers he brushed the Judge's white forelock over his brow. The face that had lain against the concrete all night was a nightmarish thing to look at, but McNally took the Judge by the hand and bending low placed a kiss on the brow of the old warrior who had tempted death so many times during the terrible, terrible war they had endured.

"My God, old man, I'm going to miss you," he said as the same fingers that had straightened the hair closed the gray eyes of the now surprisingly feeble-looking body of an old, old man. The Judge looked like he had shrunk and McNally realized with a start that the skin on the hand he was holding wasn't any more wrinkled than the skin of his own. Leaning down and whispering he said, "You go on down the road ahead of us, old friend. Get the place ready and the bar set up and we'll all be wandering the same path soon. You won't be alone long!" McNally's tears fell on the Judge's shoulders and slowly seeped into the fabric of his polo shirt.

They called for undertaker Sullivan who brought a stretcher in and the two police officers and McNally helped to carry the Judge to the funeral home wagon outside. McNally thanked the officers and walked up the walk to the front door. Somehow he was going to have to get bond set for John so he could come to the funeral.

# Chapter 20

The news of the judge's death spread around the town and countryside with the speed stories only achieved in rural small town neighborhoods can. John was in his cell that Saturday evening around seven thirty, thinking about going to bed, listening to the Mexicans jabbering in Spanish, and worrying about his grandson's marital problems. He had to talk to Mac and find out how he could go about getting bail. He needed to get out and be with the boy. The inmates in his cell block had been in an argument about something and John couldn't figure what. They were all in a huddle around the front of the white boy's cell. The little redneck was back in his cell scrubbing his commode with his toothbrush and toothpaste and John realized the Mexicans were trying to keep the jailers from noticing what he was doing. Horatio looked up and saw John looking so he moved away from them and came into the cell with John to get a magazine.

"What's the knucklehead doing scrubbing his pot?" John asked.

"When he gets it clean, man, he gonna make some hooch in there this weekend. The jailers are short staffed and that girl Sharon is gonna be in the pod control. She don't give a damn and maybe we can get the stuff to the right place before she goes off the shift on Tuesday," he said with a smile. "We got all the fruit saved from the last couple of days and a good stash of sugar. That cracker's old man is a moonshiner and he can make a good turn. You want in on it?"

"No, but thank you," John answered. "I don't do too good with alcohol. Besides, big as I am it would take a gallon to do me any good."

Horatio smiled and nodded as he folded a hotrod magazine under his arm. "Gotta go help make the screen for him. I could use a buzz, man!"

John brushed his teeth and then washed his face with his washcloth. Boredom was setting in but no worse than in the Launching Pad. He really missed taking his walks. The intercom started cracking and he could hear the jailer was saying something. Horatio walked to his cell and told him to get out there, they wanted to talk to him. John got up and shuffled out to the door. He bent down to the speaker and pushed the *talk* button. Sharon, the jailer who had just come on duty, told him he had an attorney visit and he should get ready to be brought out.

Horatio marveled. "Damn, man, you must have some clout somewhere, man. Get a lawyer to come see you on a Saturday evening."

John went back to his cell and put on his orange shirt. Two jailers from downstairs got off the pod elevator and came to his cell-block door. When the bolts inside the door made their groaning sound and finally went *thunk* John stepped through the door and they shut it behind him. The waist belt, shackles, and cuffs went back on and they took him down in the elevator to the hallway that led to the visiting room. They unlocked the door into the visiting area and there was McNally dressed in his golf clothes looking at him through the inch-thick glass. The jailers backed out into the hall and reminded him they would be just a short way down the hall. John slid the chair back by grabbing the back of it with his two hands that were secured by the cuffs and the belt. McNally looked rough.

"What happened to get you in here, Mac?" John asked feeling a sinking sensation in his stomach and thinking Davy may have done something really stupid.

Mac looked up, looked him in the eye, and said, "Our old friend the Judge is gone, John. Anna found him dead on their back porch this afternoon when she got back from a shopping trip with her friends. He died sometime last evening drinking alone on his back porch."

The big man just looked at McNally and showed no emotion except his right eye twitched a little. They sat there looking at one another for half a minute. Finally, John leaned back looking up at the ceiling. A long sigh escaped him. Within a few seconds he leaned forward and put his elbows on his knees and looked up at Mac. "He was the best one of us. Made the most out of himself."

Mac had tears in his eyes and turned sideways in his chair and crossed his legs, putting his middle finger knuckle in his mouth. John asked, "Is Anna okay?"

McNally turned back to John and reached for his handkerchief that was gone since he had given it to Anna at the house. He dried his eyes on his sleeves and said, "Yeah, she's got Helen with her. You know how good she is when she takes over in times like this. The funeral is probably going to be on Tuesday."

John asked, "Is there any chance you can get me out of here on Monday? I really am gonna need to go to his funeral."

"I'll have to ask for a bond hearing Monday. I'm sure I can get you out. Hell, John, I'll post your bond myself if you promise you won't knock the teeth out of any more Sheriffs or such," McNally said as he managed a red-eyed smile.

"Did Davy call you, Mac?" John asked.

"No. Haven't heard from him. Why?"

"His wife took off with another young feller and he needs some help. I was fixing to try to get word to you on Monday to help me figure out how to get out of here to help him. I can't believe Kenneth is gone!"

"He would have been gone fifty years ago just like Speedy and I would have too, if you hadn't been there with us. None of us would have made it if you hadn't pulled us through so don't talk to me about who the best of us is. Damn right, Kenneth was a good one, but he is gone and I need you to help me help Anna survive the funeral like he would have wanted us to. It's *my* turn to get you out of this mess so you *have* to listen to *me!* It's my turn to be the hero if you can stand for that to happen, John!"

"Just tell me what you want me to do and say and I'll do it. Whatever it takes, except I won't say I am sorry for mashing the Sheriff's face!"

"I'll take care of the Sheriff's hash and get Davy any help he needs. You have to do what I tell you to and keep your head out of your ass and your foot out of your mouth. Do you understand me, John? I'm going to lay down a legal masterpiece on your behalf but, by damn, I'm in charge! Do you understand, soldier?"

"Yes, sir!" John barked. If his hands hadn't been hogtied to his waist he would have saluted.

"Be ready to go to court with me Monday morning around eight. I'll call Davy tonight and have him come see you at visiting tomorrow. I have a lot of work to do."

With that he got up and left. John called to the jailers who took him back to his cell block where the juice was cooking in the redneck's urn. Horatio looked at John when he lay down on the bunk. John put his pillow over his head and let out a long sigh.

"Everything okay, Tio Juan?" the El Salvadoran asked.

"I got to get out of here," John answered without removing the pillow from his face.

"Man oh man, don't everybody? This place is'nt so bad though. You go to jail in my country and you die in a couple of months. My old man died in jail there. The Kings gang tortured him to death, those hijos de putas!"

John pulled the pillow off his head and looked at Horatio: "Life is like a big dirt sandwich and every day, you got to get up and take a big bite. The sooner you decide you can take the taste and smile the easier things get."

"Man, you are one crude old man sometimes," he answered. "Why don't you go to sleep, Tio Juan? I'm going to scare up a card game."

# Chapter 21

The medical examiner checked out the Judge's body late on Saturday evening and found no reason to suspect anything other than natural causes had contributed to the death. McNally and Helen helped Anna to make all the arrangements with Sullivan's Funeral Home. Anna decided to relent on her own feelings and honored her husband's wishes to be cremated. So, after a long tear-filled good-bye at the funeral home on Sunday morning, Mr. Sullivan took the body down to the crematorium and the Judge was reduced to ashes. Anna picked out an urn with a simple flower design on the side. She thought they looked like irises, his favorite flower.

A former Olympic champion in the decathlon, the Presbyterian minister Robert Pensilschwietzer would organize a memorial service for late Tuesday afternoon at the VFW Lodge with a meal provided by the women's group. Pensilschwietzer would also conduct a private burial service scheduled for Wednesday morning at eleven. The local VFW wanted to take part in the funeral with a fitting tribute to one of their own.

On Sunday morning John was in his cell block eating breakfast with Horatio. Davy was at home waking up to an empty house. McNally and the two women drove to the McNally residence. The women went to the family room and Mac found his address and phone number book, picked up the phone and dialed Davy's number. On the fourth ring the young fellow answered. Mac told him about the details of the Judge's death and then relayed his intent to get a bond hearing for John in the morning. Davy said he didn't have the money to post a big bond but Mac told him not to even think about it. He personally would take care of those details with no problem. Then Mac broke the ice and told Davy that John had spilled the beans about Lizzy leaving. Mac told Davy he would help him out with that too if he wanted. Davy acknowledged that he would be grateful for Mac's guidance.

"Why don't you come over to the house now?" Mac asked him. "I need your help, son, to help your grandfather. I am going to need your help to control him until I can get this trial figured out to his best advantage. I need to talk to you about getting a game plan together."

"He can come stay right here for now since Lizzy is gone. I don't expect she's coming back and I don't think I could take her back now anyway, Mac," the young man confided.

"We'll work all that out soon, Davy. It would be good for him to stay at your place with you. I'd like for you to come over to my house this morning and we'll talk for a while if you can. Then I'm going to need you to go down to the jail this afternoon at visiting and let him know you and I are working together. That'll ease his mind and get him motivated." Davy nodded in agreement.

"You can tell him you need him to stay with you for a while. Need some help around the house or something. That'll give him a mission. Your granddaddy loves a mission and a good fight. Hell, we might have him back working stone with you and your crew come springtime. That'd probably do you both good!"

The young stone mason smiled at the thought. Davy told Mac he'd take a shower, get cleaned up and be over in about an hour or so.

"Okay, I'll get some lunch for us so just come on soon as you can," Mac said.

"Thanks, Mac," Davy said as he hung up the phone.

Helen was busy helping Anna call everyone they could think of to let them know the schedule of events. Anna's son and daughter were on the way and would be in later in the afternoon. Mac went down to the strip mall and brought some Chinese food home for lunch, knowing Anna was fond of shrimp lo mein. Then he stopped at the KFC and bought a large bucket of Original Recipe. When he got home, Davy's Nissan pickup was in the driveway. He took the food in and set it on the kitchen counter. The women had Davy cornered in the family room. Davy was doing his best to offer his sympathy to Anna and fumbling all over himself in the process. He wasn't used to talking to sophisticated older women.

"This is a fine young man here, Mac, and I understand he may be single soon," Helen said.

"Yeah, he's just like most of the young men of the day. I'm going to help him through the messy part and get him back on the right track. His mean old granddady is the one I have the most worry with at this time!" the lawyer answered.

Anna came to Davy's rescue. "Well, I have spent the last forty-five years hearing how John saved my husband's life and I know very little else. I have always wondered so much," Turning to McNally, she asked with a very serious look on her face, "Kenneth never would tell me what happened on that awful beach on D-day. How was it that John saved you boys? What did he do? Kenneth almost worshiped him and called him a 'great American hero' and such. Can't you tell us?" Mac leaned back in his chair and looked at her over his coffee cup. "I would really rather not," he said nervously.

Davy spoke up. "I heard my dad, John Jr., say a million times that my Granddaddy saved a lot of people and killed a whole bunch of Germans and North Koreans. I've always wondered what the real story is. He looked up and saw a tear in Anna's eye starting to form.

McNally was clearly uncomfortable and a few quiet moments passed. "In light of your extreme confidential natures and the finality of this moment of Kenneth's passing, I'll tell you my version of the account, but it must never be repeated." He looked back and forth between the women and they both nodded in agreement. He looked at Davy and said, "Do I have your word, young man?"

"No sir. Not under those conditions. If I ever have children, I may want to tell them about their great-granddaddy. My generation needs to know what you men did for the world. I'll give you my word I won't never speak of it until all the people you mention are gone," the young man stated firmly.

"My, my, my!" exclaimed Helen. "Maybe you should teach that young man to be a lawyer, Mac. Very well said, Davy."

Mac looked at them and said, "I agree to your terms, Davy. I suppose there might be a need to relay what a man your grandfather was in his day. I'm sure he would never tell you."

"We were four young men off to save the world and kick Adolph Hitler's ass. We were packed together on a transport boat crossing the English Channel and the sea was extremely rough. It seemed that everything in the world that could float or fly was headed the same way we were. I was so damn scared and seasick from the ride I wanted to die before we got there. Threw up all the way.

"Kenneth and Speedy smoked every cigarette they had. John sat there like he was in a trance. I think he was praying. You know he is part Shawnee Indian don't you, of course. His great-grandmother on his mother's side was the daughter of the Shawnee Chief Kill Buck, the Indian that burned Fort Seybert and the Locust Post settlements over in West Virginia. Kenneth used to say that's where John got his sixth sense, from his Indian blood.

"When we got several hundred yards from the beach we had to climb down the rope ladders to jump on the landing craft but the seas were so rough the little landing crafts were heaving up and down like some carnival ride gone wild. I got to the bottom of the rope ladder and thought it was just a couple of feet to the deck but when I dropped off I must have fallen ten feet and turned my ankle. Thank God John didn't land on me when he hit. It was a real mess with guys falling and pitching around. Once we got headed into the beach bullets started banging off the side of the boat. For some reason it really shocked and surprised me that the Germans were shooting at us!

"We finally got close to the beach and the German rifles killed some of the men before they could get off the boat. One boy from Georgia, a Robinson boy, got shot in the head and fell on Kenneth. John shoved his body away and pushed all our heads down and held us there. Along with my rifle and some grenades I was carrying belts of machine gun bullets and so was Kenneth and Speedy. John being so damn big was carrying a machine gun too. When it came time to step off the boat a lot of the men just plain sank because the water was over their heads. Drowned with all their gear and weaponry they were carrying pulling them down. They didn't have a chance.

"I got shoved off the boat and went under down to the bottom. I was about to pass out and drown when a huge hand grabbed me by the back of the neck and pulled me up. John had me in one hand and Kenneth in the other. Speedy was riding on his back like a cowboy on a plow horse! He was moving through the water with his nose up in the air like some kind of sea monster. The largest percentage of the men on our boat that were killed in the water weren't killed by the Germans. They drowned. The ones that didn't drown were shot in the water. Only about half of the troops made it up on the beach.

"There was a big post, fatter than a telephone pole and wider than a man's head, in the water ahead of us. John headed for it. He was going through the water like a tank. So damn fast I swear we were leaving a wake. I felt the bottom under my feet and started bouncing along trying to help him. Bullets were smacking the water all around us and how we were not hit I'll never understand. Must have simply been God's will. John got right behind that big post in the water and put his head close up behind it and screamed for us to line up behind him. You have to understand. When any kind of a fight starts he is incomparable! He senses what to do. He saved our lives so many times!"

McNally had tears running down his cheeks.

"Bullets tore off both sides of that post, sending splinters flying into the air past our ears. The water literally churned with bullets on each side of us. All of a sudden the shooting stopped and John roared, 'They're changing belts! Let's rush them!' He went through the hellish barbed wire they had strung in the water like a wild bull and ran up out of the water, across the open sand, right up to a concrete pillbox just as those Germans got loaded. There were only two of them in there and before they could fire John tossed a grenade in on them."

"We rolled down into that concrete pillbox and John reached out, picked up the dead Germans that were still twitching around and stacked their bodies in front of us. We caught our breath and then John turned the German machine gun around and fired it up the hill at some other Germans up there who were shooting at us. He killed a bunch of them with their own gun! He fired that damn thing until the barrel glowed and he ran out of bullets. Then he got his own machine gun going and Kenneth and Speedy, one on each side of him, started in with their rifles and were firing with deadly accuracy. All those days shooting squirrels as kids paid off. They made the Germans pay with deadly accuracy. I couldn't do much of anything except lie there behind them holding my ears. Hot brass was bouncing everywhere and the Germans up on the hill were shooting back.

"John finally ran out of bullets. There were dead men and parts of dead men everywhere, the most awful carnage Hell could conjure in the Devil's wildest dreams on the sand and mud. Fine American boys running into the jaws of Satan and beating him back at a terrible expense.

"Finally, the shooting died down and we were able to get up the hill. John picked up ammo off of dead GIs and went up and up the hill like a killing machine. He was the consummate warrior and we followed him for what seemed an eternity. I absolutely have no idea why he wasn't shot 1,000 times. Like I said, God's will. Hundreds of men were following him and I was just trying to put one foot in front of the other with my sprained ankle swelling. I was desperately afraid they would leave me behind. John was the biggest target on the beach and never got hit. The canteen on his hip got a hole shot through it and he lost all his water.

"Kenneth and Speedy gave a good account of themselves too. I'll admit I was a follower and would never have made it if I hadn't been with those three men.

"I did have one skill that proved to be my saving grace later on. I had taken French in old Possum Will's French class in high school and managed to learn the language fairly well. It was a good tool to show off with. That turned out to help us immensely in the awful days and weeks and then months that followed. There were too many other things that happened after that that you couldn't and shouldn't want to hear about. John led us through. It's almost unbelievable that four men from the same little town in the Appalachian Mountains waded through Hell on D-day and made it up on the hills without being killed.

"My ankle was swollen and hurt me badly for days. We fought our way into the scrub brush where we flushed five Germans out of a little barn. One of them opened up on us with a rifle and Speedy went down. Kenneth killed that German with a quick snap shot and the others ran. Speedy never even hollered. Kenneth and I dragged him into the barn and he was losing a lot of blood. John went after those Germans and I thought for sure they would turn on him and kill him but he was like a hound after a black bear. We heard three shots over the hill and after a few minutes John came back. That's when I noticed he had bad cuts on his chest and I thought he was shot but that was where he had plowed through the barbed wire in the water. A medic came up from the beach and he took over Speedy who still hadn't even said a word until then.

"'Reckon my days stealing second base is over now. You boys will have to come up with another name for me besides Speedy,' he said. It was the strangest and bravest thing I ever heard anyone say. Then the medic pulled out a needle to give him a shot and he went off cussing like you never heard. He was scared to death of a needle and as far as I know he still is. Never uttered one complaint when his leg was shot off but he is literally scared to death of a little needle. Kenneth and I held him while the medic stuck him and he passed out.

111

"A sergeant came by with four men and ordered us to fall in with him and his men. One of the hardest things I ever did was to leave Speedy there. He had to suffer on the beach in a makeshift hospital for two days before they could get him out. His leg got infected and they had to take it off. I didn't see him for two years but I wrote to him often. He told me he still has all those letters. He wrote two of them to me from the hospital. He joked in one of his letters and said he made a boy from Massachusetts take his leg and throw it in the English Channel. Said he couldn't stand to think any part of him was buried in France. He failed old Poss Will's French class and he thought the leg would maybe bring him bad luck later if they left it in France. Most absurd thing I ever heard of! Many times in the following months I would have given a leg to join him or gladly traded places with him.

"John was the man that saved us and got us through. Now he is in jail. Speedy runs his restaurant and keeps to himself. Kenneth is gone. I have a chance to save John from the disgrace of dying in jail. Now, I get a chance to be his warrior. And somehow I will."

There were no dry eyes in the room as he paused in his reflections.

Davy spoke up. "Whenever I would ask him about it when I was little he would say that he wasn't a brave man. He said he was scared to death the whole time he was in the war. Said Eisenhower dumped him out on a beach where there was no choice but to fight. No place to run. He used to wake up at night and go out in the kitchen and bend over sitting in his chair moaning and Gramma Fern would stand behind him rubbing his neck and back. She would see me peek out of my room and put her finger over her lips telling me to be quiet. I would go back to my bed and cry without making any sound because I knew if there was something in the world that could scare my granddady like that then I was lost and didn't have a chance. Gramma Fern would come into my bedroom after she got Granddaddy John back to bed and crawl in beside me and hug me. She was a fine woman."

"That she was, Davy. That she was. The luckiest day of John's life is the day he married Fern. He was home on leave and he really was a handsome cuss in those days. Especially in his uniform. He would never have gotten a woman like that if there hadn't been such a shortage of men. She was working at Woolworth's behind the counter and I guess she saw the courage and goodness in him. You know she was born up on the mountain too. I don't think they dated more than two months when he had to go back on duty. They ran off to Hagerstown, Maryland, and got married. Her daddy was furious! He was a good man, Davy. He died the next year of pneumonia and his wife, your great-grandmother, went the very next year from cancer."

"Granddaddy used to come into my room sometime at night and talk to me about things like honor and doing the right thing. When I would ask him about being a war hero he would laugh and say he had done the best he could. I could smell liquor on his breath. He used to tell me stories about a man he had read about in one of those soldier magazines. He was from Finland. I remember the stories well because John thought the man was the greatest hero that had ever fought. Had a strange name but John knew it well. Kauko something or the other. This Kauko guy was from some little town by the name of Humppila. I always thought that was such a neat sounding name for a town and liked to get Grampap to say it. Humppila. I looked it up on the map and it is a real place about a hundred miles above Helsinki. Granddaddy said this man fought the Russians and protected his homeland with nothing but a rifle and a set of skis. Him and a small bunch of his countrymen kept the entire Russian army out of Finland. Granddaddy said they were the bravest and toughest men he ever heard of and he said he read where all their war dead were brought back to their own hometowns and buried in graves they keep neat as a pin even until this day. John said he always wanted to visit that Kauko's guys grave so he could pay respect to him."

"I think you should take him there sometime, Davy," Anna said tearfully.

The doorbell rang and pulled them out of their reverie, breaking the spell of the moment. Looking at the women, Mac wiped his face with his hands and realized he was sweating profusely. He was only too glad to have an excuse to quit this discussion and said, "I'll go see who is here."

At the door Mac found Reverend Pencilschwietzer and his wife smiling but concerned. The pastor looked like the poster child for a senior citizen vitamin company and his wife looked like a college cheerleader. Preachers were annoying to Mac but in this instance he was glad to have any distraction.

Pencilschwietzer was a unique man among men -- tall and lean as a sapling with the strong, healthy, hearty look of an outdoorsman and always tanned like he had just come from a golf course in Myrtle Beach. He could eat like a horse and never gain a pound. His wife Connie was mid-thirties but looked like she was twenty with strawberry-blonde hair and flashing green eyes. She was always wearing shirts she had decorated with needlepoint. Connie was a bird-watching fanatic and an aspiring artist. The shirt she was wearing had an intricate Scarlet Tanager sewn on the shoulder and McNally noticed she had little silver birds as earrings. McNally thought they must have nothing but dried asparagus shoots and wheat germ in their cupboards along with birdseed and Cream of Wheat. Pencilschwietzer had been the 1968 pole-vaulting champion of the world out of a small Midwest parochial school and his pictures were on Wheaties boxes for years. It caused quite a stir when he interviewed for the local Presbyterian Church pastorate. The job came open after the former pastor died suddenly of a heart attack at a benefit spaghetti supper. He had choked on a meatball old Mrs. Scoggins made and fell over on his plate dead as a mackerel. Pencilschwietzer had won the job hands down. He and his wife were a perfect fit for the small life community, which they referred to as "quaint" to their friends in Chicago. One of the search committee members noted he didn't like meatballs so there was little likelihood he would choke like the last preacher did.

"Well, what a surprise, Reverend Bob. And Ms. Connie, how good to see you. Come in, come in," Mac oozed. "The ladies are in the family room."

Reverend Bob and Connie shook hands with Mac as they entered the house. Mac led them to the family room where Connie hugged Helen and Anna in turn and Reverend Bob shook hands with them. Mac was relieved they were there. He was off the hook with the war stories. After an acceptable few minutes he rose from his chair and gathered the dishes and excused himself to the kitchen.

Davy thanked Mac and bid everyone a good afternoon, leaving to go visit John. Mac would have to suffer through the formalities of having a preacher in the house by himself. Pencilschwietzer was always preaching against the evils of drinking liquor to excess but Mac knew if he offered him a drink of his twelve-year-old Scotch the preacher would drain the bottle for him. But then again, Mac thought, it would be a novel time to get drunk with a preacher. They always said, "Wherever you can find four Presbyterians you are bound to find a fifth!"

Bob and Connie prided themselves in their skills visiting and socializing with church members. When Mac offered the little shooter glass of Scotch Reverend Bob didn't turn it down. They talked to Anna about God's great plan and the philosophical meanings of life and death. As the conversation eventually turned to lighter subjects Helen commented on the cross-stitched Tanager on Connie's blouse. Connie talked about her infatuation with birds and then dropped a bomb on Mac.

"Mac, aren't you representing that man, John Dean? The man that beat up the Sheriff?"

"Yes, I am. He is the grandfather of the young man who just left, Davy Dean. Why do you ask, Connie?" Mac inquired with eyebrow raised.

"Well, I have been thinking it might not be my business but I have an acquaintance, sort of, who I have been counseling. I met her through our mutual interest in birds. We met in the grocery store when both of us were buying birdseed." Connie looked to Bob for guidance and Reverend Bob just nodded for her to keep on and took another sip of Mac's Scotch. "Her name is Mary Ann Bartley and I have been trying to get her to come to our church. She lives in the house on the corner where that awful wreck happened between the cement truck and that poor old man who lives at the Brethren Home. She owns the house where Mr. Dean carried the victim to and where the assault on the Sheriff took place."

Connie stopped like she was betraying a friend and Bob patted her on the knee and told her, "Connie, go ahead and tell them. The truth should not be kept hidden."

"Mary Ann told me confidentially that she has a very explicit videotape of the whole thing she made with her camcorder. So I asked to see it. I mean, she has it all on there! The Sheriff was so nasty to Mr. Dean after what he had been through saving the other old man like he did! If you watch the tape, Mr. Dean was nothing short of heroic! But he did really hit the Sheriff hard," she admitted apologetically.

Mac just about fell off his chair, "Great Scott, madam!"

Connie reached in her purse and pulled out a VCR tape and handed it to Mac. "Mary Ann made me an extra copy of it. She has the original. I told her I wanted to give it to you because you are representing Mr. Dean. Mary Ann thinks he is like some white knight or something. She has been writing letters to him at jail and all sorts of things.

Mac walked over to the TV set and flipped it on. He adjusted the channels and got the VCR going and inserted the tape. When they finished watching it Mac gave them strict orders not to tell anyone. The great defense of John Dean had just gotten much easier for him and he recognized and savored the amount of sport he could have with his legal adversaries.

"Does anyone other than you two and this Mary Ann know about this?" Mac asked. "Mary Ann said she hadn't told anyone else. I'm sure she hasn't. She has no other friends that I know of with the exception of her bird friends and I am the only one that is even in this part of the country," Connie said.

"We absolutely, positively want to keep it that way. Can we go see this young lady now?" he excitedly asked.

Connie and the reverend said they could but Bob, who was on his third glass of Mac's Scotch, said Connie would have to drive them. Anna and Helen said to go on and not worry about them because Anna's children would arrive soon and they wanted what was best for John.

# Chapter 22

To John's great relief the memorial service was held Tuesday at the VFW instead of the church. The Sheriff showed up with his once handsome face looking like it had gone fifteen rounds with Mike Tyson. He had several deputies with him and Mac noticed the looks of surprise on their faces when John joined Mac, Davy, Speedy, and Ben Dean when they stood up as the honorary pall bearers. The Commonwealth Attorney, Charles Grimes, did not miss that point either.

It was a full house. Pensilschwietzer was in rare form. Mac was surprised to hear such an accurate account of his old friend's life. Sullivan, the funeral home director, was flitting here and there making sure Anna and her children were taken care of. This was a big one for him too. Flower arrangements surrounded the urn containing the ashes of the judge. The urn was displayed on an oak table in the front on a makeshift stage. There must have been $5,000 worth of flower arrangements around the podium. Pencilschwietzer looked like he was standing in a floral show exhibit while he preached out the message he wanted to deliver to the grieving souls.

Helen had helped Anna to make a photo display of pictures from Kenneth's life. Grade school photos showed a freckled, smiling, and happy boy with scarce a care in the world. His high school graduation picture showed a handsome, young, fresh-faced man ready to take on the world. Then there was a picture of the four classmates in their uniforms taken in England shortly before D-day. John had a buxom dark-haired English girl hanging on him and he was smiling with a cigar hanging from the corner of his mouth. Such handsome lads they had been, gone off to fight the war. A picture of Kenneth and Anna on their wedding day showed a much more serious and matured man. Then there were the pictures of him holding his children when they were born. He looked so proud and strong and responsible. Anna's favorite picture taken of his graduation from the University of Virginia Law School in Charlottesville in front of Mr. Jefferson's Rotunda, standing on the beautiful lawn with the magnolias in full bloom. Lastly, there was a very distinguished painting of him in his cloak presiding over court. This picture had been commissioned some time back by the local BAR Association and hung on display permanently on the courtroom wall.

Anna had asked Ben Dean and his band to play "Oh, Shenandoah," the Judge's favorite song. Ben had asked Vernon Hughes and his pretty black haired wife Kelley to help him sing. Kelley sang the lead and Vernon sang tenor with Ben carrying the baritone. They had worked up a version with the guitar playing solo through the introduction of the song with Ben's violin and Vernon's mandolin hauntingly coming in, and then the entire band softly bringing the old melody to a conclusion. It was masterfully done and a work of art. Vernon and Kelley sang another song at Pencilschwietzer's request. A song the Hughes' had written entitled "Trust Jesus". John thought it was the finest song he had ever heard.

The president of the local VFW spoke almost as long as Pencilschwietzer did and talked about the sacrifices made by the Judge and his generation. He passionately asked those in attendance to never forget what Kenneth Crawford had achieved in his life: a lifetime filled with service, duty, honor, and love. Another VFW member played "Taps" on the bugle and there were many tear dimmed eyes in the crowd. Anna was beautiful and stoic during the whole service although her daughter sobbed uncontrollably while Anna stroked the back of her auburn hair.

When it was finally over everyone was invited to a dinner in the VFW social hall located in the basement. The women of the church had prepared a huge carry-in feast and the VFW president welcomed all. The representatives of the Sheriff's department declined to attend but the Commonwealth's Attorney did. John was unconcerned about Grimes' presence and ate several plates full. He then volunteered to clean out a Crock-Pot in which one of the ladies had brought Swiss steak with dark-brown gravy. She gave him a big spoon and directed him to a corner of the kitchen where he took two slices of homemade bread and swabbed out every bit of it. He looked at the women watching him and said, "Jail food ain't bad and it's almost as good as the Brethren Home food, but you

Presbyterians got them all beat except you like salt too much. I could do without some of the salt but this is like dying and going to heaven." He turned his attention to cleaning out a scalloped potato pan.

John looked up from his preoccupation with the potato pan and saw Sarah Smith, Maybelle McCoy, and bucktoothed Mary from the Brethren Home coming toward him. He put the pan down on the counter. Sarah walked over to him and said, "You have gravy on your chin, John. Look there, you spilled some on your shirt too!"

John could feel his face getting red. He unconsciously checked his fly to make sure it wasn't open. Mary picked up a roll of paper towels and came to his rescue saying, "Just you bend down here, Mr. John. I'll get you fixed up." John bent down to her and she wiped his chin off and then dabbed at the spill on his shirt.

Maybelle patted him on the arm and said, "We've been missing you at the home, John. Have you been all right? We've been worried about you."

"Thank you for your concerns but I have been fine. Jail ain't bad. Good bunch of guys to play cards with and nobody cares to point out my deficiencies," he said looking Sarah Smith in the eye.

While John was visiting with the girls in the kitchen Charles Grimes made his way over to Mac who was refilling his coffee cup from the large canister. "I'm glad to see you got your client bonded out so he could be here, Mac."

"Only fitting since he is such a harmless old war dog. If it weren't for him neither Kenneth nor I would have lived through D-day," Mac responded.

"While that fact carries merit and sentimental value, malicious wounding of our Sheriff with such clear-cut testimony makes him a threat to society, I would think. Our Sheriff wants blood on this one. He not only wants it he demands it! He's not going to settle for anything less, Mac, and Investigator Wilkins has a report lying on my desk with the I's dotted and the T's crossed."

Mac stirred cream into his coffee and turned to face Mr. Grimes. "If my friend and client, Mr. Dean, loses and is sentenced to jail then he will have a place to stay with free medical care for the rest of his life which probably won't be more than a couple of years. Against my advice he wants his day in court so there will be neither pleas sought nor defenses of insanity. John says your Sheriff provoked his actions and he wants to tell the jury his version."

"Come on, Mac. You know I don't want to slam-dunk an old man like Mr. Dean but he really messed up Mark's face. Can't you plead an insanity defense? I understand he's had some mental issues in years past. Can't we go that route and save all of us unnecessary time and worry? We'll get him some probation and counseling and chalk all this up to insanity. Now doesn't that make sense?"

"He had some bouts with depression like most of us who lived through that hell in Germany," Mac answered. "He stayed on with the army at the end of the war because he didn't think he had anyone to come home to and really he didn't. I think he found relief and security in the army way of life. He would never say it but I think he stayed on because he felt himself unfit to reenter the community. It is hard to click the kill switch on and off. He knew he was in his element as a soldier. Let me tell you something, Grimes. That man was the "Terrible Swift Sword" of this nation. Then Uncle Sam gave him his reward and sent him to Korea where he distinguished himself many times in battle there. One day he just up and retired and came home with no real skills other than a strong back. That's when the depression problems surfaced. His wife and little boy suffered along with him as he mostly drank and slid into a hole. Speedy Spencer had a friend who was a stone mason who needed help and it was Speedy that got John a job laying stone. He took to it like a duck to water and somehow he quit drinking. His wife, Fern, got him straightened out on that, thank God. John and his crew did all the stone work in the front of this building. His grandson Davy who was here today took over the business when John quit three years ago after Fern died. He's not crazy, Charles. Just hardheaded as a goat and firm in his convictions."

"Well, then, Mac, convictions are what he shall have. It's not my concern what he did during his life. There simply is no defense for his actions and the Sheriff wants his head on his wall. Did you look at Mark's face today? Three-fourths of the women in this county are mad as wet hens about what your client did to the Sheriff's pretty face."

"I know, Charles. You and the Sheriff are the darlings of the local Republican Party and election year is coming up and you need to let people think your're doing your jobs. It would be a shame to put John Dean in jail for what will essentially be a life sentence but if that's what the cards have in store, so be it. I can't talk him into any plea so let's see what a jury will do with it," Mac said. "I am growing too weary to put up much of a fight trying to keep such a leaky vessel as this case afloat!"

"I'll see you later, Mr. McNally," Grimes said in disgust. "If the old bastard wants jail I'll gladly accommodate him!"

Mac watched him go. "After all these years I'm going to give the local Republicans something to remember me by," Mac mused. "If I can just keep everybody quiet and calm until the trial, I'm going to break it off in them and leave it hanging" Mac looked back in the kitchen and saw the black girl with the strange teeth reach up and hug John around the neck. Mac saw John hug her back and noticed his large hand grab the girl in the backside. She pulled away from him, said something, and then hugged him again. John was smiling from ear to ear. Davy saw it too and headed back into the kitchen to run interference on whatever was going on there. Probably a great move in Mac's view. Mac turned and looked for Helen. It was time to go home and find a tall glass of rum. Captain Morgan's Private Stock with a slice of lime would do nicely, he thought. He wanted to settle back in his chair and watch the fireplace this evening. And drink until he passed out.

# Chapter 23

John's move in with Davy was completed and they were getting used to each other. Davy liked to stay up a lot later than John did and John finally realized he didn't have to stay up to please his grandson. Davy found out John could mostly take care of himself if he let him. It was January and cold so there were only a few days fit for laying stone. Davy went around looking at jobs and lining up work for when the weather broke in the spring and he would take John with him. He spent the bad weather days in his leather shop making guitar straps, a profitable little business and hobby he had on the side. He also made straps for banjos and mandolins but there was a much larger demand for his guitar products. He wholesaled them to Ben Dean, who turned around and sold them at bluegrass festivals and county fairs he had booked in the summer with his band.

John would come out and sit in an old green recliner in the shop and keep the little woodstove going to warm them as Davy worked leather. They listened to a lot of radio programs. For the most part they enjoyed each other's company and seldom argued. Davy was missing Lizzy—longing for her one minute and hating her guts the next. Even though she had snaked him like she had, he spent most of his waking hours thinking about her and what she and the Morris boy were probably doing together. When she wanted it, Lizzy was a wildcat in bed and the thoughts of them together intimately both confounded him and, at times, to his great confusion, aroused him. Sometimes he had to walk outside and get alone for a while when the overpowering emotions would overtake him. Feelings of inadequacy embarrassed him tremendously.

Maybe Lizzy was right. Maybe it was his fault and he wasn't man enough to hold her. That one had stung him, and rejection haunted him day and night. The slow, cold, dreary days of January didn't tend to help his mood but the days did grind on. Sometimes his emotions got the better of him and to his great embarassment he went into his room and sobbed uncontrollably. This would only happen when he was alone and even then it humiliated him to lose control. He would realize afterward that it did make him feel better to blow it on out. He looked at it kind of like a steam valve on the top of his grandmother's old pressure canner: best to let that stuff out instead of exploding.

John liked to listen to Rush Limbaugh on the radio. He thought Limbaugh was right about most things he talked about even if he was essentially a loudmouth smart ass. Davy particularly got a kick out of Limbaugh's "Kennedy Updates" and his "Mike Tyson Updates." John had been a Democrat like his Daddy had told him to be because "Democrats was for the poor man." John had voted for John Kennedy and admired him very much. He looked forward to supporting Bobby Kennedy until that lunatic Sirhan Sirhan had done him in. Teddy Kennedy was another matter altogether and John detested him. He thought it hilarious and he laughed each time Limbaugh make his crude jokes about Senator Kennedy. "That spoon-fed spoiled brat deserves to be tarred and feathered along with that nasty Barney Frank!" John would roar. "Can't the New England states do better for themselves than to elect horses asses like those two? I aim to go to Massachusetts and go door to door just to find out what caliber of idiots could elect a disgusting fool like Barney Frank."

Anna Crawford had been bringing food over for them regularly. When Davy told her he was worried she was doing too much for them she said she needed something to do with herself until springtime and her garden was suitable for planting. "You silly boys. Can't you let me feel needed?" she teased even though she knew she needed to do it more for herself than for the Dean bachelors. "My children have gone on back to their lives so I have decided to adopt you two stray tomcat Dean boys!" she would joke. The food she brought was always welcome and there were seldom any leftovers. Between Anna and the deli at the Piggly Wiggly they kept fed and the gloomy days of January slid on by as John's trial loomed ever closer.

Mac started the legal ball rolling with the separation of Davy and Lizzy. He merely called her at work and told her he was representing Davy and wanted to know if she had a lawyer. She told him she was just glad to be gone from Davy Dean and knew she was in a position of being on the short end of the entire deal financially but she needed her freedom. Mac told her he admired her honesty and if she would sign a few papers for him he could make it very easy for the both of them to just go on about their respective lives. Much to his surprise Lizzy showed up at his office that same day and signed the house and all other property over to Davy with no argument whatsoever. She had already gotten all her furniture, clothing, and personal items she wanted out of the house. Mac smiled as she told him she was in the mood to travel far and light and bragged that her new beau was taking her on a cruise to the Bahamas in April, something she could never have gotten Davy to do. Mac told her he wished her well and out the door she swished. As she strutted out the door and down the walk Mac decided she looked really good from behind in those tight jeans, even if a bit trailer park trashy. Mac laughed as he thought, "I might be an old rooster these days but I still have occasional ideas of hopping up on the fence and crowing!"

Detective Wilkins was very sure his investigation was thorough and made an air-tight case against Mr. Dean. He had reviewed every detail with the Commonwealth's Attorney and assured the Sheriff he had all the bases in the case covered. The only detail he wished he could have nailed down was interviewing the owner of the house near where the assault had taken place. He had been out there a couple of times and knew the woman who lived there was at home. A couple of kids playing football next door told him that she was crazy and they called her Spider-Woman because they said she looked like a big, fat spider. Wilkins decided there was no reason to pursue it further. The Sheriff reviewed Wilkins' work and agreed he had done a good job. Mr. Grimes made copies of the final report and at Mac's request forwarded all the information as required under the rules of discovery. Mac read over the reports, especially the statement made by the Sheriff at the hospital. The medical bill thus far for the Sheriff's injuries stood at $16,411.

Commonwealth's Attorney Grimes had drafted a plea agreement he planned to offer McNally to take to his client even though Mac had told him Dean wouldn't take any deals. Grimes offered a ten-year sentence with nine years suspended for the felony charge in regards to the attack on the Sheriff. He also expected Mr. Dean to be made responsible for the medical expenses that worker's comp was now covering, not to mention possible future civil suits and the cost of the court. On the misdemeanor assault and battery charge of Mr. Zetty, the cement truck driver, he would settle for a one-year sentence to run concurrently with the felony charge along with the cost of the court. Grimes kept thinking about the trial and what a dumb ass this old Dean man must be. How did he think he would do anything but spend the rest of his life in jail? A jury trial is always a crap shoot. The old man could end up getting ten years to serve!

Did McNally have some sort of ace in the hole? McNally had been the best defense attorney in the area for a long time and his reputation was very much alive in the legal community, but he hadn't been in the trenches for at least ten years. He had several young guys in his firm to do all those slimy jobs now. Grimes thought it would be sweet to make McNally, the local head of the Democratic Party, look bad in an election year, especially if he could convict one of McNally's old worn-out war dog friends. Mac had milked the political war hero crowd for years by bringing those fossils out in their uniforms and parading them around. What are you thinking, Mr. McNally?

Grimes read over the Sheriff's statement again about how he had been questioning the old man and asking him if he was all right. Sheriff Watson had written, "I walked up to the porch and asked Mr. Dean if he thought Mr. Rennick's age had anything to do with the wreck. I must have hit a nerve with him because the next thing I knew he suddenly lashed out and slugged me in the face. I had no warning whatsoever. I drew my gun and was able to back him off and keep him from killing me. As I lay on the ground with my gun on him he begged me to shoot him. I think he was trying to commit suicide by police officer. I think he planned it as I walked up to him. Thank the good Lord I was able to keep my wits about me even though I was hurt so badly. I suppose I reverted to my training."

Grimes had looked at many of the Sheriff's written reports over the years and the sentence structure looked like someone else had written it. He made a mental note to ask Mark about that point. Grimes remembered then that the statement had been drafted in the hospital shortly after the event. You couldn't expect someone to feel literary at a time like that. Oh, well, the prosecutor thought, there was no way out of this one for the defense unless the Sheriff was lying and it was preposterous to doubt him. Once the charming Sheriff went on stand with the scars and bruises still left on his face it didn't matter what jury was picked. From that moment on this trial would be over.

The trial was set for February 2, Groundhog Day. Ha! Mac thought it was a fine day for coming out and seeing what your shadow looks like!

He was going to make it six more weeks of winter for the Republicans. Hopefully a winter that would stretch until election day. Mac was tired of what he perceived to be their cocky, good-ole-boy relationships and attitudes. They needed to be shook up! Let the games begin, he thought with a slight smile. He decided he might well retire after this one himself. If things went South he might have to when everything was said and done. There was a lot on the line here besides John Dean's sorry big behind.

# Chapter 24

The night before the trial it snowed six inches and the wind blew hard, pushing up deep drifts. The temperature dropped to five degrees Fahrenheit and Davy was nervous. John went to bed as usual without much comment just like it was any other night. He had said over and over, "Whatever happens just happens. Don't worry about it. The worst thing that could happen is they throw me in jail and have to take care of me for the rest of my life. So, don't you be worrying about it, Davy."

Davy kept thinking Mac would get his grandfather off somehow. Mac was so doggone smart and he was still awful slick in the young man's eyes. How this thing had ever happened in the first place was still beyond him. The realization that his grandfather was, in fact, a man prone to great violence surprised Davy each time he thought about the story Mac had told over at his house the Sunday afternoon following the Judge's death. It had helped him to understand his grandfather's behavior over the years. The old man had been grumpy and kind of scary to him when he was a child growing up. He had listened to the grownups talking from time to time as they were riding in the car or while he was playing with his toys and they were sitting around drinking coffee. They talked about what sounded like "War-a-war too and War-a-war won" and names like Hitler, Ike, Roosevelt, Patton, Hoover were all familiar to him. Davy wondered and worried about the atom bomb they talked about and the Russians with their Iron Curtain. The only big curtain he had ever seen was at the movie theater and he had wondered how they got a curtain made of iron to slide back and forth. Those Russians must be smart and mean, he figured from listening to the grownups talk. Davy had heard John say on several occasions: "I wish the government would have let Patton go on up there to Moscow and kill Joe Stalin and his old Red Army. Maybe if they would have gone ahead and done it that mean-looking man Khrushchev wouldn't be on the news every evening acting so smart."

He had a vague idea as a little boy that his grandfather had fought the Germans and North Koreans and had killed some of them. To little boy Davy, John had been the personification of manhood: gruff, slightly scary, and infinitely strong. He liked to go with his grandmother to take Grampap lunch when he was laying stone close to home. John would let him play with the trowel and show him how to set a rock in place and how to hit it just right and make it break in a useful form. Most kids look at their grandfathers like heroes but John had been Davy's surrogate father while his own Dad, John Jr., was off on his own adventures. Davy thought a lot about those days and looked at his grandfather in a different light now that Mac had given him a little bit of an idea what kind of man John had been during the war. He was proud of him. Always had been.

During his nightly prayers he asked Jesus to help John through this last battle with the law. He prayed for Lizzy too, and asked the Lord to give her the happiness she had never found with him. It was late when Davy finally fell asleep listening to the snowy wind blow and wondering what Lizzy was doing. He could hear John snoring, sounding like a hibernating bear growling low in his dreams of summer grass and trees full of ripe apples.

The morning of the trial broke clear and cold. Davy was up at daylight shoveling snow out of the driveway and off the porch. The wind had blown most of the snow out of his yard and deposited it in a huge drift out behind his shop. He was lucky the wind had come from the southwest pushing the snow away from the front. With the help of a Lion's Club broom he had bought off of Sullivan the undertaker he soon had the truck ready to go. The state VDOT trucks had already been through and plowed the road open. The biggest job he had was shoveling the snow piled up across the entrance to his driveway that had stacked up along the sides of the road in the wake of the big trucks.

Back in the house he heard John in the shower. Davy had given him orders to clean up for the trial. It had been no easy task to find a white shirt that fit and a tie Mac had ordered to make the big defendant presentable. Davy had polished John's shoes and belt. They had gone over to Junior's Barbershop on Monday and both of them had gotten haircuts. John still had a full head of hair he had Junior cut short and then he had him give him a close shave also. Junior told John they should have given him a medal for smacking Sheriff Watson. He didn't like the Sheriff because he had given him a speeding ticket when the Sheriff had been a state trooper, way back before he got elected. "I never voted for the son of a bitch neither. He handed me one of those silly helium balloons when I walked by the Republican booth at the county fair. Well, I took it outside and let the darn thing fly off into the night!" John grunted and Davy looked up and smiled while he was looking through a "Field & Stream" magazine from the barber's reading rack.

"What was it like staying in jail, Mr. Dean?" the diminutive barber asked.

"Food was good but not enough for me. Met a Mexican in there named Horatio who played a mean hand of cards. Had a good shower every day and a warm place to crap. 'Bout the same as the Brethren Home except a hell of a lot cheaper. I about halfway wish they would put me back in there. Davy don't play cards near as good as that Mexican does."

Davy laughed out loud and shook his head. Junior had raised his eyebrows so high he looked like a little barn owl as he trimmed the hair out of John's left ear.

They got dressed and loaded into the little truck. John seemed to fit in it better these days and Davy noticed the old man had lost a good bit of his belly. He had been taking long walks twice a day right on schedule and his whole outlook seemed better. Davy thought he had never known his grandfather to be so calm and peaceful.

Davy drove them to Speedy's restaurant and cautioned John about not eating too much. He didn't want him to go into court feeling like his guts were going to explode and passing gas like a mule. John had only four eggs over easy, three pieces of toast with butter and jelly, two big slices of fried scrapple and two refills of coffee. For him that wasn't extravagant and Nell made over him like he was a little boy headed off to his first day in kindergarten. Speedy and Nell both wished him luck in court and Speedy said he would be in the courtroom as soon as they got the breakfast rush finished.

Davy watched Speedy walk back into the kitchen carrying a stack of dishes and thought it was a fine thing he could walk with a wooden leg as well as he could. Before he knew it the famous big clock that Speedy had made himself and hung behind the counter with a plugged shotgun as the minute hand and a heavy barreled revolver for the hour hand said it was eight thirty. Davy was prodding John to get a move on because they had to be there at nine o'clock. John laughed. "I bet they don't start without us!"

"They'll throw you in jail for contempt of the court if you are late," Speedy said.

Kicking the snow off their feet they crawled back into the Nissan pickup and headed up the slick road behind a VDOT truck spreading salt and made their way to the Cambridge County Courthouse. Mac was waiting for them when they walked into the courtroom. He was carrying a notebook and a file in a large manila jacket labeled simply, "John Dean Case." He also had a leather briefcase with him. Davy took a seat on the front row of the oak benches.

McNally motioned for John to come on up front and join him. John walked through the little swinging saloon-type of doors taking a chair beside Mac at a large oak table with a water pitcher and a stack of Dixie cups beside it. To the left of their table and on the other side of the room was an identical table where the Commonwealth's Attorney, Mr. Grimes, was studiously studying a paper on top of a large, thick stack of manila case files. Davy observed that Grimes must have a number of other cases to handle later in the day. Between the two tables was a raised podium with a small desk and chair that faced the Judge. It was surrounded on three sides with an oak wall approximately three feet high. It was obvious that was where all the testifying would be done. The Judge's bench was very high in the front of the courtroom and was equipped with desk space on the Judge's left hand for the clerk of the circuit court. Beside the clerk was a smaller desk for the court recorder. The Judge could enter from a door directly behind his chair. To the Judge's right there were twelve seats for the jurors so they could see and hear every testimony and interaction among the Judge, the attorneys, and the witnesses.

A local newspaper reporter was interviewing the Sheriff on the far side of the room. Davy thought the reporter looked like a cross between a possum and Larry of the Three Stooges. The uniformed bailiff was up in front next to the door where the Judge would soon enter. There were two other uniformed deputies with the Sheriff. Investigator Wilkins was sitting beside his boss the Sheriff as the newspaperman laughed and joked with them. His feral eyes seemed to gleam when the Sheriff whispered something in his ear and pointed toward Mac and John. Davy could see the Sheriff still had a black eye and his nose was swelled up and very different looking from the nose he had sported before the fateful day of the wreck.

There was a stir in the back of the court and Rennick was wheeled in with his arms in a cast. John recognized the nurse pushing him as the resident nurse from the Launching Pad. Behind her came the director, Donald Bowman, with a stern look on his face. He looked like he was ready to testify to the world that John's behavior was not indicative of the residents living in his establishment. People kept coming in and many of them were there to support John. He looked back as his sister Mary Alice Dean from Richmond came in, boldly walked to the front and hugged her brother who stood tall and stiff. Then she went to the back of the room and sat down in the back bench. Finally the door behind the Judge's bench popped open and the bailiff snapped to attention. A tall, gray-haired man wearing a robe entered quickly and took his seat at the Judge's chair as the bailiff announced, "All rise! The Court of Cambridge County is now in session. Silence is commanded. The Honorable Judge John Jacobs is presiding. God save the Commonwealth and God save the union. Please be seated."

John leaned over and whispered to Mac, "Who is this little Judge? I never heard of him."

"Old friend of mine. From down Lexington. Good man and a VMI graduate. Now be quiet and do exactly like I told you to," the cagey old prosecutor whispered in John's ear.

"Good morning, Mr. McNally. Good morning, Mr. Grimes," the Judge said nodding to each. "We have some serious charges to address this morning, gentlemen, and I understand we are to have the jury to come in to hear the case?" he asked looking back and forth between the adversaries.

"That is correct, Your Honor," Grimes responded.

"Well, then, bailiff, since both of the parties have agreed to accept the jury we empanelled yesterday would you please bring in the jurors," the Judge commanded. "Motions have been properly made and all witnesses that are here to testify are to be excluded from the courtroom."

Grimes asked, "Your Honor, since it is so difficult for Mr. Rennick to be moved I plan to call him first."

"Okay, then, madam," the Judge indicated to Rennick's nurse. "You can stay right where you are for a few minutes, if that is okay with you Mr. McNally."

Standing up to address the Judge, Mac agreed. "Absolutely, Your Honor,"

The bailiff exited to round up the jury and Davy noticed Rennick smile with what he thought was a sarcastic look on his face. No wonder Grampa didn't like that guy!

# Chapter 25

Jury selection was usually a tedious process but this day it went expeditiously. Mack and Grimes agreed to use the jury selected for the previous day's trial. Mack knew each of them personally and he was pleased with the mix. The jury comprised of seven men and five women who solemnly filed into the courtroom and took their seats. John recognized two of the men as having been classmates in high school a year or two behind him and one of the women he was pretty sure worked at the Food Lion grocery store. They all looked serious. Judge Jacobs bid good morning to them and turned to the clerk of the court. The Judge said, "Would you read the charges, please."

Ronald Cloud, the clerk of the court, was an extremely handsome man and looked something like what the old-timers called a "riverboat gambler" type of fellow. He was a bachelor and many of the female constituents of the county, married and single, had spent intimate time with him. The clerk had that Rhett Butler style to him. Mr. Cloud stood up and read from a typed piece of paper. "Mr. John Andrew Dean has been indicted with a Class 4 Felony for the malicious wounding of a police officer. He is also charged with assault and battery, a Class 1 Misdemeanor."

The clerk took his seat and the Judge leaned forward in his chair. "Members of the jury, with the preliminary instructions in mind we discussed yesterday we'll proceed with opening statements. Both parties have agreed to expedite the proceedings. If you have no further questions we will begin shortly."

The Judge called all the witnesses for the Commonwealth, read their names, and had them stand. "Mr. McNally has made a motion all witnesses shall be excluded. You will wait in our waiting rooms and hear none of the testimony. I am ordering you not to discuss any events of the trial with anyone until you are called to testify. Bailiff, would you see these folks to their quarters please?"

After the witnesses had filed out the Judge nodded toward Mr. Grimes, who promptly got up and stepped toward the jury. "Ladies and gentlemen of the jury, I am the Commonwealth's Attorney for Cambridge County. It is my duty to prosecute John Andrew Dean who is a senior citizen and a veteran of World War II and the Korean War. He is a retired veteran of the United States Army with several Purple Hearts to his credit with enough Silver Stars and Bronze Stars to decorate a Christmas tree. For the last couple of decades he has been a resident of this county and has been a self-employed stone mason. He is a man who has served his country with valor and courage and a man who has seen great violence in turbulent times. I am prosecuting him for two violent criminal acts.

"The first act occurred on the afternoon of December 7, 1994, at the scene of a collision between an automobile driven by a neighbor of Mr. Dean's and a cement truck. It happened here in our town. What then took place was a bizarre sequence of events that in themselves are remarkable and tragic. Mr. Rennick ran a red light and was struck full broadside on the passenger side by the cement truck driven by Mr. Zetty. Mr. Dean was the first person on the scene. In the process of removing the unconscious, injured Mr. Rennick from his burning car Mr. Dean turned on Mr. Barry Zetty, the innocent driver of the cement truck who was trying to assist, and backhanded him in the face, knocking him to the ground but otherwise not injuring him. Mr. Dean then extracted Mr. Rennick from the wreck and removed him to the safety of the porch of an adjacent residence where they waited for medical and police assistance.

"The second act occurred when Sheriff Mark Watson, who was headed to his home because he wasn't feeling well that day, ran up on the accident scene. Being the public servant that he is, even though he was sick, he stopped to render assistance. He heroically took care of the burning automobile and then after rescue personnel had taken Mr. Rennick away he attempted to interview Mr. Dean who was still sitting on the porch of the unoccupied residence. The Sheriff only wanted to make sure Mr. Dean was okay and possibly offer him a ride home when Mr. Dean struck the Sheriff full in the face with his fist. Even though the Sheriff was nearly knocked unconscious he was able to draw his weapon and keep Mr. Dean at bay until other law enforcement officers arrived.

"You will hear testimony from Barry Zetty. You will hear evidence by Thomas Rennick. You will hear evidence by Sheriff Mark Watson, the elected Sheriff of Cambridge County, and see the grievous damage done to his person. You will hear the recount of the arrest by Cambridge City Police Officer James Lantz. You will hear testimony of fact from Detective Joseph Wilkins who has conducted the formal investigation of these crimes. It is not a complicated case. There is no doubt Mr. Dean did the acts that he is charged with. He will admit that he did them. The only mystery you could solve for us is why any sane citizen, as Mr. Dean purports to be, would act in such a violent and terrible manner causing so much pain and suffering for a local public servant and a victim of a terrific auto accident.

"Thank you very much."

The Commonwealth's Attorney turned back to his seat. He immediately poured himself a cup of water. Davy noticed his hand holding the paper cup shook as he poured the water.

The Judge looked at Mac and said, "Mr. McNally."

Mac rose from his chair and put his hand on John's huge shoulders. He smiled and looked up at the wood carved panel behind the Judge and pointed to it. "Wisdom, justice, mercy, and public service," he read to the jury.

"Please look up there with me, ladies and gentlemen of the jury. Read those great words with me. Wisdom, justice, mercy, and public service." Davy saw the lips of one of the women in the jury read along with him.

"This morning I am representing my lifelong classmate, friend, and fellow soldier. He is a hunting companion, a member of our community, and a great American public servant himself. Mr. John Andrew Dean is seated with me at the counsel table. I want to tell you where we are in this case, what the issues are, and where this case will lead.

"John is seventy-one-years-old and was born up on the Shenandoah Mountain on the West Virginia border. He is a local man and was a classmate of mine in school. His father fought in World War I. His grandfather fought in the Civil War on the side of the Confederacy. Two of his grandfather's brothers, John's great-uncles, fought and died in that same war on the side of the Confederacy. His grandfather back four generations was a Shawnee chief named Kill Buck whose portrait is hung in the town museum and was a great warrior. Back eight generations ago his grandfather immigrated from the Scotch-Irish Highlands to America, fought in George Washington's army and rose to the rank of captain. Mr. Dean's son is a veteran of the Vietnam War. In other words, violence is no stranger to the Dean family. John lost his wife Fern two years ago. But let's talk about public service. On the beaches of Normandy, John Dean carried me and two other local men out of the water, where we would surely have drowned, during the D-day invasion. His leadership abilities in the face of great danger were superlative. I know. He saved my life several times while living the nightmare and horrors of World War II.

"John came back to our community after serving twenty years in the U.S. Army where he rose to the rank of sergeant. He also served in the Korean conflict where he saw considerable action. For the last thirty years he has been a stone mason and his work is known far and wide throughout the valley.

"John has no criminal history. He did have some problems with depression years past, and he does take medication on a daily basis. He emphatically stated to me he does not want anyone to feel sorry for him. He makes no excuses for his actions and eagerly anticipates these proceedings. I have seen John commit tremendous acts of violence on behalf of our great nation, but I have never known him to lift a hand unprovoked and I have known him for sixty years. My client does not deny his actions. I expect Mr. Gaines will be only too happy to graphically demonstrate the particulars. All I would ask of you is to hold judgment on behalf of the defendant until you've heard all of the evidence. Then and only then, at that time, I beg you to allow yourselves to form an opinion as to what degree this man is truly guilty or innocent of these charges while remembering the words carved in oak before you. 'Wisdom, justice, mercy, and public service.' Thank you very much."

"Call your first witness, Mr. Gaines," the Judge said in a firm voice.

# Chapter 26

Charles Grimes, the Commonwealth's Attorney, stood up at his table and said, "The commonwealth calls Thomas Rennick."

Rennick was wheeled to the podium by his nurse and a microphone placed on his lap. The following is a court transcript of the testimony.

**WITNESS THOMAS RENNICK.**

**DIRECT EXAMINATION BY MR. GRIMES.**

Q.   Would you state your name, please?

A.   Thomas Rennick.

Q.   Where do you live, Mr. Rennick?

A.   I live in the Brethren Home here in town.

MR. GRIMES:   Can everyone hear? Nurse, could you get the microphone closer to him so the jury can pick up his voice better? Thank you.

Q.   Mr. Rennick. You were charged with reckless driving in reference to the accident you were involved in on December 7, 1994. Would you tell the court the disposition of that charge?

A.   I pled guilty in district court to improper driving and paid a fine of $100 plus court costs. My license to drive has been suspended. I do not plan to drive again even if I am ever physically able.

Q.   So, you make no bones about it, Mr. Rennick. The accident was caused by your running a red light. Correct?

A.   That is correct but in my own defense the sun was wicked that day and I was looking directly into it.

Q.   Do you remember anything about the events immediately after the accident?

A.   I remember John Dean holding me on his lap in somebody's yard. I had his coat wrapped around me and I remember the clouds in the sky looking pink.

Q.   Do you remember anything else at all?

A.   I remember John Dean telling me he would give me some of his deer bologna if I pulled through.

## NOTE:   THE JURY AND THE COURT LAUGHED AT THIS REMARK.

Q.   And do you see the man you are referring to in this court?

A.   Yes, he's sitting at the table.

COURT:   Let the record show Mr. Rennick pointed out the defendant.

Q.   How do you know John Dean?

A.   He lived four doors down from me at the Brethren Home before all this happened.

Q.   Have you ever had any conflicts with Mr. Dean in the past?

A.   Yes I have.

Q.   And what was the nature of your conflicts?

A.  To tell you the truth I was picking on him and trying to get under his skin and I succeeded.

Q.  And what took place?

A.  John put his hand around my neck and pretty much told me he would kick my ass if I didn't knock it off.

Q.  So, Mr. Rennick, you are saying Mr. Dean assaulted you?

A.  Some of you lawyers might call it that but the truth is I got what I was asking for and he didn't hurt me. He could have and I thought he was going to. I got his point.

MR. GRIMES: No further questions, Your Honor.

## CROSS-EXAMINATION BY MR. MCNALLY

Q.  Mr. Rennick, do you like John Dean?

A.  For a Southern redneck giant he is okay. I was jealous of him just like most of the rest of the folks at the home because he has that grandson who came to see him regularly and took him places. Most of us don't have anyone who doesn't wish we would just go on and die so they can get at our money before the home gets it all. As much as I hate to admit it I suppose he probably saved my life at the wreck.

Q.  Have you ever known Mr. Dean to act aggressively to anyone who did not provoke him?

A.  No, I have not.

MR. MCNALLY: I have no further questions for this witness, Your Honor.

COURT:  Do you wish to redirect, Mr. Grimes?

MR. GRIMES:  I have no further questions.

COURT:  May this witness be excused?

MR. GRIMES:  Yes, Your Honor.

COURT: Thank you, Mr. Rennick.

MR. GRIMES: I'm going to call Barry Zetty.

## WITNESS BARRY ZETTY

## DIRECT EXAMINATION BY MR. GRIMES.

Q. State your name for the court, please.

A. My name is Barry Zetty.

Q. You have been sworn, earlier today, to tell the truth?

A. That's correct.

Q. What do you do for a living?

A. I drive a cement truck for Hard Hat Concrete.

Q. Could you describe what happened to you on December 7, 1994?

A. I was coming back into the plant to get another load. We were pouring the floor for a dairy barn east of town at the Paulson's Dairy farm. I was coming through the intersection at Plum Avenue and Twelfth Street. I had the green light all the way and thank the Lord I was running the speed limit which is 25 mph there. A big Oldsmobile ran through the light headed west and there was nothing I could do about it. I just hit him broadsides. It was a terrible collision.

Q. Were you injured?

A. I bumped my head real hard on the steering wheel and I still got some bruises from the seatbelt. Thank God, I was wearing my seatbelts cause sometimes I forget to.

Q. When you got out of your truck what did you see?

A. Well, I thought whoever was driving that Oldsmobile was probably either dead or hurt real bad. I saw this great big old man come hustling up to the car. I ran over there and I guess I was awful excited. There was blood and glass all over the old man behind the wheel and one of those new air bags had gone off. Probably saved his life. The big fellow reached in and cut off the ignition. Then smoke and a little fire came out from under the hood. I started screaming that we should get him out of there.

Q.   Do you see the man who was trying to assist Mr. Rennick?

A.   Yes, he is sitting right there. He is so big it's hard to miss him.

COURT:   Let the record show Mr. Zetty identified the defendant, John Dean, as being the man at the wreck.

Q.   What happened then?

A.   I guess I got really excited and since then I have thought about it a lot and I don't think I was helping Mr. Dean much by being hyper like I get.

Q.   Just answer my questions, Mr. Zetty and don't add other words, please. What happened then?

A.   Mr. Dean backhanded me and knocked me backward. I tripped and fell on the ground. He got his pocketknife out and cut the seatbelt around the man in the car and lifted him out the window like he was a rag doll or something. The fire was really coming out from under the hood by then. I ran back to my truck to get my fire extinguisher. I looked all through the truck but then I remembered I had taken it out and had it by my woodstove at home. Mr. Hardesty, my boss, wrote me up for that when he found out.

MR. GRIMES:   Your Honor, would you instruct the witness to limit his answers to my questions?

COURT:   May I remind you, Mr. Grimes, that he is *your* witness. You control him. Mr. Zetty, try to limit your answers simply to what you have been asked.

Q.   Did you see a police vehicle arrive?

A.   Yeah, I seen the Sheriff, Mark Watson, pull up.

Q.   What happened then?

A.   I could see Mr. Dean holding Mr. Rennick wrapped up in his coat over on the porch of the house on the corner. The Sheriff couldn't get his fire extinguisher to work and then the fire truck got there and put out the fire. The squad got there and they took Mr. Rennick away and the Sheriff went over to talk to Mr. Dean. I was still pretty hot about him swatting me like he did so I wanted to make sure the Sheriff knew I was mad. All of a sudden I seen Mr. Dean hit the Sheriff in the face and he come a'sailin backward on the ground. I took off running because I figured that old man was mad about something and I thought he had killed the Sheriff he hit him so hard.

Q.   What happened then?

A.   Then a city cop come tearing in with another Deputy and that new boy on the force, Officer Lantz, went over there with the other Deputy that had got there right behind him and arrested Mr. Dean. They couldn't get handcuffs on him because they wouldn't fit. They took some of those rubber bands they got around his wrists and they had a hard time getting him in the back seat.

Q.   Was he refusing to get in the car?

A.   No. He was trying to get in but the door was kinda little for him. He is a big man in case you haven't noticed.

MR. GRIMES:   I have no further questions, Your Honor.

COURT:   Mr. McNally, cross-examine this witness if you wish to.

MCNALLY:   Absolutely, sir. I don't want to miss this encounter.


## CROSS-EXAMINATION BY MR. MCNALLY.

Q.   Mr. Zetty, let's get right to the point. Do you think John Dean meant to hurt you when he more or less shooed you away from that burning car?

A.   You're probably right. He really didn't hit me hard. Not like he hit that Sheriff, thank God.

Q.   Did Mr. Dean cause you any injury, however slight?

A.   No, I guess not.

Q.   What do you mean? "I guess not," Did he injure you at all?

A.   No, he didn't.

Q.   So, Mr. Zetty, what Mr. Dean did when he made contact with you, in all truth he actually put you into a safer situation away from the burning car, isn't that right?

A.   Well, I'll tell you, Mr. McNally, I been to the races and I seen cars catch fire there and I was scared that car was gonna flame up in a big fireball like I seen 'em do. I would be lying if I said I wasn't glad to be away from it even though I was mad cause he swatted me a little.

Q.   So in your best estimate, Mr. Zetty, do you think John Dean meant to hurt you with the actions he took to move you away from him so he could assist Mr. Rennick?

A.   I suppose he didn't, no. Like I said, I was mad at first mostly cause it kinda hurt my feelings some. He did a good job getting that man out of that car and taking care of him.

Q.   You said in your testimony that when Mr. Dean swatted you "you tripped and fell on the ground." Mr. Dean did not intend to knock you down, did he?

A.   Oh, no sir. When he made contact with me I had already started to turn to back off and got my feet tangled up. That is why I fell.

Q.   So what you're telling the court is that Mr. Dean more or less just shooed you away like a person would shoo away a pet or something like that?

A.   Yes, sir. Something like that.

MR. MCNALLY:   No further questions, Your Honor.

COURT:   Mr. Grimes, do you wish to reexamine this witness.

MR. GRIMES:   Yes, sir, I do.


## RE-EXAMINATION OF BARRY ZETTY BY MR. GRIMES

Q.   Mr. Zetty, John Dean did in fact swing his arm at you, did he not?

A.   Yes, sir.

Q.   And when he swung his arm at you he did in fact strike you with that arm, didn't he?

A.   Yes, he did.

Q.   And even though you say you "got your feet crossed up," what caused you to fall to the ground was the impact of Mr. Dean's blow, isn't that correct, Mr. Zetty?

A.   Yes, sir. That's correct.

MR. GRIMES:   That's all my questions and this witness can be excused.

COURT:   Thank you, Mr. Zetty. You may leave or remain in the courtroom if you so desire. The court will take a fifteen-minute recess.

BAILIFF:   All rise.


When the Commonwealth's Attorney went to his room off to the side of the courtroom he called the Sheriff and Investigator Wilkins in with him. He jumped all over Wilkins demanding to know why he hadn't interviewed Mr. Zetty to the point of at least knowing what he was going to say. Rennick had not been the effective witness he wanted either. As a matter of fact, both witnesses thus far had damaged rather than strengthened his position. Wilkins got mad and told Grimes maybe he should have talked to the witnesses himself before the trial date. Grimes became furious and stormed out the door saying that he had been assured by the Sheriff that the case was a slam dunk and nothing to worry about. Sheriff Watson didn't say a word. Old man McNally was going to get his shot at questioning him too in a short while and the Sheriff was getting nervous.

# Chapter 27

**WITNESS DETECTIVE WILKINS.**

**DIRECT EXAMINATION BY MR. GRIMES**

Q.    State your name and occupation for the jury.

A.    My name is Joseph Wilkins and I am a Detective for the Cambridge County Sheriff's Office.

Q.    Did you investigate the circumstances surrounding the injury of Sheriff Mark Watson on December 7, 1994?

A.    Yes, I did.

Q.    And you interviewed the Sheriff and filed the reports associated with this incident?

A.    Yes, I did.

Q.    And you brought charges of reckless driving against Mr. Rennick which resulted in a conviction of the same charge?

A.    Yes, I did.

Q.    Did you take photographs of the injuries the Sheriff sustained?

A.    Yes, I did.

Q. Do you have those photos with you now?

A. Here they are.

Q. Are these photos accurate representations of the events in question?

A. Yes they are.

MR. GRIMES: Your Honor I would move to admit these photos as evidence.

COURT: Show them to Mr. McNally. What number will these be? They will be prosecution exhibits number 1, number 2, and number 3. Thank you.

MR. MCNALLY: No objection, Your Honor.

COURT: Show them to the jury, Mr. Grimes.

Q. Did you interview Mr. Dean?

A. I saw him at the jail at the time of arrest. He was in custody and with all the stress he had been under I elected not to attempt to interview him at that time. I made that decision after talking to Officer Lantz who had made very good notes of what Mr. Dean had voluntarily stated to him during the transport to the jail. I called Mr. McNally the next day to try to schedule an interview because I had heard he was going to represent Mr. Dean.

Q. And what did Mr. McNally tell you?

A. He said his client had nothing to talk to me about so it was no use attempting anything further.

MR. GRIMES: Answer any questions Mr. McNally has for you.


**CROSS-EXAMINATION OF JOSEPH WILKINS BY MR. MCNALLY.**

Q. Detective Wilkins, you didn't see the Sheriff the evening of December 7, did you?

A. No, I did not.

Q. These photos you just introduced as evidence are so impressive! All blown up to such gigantic proportions. I don't believe I have ever seen such a large nose as on this one. And the Sheriff's gums look rather nasty blown up to eight inches long. Looks kind of like a hockey player's face after a little rough fun on the ice.

MR. GRIMES   Objection, Your Honor! And I move to stike.

COURT   Objection sustained. Mr. McNally this is not a circus. Try anything similar and I will hold you in contempt of court.

MR. MCNALLY   Of course, Your Honor. My apologies.

Q. When did you take these graphic photos if you didn't see him that evening?

A. I took them at 7:00 A.M. on the eighth.

Q. When did you find out you would be the person to handle the case?

A. I was contacted by Major Mike Thompson who told me he had been in to see the Sheriff and had taken the written statement that is in my file. He said I was to handle the case by the Sheriff's direct orders.

MR. MCNALLY:   I have no further questions, Your Honor.

COURT:   Mr. Grimes, do you wish to redirect?

MR. GRIMES:   No, Your Honor, and I would ask that this witness remain.

COURT:   Okay, Detective Wilkins, please remain in the witness room and I will remind you not to discuss your testimony with anyone. Call your next witness, Mr. Grimes.

MR. GRIMES:   The Commonwealth calls Ms. Jody Cline.

## *WITNESS JODY CLINE.*

## DIRECT EXAMINATION BY MR. GRIMES.

Q.  State your name and age for the jury, please.

A.  Jody Cline and I am twenty-seven-years-old.

Q.  And what do you do for a living, Ms. Cline?

A.  I am a full-time emergency medical technician employed by Cambridge County Fire and Rescue.

Q.  Were you working on December 7, 1994?

A.  Yes, I was.

Q.  Did you respond to a wreck at the intersection of Plum Avenue and Twelfth Street?

A.  Yes, I did.

Q.  Did you witness an altercation between the Sheriff and another man?

A.  Yes, I did.

Q.  Do you see that man in this court now?

A.  Yes, he is sitting right there next to Mr. McNally. I know him. His name is Mr. Dean.

COURT:  Let the record show Ms. Cline identified the defendant, Mr. Dean.

Q.  Tell the jury what happened.

A.  We had loaded up Mr. Rennick, the driver of the Oldsmobile. He was hurt badly. I checked out Mr. Dean and his vitals were fine. I asked him if he felt okay and he said he would be okay and walk on home after he had sat there for a while. He looked very tired but he seemed all right.

Q.  What did you see then?

A.   Sheriff Mark Watson walked from the wreck scene over to where Mr. Dean was sitting on the porch of that old house on the corner and started talking to him. I was watching and after they had talked for just a short while Mr. Dean hit Mark in the face, knocking him backward on his back. He really hit him hard. I saw Mark draw his gun and aim it at Mr. Dean. The cement truck driver was walking toward them when all this took place. When Mr. Dean hit Mark the cement truck man came running at us yelling that Mr. Dean had killed the Sheriff. That's when the city police officer, James Lantz, pulled up. We had another unit arriving at the scene so we took off with our victim.

Q.   So you didn't hear anything the Sheriff said to Mr. Dean?

A.   No, sir. They were fifty yards away from us at least. The only person that could have heard was the truck driver who was pretty freaked out at the time.

Q.   You saw no body language from the Sheriff that would indicate he was in a confrontational argument with the defendant?

MR. MCNALLY:   I object, Your Honor. Calls for speculation on the part of the witness.

COURT:   I disagree, Mr. McNally. She can testify to what she saw. You may want to rephrase, Mr. Grimes.

Q.   Okay, Ms. Cline, did you see anything that would alarm you or cause you to have concern for the Sheriff?

A.   I was just watching Mark. They were talking and Mark was leaning in toward him when Mr. Dean hit him. That's all.

MR. GRIMES:   No further questions for this witness, Your Honor.

COURT:   Your cross, Mr. McNally.


## CROSS-EXAMINATION OF JODY CLINE BY MR. MCNALLY.

Q.   Ms. Cline, are you married?

MR. GRIMES:   I object, Your Honor! What does Ms. Cline's marital status have to do with anything that is remotely related to this case?

MR. MCNALLY:   If I may proceed it will become very relevant, Your Honor.

COURT:   Go ahead, Mr. McNally, but don't try my patience with smoke screens. Answer his questions, Ms. Cline.

A.   Yes, I am. But I'm separated from my husband at this time.

Q.   And how long have you been separated?

MR. GRIMES:   Your Honor....

COURT:   Your continuing objection is noted Mr. Grimes. Mr. McNally, this line of questioning had better be fruitful and get to the point. Answer his question, Ms. Cline.

A.   I, or we, have been separated since around the first of October.

Q.   Thank you, Ms. Cline. I noticed when you answered the questions Mr. Grimes just asked you consistently referred to the High Sheriff as "Mark." Are you now or have you ever been romantically involved with the Sheriff, Mark Watson?

A.   Not now, but I was.

Q.   Were you with Mark Watson the night prior to the wreck? December 6?

A.   Yes.

Q.   Where had you gone?

A.   We had driven down to Tyson's Corner and went to a bar.

Q.   Did you have alcoholic drinks that night?

A.   Yes. Mark actually had a little too much to drink so I drove us home. We got home around....

MR. GRIMES:   Your Honor, I must object! The Sheriff's activities the previous day serve no purpose to finding the truth in this case and only serve to tarnish our Sheriff's integrity. Where is all this misinformation leading to?

MR. MCNALLY:   Don't you think the frame of mind and physical well being of the Sheriff at the time of the alleged offense charged against Mr.

Dean here is important to the jury's perception of the truth of the events of that day?

COURT:  I overrule your objection and want to hear myself where this testimony is going. I think it is highly relevant.

Q.  Ms. Cline, I know this is the last thing you were prepared to deal with today, but. I need to know,the jury needs to know: How intoxicated was the Sheriff the night before this incident?

A.  He had a pint bottle of Scotch in the car and he sipped on that all the way back to Cambridge. He threw the empty bottle out the window at a caution sign. That was after he drank two pitchers of beer. I had to drag him into his bed at his house that night. He wanted me to stay. He had thrown up in the yard and I told him I had to be on duty at eight in the morning. It was two thirty then. He was very drunk. I haven't gone out with him since.

Q.  Did he call you the next day?

A.  Yes, around twelve thirty. He wanted me to come over but I told him I was working and had to finish my shift.

Q.  Did he talk okay then?

A.  His speech was still slurred a little and he said he had a hangover. I was really kind of offended and told him he just needed to go back to bed. He laughed and said he was having a beer for breakfast.

Q.  So, were you surprised to see him at the scene of the accident?

A.  Very surprised.

Q.  Did you notice anything that would indicate the Sheriff was in a foul humor when he went over to talk to Mr. Dean?

A.  Well, I was shocked to see him on the scene. I figured he would take the day off after I talked to him on the phone that morning and told him to go back to bed. When he passed me as I was helping to get Mr. Rennick into the van he didn't even speak to me. Actually, I was glad I didn't have to talk to him. I had seen another side of him that I definitely didn't like.

MCNALLY:   Thank you for your honest statement today, Ms. Cline. No further questions, Your Honor.

COURT:   Do you wish to redirect, Mr. Grimes?

MR. GRIMES:   Yes, I do, Your Honor   .

## REDIRECT EXAMINATION OF JODY CLINE BY MR. GRIMES.

Q.   Ms. Cline, for the record, were you interviewed by Detective Wilkins in reference to this case prior to coming here today?

A.   Yes, sir.

Q.   Then why is it that you did not disclose the facts of your former relations with the Sheriff?

A.   Nobody asked me.

Q.   As you have testified, you had no personal direct contact with our Sheriff while he was working the accident, did you?

A.   No, I didn't.

MR. GRIMES:   No further questions, Your Honor. As far as I am concerned this witness may be excused.

COURT:   Mr. McNally?

MR. MCNALLY:   I may wish to recall her, Your Honor.

COURT:   Thank you, Ms. Cline, you will need to stay in the courtroom. Mr. Grimes, your next witness?

MR. GRIMES:   The Commonwealth calls Sheriff Mark Watson.

# Chapter 28

## DIRECT EXAMINATION OF SHERIFF MARK WATSON BY MR. GRIMES

COURT:    Clerk, this witness has been sworn?

Clerk:    No, he needs to be sworn.

Court:    Sheriff Watson, do you solemnly swear to tell the truth?

Sheriff Watson    I do, sir.

Court    Proceed, Mr. Grimes.

Q.    Good morning, Sheriff. Would you state your name and tell the jury who you are, sir?

A.    My name is Mark Watson and I have been the Sheriff of Cambridge County for seven years.

Q.    Sheriff Watson, on December 7, 1994, did you encounter a wreck at the intersection of Plum Avenue and Twelfth Street?

A.    Yes, I did.

Q.    Tell us about what happened that day.

A.   I had not been feeling well and had the flu so I didn't leave my home for work until around noon. I made a couple of stops, felt bad again and was heading home when I ran up on the accident.

Q.   Had you been dispatched to the wreck?

A.   No, it was just a happenstance that I was driving that particular route at that particular time and encountered the accident.

Q.   What action did you take?

A.   I called in to dispatch on the radio and made them aware I was out at the scene of the wreck and to expedite a city unit and a rescue unit to take the call since it was in the town limits. It is customary for their personnel to handle traffic inside the town limits even though I have jurisdiction over the county and the city.

Q.   You said you were ill. Had you taken any medication that day?

A.   Nothing but some aspirin.

Q.   What actions did you take then?

A.   I checked the vehicle for occupants and then went to my car to get a fire extinguisher. Flames were coming out from under the hood and I wanted to get that stopped if possible. My fire extinguisher malfunctioned and I was unable to get it to work. Fortunately, fire and rescue arrived and they were able to get the fire out quickly. The city police units had not arrived at that time so I decided to try to sort out some facts of the details of the accident. The squad was just taking the Rennick man and I walked over to the porch to check on Mr. Dean's welfare.

Q.   Tell us about your encounter with Mr. Dean.

A.   I had talked to Mr. Zetty briefly and he told me that Mr. Dean had backhanded him when Mr. Dean was trying to assist in caring for Mr. Rennick. I walked over to Mr. Dean where he was sitting on the porch of that old house on the corner. That's where he had carried the victim. I asked him if he was okay and he said he was fine. I asked him if he thought Mr. Rennick's age might have contributed to the accident. I must have hit a sensitive issue. I asked him if he had hit Mr. Zetty and he said, "Yes, I might hit him again if he comes near me." I decided to take Mr. Dean into my custody on a protective civil arrest so I pulled out my handcuffs and the next thing I knew, totally out of the blue, he slugged me in the face. I thought he was going to kill me and I feared for my life. I pulled out my pistol to stop any further aggressive action on his part, to protect myself, you know. He said something like, "Go ahead and shoot me."

I thought to myself that maybe he was trying to commit suicide by forcing a police officer to shoot him. Thank God, I didn't have to. Then Officer Lantz arrived and he took Mr. Dean and I was transported to the hospital by the squad. I was in severe pain and don't remember a whole lot.

MR. GRIMES:   Nothing further, Your Honor.

COURT:   Mr. McNally, you may cross-examine the witness.

## CROSS-EXAMINATION OF SHERIFF WATSON.

MR. MCNALLY:   Thank you, Your Honor.

Q.   Mr. Watson, where were you the night before this wreck…

MR. GRIMES:   Your Honor, I most strenuously object. This act is of its own account and this night before questioning is irrelevant. Why don't we take into account the Sheriff's whereabouts six months earlier or a year?

COURT:   I disagree, Mr. Grimes. His physical condition at the time of this incident is important to the jury's perception of what happened. Answer the question, Sheriff Watson.

A.   I believe I may have been out to eat with a friend.

Q.   Did you have any alcoholic beverages that evening?

A.   That was a long time ago and I really haven't thought about it. I think we may have driven down to northern Virginia. I am not sure. It is possible I may have had a beer with dinner.

Q.   What time did you get to bed that night?

A.   I do not remember.

Q.   You don't remember or you don't want to remember, Sheriff?

MR. GRIMES:   I object, Your Honor. Mr. McNally is badgering the Sheriff of Cambridge County!

COURT:   Objection sustained. Mr. McNally, I want no more of that! The jury will disregard the last question by Mr. McNally.

Q.   You are under oath, Sheriff Watson. You truly don't remember what you did on the night of December 6, 1994?

A.   No, I'm not sure.

Q.   Well, sir, let's focus on the morning of the seventh of December. What time did you get up that morning?

MR. GRIMES:   Your Honor, I object!

COURT:   Objection overruled!

Q.   I repeat, Sheriff Watson. What time did you get up that morning?

A.   Uh, I, ah. I don't remember.

Q.   Did you drink any alcoholic drinks that day prior to the wreck?

A.   No, I did not. I went to work!

Q.   You went to work that day and took a couple of aspirins and you still felt bad so you decided to go home and then you ran up on this wreck?

A.   Something like that. I went through hell that evening in the hospital. Things are not clear.

Q.   Things are not clear but you can testify under oath exactly what you said to Mr. Dean and what Mr. Dean said to you but you can't remember what approximate time you went to bed the night before or got up that morning? How can that be, Sheriff?

MR. GRIMES:   Your Honor, he is badgering my witness.

COURT:   He is the Sheriff. He ought to be able to take some badgering and survive. Answer the questions, Sheriff, and remember you are *under oath.*

Q.   You didn't say anything else to Mr. Dean?

A.    Not that I can recall. I do remember saying exactly what I testified to saying. I do remember him saying exactly what I testified he said.

Q.    Did you make a phone call to Ms. Jody Cline the morning of December 7, 1994?

A.    I don't recall.

Q.    Well, let me help you to remember a little, Sheriff. Here are the phone records of Ms. Cline's cellular telephone. Isn't 540-555-4201 your cellular phone number?

A.    Yes, it is.

Q.    It says right here that a phone call was made from your car phone to her cellular phone at exactly 12:17 P.M. Is that when you told her you had had a beer for breakfast and you wanted her to come over to your apartment?

A.    I don't recall.

Q.    I expect you don't, Sheriff. One final question. Were you under the influence of alcohol when this event took place?

A.    Absolutely not!

Q.    You can testify clearly that you think my client was angry at you for being insensitive to his age and was trying to get you to shoot him to put him out of his misery. Is that what you are telling this court?

A.    Yes!

MR. MCNALLY:    Nothing further, Your Honor.

COURT:    Redirect, Mr. Grimes?

MR. GRIMES:    Nothing further, Your Honor.

COURT:    Do either one of you gentlemen wish to hold this witness?

MCNALLY:    Yes, Your Honor. We may wish to call him later.

COURT:    Sheriff Watson, you must remain. Do not discuss your testimony in any way or by any means with anyone, Sir. Do you understand me?

SHERIFF WATSON:   Yes, sir.

COURT:   Call your next witness, Mr. Grimes.

MR. GRIMES:   The Commonwealth calls Officer James Lantz

COURT:   Mr. Lantz, go before the clerk to be sworn, please.

(Clerk swears in officer Lantz.)


## DIRECT EXAMINATION OF JAMES LANTZ BY ME. GRIMES.

Q.   State your name for the court, please.

A.   James Lantz.

Q.   How are you employed?

A.   I am a Cambridge Township Police Officer.

Q.   And were you on patrol on December 7 of 1994?

A.   Yes, I was.

Q.   Did you answer a call at the intersection of Plum and Twelfth?

A.   Yes, I did.

Q.   Would you tell the court what happened when you arrived at that location?

A.   Well, when I got there I saw fire and rescue had put the fire out on the wrecked Oldsmobile. I had hardly gotten out of the car when Mr. Zetty, the cement truck driver, came running from the yard of the old house there on the corner yelling that someone had killed the Sheriff.

Q.   Can you remember what he was yelling?

A.   Yes Sir, pretty close. He was yelling something to the effect, I think it was, ah. I don't like to quote people unless I get it perfect.

Q.   That is a good trait in a police officer and I know I am putting you on the spot but can you remember to the best of your recollection what Mr. Zetty was screaming?

MCNALLY: I object, Your Honor. The Commonwealth already interviewed Mr. Zetty and had the chance to ask him directly. What Mr. Zetty was yelling is hearsay.

COURT: I will allow Officer Lantz to say what he heard when he got out of his patrol car under the Excited Utterance Exception.

Q. What did you hear when you got out of your patrol car?

A. To the best of my memory Mr. Zetty was yelling, "He killed the Sheriff! He killed the Sheriff! If he killed one person he'll kill another!" Something like that. That is pretty close.

Q. What did you do then?

A. I went running toward the yard. I could see Mark, I mean Sheriff Watson, lying on the ground and he had his pistol drawn, aiming it at this big old man sitting on the steps of the house.

Q. What action did you take then?

A. I took Mr. Dean into custody and called the squad in for the Sheriff. We couldn't get Mr. Dean handcuffed because his wrists were too big so I got one of the other guys to bring some flex cuffs and put them on him.

Q. Did Mr. Dean make any comments?

A. He said he was all right. I told him he was under arrest for hitting the Sheriff and he said that was okay with him. I put him in the cage of my cruiser. Had to put him in sideways because he is so large.

Q. Do you see that person in the courtroom now?

A. Yes. He's sitting next to Mr. McNally.

COURT: Let the record show Officer Lantz identified the defendant, Mr. Dean.

Q. Did Mr. Dean make any voluntary comments on the way to the jail?

A. He insisted over and over that Sheriff Watson was drunk. He even told the magistrate that.

Q. Well, Officer Lantz, was Sheriff Watson drunk?

A. I don't know about that. I didn't examine him. I mean who would suppose the Sheriff was drunk?

Q. Did Mr. Dean make any other statements?

A. It was very clear he didn't like the Sheriff. Made several references to the Sheriff's bicycling pants.

MR. GRIMES: No further questions for this witness, Your Honor.

COURT: Answer any questions Mr. McNally has.

## CROSS-EXAMINATION OF OFFICER JAMES LANTZ BY MR. MCNALLY.

Q. Good morning, Officer Lantz.

A. Good morning, Mr. McNally.

Q. Officer Lantz, I know it makes you uncomfortable stating what other people said. I think that is because of your basic honesty. Honesty is a wonderful thing. Especially in a police officer. Wouldn't you say so, Mr. Lantz?

A. Yes, sir. The most important thing. A man ain't no better than his word.

Q. Good then. Did you think Mr. Dean was dangerous when you were handcuffing him?

A. Well, I saw what he had done to the Sheriff but he didn't give me any trouble. In fact, he was very respectful to me.

Q. Did he ride peacefully to jail?

A. Yes, sir.

Q. Now, Mr. Lantz, you answered Mr. Grimes' questions about what Mr. Dean supposedly said in the cage of your car. Would you take your time and tell the jury everything you can remember Mr. Dean saying about the Sheriff?

A.   He said something about the Sheriff shouldn't be the Sheriff if he didn't want to do his job. He asked me if he was the same man who did all those commercials telling senior citizens how to be safe. He asked me if he was the same Sheriff that made all those TV commercials in those, um…. This is his words not mine but he said, " *queer*-looking bicycle pants."

Q.   When you came running over to the Sheriff you had another Deputy with you. What became of him?

A.   That was Deputy Baylor. I think he took care of the Sheriff's gun belt when the squad took him. He kinda just took care of the Sheriff after we got Mr. Dean cuffed.

Q.   Did Mr. Dean tell you anything else?

A.   Not that I remember, Sir, just small talk. Oh, he did say he was in the invasion of Normandy with you and Judge Crawford. I told him I been over in Desert Storm. He asked me who my Daddy is, I think.

MR. MCNALLY   Thank you for your testimony and thank you for your service to this great country. No further questions.

COURT:   Redirect, Mr. Grimes?

MR. GRIMES:   No. Your Honor, and this witness can be excused.

MR. MCNALLY:   Likewise, Your Honor.

COURT:   You may be excused, Mr. Lantz, and thank you for your testimony. I will remind you not to discuss your testimony with anyone until this case is terminated.

# Chapter 29

<u>**DIRECT EXAMINATION OF DR. PEDRO GOMEZ BY MR. GRIMES.**</u>

COURT:    Please step over to the clerk to be sworn.

(Clerk swears in witness.)

COURT:    You may interview the witness, Mr. Grimes.

Q.    State your name and occupation, sir.

A.    My name is Dr. Pedro Gomez. I am what we call in the medical world an eye, ear, nose, and throat specialist.

Q.    Where did you practice and for how long?

A.    Here in Cambridge for the past four years. Prior to that I practiced in Roanoke for twelve years. That's also where I did my residency.

Q.    Did you care for Sheriff Mark Watson?

A.    Yes, I did.

Q.    What date did you first see Mr. Watson?

A.    On December 7 of this past year.

Q.    Could you explain the extent of the Sheriff's injuries?

A.    I have these photographs of his injuries that explain most of what I think you're looking for.

Q.    And these photos are a part of your file, is that correct?

A.    Yes, sir. They are.

COURT:    Show them to Mr. McNally, Mr. Grimes.

MR. GRIMES:    I move to enter them as evidence, Your Honor.

COURT:    Do you have any objection, Mr. McNally?

MR. MCNALLY:    None, Your Honor.

COURT:    What's there, four of them? Label them item number 4, number 5, number 6, and number 7. Show them to the jury, Mr. Grimes.

Q.    Do you have a report listing the Sheriff's injuries?

A.    Yes, I do.

Q.    May I see that also?

A.    Here, sir.

MR. GRIMES:    I move to introduce this report as evidence, Your Honor.

COURT:    Please show it to Mr. McNally. That will be labeled as item number 8 unless Mr. McNally objects. Please show it to the jury.

MR. MCNALLY:    No objection, Your Honor.

Q.    Dr. Gomez, Mr. McNally has stipulated to your expertise during pretrial hearings. How long have you been practicing in this particular field?

A.    I suppose it is close to twenty-two years since I escaped from Cuba and passed the exams here. Before that I was a doctor of medicine in Cuba for five years.

Q.    Would you briefly explain to the jury in layman's terms what kind of injuries the Sheriff sustained? In other words, just explain all the technical terms on your report in common terms so we can understand as close as possible the extent of his injuries.

A.   His nose was more or less crushed and his sinus passages were damaged. His front teeth were both knocked back into the roof of his mouth. His upper lip had a two-inch gash running horizontally on the inside that required eight stitches. He had chips of bone and cartilage floating in his upper gum that had to be removed. I've seen worse but the damage was significant.

Q.   Will the Sheriff have any permanent damage from these injuries?

A.   We were able to do root canals on his front teeth and saved them both. They'll probably turn brown with time, or at least darker. Breathing through his nose should be completely restored and corrected with time. If he chooses to have plastic surgery we can get his nose looking very close to the way it looked prior to the injury. If not, his nose will more than likely have a slight hump in it just below the eyes.

Q.   Would you say the Sheriff has been put through a lot of pain?

MR. MCNALLY:   I object, Your Honor. He can ask the Sheriff that question if he wants to. He wasn't released.

COURT:   Objection overruled. The Doctor treated him and he can testify to his expert opinion about his patients condition and its ramification.

A.   Yes. It was a painful injury I gave him significant doses of prescription pain relievers.

Q.   Could this injury have been life threatening?

A.   Highly unlikely but possible.

MR. GRIMES:   No further questions, Your Honor.

COURT:   Mr. McNally, your witness.

## CROSS-EXAMINATION OF DR. GOMEZ BY MR. MCNALLY.

Q.   Dr. Gomez, what time did you see the Sheriff on the evening of December the seventh?

A.   I first saw him around four thirty in the afternoon.

Q.    What time did you treat him?

A.    I wasn't able to treat him until early the next morning.

Q.    Why didn't you treat him right away? I'm no doctor but it seems that in this type of situation you would want to get to it immediately.

A.    Well, one of the reasons was that some of the swelling had to be alleviated before we could start.

Q.    What were the other reasons?

A.    Another reason was he wasn't feeling well and I needed to get him settled down some and calm. He was extremely upset.

Q.    Was another reason his blood/alcohol content?

MR. GRIMES:    I object, Your Honor. This is just a tactic to mislead the jury!

COURT:    Objection overruled, Mr. Grimes. This is your witness and you yourself opened the door. Answer Mr. McNally's question, Dr. Gomez.

A.    His blood/alcohol content was too high to administer anesthetics.

Q.    Well, I suppose you drew blood from him? How did you know how high his blood/alcohol content was at the time?

A.    I believe there are doctor/client privilege issues here.

Q.    Dr. Gomez, can you please look at and identify this document.

A.    It is our hospital medical chart on patient Mark Watson on December 7th, 1994.

Q.    How do you know this?

A.    Because I filled it out

Q.    Can you please tell the court what Mark Watson's Blood Alcohol Content was according to this document?

A.    It was .07.

MR. MCNALLY   Your Honor I would like to introduce this document as defense evidence Number 1.

COURT   Show the document to Mr. Grimes. Okay, absent any objections we will enter it into evidence as Defense Exhibit #1. Please show it to the Jury.

Q.   That's one point less than considered the presumed drunk driving level, correct?

A.   That's what I understand.

Q.   Did the Sheriff say anything offensive to you that evening.

A.   Yes he did.

Q.   What did he say?

A.   I attempted to have a look up his nasal passages and he cursed me. He called me a "wetback" and a "son of a bitch" and took the Lord's name in vain, which I will not even repeat for you even under penalty of jail.

MR. MCNALLY:   I have no further questions for this man.

COURT:   Mr. Grimes, do you wish to redirect?

MR. GRIMES:   No, Your Honor. As far as I am concerned this witness may be excused.

MR. MCNALLY:   I would ask this witness remain, Your Honor.

COURT:   Dr. Gomez, you will return to the waiting room and let me warn you not to discuss your testimony with anyone.

MR. GRIMES:   The Commonwealth rests, Your Honor.

COURT:   This court will take a recess for lunch and reconvene at one thirty. Ladies and gentlemen of the Jury, would you please exit to your lounge?

BAILIFF:   All rise.

The Commonwealth's Attorney was visibly upset. He motioned for the bailiff and whispered something in his ear. The bailiff left quickly out the side door as Mr. Grimes leaned back in his chair and looked up at the ceiling.

# Chapter 30

Grimes went fuming into the witness rooms where the witnesses were excluded, away from the courtroom testimony. He got the Sheriff's and Wilkins' attention and motioned for them to follow him. He took them down the back steps and into his office through the private entrance in the back hallway. He slammed the door shut and put his finger under the broken nose of the Sheriff.

"What kind-of-a idiot are you? When we get out of this trial I will never believe another word either one of you dumb asses tell me. I just heard testimony that may very well get you charged with perjury, Mark. I think your lunacy and drunken ineptness have ruined us all! Now get the hell out of my office! Now!!"

The two men looked at him in disbelief with Mark Watson's face drained of color. Grimes said softly, "I mean it! Get out of here now! I have never been so embarrassed and humiliated in my entire life. Now please leave me alone!" The Sheriff and his investigator exited the office without a further word.

John's sister, Aunt Mary Alice, grabbed John in the lobby and standing on her tiptoes kissed him on the cheek. "What am I going to do with you? You've been fighting so long. I thought I could quit worrying about you when you came home from Korea and now after all these years you're still fighting."

"It's a Dean family tradition, Mary Alice. You know that. Deans never worried so much about a little scuffle like these people do nowadays,"

John said as he hugged her back. He suddenly had a tear in his eye vividly remembering the last hug he had had from his sister. It had been at Fern's funeral and he didn't want to accept it then. Now he let her hold him for a moment and then he hugged her back.

"I gotta go with Mac to talk about the trial. After this is over come see me, please. And, Mary Alice, thanks so much for coming. I'll be all right," he blurted out as he pushed out the door after Mac.

"I have those things you want in the trunk of my car. Those dreadful things we have been fighting over all these years. I want to give them back to you. I want to have a brother again," she said and then burst into tears. "I'm so very sorry!"

John took her in his arms and held her, looking very uncomfortable as his sister sobbed openly in front of everyone. "Mary Alice, we'll talk about all this later. I have to go talk to Mac now. I don't have much time for this now."

John broke free from Mary Alice and Mac gave her his handkerchief. The three men filed out the door and down the courthouse steps.

"What the hell is going on in there, Mac?" Davy asked McNally as they hustled down the sidewalk that had been shoveled clean of the new snow. "Is that all they have? Seemed like every witness that testified went contrary to what that Commonwealth Attorney wanted. He was pissed a couple of times! You could see it!"

"What do you mean is that all they have?" Mac asked brusquely. "There's been testimony that your grandfather here slugged the elected Sheriff of this county while he was doing his job, crushing the front of his face causing disfiguring permanent damage. Isn't that enough for you?"

John shook his huge head and said, "That Cuban doctor said he was drunk! Don't that amount to nothing?"

"Damn it, John! How many times do I have to tell you? The Sheriff is not on trial here! You are! And you're just dying to get up on the stand and rail on and on saying --God only knows what you might say! Or what Grimes might trip you up with and make you mad enough to say! Stupid things in front of this jury to make you look like the Big Bad Wolf with rabies and the Sheriff look like lovable Ole Yeller the dog when all he did was steel a couple of ham biscuits. Just because you want everybody to know that the Sheriff was drunk and said something that insulted that huge block of Southern honor you carry around on your shoulders, it still don't make it right that you hit him! Can't you boys understand me? Let's go get some lunch and think about this thing."

John and Davy followed him out the large heavy doors of the courthouse and across the street. Mac led them to the front door of a small restaurant and started to go in.

"Hey, Mac, I can't go in here," John announced in the entrance. Mac stopped in his tracks in the doorway and looked at him like he was crazy. "Really, Mac. The Greek guy that runs this place will spit in anything he cooks for me."

"He ain't lying, Mac. I heard about it," Davy volunteered.

"What the hell did you do to old Mavriorgos?" McNally asked incredulously.

"Oh, he bet me I couldn't eat thirty hot dogs one afternoon when I came in here so I ate them and asked for more. Really pissed him off. He ran me out the door and I don't want to go back in there," John stated.

Mac looked at John incredulously as Davy nodded his head in agreement with his grandfather. It was Mac's turn to shake his head and said in a tone of resignation, "Is there anybody you haven't pissed off in this town someway or somehow? Damn! Come on then. We'll have to walk up to Casey Jones' Locker."

Mac took off walking briskly with Davy and John following. Turning his head over his shoulder as he kept walking, Mac asked, "You ate thirty of those damn smelly hot dogs with all that spicy chili and onions on them? All at one sitting? Just thinking about eating thirty of those gut grenades makes me want to throw up."

"I ate them all in twenty-two minutes on the clock. Waitress timed me. Hell, I could've ate fifty if I had tried or really wanted to. Drank a six-pack of his warm Dr. Peppers too," John said. "The cold ones make my head hurt."

"As I just said, that makes me want to throw up just thinking about it," McNally observed. "Old Mavriorgos probably doesn't like you then. Tight as that old fart is. He owns most of the slum rental property in town. I've handled a lot of legal work for him." Davy grinned as the three hustled up the sidewalk.

They went in to a little diner that was really a train car someone had hauled into town years earlier and built a little restaurant into it and then around it. The locals still called it Casey Jones' Locker like the original owner had called it even though the new owner named it Fat Boy's Caboose.

"I don't much like the new name of this place," John complained.

"Why not?" McNally asked.

"Fatboy's Caboose sounds like the backside of one of those funny boys I seen when I got off the boat in San Francisco one time," John stated.

"I can see I need to send you to one of these new sensitivity training seminars the BAR Association is always demanding I go to!" Mac exclaimed. "Don't go making any reference to homosexuals when you get on the stand this afternoon. I can hear Grimes getting you to say, 'That Sheriff talked to me like a little queer,' or something offensive like that. You can't say that kind of garbage in today's world, John."

Mac and Davy had cheeseburgers and fries and John ordered the meatloaf special with mashed potatoes and gravy. They talked over the morning's testimony. Davy and John kept telling Mac how well he had done but Mac told them over and over they were still deep in trouble.

"How in the world did you know about that rescue squad girl laying around with the Sheriff?" Davy asked.

"Yeah, I'd like to know that myself," John said. "She was a good-looking little honey. I don't blame the Sheriff for whacking her."

"You don't live in a little town like this for all these years and write wills and represent people in divorce cases without knowing who's playing hide-the-salami with whom," Mac said without thinking.

"I guess you knew Lizzy was running around on me way before I did then, huh! Like half of the rest of the guys I run into tell me they knew about it for months," Davy said with a huff as a dark cloud settled over his brow.

Looking at Davy around his hamburger bun and conceding his unintentional verbal mistake Mac answered, "No, son. I didn't have a clue on that one. She fooled us all, she did. I would have warned you if I'd known about something like that."

John just kept eating his meatloaf and then said, "Forget about her, boy. When I was your age I used to grind those little girls just like grinding hamburger. But now I'd just rather have a hamburger."

"If that's the case why didn't you order a hamburger instead of that green-looking meatloaf? And why am I representing a pervert like you, John Dean?" Mac laughed and so did John. Davy managed a forlorn smile.

Mac had achieved his mission over lunch. He had John well warned, laughing and relaxed. They talked and joked while finishing their lunches and John had to have a piece of French apple pie and a scoop of ice cream. Once done they had to hustle to get back to court on time. When they entered the courtroom they passed the Sheriff and two of his men in the hall. They didn't look happy and glared at the three of them with their arms crossed. Mac smiled at the Sheriff and said, "Can't wait until this is over, can you Sheriff?" If glares were bullets Mac would have been more than adequately ventilated. The Sheriff didn't bother to answer.

"I wonder if he knows how bad he's messed in his nest?" John asked McNally as they walked down the hallway toward the courtroom.

"Yeah, well, it's gonna get worse for him here in just a little while. You remember the things we talked about, John. Don't get mad no matter what Grimes says to you. He's going to try to piss you off and make you show your ass in front of the jury. Don't you let him! You hear me, John? Your grandson needs you with him. Not in the jail where you will be if you let that Commonwealth's Attorney get under your skin."

They hadn't been in their seats more than a couple of minutes when the bailiff came back in and looked at the ancient wall clock that read 1:29. The Judge obviously liked schedules kept tight. Mac turned to John and said, "Okay, John. We have been over what I am going to ask you. Any questions?"

"No. I'm going to be all right. It don't much matter anyhow," he answered.

"That's where you are wrong, John. It does matter and my butt is on the line here too!" he said. "You do your job, soldier! And that, Sergeant, is an order! You saved my tail because I was smart enough to listen to you on the battlefield. This courtroom has been my battlefield for forty years. You want to survive, soldier, you be smart enough to listen to me!"

"All rise for the Judge!" the bailiff roared.

John stood up and the Judge entered in his black robe and took his seat.

"Thanks, Mac," John whispered. "I'll try to do good for you."

# Chapter 31

The Defense

## TRANSCRIPTS OF THE COMMONWEALTH VS JOHN ANDREW DEAN

COURT: Ladies and gentlemen of the jury, I trust you had a good break and an acceptable lunch. You have heard the Commonwealth's case against Mr. Dean charged with the malicious wounding of a police officer and another count of assault and battery. Now if you will give your attention to Mr. McNally for the defense of Mr. Dean.

COURT: Call your witness, Mr. McNally.

MR. MCNALLY: Defense calls Mary Ann Bartley, Your Honor. She has not been sworn as of yet.

COURT: Ms. Bartley, would you stand in front of the clerk to be sworn, please?

CLERK: Do you promise to tell the truth, the whole truth so help you God?

MS. BARTLEY: Yes,

COURT: Please be seated in the witness stand and answer any questions Mr. McNally has.

## DIRECT EXAMINATION OF MARY ANN BARTLEY BY MR. MCNALLY.

Q.   Would you state your name for the jury?

A.   Mary Ann Bartley.

Q.   Ms. Bartley, what is your educational background?

A.   I have a bachelor's degree in sociology from Old Dominion University.

Q.   Where do you live, Ms. Bartley?

A.   I live at 712 Plum Avenue. Right at the corner of Plum and Twelfth Street here in Cambridge.

Q.   I would like to draw your attention to the afternoon of December 7 of this past fall. Were you at home that afternoon?

A.   Yes.

Q.   Did anything unusual take place that afternoon?

A.   Yes, that was the afternoon of the wreck between the cement truck and the old man in the Oldsmobile.

Q.   Tell us what happened, Mary Ann.

A.   I was getting ready to film the birds at my backyard birdfeeder with my VHS camcorder. I heard brakes squealing and a terrific *thump* sound from out in front of the house. I got out of my chair and went to the front door and saw the cement truck driver climb out of his truck and run over to the Oldsmobile. A very large older man was already at the driver's door.

Q.   Do you see this "very large older man" in the courtroom?

A.   Yes, sir. He is sitting next to you.

COURT:   Let the record reflect she identified the defendant, Mr. Dean.

Q.   What did you do then, Ms. Bartley?

173

A.    I turned my camera on the action and started filming the whole thing. I have everything on tape. I have a really good Sony camcorder, practically the best money can buy. I needed the best to capture my birds, both sight and sound. It didn't have any difficulty picking up everything.

Q.    Do you have this tape you speak of with you?

A.    Yes, I do.

MR. MCNALLY:    Your Honor, I move to admit this tape into evidence as defense exhibit #1.

COURT:    Mr. Grimes?

MR. GRIMES:    Your Honor, I have not seen this tape and until this moment, did not know of its existence. May I approach the bench?

COURT:    I want to see both of you in my chambers.

BAILIFF:    All rise

In the Judges chambers the Judge moved quickly to take a seat behind his mahogany desk. Mac took a seat to his right and Grimes remained standing in front of the Judges desk.

"Judge, I have not seen this tape nor have I known of its existence and…"

The Judge interrupted the prosecutor and asked, "McNally, how long have you known about this videotape?"

"Since a day or so after Judge Crawford's death."

"Then why in the world didn't you come forward with it? The prosecution is entitled to examine it, particularly related to issues of its validity," the Judge chastised.

"Your Honor, with all due respect the videotape is only an extension of the testimony of the witness, Ms. Bartley," Mac implored.

"If the videotape is as McNally says, merely repeating the testimony of the witness, then in the interest of judicial economy there is no reason to play the tape for the Jury. In fact, I will stipulate to the witnesses' version of the events," Grimes fumed.

The Judge got a sly sort of a smile on his face and said, "If this were a law school hypothetical you'd be right! However, as we all know, witness recollections of events can be colored. I am leaning toward the feeling that it's in the best interest of the Jury and justice that the videotape be shown in open court."

"Judge, I am appalled at the conduct of Mr. McNally and feel like he should be censored by the BAR at some time in the future. I would, however, with the best interests of the court in mind ask to view the video here in your chambers prior to allowing it in the courtroom," Grimes said.

"Well, Gentlemen, if you wish to proceed I will allow you your request. Mr. McNally, do you have any other surprises I should know about now?" the Judge asked with the ghost of a smile on his face.

"No, Your Honor, and I didn't regard the videotape as a surprise. It backs up what the witness states in the same manner a photograph would. Mr. Grimes has gone out of his way to inform me some time ago that he and the Sheriff's men had a case with the I's dotted and the T's crossed…."

"That is enough, McNally!" the Judge snarled.

The Bailiff was summonsed and a large television was rolled into the Judge's chambers on a tall rectangular stand with a VCR player on a lower shelf. After some fiddling with the wires the tape was inserted and suddenly they were looking through the screen door of Mary Ann Bartley. Grimes was visibly angered when he saw the Sheriff's performance. He actually flinched when John Dean's fist connected solidly with Watson's face. When it was over he smiled meanly and said, "Lets do let the Jury take a look. I believe it may serve to convict your client, Mr. McNally."

"Let's let them see the truth and decide then," McNally said. They went back to the courtroom and the Bailiff had them rise for the Judge. When everyone was settled the Judge began again.

COURT:     That tape will be labeled, what, defense exhibit number 1, I think?

MR. MCNALLY:     No, Your Honor, this will be number two. The hospital document proving the high blood alcohol content of the Sheriff was #1.

COURT:     Okay, label it defense Item #2.

The tape was played and the jury saw firsthand the entire story in detail. They watched as John carried Rennick to the steps of the porch and tried to calm him, even wrapping his coat around the injured man. One of the women on the panel shook her head in disbelief when she heard the

Sheriff's slurred speech and hateful attitude. Everything played out on the large television screen in front of them and it ran like the evening news. Mary Ann was talented with the camera. It had the effect Mac wanted on the jury and made the Sheriff look terrible. Mac thought one of the men on the jury wanted to cheer when John belted the Sheriff in the mouth. Then Mary Ann zeroed in on the muzzle of the Sheriff's gun. It was chilling, peering over John's shoulders at the pusillanimous lawman lying there whimpering with the gun in his hand and the little round evil looking black muzzle bouncing around aimed at the old man. All the sights and sounds were there right in front of them.

When it was over two of the male jurors leaned back in their chairs, crossed their legs and folded their arms. Mac, who was a master at reading body language, was very satisfied. The person on whom the film had the most profound effect was John's sister, Mary Alice, who wept openly after it had played. She had to get up and exit the courtroom.

Q.    And you have had exclusive possession of this tape since you filmed it?

A.    Yes. I made a copy immediately and put the original in my safe at home. This is the first time I have watched this original tape since the first day. I always make copies of everything because you never know when you might drop a tape or spill something on it or it might get torn up in the VCR machine.

Q.    So this tape we just witnessed is in fact the original accurate record of the drama that played out in your front yard on December 7, 1994?

A.    Yes, it is.

Q.    And this tape has not been altered or changed in any way from the moment it was created?

A.    No, it has not.

MR. MCNALLY:    Thank you so very much, Ms. Bartley. No further questions, Your Honor.

COURT:    Answer any questions Mr. Grimes may have, Ms. Bartley.

## CROSS-EXAMINATION OF MARY JANE BARTLEY BY MR. GRIMES.

Q. Ms. Bartley, were you interviewed or contacted by Investigator Wilkins or anyone from the Sheriff's Office in reference to what you have testified to this afternoon?

A. No, I was not.

Q. Are you home most every day, during the day?

A. Most of the time. I go to the store now and then and I have become active at the Presbyterian Church.

Q. Is your telephone number listed in the local phone book?

A. Yes.

Q. Have you received any phone calls from the Sheriff's Office since December the seventh of last year?

A. No, I have not. I don't have an answering machine so I don't know about whenever I wasn't at home. Sometimes I turn the ringer off because I like to concentrate when I read and I hate those phone solicitors. They drive me crazy. Sometimes I leave the ringer off for a couple of days when I forget to turn it back on.

Q. Are you employed anywhere?

A. No. But I'm going to be busy soon. I'll be starting to do a lot of volunteer work soon with the women's group at the church.

Q. How do you support yourself?

A. I receive money from my father's estate periodically.

Q. You had this tape all this time. Did you show it to anyone else?

A. I showed the copy of the original to Connie Pencilschwietzer, my pastor's wife. She's the one who introduced me to Mr. McNally.

Q. And when was that? Yesterday? Last week? The day after the wreck?

A. No. It was probably about the middle of January. About three weeks ago. Right after the other Judge died.

Q. Were you ever home when Investigator Wilkins knocked on your door?

A. Once I was.

Q. Then why didn't you speak to him? Surely an educated woman like yourself realizes what kind of powerful evidence you possessed? Why didn't you talk to the Sheriff's Office?

A. I was in the shower and by the time I got out and got my bathrobe on he was already in his car and leaving. I started to call them for a couple of days after the accident. And the investigator left his business card on my door. But I kept watching the tape over and over. I mean I get emotional when I think about it. I'm getting emotional now. May I have a tissue, please?

MR. GRIMES: Yes, yes. By all means. Here you go. Continue when you are ready, Ms. Bartley.

A. Well, I mean, the giant, Mr. Dean, saved the old man in the car. It was obvious the cement truck driver was freaking out and in the way, causing a problem, so the giant, I mean Mr. Dean, did the only sensible thing. He shooed him away like a fly or something bothersome so he could do what he had to do....

MR. GRIMES: Thank you, Thank you, That's all I needed to know, Ms. Bartley I just wanted to know why you didn't turn over the tape?

COURT: First, I'd like to hear her finish her statement. I want to hear what she has to say. Go ahead, Ms. Bartley. Bailiff, get her a box of tissues over here.

A. Anyway, I watched that film over and over again and all I could think of was that nobody would believe me. I thought the tape might help the giant and I couldn't bear to think that I would let him down. I think they should give him a trophy for saving the other old man's life!

MR. GRIMES: That will be all, Your Honor.

COURT: Do you wish to Redirect, Mr. McNally?

MR. MCNALLY: Yes, briefly, Your Honor.

## REDIRECT EXAMINATION OF MARY ANN BARTLEY BY MR. MCNALLY.

Q.   You pretty much stay to yourself, don't you Ms. Bartley?

A.   Yes, I do. But lately I have met a good friend in Mrs. Pensilschwietzer. She's helping me and I'm actually finding great relief in the gospel. I hope to be baptized soon.

Q.   Well, good for you, Mary Ann! Did you ever think positively about Sheriff Watson?

A.   Yes, I voted for him twice but never again.

Q.   Why didn't you speak to the investigator when he came by.

A.   Because, like I said, I was in the shower and he didn't stay on the porch long. It was cold that day. But then I got to thinking he's probably as out of control as his boss is.

MR. GRIMES:   I object, Your Honor!

COURT:   Objection sustained. The jury will disregard the witnesses last statement.

MR. MCNALLY:   I have no further questions, Your Honor.

COURT:   May this witness be excused?

MR. GRIMES:   Yes, sir.

MR. MCNALLY:   Yes, Your Honor.

COURT:   You may be excused, Ms. Bartley. Thank you for your testimony and you may leave or you may remain in the court if you desire. Call your next witness, Mr. McNally.

MR. MCNALLY:   The defense calls the defendant, Mr. John Dean.

# Chapter 32

<u>**DEFENSE CALLS JOHN ANDREW DEAN**</u>

COURT:   Mr. Dean, you have not been sworn before this court. Raise your right hand.

CLERK:   Do you swear to tell the truth, the whole truth, so help you God?

MR. DEAN:   Yes, I do.

COURT:   Have a seat in the witness stand.

MR. DEAN:   Your Honor, I don't fit in there.

COURT:   I see what you mean, Mr. Dean. Bailiff, would you bring a chair and set it right there in front of the jury. Get a sturdy one while you are at it. Stretch that wire over there and put the microphone in front of him. Okay. Is that comfortable, Mr. Dean?

MR. DEAN:   Yes, sir. This will work. Pardon me. I'm sorry, Your Honor. Thank you.

<u>**DIRECT EXAMINATION OF JOHN ANDREW DEAN BY MR. MCNALLY.**</u>

Q.   State your name for the jury.

A.  John Andrew Dean

Q.  How old are you, Mr. Dean?

A.  Seventy-one.

Q.  Where were you on the afternoon of December the seventh of last year?

A.  I was taking a walk down Twelfth Street here in town.

Q.  Why were you taking a walk, Mr. Dean?

A.  Exercise. My grandson got me interested in doing things I like to do and walking every day helps me do it.

Q.  Where were you living at the time?

A.  The Brethren Home.

Q.  Did you know Thomas Rennick, one of the other residents?

A.  Yes, I know him. I suppose you mean before the wreck.

Q.  Correct, Mr. Dean. Did you and Mr. Rennick have a relationship?

A.  I guess I really despised the little Yankee. He's from New Jersey and I suppose he and I have had different upbringings. He likes to make sarcastic remarks about people. He's a chore to be around sometimes.

Q.  Do you have a driver's license, Mr. Dean?

A.  No. Not anymore.

Q.  Wouldn't you like to still drive?

A.  Yes, I would but the doctor told me he wouldn't allow me to drive because of the medication I was on. I'm still on it now and to tell you the truth I don't think I would be a really safe driver now anyway. Reaction time is so slow anymore. I daydream too much sometimes too. Some folks my age are excellent drivers but I ain't. Never was real good at it.

Q.  What kind of medication were you on, Mr. Dean?

A.   After my wife Fern died two years ago I had some problem with depression. I was on medication for that called Prozac which is an antidepressant. I've had it before. They called it post-traumatic stress syndrome or battle fatigue, something like that. I'm retired from the U.S. Army and saw a lot of intense action in World War II and in the Korean War that haunts me from time to time. That's really what convinced me to sell my house and move into the Launching Pad after my wife passed on.

Q.   What is this Launching Pad you just referred to?

A.   Er, ah, sorry. That's what I call the Brethren Home. *Jesus' Launching Pad.* I went there to die. Worn out and tired. My grandson didn't let me. He baited me back into the world of the living.

Q.   So, Mr. Dean, did you ever have any conflicts with Mr. Rennick at the Launching Pad?

A.   Yes, nothing much. He kept picking on me, trying to belittle me in front of the other residents and I let him know he needed to quit it.

Q.   What did you do to him?

A.   Put my hand on his shoulders and told him to knock it off. He got the hint.

Q.   Did you know Mr. Rennick still had a car and drove around town?

A.   Yes. And he's another example of old people who need to realize their limitations. I think he is the fourth person living there that's had an accident since I been there. His was the most serious. I mean, if you are capable of driving in your later years more power to you. I just know in my heart that I'm a hazard simply walking past people much less driving a two-ton vehicle up and down the roads. Too much traffic now. Not like it was when I was a kid.

Q.   Let's get back to December 7. In your own words tell the court what happened.

A.   I was walking along the sidewalk, minding my own business, when I heard tires squeal. Looked up and seen the cement truck hit Rennick's Oldsmobile in the side. It was clear Rennick had run the red light. I figured he was probably killed because the impact was tremendous. Knocked the car a good ways. I run up to the car and looked inside and seen that air bag they put in some of them cars these days had come out. Rennick's arms looked like they was broke.

Q.   You've seen many people in physical and mental distress in your lifetime, haven't you John?

A.   I've seen just about everything you can see from shot off, blown up, burned and broken in every way you can imagine. I ain't proud of it, but sir, I have killed a lot of people in this world on behalf of the United States of America. I am no stranger to broken bodies and how they got to be broken. I also saved a lot of people in my time. I've also done the dirtiest jobs a democracy needs done on a regular basis to keep its people free and civilized.

Q.   You were at the door of the car looking in at Mr. Rennick, assessing the situation. What happened then?

A.   The cement truck driver came running up and he looked in the car and got really upset, started pounding me on the shoulders and back yelling for me to do something. He was screaming about getting Rennick out of there and he was all over me. Then the car caught fire up under the hood and I knew he had to come out of the car no matter how broke up he was. Burning is horrible. I seen it lots of times.

Q.   Now, John, you have heard the testimony of Mr. Zetty, the cement truck driver. We've seen the videotape of what happened that day. It is clear Mr. Zetty is a nice person and I am sure his intentions were good. Why did you take the action you did toward him?

A.   I couldn't think with him squawking around like he was. I had no intention of hurting him. I just needed to get his attention and get him out of the way and quick. Maybe I did it with too much force and if I did, I apologize. In my mind I had to get him out of the way so I could do what had to be done before the car burnt up. I've seen vehicles burn up before and you don't want to be trapped in them or right beside of them when they do, I can tell you that. Can I get a drink of water?

COURT:   Bailiff, would you please assist Mr. Dean?

Q.   John, to end up on this point, did you intend to hurt Mr. Zetty in any way when you took the actions you did to get him to back off so you could tend to the emergency with Mr. Rennick?

A.    No, I did not. Watching the film it surprised me on how far back I knocked him. I suppose I have to still be careful as big as I am.

Q.    John, with your imposing physical size and strength, what actions have you learned to take in order to protect those around you?

A.    The hardest I ever been hit in my life was by a Marine from Montana who was about five foot four inches tall in a bar fight in Korea. But generally speaking, big people like me have to be careful of our size and strength. You can hurt someone real easy without meaning to. Bull in the china closet sort of thing. Guess I forget sometimes now. You don't drive a Mack Truck like you drive a sports car, is what I'm trying to say, without tearing up something.

Q.    We all saw the film where you carried Mr. Rennick over to Ms. Bartley's porch and wrapped him in your coat. Why did you do that? With the coat I mean?

A.    Shock, man. Shock will kill people when they shouldn't die. You gotta keep them warm if you can. That's why I told him that nonsense about givin' him a whole stick of deer bologna. Needed to get him thinking about something else and I know he really likes my deer bologna although he probably wouldn't admit it. I have a stick saved for him though in the freezer because I promised him…...

MR. GRIMES:    Your Honor, this is very noble of him but irrelevant to the case.

COURT:    I agree. While all this is very interesting let's move along on pertinent details, Mr. McNally.

Q.    What did you notice when the Sheriff came walking up to you?

A.    I noticed he wasn't walking the best. First thing I thought was that he must be sick or something 'cause he staggered a little.

Q.    Did you know the Sheriff before this incident?

A.    I seen him on the television in them bicycle shorts and his little helmet all the time. The local news girl puts him on every other day it seems leading up to an election. I've seen him on the TV doing those little things about how he is concerned about us senior citizens and telling us ways to protect ourselves. I thought he was really worried about us from watching them things. To answer your question direct, my answer is *no.* I have never talked to the man. I walked by him at the county fair where he was passing out them blue balloons full of helium or hot air—whatever it is them Republicans blow into them—but he was tied up talking to some young girls then.

Q.  Why did you hit him, John? The tape clearly shows what happened and what was said, but I want you to tell the jury why you did what you did.

A.    First reason, I could smell the liquor on his breath, his speech was slurred, and he was unsteady on his feet. Shouldn't no police officer ever be in that condition while on duty. It was a disgrace and shows a total lack of respect to the badge and what it should stand for. Second reason, he insulted me and disappointed me. I expected better of this elected man who was supposed to be a friend to old people, asking me if I was a hero or just stupid! Third reason, he was trying to make an unlawful arrest on me.

Q.   What made you perceive it as an unlawful arrest?

A.    I listen to a show in the evening on the radio called *It's the Law.* A lawyer from Richmond that does all those TV commercials about representing victims of tractor trailer accidents talks about the law, that Bill Bralley fellow. He said one evening that in Virginia it's illegal for a cop to arrest you on a misdemeanor that didn't happen in his presence. I didn't think I had assaulted the truck driver anyway and when that happened the Sheriff wasn't even there yet. I felt certain that if he wanted to arrest me he needed to go see a magistrate and get a warrant. I have fought for this great nation all my life. I be daggoned if I let someone violate the freedoms I fought for even if he is the Sheriff! He sat right here in this here witness box while ago and said he tried to make a civil arrest on me. He never said that and it was a lie! The tape that Mary Ann Bartley made proves it! If I heard Bralley right, the Sheriff was violating my civil rights by trying to make a custodial arrest on me in regards to a misdemeanor that did not happen in his presence. I had the right to prevent that by the Code of Virginia!

Q.   What did you think when he aimed the gun at you?

A. Lord knows, that ain't the first time I had a gun aimed at me. I thought he was going to kill me and he probably would have done us all a big favor if he had. I was just too tired to try to do anything else about it so I just set there. I ain't afraid to die. In a way I kind of look forward to it. I ain't sure about Heaven and all but I ain't afraid to die.

Q. So you are a Christian then?

A. Probably not a very good one but I try to be....

GRIMES    I object, Your Honor.

COURT    Objection sustained.

Q. When Officer Lantz arrived and took you into custody you didn't resist then. Why not?

A. I was just glad to get out from in front of that pistol barrel. I was afraid he would just gut-shoot me and it would hurt like hell. A stomach wound is hellish! Also, Officer Lantz couldn't have done anything else except arrest me from what he seen when he got there. What he found when he got there had to look like a felony to him. A cop can do that, arrest you for something he thinks you done while not in his presence, if it makes the felony grade. Officer Lantz treated me with respect. He's a good young man.

MR. MCNALLY:   That's all the questions I have at this time, Your Honor.

COURT:   Thank you, Mr. Dean. The court will take a fifteen-minute recess.

BAILIFF:   All rise!

# Chapter 33

COURT:    You are still under oath, Mr. Dean. Answer any questions Mr. Grimes may have for you.

## CROSS-EXAMINATION OF JOHN ANDREW DEAN BY MR. GRIMES.

Q.    So, Mr. Dean, I am asking you to give me a simple yes or no answer to all my questions. Just yes or no and nothing more. You were angry with the Sheriff?

A.    Yes, but…..

Q.    Your Honor, please instruct the witness to answer simply yes or no.

COURT    Mr. Dean, I understand it may be difficult for you to do so but answer only yes or no.

A.    Yes, Sir. To answer the persecutor, sorry, I mean the prosecutor, Mr. Grimes….Yes.

Q.    You alluded to this great country and the rights you have fought for when you were in the army. Don't you think the Sheriff has the right not to be struck in the face?

A.    Yes.

Q. Did you strike Mr. Zetty and knock him to the ground?

A. Yes.

Q. Did you hit the Sheriff in the face with your fist?

A. Yes.

Q. Couldn't you have merely gone along with him and protested in a civil manner?

A. Yes.

Q. You've been trained to use violence, correct?

A. Yes.

Q. You have used it to settle personal disputes before, haven't you?

A. Yes.

Q. Were you ever disciplined for violent activity in the military, Mr. Dean?

A. Yes, Sir. Fighting outside of a club in Korea.

Q. Mr. Dean, are your senses as acute as they were when you were a young man?

A. I don't understand the question.

Q. Okay, you don't hear as well as you did when you were, say, twenty years old?

A. No.

Q. You don't see or smell as well either, do you?

A. No, but I know what I seen and heard that day! And furthermore......

MR. GRIMES: No more questions, Your Honor.

COURT: Mr. McNally, do you wish to redirect?

MR. MCNALLY: Yes I do, Your Honor.

## REDIRECT EXAMINATION OF JOHN ANDREW DEAN BY MR. MCNALLY.

Q. You just testified that you were angry with the Sheriff. Can you explain that fact?

A. I was angry with him for several reasons. First, he disgusted me by his unprofessional behavior, second, by the things he said to me, and third, he was trying to arrest me on a charge I don't think he could legally make!

Q. Mr. Dean, if you had it to do over would you hit the Sheriff again?

A. No, I would not.

Q. Why not?

A. For two reasons. First, I know I put a lot of people I care about in a bad situation because of my actions and, secondly, I would have loved to have him take me in front of that little magistrate on duty that day. He's tough! He would've thrown both of us in jail with all those Mexicans in there and those guys would have really fixed the Sheriff good. They hate his guts!

Q. If you walk out of here today instead of having to go to jail where will you go?

A. I'll live with my grandson Davy. We might go up to Alaska to visit his father, my son. I would also like to travel to Finland.

Q. Have you been in any trouble since you retired from the army?

A. Just that depression problem I had and some alcohol abuse caused me to do some stupid things I hardly remember. Nothing else. Reckon all the hell I been through someone could forgive me a little for that. I hope so. I ain't never intentionally hurt nobody except the Sheriff since I was done fighting in Korea.

Q. One more question, Mr. Dean. Were you ever in France?

A. Yes, sir. I was one of the fellows who stormed the beach in Normandy on D-day with you, Speedy Spencer, and the deceased Judge Kenneth Crawford and I still have the barbed wire scars on my chest to prove it.

MR. MCNALLY:    No further questions.

COURT:   Mr. Grimes, do you wish to redirect?

MR. GRIMES:   Yes, Your Honor, I do.


## REDIRECT EXAMINATION OF JOHN DEAN BY MR. GRIMES.

Q.   Yes or No answer, Mr. Dean. You just said you intentionally hurt Sheriff Watson, didn't you?

A.   Yes.

Q.   You believe you would be proud to defend yourself or another person having their constitutional rights violated, correct?

A.   Yes.

Q.   And you believe your rights were violated by the Sheriff, correct?

A.   Yes.

MR. GRIMES:   I have no further questions.

COURT:   Mr. Dean, you may step down. Any more witnesses, Mr. McNally?

MR. MCNALLY:   Defense rests.

COURT:   We will take a short recess and then come back for closing arguments.

BAILIFF:   All rise!

# Chapter 34

COURT: Ladies and gentlemen of the jury, we will now hear closing arguments from Mr. McNally. You may begin, Sir.

## CLOSING ARGUMENT PRESENTED BY MR. MCNALLY.

MR. MCNALLY: First of all I want to thank you for your service here today. It is the greatest responsibility of all of our citizens to serve as jurors when called upon to ensure justice is served in our county court system. Today, your choices here today will decide the fate of John Dean, a Grandfather, a Veteran, and a member of this community. There will be no other Juries after you make your decision today. The only appeal after circuit court in the Commonwealth of Virginia are appeals of procedure. The facts of this case will never be heard again by a Jury. You hold immense power over the lives of the people who are accused of crimes in our county.

Do you remember my opening statements? I had you look at the words carved in oak there on the wall behind the Judge. Look at them again. "Wisdom, Justice, Mercy, and Public Service." Let's take them one by one and examine how each relates to this case.

First, let's examine Public Service. John's life has been the ultimate in this category. He has wielded and used the terrible swift sword of freedom we sing about in our national anthem. John Dean has carried our flag onto the ground of our enemies who sought to annihilate us. John has done the noble duties our armed forces are called upon to carry out so courts like this one can convene. How do I know that? I rode his back out of the English Channel and up onto the beaches of hell. Right into the teeth of the German guns. The most frightening hell a person can imagine. That man sitting there was like three John Wayne movies packed into one. I can personally testify to you that he is a great American hero.

Justice. Would it be just to put this noble man in prison because he tried to protect himself from a drunken man with a badge who was attempting to make an illegal arrest on his person? You have heard the testimony of the doctor. The Sheriff's blood/alcohol content was nearly enough to statutorily convict him of driving under the influence in this state. But the Sheriff is not on trial here, is he? Maybe he should be. You saw the film. Put yourselves in the shoes of John there that day. Several of you could at once you know! What size do you wear, John? Seventeen? Think how you would feel if someone, who is not only sworn to serve and protect you but is elected by the people to serve and protect you, insulted you and got in your face like what we witnessed through the lens of Ms. Bartley's camcorder. Ugly is the word I would use to describe the Sheriff's behavior! Ugly! And here was John. Seventy-one years old. Taking a walk so he can do the one thing in life that brings him hope and happiness. Trying to keep himself fit so he can take part in his Grandson's life. And take part in life himself. Walking along minding his own business on a cool December evening and suddenly he is once more thrust into a life or death situation. A person who has picked on him and abused him in front of others is mortally stricken in an automobile wreck. He tries to assess an emergency situation as he has done numerous times in his life. An overly panicking man is pounding on his back demanding he do something with fiery wreckage and a severely wounded broken man in front of him. He tries to take action, as every fiber of his body has learned and been conditioned to do. But first, so that he can do what needs to be done, he has to rid himself of a distraction that would otherwise prevent him from saving the injured man's life. He merely swatted at Mr. Zetty to make him back off. If you or I would have done the same thing Mr. Zetty would hardly have felt it. But from John's arm? I don't think anyone who has watched the film would think John Dean meant to hurt or attack Mr. Zetty in any way. You heard Mr. Zetty himself state that he didn't think John meant to hurt him. In fact, Zetty stated, and I quote, "I was mad because he had swatted me a little." Ladies and gentlemen of the jury, there is no way this act *swatting someone a little* can be considered a Class I misdemeanor or meet the criteria of assault and battery. Not enough to put a seventy-one-year-old man in jail for a year that could well be his last on earth! Keep in mind he already spent Christmas in jail. Possibly his last.

Mercy. The most gracious and important element to consider. What role does mercy play in your job to decide what to do with this situation? The State is going to try to take all the human emotion out of the events of December 7. The prosecutor will try to make you think solely about John Dean hitting the Sheriff and the Sheriff being hurt. Period. I say mercy, along with common sense, plays a huge role in the fair conclusion of this trial. Mercy is the element you must show toward this man who had just saved a man's life. Mercy is the element you must consider when you think about the old man sitting there, who has served this great country so valiantly, having to sit there while his adrenaline is still pumping and listen to a police officer insult the very core of his existence. His strong Southern pride run into the ground by the mouth of a drunk in a uniform. And then, to be arrested when he correctly surmised that the Sheriff had no legal right to do so! Show him mercy, ladies and gentlemen. If there were no room for it in this courtroom, why would it be important enough to be inscribed in oak behind the Judge's head to be remembered?

Wisdom. The last inscription from the wall we need to examine. How wise was it for Mr. Rennick to run the red light? John Dean did not factor in that horrendous mistake by Rennick. How wise was it for Mr. Zetty to lose his ability to control himself when a man's life was on the line? I am sure John Dean would have preferred him to at least control himself during an emergency. How wise was it for the Sheriff to be driving a vehicle, much less a government-owned vehicle, under the influence of alcohol? How wise was it for the Sheriff to act the impertinent fool you saw on the film and insult and belittle the only hero of that cold December day, December the 7th, the anniversary of the Japanese bombing Pearl Harbor? John Dean acted out of reflex. He was sitting on the steps of Ms. Bartley's house collecting himself for the walk home. He didn't ask the Sheriff to come over to talk to him. He didn't seek any of this mess.

I hope you have the *Wisdom* to acquit this fine man of these charges. If not an acquittal than give him the benefit of the doubt and save him from what will amount to life in prison.

Thank you for your service.

COURT:     Thank you, Mr. McNally. Your turn, Mr. Grimes.


## CLOSING ARGUMENTS PRESENTED BY MR. GRIMES.

Ladies and gentlemen of the jury, I too would like to thank you for your service here today. You have seen some extraordinary evidence in this courtroom. I beg you, do not let it distract you from the reason we are here. Mr. McNally would have you believe that the defendant is a lovable giant. He would have you view the accused as a grandfather someone should feel sorry for. A grandfather who has committed the Felony of Malicious Wounding. The elements of malicious wounding are: anyone who wounds any person or by any means causes him bodily injury with the intent to maim, disfigure, disable, or kill. If you listen to Mr. McNally and his pleas for mercy you would think that his client must be an angel. You've heard how the defendant has been trained in combat. In fact, he admitted he has a history of using violence to settle personal disputes. If we use Mr. McNally's logic, any man should be allowed a free reign to commit violence on another person for any perceived slight or affront to his sensitive ego! Mark Watson had too much to drink the night before. I won't insult your intelligence by hinting that he didn't. The medical evidence presented has shown that he did. The film does show he was, to quote the defence "ugly." But, this doesn't give Mr. Dean the right to be the judge, jury and executioner to the Sheriff. That's the job of the Court System. If Mr. Dean had hit one centimeter lower and the Sheriff's head had been tilted backward a little, he was hit with enough force that his nose could have been driven back into his brain and killed him! We could just as easily be trying Mr. Dean for murder? Think about it. No matter what the reason. No matter what cockeyed justification Mr. McNally can conjure, you cannot get around the fact his own witness, Ms. Bartley and her film so clearly showed: John Dean is guilty beyond a reasonable doubt of the felonious and malicious wounding.

Now for the second charge we cannot forget: the assault of Mr. Zetty. This assault occurred when Mr. Dean struck Mr. Zetty with enough force to knock him backward. The Defendant admitted under oath he struck Mr. Zetty.

You have heard testimony from Mr. Rennick that indicates Mr. Dean freely resorts to physical confrontation whenever a conflict arises. You heard him testify, and I quote, "He grabbed me by the back of the neck." Of course Mr. Dean sloughed it off by saying, and I quote him, "I laid my hand on the back of his neck." Do you want someone to "Lay their hand on the back of your neck to get you to get his point!" His own implication hints at pending acts of violence. If the world does not revolve the way he wants it to he resorts to violence. He must be stopped! Do you members of the Jury want to get in an argument over a shopping cart at Food Lion with Mr. Dean? Do you want to find yourself sitting next to him at a Little League game with him cheering for the other side when the score is close? I think not!

There is only one conclusion you can come to: conviction on both charges. The Commonwealth has met the criteria to prove beyond a reasonable doubt that John Dean did commit assault and battery on Barry Zetty and then did maliciously wound Sheriff Mark Watson, leaving permanent physical damage to his nose, teeth, and sinus cavities.

Thank you for your service.

COURT:   Ladies and gentlemen of the jury, you have heard the testimony and arguments of this trial. Please go back to your chambers and make your decision. The court will now take up several other matters while the jury is in deliberation.

# Chapter 35

John and Mac went into the lobby of the courthouse and Mac looked John in the eye. Said he had done the best he could do and he hoped it was enough. Speedy Spencer and Davy along with Ben Dean joined them and they all went out on the side porch into the bright sun reflecting on the new snow. It was cold out there but at least they were away from the glares of the deputies still loyal to the Sheriff. City Officer Lantz walked out the door and nodded as he passed. He took a few steps down the marble porch stairs, stopped, and turned around. Walking up to John he extended his hand and John shook it. Then he shook hands with Mac and left without saying a single word. As the group watched Officer Lantz walk away Aziz came around the courthouse on the brick sidewalk with his hands pushed down in his pockets.

"There comes the old goat roper, himself!" John exclaimed.

"I must not be too late. They have not locked your worthless carcass in the jail and thrown the key away yet," Aziz countered. "I drive two hours to stand beside you in your hour of need and all you do is insult me. Of course, you and Mac both fought the Germans on behalf of the Jews who are my natural enemies. What kind of friends could you be to me? Nevertheless, I am here to help Ben and the boys break you out if they lock you up."

John shook hands with Aziz and Aziz pulled the old mountain man into his arms and hugged him. Ben Dean lit a cigarette and John asked him for one even though he hadn't smoked for years. Davy asked Mac how long he thought the jury would take and Mac said he had no idea.

He said he couldn't get a good read on them. Mac was worried Grimes had been effective during his last arguments. They would just have to wait and see. After half an hour of small talk and second guessing everything they could think of the bailiff stuck his head out the door and said the jury had reached a decision.

Everybody packed back into the courtroom and the Sheriff was whispering to the newspaper reporter over in the far corner surrounded by several somber-faced deputies. The Judge nodded to the bailiff who went over and escorted the jury back in. The Judge waited until everybody got settled and then boomed in a firm voice, "Mr. Dean, please stand. Has the jury reached a decision?"

The tall distinguished looking schoolteacher who was the foreman of the jury stood up and said, "Yes, we have, Your Honor."

The Judge asked the clerk, "On the misdemeanor charge of assault and battery against Barry Zetty what did the jury find?"

"Guilty, Your Honor," came the reply from Circuit Clerk Ronald Cloud.

"And on the felony charge of malicious wounding of a police officer how did the jury decide?" the Judge asked.

"The jury finds Mr. Dean not guilty Your Honor," the clerk stated.

Then the Judge took control and addressed the jury. "This is a bifurcated trial. You have found Mr. Dean guilty of assault and battery. Now we will hear from the prosecution and the defense in relation to what punishment should be meted against Mr. Dean.

Mac presented the facts of the case to the jury from his side, citing any amount of time for John to serve would be improper. He reminded the jury of all the testimony that had made John look like a hero and tried to paint a picture of him as a victim of circumstance. He put Davy on the stand and he was allowed to tell the jury he would look after his grandfather and keep him out of trouble. Davy asked the jury not to put his grandfather in jail. Mac made a good show.

Grimes reviewed the opposite side of the story and told the jury he felt John Dean needed to know he couldn't indiscriminately hand out physical violence to the citizens of Cambridge County. He said McNally was overly dramatic, suggesting that even the full year in jail would not be appropriate. Grimes asked for them to impose the maximum sentence the misdemeanor allowed: one year in jail and a $2,500 fine.

The jury went back to their room and came out an hour later and sentenced John to six months in jail with six months suspended. They fined

John $1,000 and suspended $900 and recommended he be on one year of unsupervised probation. In their minds the jury hung the year over his head along with the $900: if he got in any more trouble he would have to serve the time and cough up the money. A fair incentive for the convicted to keep his hands off of people and behave himself.

The Judge agreed with the verdict and that was the end of it. He promptly called for a fifteen-minute recess before the jury tackled the next case on the docket and exited through his door behind his seat. The bailiff escorted the jury out the side door.

McNally was upset. He thought the conviction had been unmerited but he knew they were lucky to be walking out with John in tow. John was smiling from ear to ear. Grimes hardly batted an eye and immediately went to digging in his briefcase, pulling another thick folder out onto the oak table. McNally was ushering John toward the exit when the door on the side of the courtroom flew open and Steve the jailor came through herding Crazyeyes who was cursing and snarling. When Crazyeyes saw John and Mac he blurted out, "Hey, man! You get off? I knew you would. Hey! Hey! Alpha dog attorney, I needs to talk at you!"

Mac grabbed John by the sleeve and led him out of the courtroom. The other deputies in the courtroom went to the aid of Steve, leaving the Sheriff and the newspaper reporter standing alone. Mark Watson, peering out of the witness room, looked deflated to say the least. The reporter came out chasing Mac and John into the lobby.

"Mr. McNally, are you pleased with the verdict?" the feral-looking reporter asked.

"Well, certainly I'm pleased my client will not be spending any more time in jail but I feel like the jury erred by not vindicating him totally," McNally responded.

"Do you anticipate any civil suits from your client against the Sheriff?" the reporter asked. "Especially since your client was found not guilty of assaulting him?"

"I think the Sheriff should be concerned about Mr. Dean seeking relief against him in a federal venue. We are considering filing against Mr. Watson for depriving Mr. Dean of his Constitutional rights. Even though this jury found Mr. Dean guilty of assaulting Mr. Zetty, I feel confident that that issue can be resolved in federal court away from all the uniformed deputies and Mr. Grimes' merry men. Now, good day to you, sir," Mac said.

Aunt Mary Alice was standing waiting with Davy, Ben, and Aziz in the lobby at the door. She gave Mac and John big teary hugs and kisses. Anna Crawford and Helen McNally announced to the entire group they were holding a party at Anna's house and their feelings would be hurt if everybody didn't come. The Reverend and Mrs. Pencilschwietzer had left with Mary Ann Bartley to get everything ready. The entire group headed out into the bright February sun reflecting off the melting snow.

All of a sudden behind them the courthouse door erupted open and here came Crazyeyes running like a deer. He hit the snow with ten foot strides. One side of his shackles was flapping in the wind and he was looking like the old Hertz Rent-a-Car commercials where O. J. Simpson was running through an airport. Then out came the cavalry with two young deputies in the lead. Steve the jailer came storming out with his nose bleeding down the front of his uniform. McNally grabbed John's arm and said, "Don't even think about getting involved!"

John bellowed, "Run, boy, run!" and the whole crowd was watching with interest when one of the deputies tackled Crazyeyes in a snow bank and the rest piled on. They dragged him back into the courthouse kicking and screaming, snow packed in his shirt.

The newspaper man had caught a couple of action shots as Sheriff Mark Watson appeared on the courthouse steps and grabbed the escapee by the collar. Aziz took John's elbow and said, "Let's get out of here before something else happens."

The entire group drifted toward their cars. The sun was out shining bright and warm and the snow was turning to dirty slush along the sidewalks. When Davy and John got to the truck John reached under the seat and pulled out a paper bag with his last stick of deer bologna in it and asked Davy to drive over to the Brethren Home. When they pulled into the lot John asked Davy to wait in the truck.

"Maybe I better go with you, Grampap. You might need a witness."

John headed in the front door with the paper bag under his arm with Davy in tow. Marching down the hall he hoped he wouldn't encounter Donald Bowman and luckily he didn't. John went straight down to Rennick's room and the door was cracked open. The television was on the ABC evening news and Peter Jennings was talking to President Clinton. Rennick was sitting in his wheelchair with his back to the door. John rapped his knuckles on the door and Rennick turned his head enough to see him.

"Well, Mr. Dean. Did you come to gloat or to deliver on your promise," the pink-faced man said with a smile on his face. "You gave them the slip today. I just heard it on the news. Congratulations! Come on in and sit on the bed. Even us Yankee agitators like a little company every once in a while."

"I brung you the deer bologna I promised you, Rennick. I have a little get-together I need to get to so I can't stay," John said as he laid the bag on Rennick's lap.

Rennick toyed with the bag and looked at the stick of bologna. "I'll enjoy this. Thank you very much, John. And thank you for pulling my feeble ass out of my burning Oldsmobile."

"You would've done it for me, wouldn't you?" John asked.

"Actually, if our positions would have been reversed that day I probably would have kept on walking. I'm not going to lie to you, John. A hero I am not. Besides, there is no way I could ever pull you out of a recliner much less a wrecked car," the little man truthfully stated.

John laughed, got up, and walked to the door. "At least you're honest most of the time, except when you ain't playing cards with the women. See you in Hell, Rennick."

Rennick burst out laughing. John and Davy walked down the hall and out into the cold February evening air.

Later that night after a very nice party, John was surprised by Mary Jane Bartley who shyly presented him with his old cane she had retrieved from the pile of leaves beside the wreck. Davy and John finally made it home around nine o'clock. John took off his clothes and hung them on a hook on the back of his bedroom door. He put on his bathrobe and went into the living room and sat down on the recliner. Davy came in and cut on the television. *Law & Order* was on. Davy looked at John and asked, "What're we gonna do now, Grampap? Now that all the excitement's over."

"Let's cash in everything we got, get a bigger truck, and head up to Alaska to find your daddy," John said. "We got nothing here to hold us. Since I ain't gonna to be dumping all my money down that Launching Pad every month I can probably come up with around $200,000 cash. That along with my Social Security check and my pension ought to be enough for us to have some fun. I'm tired of not having no fun. What if I give it all to you and you kinda look out for me. What do you say?"

"You're serious, aren't you!" Davy said.

"Serious as a heart attack, boy! You think about it. I always wanted to go salmon fishing and shoot a grizzly bear," John drawled. "I want to see your daddy before I check out of here too. But before we go to Alaska, I want to go to Humppila, Finland. I want to visit Kauko's grave and pay my respects to the best soldier I ever heard of. Those stories I read about him gave me courage when times for me was awful dark. You know what they say one of them Finnish boys said when only about a hundred Finnish boys seen a thousand Russians coming at them across a snowy field? One of them boys stood up and said, 'The only question I have is where we going to bury all of them!' Ha! Those men had some balls! Stories of their courage made me know I could do the things I done. I hear the fishing is good in those lakes up there too. I got a hankering to do some fishing. We can come back from there and then head to Alaska when summer hits."

"You amaze me with the ideas that do bounce around in your brain! I think tomorrow we need to clean all our guns and get some things organized around here."

# Part 2
# Travelers

# Chapter 36

John woke up in the middle of the night with a scalding stomach ache. He had known he shouldn't eat the seafood salad with red onions and spinach at the party at Mac's house last evening. He had eaten a lot of it too. Nausea washed over him and he rushed to the bathroom just in time, making an ungodly noise as he retched over and over. Then the diarrhea hit him. Davy got up and came wandering down the hallway with a groggy look of alarm.

Knocking lightly on the door with his knuckles he asked with concern, "You all right in there, Grampap?"

"Yeah. Don't pay no attention to me. Just cleaning out the pipes," the old man answered. "Made a hog out of myself again at the party and am paying for it now. Can't handle onions no more. It just ain't fair! As much as I like them they sure don't care for me," he commented wryly as he let fly again.

"Darn, Grampap! You smell like the broth off of Hell!" Davy exclaimed as he retreated down the hallway and back into his room. He shut his bedroom door and John saw the light shining under the door go off. A little while later John got himself under control, brushed his teeth, and got a little drink of water. He knew he would have a terrible time getting back to sleep. Nothing is worse than a night without sleep, he thought, just lying there trapped within the confines of your skull with a lifetime of memories bouncing around between your ears. He wished he had a shot of paregoric to calm his guts. It would help him go back to sleep too. He liked the taste of it and hadn't had any for years. His aunt had given it to him as a boy when he had stomach troubles, mixing it with sugar and dissolving it in warm water. It always made his belly quit hurting and put him back to sleep in a dreamy sort of way. The old family doctor, Dr. Frank Reedy, had handed the opiate out like Halloween candy for a couple of dollars a bottle. Now the doctors were reluctant to give a prescription for any of the stuff, saying it was too addictive. John didn't think it was addictive or else half of Cambridge would have been hanging around Doc Reedy's until he died around 1960. It sure did work when nothing else would when you had gut pains.

John went back to his bed and laid down, trying to return to a safe well of unconsciousness. His thoughts drifted back to the trial and a smile of satisfaction turned up the corners of his lips. That bicycle-riding Sheriff was going to have a sore ass for a while to place on the banana seat of that bicycle he rides. He was just too used to strutting around doing his imitation of a bantam rooster in charge of the barnyard. Now he would have to live with his newly clipped wing feathers. John chuckled to himself and wondered if it would have any effect on the Sheriff's political career. Probably not. People tend to vote for people already in office and who was going to find someone to run against him anyway? Maybe a new state trooper would move into the county and see an opportunity worth taking.

John shut his eyes and tried to say his prayers. He felt compelled to talk to God but it made him feel very uncomfortable at the same time. His father had had an old hound around the cabin on the mountain when he was a little boy. A great brown and black, rangy, and bony fellow named Buck. John's father kicked the dog or talked rough to him every time he got near him, resulting in the dog cowering in front of him all the time, which only served to make the old man feel like kicking him more. Buck would come up to someone, crawling on his belly whining, then roll over on his back in a subservient posture just hoping that someone might scratch his belly or be kind enough to pat him on the head. John would save rare scraps of meat for Buck when he could and loved to pet him when his father wasn't looking.

Buck was John's ally and his only confidant most of the time in the isolation of their mountain farm. His sister, Mary Alice, wasn't much of a companion. A tattletale spoiled brat and who their father thought could do no wrong. Buck had become afflicted with some sort of uncontrollable mange and large chunks of his hair had fallen out with scabs covering portions of his belly and sides. John held Buck while his father rubbed axle grease mixed with iodine on the sores, trying to heal the old dog but nothing worked. The treatment only made the dog look like a greasy, nasty, repulsive creature from a horror story. One day after eating a lunch of turnips and cornbread, John and his father were walking up the mountain to cut firewood. John was carrying the crosscut saw and the old man was carrying an axe and a wedge. Old Buck was asleep in the sunshine next to the chicken house. John's father said something about the old dog suffering enough and to John's horror he watched as the old man swung the axe and planted it in Old Buck's skull. The dog quivered for a few seconds and then relaxed.

"I wish you would have used a bullet instead of the axe, Pappy!" John stammered, horrified at the grizzly sight before him.

"No need to waste a bullet on such a miserable creature as Old Buck," the mountain man had said as he wiped the axe head off on cheatgrass and broom sedge. "Drag him along into the woods. I ain't got time to dig no hole to bury his carcass and he'll draw flies if we leave him lay this close to the house."

John grabbed old Buck by his front paws and dragged the dead hound to the edge of the woods as tears ran down his cheeks. He was surprised at how light the dog's body was. Next to a white oak tree John piled rocks over old Buck and started to sob as he worked. The next thing he knew he had been kicked in the ass and knocked down face first on the ground beside the dog who was half-covered with rocks.

"What you doing crying over a worthless old sick dog that is better off now that he's dead?" the old man stormed. "A real man controls hisself and don't act so girlish!"

"Old Buck was my friend," John blurted. "I'll miss him, Pappy, that's all."

"Get over it, son! The dog's usefulness was over long ago and he was a liability to this family. Get up and finish covering him and get over here and help me get this saw a singing. We got work to do and ain't got no time sorrowing like a damned woman over an old dog I shouldn't have never allowed on this farm in the first place! Useless son of a bitch! Just like a lot of useless things I own! Now you get your useless ass up and get to it. There's work needs done!"

He couldn't understand how his father had been such a monster at times and a hero at others. One winter when John was six years old a tremendous amount of snow fell and the wind howled for days creating gigantic drifts. The winter dragged on and on and around the first of

March another huge blizzard struck the mountain. All the salt meat had been eaten. All the dried beans, chestnuts, and corn meal too. Every morning and every evening his mother's callused and emaciated hands spooned out a tablespoon of lard to him and one to his sister. That was all they had to eat; a spoon of lard a day. His father pulled on his leggings and his greatcoat. Mother asked him where he was going and he said he thought he knew where a bear was denned up. The same mean bear that had stolen one of his pigs and killed his old coon dog. The rugged man picked up his Henry lever-action rifle and stepped out the door into the wind.

Late that night John's mother and sister gathered close to the fire scared to death their father had been killed by the bear he was hunting. Or maybe he had gotten lost in the blizzard. The wind was howling fierce in the white pines around the cabin. Mother gathered her two children under a blanket and got them to sing songs of faith. John remembered singing "Come Thou Fount of Many Blessings" though he couldn't remember any of the words except "Ebenezer" and a reference to "some melodious sonnet." That's when they heard stomping outside the door and knew their Father was home. The door exploded open. A cloud of snow and wind burst its way into the small cabin along with his Father carrying the bloody hams of a bear. Soon fat juicy meat was roasting over the fire. The look of love and respect John saw his Mother give his Father was never forgotten. At that moment he had never feared and yet loved his father more. The exhausted hero his Father was that night compared to the man who had killed old Buck and treated him so badly seemed like two sides of a very rough and worn coin John could never resolve.

The entire afternoon after his father had killed old Buck John had plotted in his mind, a thousand ways to kill his father. He went to bed at night wishing for the old man's death. Now it was sixty years ago and the guilt he carried all these years from the day the tree top had fallen and killed his father sometimes was worse than his memories of war. John was sure, in the dark hours, that his prayers as a boy were the cause of his father's death. God ain't nothing to trifle with! Every time he felt like he needed to pray he would remember old Buck. Then as he began to pray he kept waiting for God's axe to drop on his own worthless head and feelings of total unworthiness would become an unbearably heavy yoke on his soul. Fern had tried over and over to get him to go to church with her. He had even refused her when she wanted to have a church wedding and had dragged her to the office of the justice of the peace for one of those quick civil services. He'd never understood the extent of how it had embarrassed her. The only time he had gone inside a church with her was at her funeral. My God, how he hated that fact now! All those Christmas Eves he had wanted to tell her why he felt unworthy of going through the doors of a church of any kind.

How could she have known the images that haunted him since a cloudy, rainy day in Germany? He couldn't bring himself to tell anyone about it. Nobody! It was the subject of countless nightmares, the ghoulish memories associated with one evening of war when he first became judge, jury, and executioner. They had fought their way through those impenetrable hedgerows into a little French town and had the Krauts on the run. A German sniper had taken up a position designed to delay the Yanks' advance and cover the German retreat. The sniper opened up on their unit from the cover of a church and knocked down three GIs in short order. One of the GIs, a boy from Kansas, had taken a round through the belly button and it had busted out his backbone. He was screaming his lungs out lying there paralyzed from the waist down, dying in the street. Although John was exhausted and had reached the point of not caring he instantly made up his mind the sniper was going to pay for his work. Crawling on his belly behind a low rock wall, he made it to the corner of the church, jumped up onto the top of a stone wall and in one motion dived headfirst through a low open window. Rolling into the corner of a small room he brought up his rifle scanning for movement, looking for a target of any kind. The room had served as a nursery for the church not too long ago. Little pictures of lambs cut out with scissors, colored with chalk, had been pinned to the bulletin board along with a picture of Jesus sitting beside a stream in a pasture. Two cribs lined one wall back to back. A chalkboard with writing in German on it looked like it was probably some scriptures or prayer or something that he couldn't read. That's when he saw blood running out from under a closet door and opened it very carefully with the end of his rifle. Sitting on the floor of the closet was a beautiful, nearly naked, dead Jewish girl with a fresh bullet hole on her forehead. Her mouth and eyes were wide open. She was wearing only a torn shirt. A thin thread holding a tiny Star of David made of cloth hung around her neck. John reached out and touched her hair and with his index finger shut her eyes and mouth.

It was obvious she had been beaten, raped, and sodomized. As quietly as he could he crept over to the door leading into the sanctuary and peering through the crack he could see the long, unforgiving pews lined all the way to the front. The massive pulpit made of polished wood stood before a partially blown-out stained-glass window. A huge brown wooden cross was suspended from the ceiling to the right of the pulpit. Parts of what was once a fine pipe organ hung broken like sewer pipes gone lunatic on the left side. Pieces of the heavy door John was crouched behind suddenly erupted in splinters stinging John's face as he instinctively cart-wheeled his body away from the hot, death-dealing lead. Spinning to the left as the deafening boom of the German's rifle roared from behind the pulpit, John found the pin on one of his hand grenades, pulled it and flung the grenade to the front of the church. He dived back to cover on the floor of the nursery and landed under a picture of Jesus with children. He clamped his hands over his ears.

The ensuing explosion was terrible but effective. The grenade had rolled to the bottom of the huge cross. The impact of the blast caused the cross to become loose from its moorings in the plaster wall and ceiling. The massive twenty-foot cross that had to weigh at least 500 pounds fell straight to the floor and then tumbled like a felled oak tree spinning on its limbs, pinning the wounded sniper on the floor beside of the now shrapnel-scarred pulpit as dust and broken plaster rained down from the ceiling. The sniper had lost his rifle but was still conscious. An evil, cold, and venomous looking German Luger pistol was just out of reach of his left hand on the floor. Blood was running out of his left ear and his right leg was twisted at a ninety-degree angle.

John walked to the front of the church his rifle on point, safety off, finger on trigger. Looking the German in the eye he said, "Don't reckon you will ever make it to Kansas to plow no fields for my buddy you killed out there, will you?" John picked up the pinned and wounded soldier's gun as the German defiantly stared at John.

"Don't reckon you had anything to do with the raping and murder of that little girl back there in the closet either, did you?"

Calmly, deliberately and coldly with no remorse John picked up the Kraut's pistol and hog-shot him with one of his own bullets, behind the sniper's ear, ending his misery and hopefully sending him to Hell.

Now, as he lay in his bed over fifty years later, he decided once again he was unworthy of even praying. He went back to the bathroom and got in the medicine cabinet. Downing a big gulp of chalky-tasting Kaopectate and a half dozen Tylenol tablets chased by another glass of water, he looked in the mirror and saw a very tired old man looking back at him who desperately needed to be forgiven by his maker. One who he was sure couldn't wait to throw him into Satan's hellfires. If only he had gone on down the road of death before Fern had, he thought as he rolled into bed and opened his well-worn copy of *Essays of Mark Twain*. Twain was always amusing and comforting somehow. At least it helped him from sinking in a valley of his inescapable memories. A spider that had made it inside for the winter crawled across the bedroom ceiling. John hoped he would make a web up in the corner and catch that irritating fly that liked to land on his nose while he was reading and buzz around the light bulb in his lamp.

He awoke at dawn with an erection. John's private parts were in proportion to the rest of him and the subject of many jokes and friendly banter among his peers. While skinny-dipping with his buddies in Cambridge he had become a legend and for a while they had called him Pony Boy, even in front of the girls at school, which made his face get hot and red. They had embarrassed him to no end, especially Mac who had a way with words and wouldn't let things be. McNally had composed a poem probably still remembered by all the boys and some of the girls who had suffered a year in Mrs. Suter's sixth-grade class. McNally was very proud of his poetic endeavors and had made sure everybody had the chance to hear him recite it.

> John, John the Mountaineer's son,
> Takes great delight in trifles.
> His shoes don't fit,
> He don't give a shit,
> Because his Jim-dog's as long as his rifle.

That Mac was a real poet! John laughed to himself as he visited the bathroom again, relieved his bladder, and his problem soon faded away. Again he chuckled at his memories remembering what a rotten little kid McNally had really been in grade school. Amazing how one child's behavior so influenced another. They didn't have indoor plumbing at Cambridge County School when he was growing up. Not until they built the new school in 1934 did they have restrooms and locker rooms. The new school was the pride and joy of the school board, the board of supervisors, and the citizens of Cambridge County. It had all started when someone wrote on the bathroom wall what was termed by the principal, Mr. Will, as "a subhuman act of vandalism." The writing was a poem about a cowboy named Piss Pot Pete. Mr. Comer, the physical education teacher, made the statement that the handwriting looked like McNally's.

The next thing Mac knew he was hauled into the office and raked over the coals. He denied everything and fended off the accusations thrown at him, especially the threats of his being sent to reform school if he was found guilty of desecrating the new building without the courage to admit his transgressions.

When Mac got home his parents returned to school with him and once again Mac was put under the most intense pressure to confess. He wouldn't break and then he tearfully persuaded his mother to believe in his innocence. Mr. Will was afraid to push it any farther for fear of Mac's father and his political connections in town turning against him. The wall was painted with two coats of fresh paint covering up the obscenity. Mr. Comer and Mr. Will popped in and out of the locker room frequently trying to nail someone in the act of writing on the wall but with no success. Of course, everyone knew Mac was guilty as hell after having heard him recite "The Ballad of Piss Pot Pete" on numerous occasions. Since no one had seen him do it and he did not confide his secrets with anyone, there was no way he could be held accountable as long as his ability to look an adult in the face and lie directly and convincingly held up. Good practice for a future lawyer.

One morning about a week later, just after the opening bell, there was a stir in the gymnasium and John looked at Mac who had heard it too and was keeping his nose in his math book. Mr. Will, Mr. Comer, and the town police chief Paul Neff, were seen with dark looks on their faces. Someone had entered the school apparently through an open window off the back porch roof. The vandalizing burglar had written with a paintbrush in bright red paint:

They paint these walls,
To hide my pen.
But the Out-House Poet
Has struck again!

John could remember being scared to death when he was taken to the principal's office to be questioned as were all the boys. The police chief found dusty footprints on top of the locker that the vandal had made upon entry, showing a crisscross tread pattern from work boots. They examined every boys boots and found no matching shoe print design. Mac's mother ensured the investigators her son had only one pair of work boots and one pair of slick-soled Sunday shoes. Mr. Will had been so sure he finally had

Mac dead to right he nearly pulled out what little hair he had left on his head. When the hard evidence, as Chief Neff had called it, pointed to someone else, Mac was exonerated.

A week later John was hired by Mac's father to help shock an acre of corn. Mac swore John to secrecy and showed him an old pair of work boots, a small paintbrush, and a pint can of red paint he had jammed down a groundhog hole in the middle of a briar patch next to the creek that flowed on the north side of old man McNally's field. John laughed again as he remembered the funny prank and how he had helped Mac place a large field stone over the groundhog hole. McNally hasn't changed much after all, John thought. After all the bad stuff I've done it seems like McNally should be the one to worry about his lifelong behavior! Not me!

Then there was the time the circus had come to town. Speedy, Mac, and John had walked to the fairground with their dimes for admission in the watch pockets of their overalls. The big board fence that encircled the fairground served to keep people from sneaking in. Mac said he wasn't going to spend his dime on admission and tried to get the other two boys to slip in with him through a loose board he knew about on the north side of the fairground. It had been raining for several days and the ground was soft and muddy. There was a big mud puddle about seventy yards from the main gate. It was the size of a small pond. Speedy and John knew they would get severe beatings if they were caught doing something like slipping into the fair. John could hear his Uncle Ned say, "I hate a thief. I respect a liar more. Don't ever let me catch you cheating someone out of money, son. Don't ever let that happen." It was the only thing his uncle had ever counseled him on. John had no other place to go and he did not want to jeopardize his status with his uncle and aunt. He lived in fear of being sent to the orphanage.

Speedy and John went around to the main entrance, paid their dimes and went around to the back of the tent to see if Mac had made it. They were just in time to see Mac slip through the fence and make a wild run for the safety of the crowd. Out of nowhere a Virginia State Trooper riding on a big gray gelding intercepted Mac and leaning down, the trooper snatched the trespasser by the back of his jacket and lifted him off the ground. With the whole crowd watching the Trooper carried Mac out through the main gate to the middle of the mud puddle and unceremoniously dropped him face-first into the muck and the brown water where he splashed around much like a drowning rat. The last Speedy and John saw of Mac that day he was running down the hill toward his home while the entire crowd laughed in approval. That rascal Mac was always a catbird! John suddenly thought with a start, "I am an old man lost in my memories. I need to live in the present."

Fixing a pot of coffee was a ritual he enjoyed doing every day. Davy had one of those new Mr. Coffee machines but John preferred to use an old stained up coffeepot he had dragged out of his storage building. He had used it for years and it did make very good coffee. As the coffee brewed John switched on the little radio-television set on the counter beside the toaster. The local news was on and darned if they weren't interviewing old pretty boy the Sheriff. There had been a domestic murder on the east side of the county during the night and the Sheriff was wasting no opportunity to get past the bad press he had just suffered and turn the locals' attention to someone else's woes and let them see him doing his job.

John looked out the window and the sun was already melting the February snow off the roof and the gutter in front of the kitchen window was leaking, forming an ice-sickle that sparkled in the clear morning sun. John dug in the refrigerator and found a package of Jimmy Dean Sausage and a half dozen eggs. He got the sausage frying in a twelve-inch cast-iron skillet Aunt Mary Alice had given back to him. Soon it was popping and sputtering along with the coffee percolating. Once the sausage was done John dropped the eggs one by one into the hot grease and fried them over easy. He put a paper towel on top of a plate beside the stove and placed the fried eggs and sausage on it to get some of the grease off them. Turning the heat way back on the frying pan he got out a bag of Martha White flour and sprinkled it around on top of the hot grease until it was completely covered. Letting it brown a little he got a gallon of milk out of the refrigerator and poured it into the mix, stirring it in carefully until he had what he thought was the right amount. The stirring continued as he shook salt and pepper into the gravy and after a while it started to thicken. When he got it right he dropped four slices of Wonder Bread into the toaster and went to wake up Davy.

"Daggone, Grampap! I'm gonna weigh as much as you do if you don't quit fixing such good breakfasts for me. I swear! Man, that smells good!" The young man was excited as he dropped two pieces of the toast on the plate, placed two eggs and two sausage patties on the bread, and then ladled several large dippers full of the white gravy on top of it all.

"Eat up, boy! We got lots of plans to make today. I feel like traveling. I was serious when I said I want to go to Finland and then to Alaska. I done decided if you got to be here in this world then you might as well have a good time and see a few places," the old man said as he loaded up his own plate.

"You gonna eat all that after being sick as you was last night?" Davy asked.

"It was that seafood salad she served on top of those red onions that done it to me. Laid me low it did, but that was last night. Breakfast like this is the best meal of the day," John answered.

"Just how am I supposed to run a masonry business and gallivant all around the world with you?" Davy asked.

"Easy," the old man stated. "You tell those people you got booked already that you won the lottery and are independently wealthy now and don't need their work. They can find someone else to get it done. I have $272, 644 in the bank. I probably won't last four years. I have a gun collection worth at least $25,000 you can have when I am gone with the exception of a couple of them I want to go somewhere else. How much money you owe on your house here?"

"I don't owe but about $18,000 on it and my pickup is paid for free and clear. I don't owe nobody else nothing," the young man answered.

"Okay, I will pay off your house and hire the Trumbo boys to mow the yard and keep the place up until say the middle of October. We talk to Mac and get him to write up a contract where you take care of me for the same amount I was paying those outlaws at that Brethren Home plus I pay for all your travel expenses. Then I write a will and leave everything to you. I'm serious. I wanna to go see this Finland country and visit the grave of the only person I ever heard of that could take out seven Russian tanks by himself. Those stories I heard about him and his brave pals gave me courage in some terrible rough times and I won't never forget it. I want to see the land and the people that could produce men like him. Do you know Finland is the only country that paid back Uncle Sam all its debts it owed us after the war was over? They wouldn't have never sided with Hitler if they wasn't more worried about that animal Stalin. Besides, I hear they got the prettiest girls in the whole world. I still like to look at them too. It won't hurt you to chase a few European skirts either! What do you say?"

"I'll think about it," Davy said as he put another piece of Wonder Bread in the toaster. He had ideas about sopping out the skillet until his grandfather beat him to it.

# Chapter 37

Davy answered the phone and was surprised to hear the childlike voice of Connie Pencilschwietzer. She asked how the two Dean men were getting along since they didn't have to worry about John's legal troubles anymore. Davy made small talk with her until she got around to the purpose of her call. Connie wanted to invite them to come by the Pencilschwietzer's home on Thursday night for dinner around six thirty. Davy couldn't think of any good excuses fast enough and before he knew it he had said something akin to "Okay" and before he knew what happened she was saying, "Oh, that's just great! Bob will be pleased you're coming and I'm going to invite a couple of other folks over too, so see you at about six fifteen then? I'm so excited! Bye-bye now! And don't you boys bring anything except yourselves. I'll have it all taken care of. I just love to cook you know. Handy thing for a preacher's wife. Bye-bye!"

When Davy told his grandfather, he really hadn't expected such a big protest. John was adamant. He did not want to go the Reverend's home at all, period. "I ain't going to no grass-eating preacher's stuffy old house!"

Davy finally put his foot down and surprisingly issued an assertive order to his grandfather: "Well, Grampap, you're going with me because I already gave her my word we was coming! And, don't forget, Grampap. They was the ones who hooked Mac up with that Mary Ann Bartley who saved your ass for you. You'd still be settin' down at that jailhouse playing cards with them Mexican boys if'n it weren't for them!"

"Bullshit," the old man exploded. "All he wants to do is to try to get you and me coming to his church every Sunday and coughing up 10 percent of everything you make! I know his type."

"Grampap, please don't embarrass me by refusing to go. They're nice folks and I already told them we was coming," Davy implored. "You're the one saying you need to have some fun in this world and wanting me to go off and fly halfway around the world to put some flowers on some Scandinavian Superman's grave. If you want me to go with you and look out for you then you need to show me you're going to meet me halfway on these kinds of things."

"So, you saying you'll go with me then? Take me up on my offer?" John asked with one eyebrow raised.

"Reckon I'd be a fool not to. But with my luck you'll probably live another twenty years, have a stroke, and end up being a big fat 300-pound baby slobbering around with me having to change your diapers and powder your butt while shoveling oatmeal and Geritol down your throat," Davy said with a laugh. John laughed too at the ridiculous image Davy had thrown out. But both of them knew what he had crudely joked about could become a frightening reality for a young man. Accepting the responsibility of caring for his Grandfather indefinitely would be a huge gamble for him, no doubt.

John held out his hand and almost reluctantly Davy gripped the old man's huge hand and they shook on it. "You don't have to worry about me staying past my welcome," the old giant said matter of factly. Davy turned and looked at him, thought about asking what he meant by that but then thought better of it. After that moment the traveling plans were mere formalities. The Dean boys were headed to Finland with one pit stop at the preacher's house and a few minor details to work out. It might as well have been written in stone. A Dean's handshake has permanent consequences.

"Where is Finland, anyways Grampap?" the young man asked. "I failed geography in the eleventh grade and had to take it over in the twelfth. The only thing I remember is that it's close to Sweden and Norway and it's supposed to be really cold up there."

"It's west of Russia and east of Sweden," John answered. "Right in between. They've caught hell from both sides for a long time. I hear they hate the Swedes almost as much as the Ruskies! It'll be lots easier finding Humppila, Finland, than it'll be for me to survive an evening with that mealy-mouthed preacher and his wife."

"I'm sure you'll be so upset the whole time you're there that you won't be able to eat any of her food, will you?" Davy needled. John picked up a little pillow off the couch and hit his grandson playfully on the head with it and said, "At least she's good to look at! If I was a younger man I would try to sport her. I doubt if that preacher is doing her any good."

Davy just shook his head and said, "I swear, old man!"

Thursday afternoon rolled around quicker than John would have liked and Davy got him to take a shower and shave. He'd done some wash that day which neither of them were good at doing. Davy had a washer and a dryer and learned fast after Lizzy left not to wash his white underwear with purple towels. He had a whole set of raspberry-colored undershorts to show for it and John loved to pick on him when he would wear a pair of them around the house. Davy got so tired of hearing about it from his grandfather that he took all of John's underwear including his white T-shirts and threw them in the washer with the same purple towels that had turned his boxers pink. Then he turned on the hot water. When John saw what Davy had done to his clothes he exploded and raised a ruckus about wasting money. Both of the Dean men were traditionally so financially tight that it was entirely against their natures to give up on perfectly good underwear even if it was purple. So it was that both of them got dressed in their Sunday best in pants and shirts that were wrinkled from not having someone around to iron properly. And, at the same time sporting pink underwear, headed to the preacher's house for dinner. John was worried something bad would happen and he would have to go to the hospital with sissy-looking shorts on but not sufficiently worried to throw away garments that were serviceable. They had a lot of wear in them even if they looked like raspberry sherbet.

The parsonage was a nice brick house only about a quarter of a mile from the church. It had a big front porch and large boxwood and red maple trees growing along a crumbling front walk. A well-kept gray 1988 Oldsmobile four-door was in the garage shining under several layers of buffed wax.

John was mumbling under his breath as Davy rang the doorbell. Connie came to the door in blue jeans and a red sweater. She looked like she was twenty-five instead of thirty-eight with all those pearly white teeth shining and welcoming them in. Her amazing green eyes sparkled when she made eye contact with Davy and shook his hand. Her hand felt soft and cool when he shook it. Pencilschwietzer was putting a piece of wood in the fireplace that already had a good bed of deep glowing coals under it. The aroma of home cooking filled the room and made John's mouth start watering in spite of himself. The preacher welcomed them in and invited them to sit down. The television was tuned to ESPN and Bob was watching a hockey game between the Red Wings and the Flyers. Connie said they were waiting on some other guests and told the men to make themselves comfortable while she finished getting dinner ready. Mary Ann Bartley came out of the kitchen wearing an apron and John noticed right away she looked like she had lost weight since he had seen her just three weeks ago at the trial.

"Certainly you men remember Mary Ann from the trial, don't you?" Connie twittered.

"Of course we do," John said, rising up to acknowledge her presence and motioning for Davy to do the same. "I want to thank you again for your help in my troubles, Ms. Bartley," John said stiffly.

Davy said a simple, "Hi, Mary Ann," which elicited a nervous fluttering of her eyelids from the large–framed, homely young woman. Suddenly appearing embarrassed and confused, she promptly turned back to the kitchen.

Connie jumped in quickly and said as she followed Mary Ann, "We need to get back in here and take care of the rest of the dinner before we burn the meatloaf! Now you men relax a bit and we'll be back here in the kitchen."

"John, how's life going living with your grandson? You guys're doing the bachelor thing these days I hear," Pencilschwietzer asked.

"Oh, we're making do just fine. We could use a little help with the clothes washing and the ironing though. Don't know any Mexican women who want some part time work do you, Reverend? You preachers are sort of sympathetic to those types, aren't you, Reverand?"

"Call me Bob, fellows. That reverend stuff gets old sometimes. I appreciate the respect but I like just being plain old Bob if that is okay with you men," the pastor answered. "I don't know any Mexican women but that doesn't mean one might not come along dripping water off her back looking for a few pesos off a couple of good-looking gringos like you two. I don't suppose you would require a green card to let her work, would you?"

Davy was relieved when John broke out laughing and said, "Bob, I think I'm going to be able to talk to you." The Red Wings scored a go-ahead goal and Bob whooped and hollered. "Like your hockey, do you?" John asked.

"Sure do! I never knew much about the game but Connie's father got me started watching it and Connie is wild about it too. It's part of being from Finland. They're nuts about it up there. Hockey, coffee and beer-drinking! Those people drink more coffee and alcohol per capita than any other country in the world."

Davy looked at John and said, "This here is a real coincidence. Me and Grampap are studying on going to Finland soon. You say Connie is from there?"

"She was born in Michigan a couple years after her parents moved here in the early 1950s. Whole bunch of Finns live up there around the lakes. Reminds them of home. Tough bunch of customers too!"

Connie stuck her head into the living room from the kitchen door and asked, "Did I hear you say the Red Wings scored?"

"Yes they did. Went up three to two. Guess where our guests want to go on a trip shortly? They want to travel to Finland," Bob said. "What's in Finland you fellows want to see? You got family over there too or something?"

Davy looked at John who said, "I want to visit a friend's grave. Ever hear of a little town named Humppila? That is where he's supposed to be buried."

Connie said in a surprised tone, "My parents are from Forssa which is only a few miles from Humppila. I have an Aunt Terttu and Uncle Heikki that live there and I used to stay with them sometimes. I remember picking wild blueberries in the forest until my fingers were all purple for days. I always wanted a little girl of my own to take home to Finland to pick blueberries but I guess the Lord has other ideas. It's just me and old Bob here so we can go most any time or anywhere we want," she said as she stroked her fingers through Bob's wavy hair. He raised his arm up to rub her forearm and glanced at her with a loving and sad look. She changed the subject quickly.

"Uncle Heikki said he was always scared of the bears in the woods but I never saw one. I think he did that just to get a rise out of me. He's such a tough old farmer a bear would probably run from him if he did see one!"

"Or he would talk it to death!" Bob said. "Friendliest man I ever met that I couldn't understand a word he said."

"What a coincidence!" Connie exclaimed. "Bob and I have been talking about going there ourselves this summer. We aren't going until late June. Don't you know there can be four or five feet of snow on the ground there now and the temperatures won't get above freezing regularly until middle of May at least?"

"No, I never thought of that," John said. "Maybe we ought to wait until then too, Davy. Can't see no tombstone in weather like that!"

"That would solve some problems for me to wait until then too," Davy responded. "I been worried about turning down the stonework job I got the bid on at the new bank over on Route 60. That job will pay real good money, Grampap. We'd have plenty of time to finish that job and be ready to leave around the middle of June. I like the idea of waiting until then."

John turned to Mrs. Pencilschweitzer and asked, "Maybe you could help us get tickets and show us the ropes. Kind of get us headed in the right way?"

"That would be no trouble at all!" Bob offered. "We went over last time two years ago on Iceland Air. That's the only way to do it. Breaks the flight up just right and that way you can avoid Heathrow or Hamburg. The airport in Reykjavik is really neat too. Connie has a cousin who owns an electronics company and has a cabin on a lake where we probably could all stay for free if you would be interested."

The doorbell rang before John could answer and much to his surprise and delight Connie greeted Mac and his wife along with the widow Anne Crawford. Dinner was wonderful and there was plenty for all. John went wild over the homemade bread Connie and Mary Ann had made. For the old man, it was a very nice evening and over before any of them wanted it to be. On the way home John told Davy, "For a preacher man, that Bob is a pretty good feller."

Driving home that night on a dark two lane road, Davy found himself suddenly missing Lizzy. Then he began to have severe doubts about what he had gotten himself into. The tremendous responsibility he had taken on by himself with his grandfather was starting to sink in. The Dean loyalty and honor would never allow him to even attempt to back out of a promise of any kind, much less one of this seriousness. Davy looked over at his grandfather who was riding with his eyes closed, half asleep and then watched as the old man snapped out of his reverie and focused back on the road ahead. A few snowflakes were falling. It would be March soon and he could get back to work. That would be good. A fat possum ran across the road just before he turned into his driveway and waddled into the corn stubble and winter wheat in the field across from his house. No lights were on and no warm woman awaited him in bed. She was probably tucked in

221

somewhere else with that worthless Morris boy. The thought of it depressed him further. The pillow was cold as he flopped down in the bed without even bothering to take his clothes off. He fell asleep thinking about Connie Pencilschwietzer's tight fitting jeans and her flashing green eyes.

# Chapter 38

March rolled by and Davy was taking John with him to work every day. The old man was really doing a good job helping with the stone and it seemed he had a new spirit to him. He was actually fun to be around and a joy to work with, talking and joking through the cool spring days. Before John retired, and the whole time he was the foreman, John had always been grudgingly serious on the job, treating everyone roughly. It was as if he was perpetually angry with their performance and mad at the rest of the world. When he had been in charge, he worked like a man possessed, like a steam engine that knew no holiday or lack of coal and water. He was the sternest of taskmasters, always pushing his workers. In frustration, Davy asked him one time when they were alone why he had that kind of attitude on the job. He didn't act like that any other time. As soon as he stepped out of his old truck in the mornings it was like he sprouted horns and grew a pointed tail in order to lead a host of demons against the forces of stone, subduing it and beating it into the form he demanded. John responded to Davy's question by saying his own father had approached all jobs in that manner and had drilled into him the idea that an iron hand was the only way to keep discipline with men. It caused a high stress level at the job site Davy had never liked. When John retired and Davy took over the crew he had allowed a much more relaxed work setting and he really didn't see any drop in their production rate. Everything ran smoothly until Davy hired Herman Harrison from Greenville. Harrison had mistaken Davy's kindness with weakness.

Harrison was a physically imposing man with a haughty attitude and the other boys on the crew were afraid of him. When Harrison came back from lunch twenty minutes late and the rest of the crew was already working Davy had looked Harrison right in the face and told him he had warned him for the last time about screwing off on the clock. Harrison cursed and squared off on Davy to the astonishment of the rest of the men. Davy pulled out his checkbook and wrote the bully a paycheck, which he figured in his head right up to the time of the confrontation. Writing out the check with hands that did not shake, he stuffed the check in Harrison's shirt pocket. Then looking him cold in the eye he told him to get off his job sight and not bother to come back. Harrison bristled up and said, "I have never been fired before and I am not going to take this from a youngster like you! You can't do this to me!"

"You done it to yourself, Mr. Harrison. Now I ain't gonna tell you again to leave. You are now officially trespassing on my job site."

Harrison clenched his fists and glared at Davy who met his glare with those ice-cold blue Dean eyes. Harrison finally threw his trowel and level in his masonry bag, turned, and stalked away without another word. From that time on Davy didn't have any problems with maintaining discipline with the rest of the crew. He had earned their respect. The work days were much more enjoyable now than when John had been the headman and Davy was a congenial but solid manager. John had always kept four or five men on the crew but Davy only had two boys working with him along with John. He had explained to them this would be his last job for the foreseeable future and told them to start making some other plans for when the job was finished. Neither of his employees, the Rawlings brothers, would have any trouble finding work with any one of several local masonry outfits if they wished and they always had work at their Uncle Bob's junkyard when they wanted it. Davy was the best in the valley at laying stone and not many of the others knew how to handle the rocks like he did. It had come naturally to him and John was very proud of the quality of his grandson's work.

Tony and Roger Rawlings had been raised by their Uncle Bobby who ran a backwoods, unlicensed junkyard and car crushing business that was always at odds with the local zoning administrator. They helped their uncle when work got slow with Davy. Bob Rawlings also sold a large quantity of moonshine made on the neighboring farm by him and his cousin Elmer Sweeney. Every Friday night they sponsored cockfights in their large metal barn behind the junkyard, drawing big crowds from all over. Tony was really glad to get his paycheck at the end of his first week back to work. Linda, his girlfriend, was on the verge of kicking him out of her mobile home for not paying the trailer payment the month before like he had promised her he would do. He had cashed his check at the bank that Friday evening and headed home with all intentions of giving her the money for the payment. He was nearly empty of gas so he stopped at the Corner Convenience & Gas on Route 60 to fill up. It was his great misfortune to run into a guy he knew from North Carolina who had a rooster for sale in a cage in the back of his van. The man had said he had to go to Tennessee to check on his mother who had diabetes problems. She had a turn for the worse, and was in the hospital getting her left foot taken off. He was really disappointed because he was sure his rooster was going to win big that night. It had been undefeated down at Big Stone Gap the week before, he lamented. "Bad timing on mom's part, I'd say."

"The only reason I would even think about selling my rooster is because I'm caught short and need cash to fill up my tanks on my van so I can make it back home to take care of Momma," he said. "If I don't go my sister will kick me out of her trailer."

Then the man hung out the bait: "You interested in making yourself a lot of money? I guarantee you will walk away with a fistful of money over at your Uncle Bob's garage tonight fighting this rooster!"

The North Carolina shyster had set the price for his prize cock at $250 and let Tony think he had stolen the bird for $200. All but thirty dollars of a paycheck he had worked all week for at hard labor on the stone crew. It cost him ten dollars for a half tank of gas so he was left with twenty to bet on Super Chicken. That night when he threw the rooster in the pit the macho-looking bird took one look at his opponent, turned and ran in fright. The ringmaster, as was appropriate with the rules of the fight, grabbed Tony's $200 rooster and wrung his neck on the spot, tossing him flopping toward the trash barrel beside one of the support posts. No cowardly, running roosters were tolerated at Bob's Garage. When Tony slinked into the trailer around one in the morning flat broke, drunk, and hungry all hell broke loose. Linda wasn't happy and the next Friday she showed up at the job site right at four o'clock. Linda was built like a refrigerator with a head, had on a T-shirt with Stone Cold Steve Austin on the front. Her face was flushed and the black roots of her dyed blonde hair was noticeable when she snatched Tony's check from Davy as soon as he wrote it. She shoved a pen in Tony's hand, and made him endorse it right there on the spot. John burst into booming laughter. He really thought that was funny. Tony hung his head in shame knowing what a ribbing he was going to have to endure in the coming weeks. Linda was wearing the Stone Cold Steve Austin T-shirt with no bra. When John took to laughing harder she asked him what he was laughing at and told him to kiss her ass which only made John hee-haw more.

"Jackasses!" she yelled as she dragged Tony over to the black, rusted-out Monte Carlo sporting a ten-foot CB antenna on the trunk roof with a tennis ball glued on the tip. John almost couldn't wait until Monday when he would have the opportunity to pour it on Tony. Tony crawled in the passenger seat of the Chevrolet and put on his seatbelt, looking at his lap with his Earnhardt hat pulled low over his eyes. Linda popped the clutch and threw dust and gravel all over John when she spun off the lot, causing him to laugh so hard Davy thought he was going to choke.

The steady labor gave John good exercise and his muscles toned back up. He was still taking long walks in the evening after work too. The company of the working men was good for him mentally and he lost a lot of his belly. The fresh air and sunshine also did him well as he worked at his own pace and the crew fell into a rhythm as the stone building began to take shape. John did much of the cutting and fitting of the rock. Davy set them in place and the Rawlings boys mixed the mud and moved around and between the Deans like worker ants.

April rolled past and the warm days of May found them nearing completion of the job. John walked around the corner of the building one day and was gone for a good while until Davy began to get concerned. He laid down his trowel and went to look for his grandfather. John was leaning on a split-rail fence around back, looking out across the open field to the edge of a forest. Pokeweed and poison ivy were trying to assert themselves along the fence. John was munching on a wild asparagus shoot he had found. Davy walked up and said, "What you looking at, Grampap?"

"Oh, just taking a good look at springtime. The dogwoods are blooming up there with the redbuds and the birds a-carrying on. I thought I heard an old turkey gobbler hollering back in the woods a while ago and I was listening to see if he would sound off again," the old giant responded. "Why? You gonna dock my pay for screwing off or something?"

"Of course not, Grampap. I was just concerned where you was at so I come around here to check on you. I thought I was supposed to do that per our agreement, look after you and all that kind of stuff," the young man answered.

John laughed and said, "Every year since I was about fifty or so I've thought about springtime and fall a little different. Christmas and Thanksgiving or the Fourth of July are the same. You don't know what I'm talking about yet. You still think you gonna live forever. When you get older the good times kind of grab you. Like the first clear crisp day of October when it's clear as a bell and the smell of frost on dusty field corn and foxtails is in the air with the crickets singing their farewell songs. The things that are worthwhile in this world, Son. You get to thinking and wondering if this'll be the last time you might get to see them. You get to thinking, 'I wonder how many more springs or falls I'll get to see.' Then you start thinking about all the people you know who are dead and gone and how it probably don't mean a thing to them anymore. I wonder if their spirits are floating around taking all this in, listening to an old man mutter and sputter around, just a laughing at us knowing for sure what we don't know yet. We been blessed. These mountains of Virginia are a favored, beautiful place on this earth, ain't it son?"

"Yes, I guess it is, Grampap. I've never been anywhere else but here so I'll have to take your word for it. Why don't you just listen for that old gobbler all you want to. You know how I am. I always do my job and checking on you is my job now too."

"Hope it's a little more than a job for you, son," John said glancing at him. Then the turkey cut loose up in the woods with a trumpeting triple gobble and came strutting out of the edge of the woods all puffed up and fanned out. They stood there and watched him. Finally John busted out laughing and said, "Run, get Tony. Tell him I got a twenty-pound rooster up here in the field I'll sell him!"

That Friday they finished the job by lunchtime and spent the afternoon cleaning up the job site. Davy refused to leave a mess at any of his jobs. All the cement bags were thrown in the dumpster and the pieces of stone left over were loaded onto the back of his truck. John had been true to his word and had taken Davy to the Dodge dealership in Staunton one Saturday and had paid the difference in cash on a trade of Davy's little Nissan truck for a 1994 Dodge Crew Cab pickup a local pharmacist had traded in on a new one. The pharmacist had a little farm and pulled a utility trailer to the dump every other week so he thought he needed a big work truck. It was a heavy-duty truck and had the factory towing package with heavy-duty suspension and all the bells and whistles. The bed looked like it had never had anything on it when they bought the truck off the Dodge dealer. It had been garage kept. John fit in this truck much better too. When he slid the passenger seat all the way back and then leaned it back a little bit more with the fancy electronic controls down on the side of the seat there was plenty of room. He was riding, as he said, "like a fat cat going to the fish market."

Roger Rawlings asked, "What you boys going to do this evening?"

"Probably go home and drink a couple of cold ones and watch television. The Braves play the Mets this evening and they got a new guy named John Rocker throwing. They say he brings the smoke," Davy answered.

"Why don't you all come over to Bob's shop and watch the chicken fights. They got a big deal happening over there tonight and it ought to be fun. A couple of guys from Alabama are supposed to be there with some big-time roosters," Roger offered. "I could take you in with me. Bob don't let uninvited people in, you know, unless they got roosters to fight."

John looked at Davy and said, "Is Tony going to enter any Olympic sprinter-brand roosters that set speed records running away? I wouldn't mind seeing that. They must be French roosters."

"Yeah, as a matter of fact I got two real good prospects I'm gonna put in the ring tonight. Why don't you come and see what it's like. You'll have a fine time, I promise," Tony responded. "When I win the big pot you won't be laughing then, you old lard ass!"

"I don't know," Davy hesitated.

"We been looking at the tube too much. Let's go!" the old man urged.

"What time you want us to be there?" Davy asked.

"Meet us over at the Country Store Market on the back way into Bob's Garage at about eight o'clock," Roger said. "We'll let you follow us in and we'll park out back in the pasture field if Bob ain't got Benny that old mean bull of his in there. Then we can get out the back gate if a fight starts."

Tony's girlfriend Linda Breeden pulled in just as Davy got his checkbook out of the console between the front seats of the big Dodge. Davy leaned forward to get a look at what T-shirt she was wearing this time. It was another wrestler, The Undertaker. John started singing Conway Twitty's song "I'm Lying Here with Linda on My Mind."

"Got a new wrestler on your shirt there this week, don't you Linda?" the old man asked.

"If I don't get Tony's check I'm gonna have a new man on my belly this weekend too!" she quipped. "You pervert. Quit staring at my titties!"

Davy turned his attention to writing the check. John said, "Why don't you tell your titties to quit staring at my eyes".

"Go jump in a lake, you prick! All you men are alike! Pigs!" She snorted.

"Oink, Oink," said John as he lit up a cigar. Even Davy laughed at that. She threw gravel all over the place again when she left in a cloud of dust. "I wish she wouldn't do that!" Davy yelled at Tony and Roger as they climbed into Roger's Subaru Brat. "And I wish you wouldn't provoke her like that, Grampap!"

"I think she secretly wants me," John said with a chuckle.

"A while back I would have thought that was funny but not anymore," Davy said.

At eight o'clock they were pulling into the Country Store Market. Tony and Roger were nowhere to be seen. John walked into the store and bought two ice-cream sandwiches and brought one out to Davy. They had eaten in Cambridge at the KFC earlier that evening. The Rawlings boys came flying down the road in their little Subaru and slid into the lot. Tony got out and when he turned John could see he had one nasty black eye taking shape. He was half drunk and Roger looked a little worried.

"Go ahead, John! Get it over with. Give me some crap! My woman knocked the hell out of me when I told her I was going to the chicken fights so I busted her one in the mouth and I left. She's awful good in the sack but I'm tired of her crap! Go ahead and get it over with. Laugh your ass off old man!," Tony said in a wild mood. "I am ready for the chicken fights! Let's go, Roger!"

"Dumb idiot!" Roger spit out at Tony. "You can bet your butt she's down at the magistrate's office getting a warrant out on you. You gonna get locked up this weekend and I ain't gonna bond you out. I ain't got the time or money for that."

John was wiping some melted ice cream off his blue shirt that had somehow missed getting sucked into his mouth. At the same time he was trying to fold up the messy paper wrapper and trying to figure out what to do with it short of tossing it on the parking lot. "If you think she is swearing out warrants for you the best thing you can do is call down there and see if she did. That way you can go turn yourself in and they will release you on one of them there personal recognizance bonds. You keep on drinking and you gonna end up in the drunk tank for the night sure as shootin'."

"Guess he knows too!" Roger reflected. "It ain't been long since Mr. John was a resident over there."

"Screw her and screw all them deputies too along with their prissy-assed Sheriff with a plastic nose! I want to go fight my roosters. Let's go," Tony said. "The law ain't gonna come down to Bob's garage anyway just to serve a damn misdemeanor warrant. Them deputies are afraid of Uncle Bob. Look at my eye! Damn thing is swelling clean shut. She hit me first anyway!" he whined.

"Yeah, like they gonna believe that story with you drinking and all," Davy observed.

"Let's go," Tony said. "You bunch of old women gonna sit around and blabber or are you going to the chicken fights? Get me another beer, Roger."

Roger took off and John looked at Davy and asked, "You reckon we ought to go on home and leave these two wild Indians to themselves this evening?"

"I never been to a chicken fight. Let's go," Davy said with a smile. "I don't expect we will stay too long but since we are here let's see what it's all about."

# Chapter 39

When they got to the red fiberglass gate Roger stopped his Subaru and plugged a spotlight into the cigarette lighter on his dash and shined it all around the pasture, making sure Benny the Bull was not in there. Tony got out and opened the gate, letting both vehicles into the grassy field behind the large metal barn that looked more like a rundown warehouse. Light was pouring out around a door in the rear and Davy could hear excited hollering and cussing coming from inside. Before they made it up to the barn the door flew open and a girl in cut off jeans and a halter top was leading a rich-looking man in a cowboy hat by the hand out into the pasture.

"Where you going with Mr. Hand, Tessie?" Tony sneered at the woman.

"None of your business, Tony, you little piss-ant!" the woman responded tartly.

"Mind your manners, boy," Mr. Hand said assertively to Tony.

"Who you callin' boy, sir?" Tony said as he entered the sawdust-covered floor without looking back. Davy looked at Roger who said, "Go on in. I have to water the weeds." John and Davy followed Tony in the door. Mr. Hand was asking Tessie who the young jerk was as she led him to a camper parked at the other end of the building.

There must have been seventy-five or eighty people around a fighting ring in the middle of the barn floor. The ring was four feet wide and about eight feet long. There were two small sets of bleachers set up on each side and plenty of standing room around them. John took a place at the end of one of the bleachers and leaned his elbow on the top seat. Davy sat down on the front row next to a couple of guys he had attended high school with. Both had red plastic cups of what Davy thought was water until one of them took a drink and snorted. "Damn, that's some powerful joy juice Bob's selling tonight!"

"Where'd you buy that stuff?" Davy inquired.

"Over in the corner," the young man answered. "See the old man pouring it for that other old redneck? Two dollars a half glass and a full one for three. It's got the kick and goes down smooth! Old Bob has a good business here. You get your money's worth."

A young man around twenty years old with a huge bulge in his lower lip due to his having packed it with what looked like half a can of rich, black Copenhagen snuff, carried a rooster with green and black tail feathers up to the far side of the pit. A husky man with a glass eye and very large tattoo-covered forearms wearing an engineer's hat carried a rooster to the near side and knelt down, holding the bird in his hands.

"Who is that feller with the glass eye?" John asked Roger who had taken a place beside him. "He looks familiar."

"You ought to know him, Mr. John," said Roger. "He's kin to you I guess. Name is Nicky Dean. Most people call him Deadeye. He sure knows his chickens. That rooster he's fighting there is a nasty-looking gentleman, ain't he?"

Both birds had long razor-sharp metal spurs attached to the backs of their legs. The pit boss took his position at the end of the pit. Bets were being wagered by nearly half the people around the ring. At a hand signal from the pit boss both men turned loose of their feathered warriors.

John was trying to see the action as both birds flashed and tumbled over and over in an amazing display of acrobatics and feathered martial arts. Most of the crowd was yelling and whooping vying for a better viewing angle. The glass-eyed man's bird suddenly sidestepped his opponent and hopped behind him, sinking both spurs in the back of the green-tailed rooster. Everyone who witnessed it knew immediately the bird was dead on his feet. The young man with the fat tobacco lip shook his head and watched as his bird heroically tried to stay on his feet until the victor grabbed the back of his opponent's neck with his beak and pushed his head to the floor.

The older man extracted his rooster from his victory position over the dead bird. The rooster spun quicker than light and planted one of the spurs he had just pulled out of his vanquished foe right in the meaty part of his glass-eyed owner's hand. Deadeye let out a yelp and the pit boss came to his rescue, grabbing the new champion. Blood spurted from Deadeye's hand as the pit boss shoved the hot-blooded rooster into a cage. Men were slapping Deadeye on the back as he wrapped a checkered handkerchief around his wounded hand to stanch the blood. John heard Deadeye say, "That there does smart a little, I'll tell you."

Davy got up and walked around to his grandfather. "I don't like this at all, Grampap. Let's get the hell out of here. Besides, you on probation and they serving moonshine here. You want to go back to jail?"

"I'd like to see a little more of it, Davy. Did you know that glass-eyed man who just won is your cousin?" John asked, hoping to raise interest in his grandson.

"I don't care if he is the king of merry old England, I ain't gonna watch this crap!" Davy said. To prove his point he walked over to the back door and went out into the night air.

Roger nudged John who had his head turned to watch Davy go.

"Where's Davy going? He gonna miss Tony's bird fight."

"I reckon he don't like this kind of stuff. He's soft-hearted toward any animal. I've seen him get tore up over killing a deer at times," John answered.

Roger gestured toward Tony who was strutting up to the ring with a big red rooster. "Look at that bird! Don't he look rank?"

"What's so special about him?" John asked with a grin. "He gonna run too? Like all of Tony's champions?"

"I don't think this one's gonna run. Tony's had this one a while. Been feeding him stuff to keep him from bleeding. Hasn't fed him at all since Thursday night. Just a little piece of peeled apple to keep his craw from drying up. He's kept him in a totally dark cage since then too. Makes them mean and hungry like a prize fighter should be."

Deadeye Dean with his bandaged hand moved toward the ring with another rooster and soon the bets were wagered heavily in favor of the glass-eyed man's bird. Tony's alcohol-augmented mouth took over and he yelled, "Bet against me, boys! Bet against me! Throw your money away!"

Then they were into it. The birds put on an amazing display of whirling, leaping agility until Tony's rooster struck like lightning and Deadeye's bird lay dead on the floor. Tony snatched up his winner and shoved him in a cage as the surprised Deadeye Dean discarded his deceased feathered warrior in the barrel at the side of the bleachers. Tony was in his glory yelling, "I'll take on all callers with my rooster! Ain't he rank?"

Roger looked at John and with a worried look on his face. "He's gonna get his ass whipped if he don't show some manners."

"Wouldn't bet against it!" John replied. "Somebody's certain to reach down in that boy's central nervous system and make a behavior adjustment on his mouth control."

Just then Tony and Roger's Uncle Bob walked up to Tony and grabbed him by the arm and whispered in his ear. Tony pulled his head back and uttered a profanity. Uncle Bob motioned for Roger and John to come with him.

"The law is out here and they wanted to come in and drag your ass out of here, Tony. I told them to stay outside and I'd see if you were here. I ain't having them tin-badge cowboys stomping this place up tonight. I got too much refreshments in the back room and them girls from Harrisonburg are here. I can't let that happen. Don't want to risk it! Tony, you're gonna walk out there and give yourself up. They showed me a fistful of warrants and some of them is green ones," the grizzled old entrepreneur said.

"I ain't going to jail tonight, Uncle Bob!" Tony yelled.

As quick as a striking snake the old man had Tony's arm behind his back with one hand and the back of his belt in the other, crow-hopping him toward the door. "I ain't having my place raided just because you're a little dumb ass either!" Bob shoved Tony through the front door and they exited into the night.

"Let's get out of here too," Roger said.

John followed him toward the back. Deadeye Dean approached them and said, "You reckon he's gonna need some bail money? I'll give you $500 for his rooster right now." To prove his point he held out five crisp hundreds.

"Make it six, Mr. Dean. You'll still be getting a deal," Roger answered.

Dean pulled out another bill and handed the cash to Roger who folded the money and put it in his shirt pocket.

Davy was waiting outside, leaning against a rusty hay rake long out of service. John explained to him what had happened to Tony and they wasted no time heading to their trucks. Roger said he was going to see if he could bail out his brother with the money he got for the rooster and John and Davy hustled out the gate and turned toward home.

"You sure didn't stay in there long. What's with that?" John asked.

"I like to go hunting. I don't mind killing a chicken for the pot but watching a bunch of idiots cheering over spilt blood is not what I call fun. It's sickening to me and I ain't gonna be a part of it," the young man answered as he drove down the narrow gravel road with dust-covered blackberry vines and poison oak lining the sides of the right of way. John noticed with disgust that some human hog had tossed two white bags of household trash against the woven wire fence at a turn in the road. Christmas gift wrapping paper was hanging out of a rip in one of the bags with Santa Clause's smiling face beaming at them in the headlights. Davy stopped, got out of the vehicle, and tossed the trash on the back of his truck. "I hate to see that kind of stuff. The more I learn about people the more I admire dogs." Davy looked for a response from John whose head was leaning against the glass of the passenger window with his mouth open. He was asleep.

# Chapter 40

The next morning Davy went to the kitchen and turned on the little thirteen-inch TV set as he loaded up the coffee maker. The local morning news was on and the newsgirl was giving the weather forecast. The coffee pot was beginning to gurgle when the newsgirl ended her meteorological report. John came padding into the kitchen like an old bear emerging from hibernation and grabbed his coffee mug. The tone of the newsgirl caused them both to stop and listen as she said, "And now turning to the story of the day and maybe the story of the decade. Tragedy has struck our community. Sheriff Mark Watson was killed by gunfire answering a domestic violence call in the early morning hours in the Rockfish Gap area in remote Northwest Cambridge County this morning. Raymond Wayne Breeden, better known in the area as Red, is being held at the Cambridge County Jail charged with the capital murder of the Sheriff. According to information provided by Major Michael Thompson, Sheriff Watson was in the area conducting an investigation around 1:00 A.M. when the department received a 911 call from Breeden's wife stating Breeden was drunk and threatening to kill her and her children. Sheriff Watson was close by and responded. According to Major Thompson, Sheriff Watson was shot as he approached the front door of the residence. When other deputies arrived they found the body of the Sheriff and the unconscious Breeden lying on top of the Sheriff. Breeden's wife had struck Breeden on the head from behind with a cast-iron tea kettle shortly after he fired the fatal shot from a high-powered rifle. More details will be revealed in a formal press statement by Major Thompson on Cambridge County's

Circuit Court steps at ten o'clock this morning. Stay tuned for breaking news."

The station shifted to an advertisement by a local automobile dealer who was wearing a coonskin hat and firing a muzzleloader at a painted piece of plywood with prices marked on it. The asinine jingle was telling you how "Moondog Raggleman of Sportsmen's Auto World" was shooting down high prices this weekend.

"Well, I guess he died a hero and will be forever honored for dying in the service of his community!" John snorted. "Nobody will dare say he was a dumb ass for walking up to a house like that with no backup or cover. His committing perjury and all the other dirt about him that came out in the trial will be forgotten and he will be the sainted hero forever of the Fraternal Order of Police."

"Damn, Grampap! You are cold, aren't you? He had to walk up to a house where a worthless drunk was terrorizing his own flesh and blood. He was protecting a woman and her little kids! It was his job. It takes a lot of guts to walk up to a house in the middle of the night like that by yourself. Particularly knowing how mean old Red Breeden can be," Davy responded. "You know Red Breeden is Tony Rawlings' girlfriend Linda's daddy by his first marriage, don't you?"

"Yeah, well, that's what Tony will get if he keeps messing with that wild woman. It was still a stupid thing for the Sheriff to do. Bad tactics. I'm surprised he went up there by himself. I can't see him doing that. Didn't think he had the guts! I guess even the most cowardly dog on occasion will run up to a bull or a bear and bark like hell just to prove to himself he's still a dog. My question is who was the Sheriff snaking up in Rockfish Hollow that he was out there in the middle of the night? I expect he kind of just ended up in the wrong place at the wrong time just like he did when he rolled up on Rennick's wreck. He didn't have no choice. Lots of good men and bad ones alike are dead and I'm still here mostly by mistake or luck of the draw. I can't tell you how many times I've missed death by less than an inch. That Sheriff should have stayed out of the bottle, kept his pecker in his pants, and stuck to riding bicycles and playing with them Special Olympics kids while showing that fake pretty-boy smile of his at the camera," John stated.

"I reckon he ain't been doing so much smiling at the camera since you altered his looks for the worse with them big knuckles of yours. And then Mac went and clipped his wings in the courtroom," Davy quipped. "Don't reckon he was feeling so confident these days."

The phone rang and Davy answered it. Roger Rawlings was on the line and said that Tony was still in jail with bail set at $20,000. Roger was lamenting the fact he couldn't raise the 10 percent for the bondsman to spring his brother out. He had the money from selling the rooster and $200 of his own. He was $1,200 short and wanted a loan for the rest. Davy put his hand over the receiver and spoke to his grandfather.

"Roger needs $1,200 more to get Tony out on bond. Magistrate set bond at twenty grand and he only has $800. What do you think?"

"I say let the little jerk stay in jail until Monday. They"ll take him over before the juvenile court judge and probably reduce his bond or even let him out on his own signature if he don't smart off. If he gets out today and screws up we'll be out of the money if we loan it to them. It won't hurt Tony none to set in there a couple of days. Maybe it'll calm him down. He's getting too big for his britches anyway."

Davy took his hand off the receiver and said into the phone, "Roger, we just can't go that much on Tony. Grampap and I're afraid if he gets out so soon before he has some time to think, he might do something really dumb. Why won't your Uncle Bob do it? He has a pile of money."

"I'll ask him again but he is pretty pissed off. That rooster Tony fought and won with was really Uncle Bob's. He like to killed me when he found out I done sold it to Deadeye Dean. Thank you all anyway. Hey, did you all hear about Red Breeden killing the Sheriff?" Roger asked.

"Yeah, we heard. We gotta go now," Davy said as he hung up.

"Dumb peckerheads," John muttered. "Time for breakfast. Let's peel some taters and get some sausage frying. I could eat a horse!"

Later in the morning Davy mowed the yard and gave John a set of pruning shears and asked him to trim the boxwoods along the driveway. At ten o'clock, as promised, Major Thompson accompanied by Commonwealth's Attorney Grimes on TV gave an emotional statement from the courthouse steps detailing the entire ordeal concerning the murder of the Sheriff. They even had Red Breeden's wife, Minnie, on the news, with her three dirty kids in their raggedy clothes hugging her. She was sporting a fat lip where old Red had backhanded her. She was saying she thought the Sheriff had saved their lives. She didn't mention the cast-iron tea kettle half full of cold coffee she had bounced off the back of old Red's skull right after he pulled the trigger on his .45-70 caliber Marlin lever-action. It blew a hole the size of a softball through the Sheriff's chest. She didn't mention she had been drunk too.

Major Thompson revealed a story of how the Sheriff had been called at home around midnight by his great-aunt Lucille Shifflett who lived alone. She was sure there was somebody in her smokehouse stealing her hams and she was frightened. She had no children and everyone knew she had willed her 400-acre mountain farm to her nephew Mark for looking after her. Sheriff Watson had called dispatch and informed them of where he was going just in case there was a problem at Aunt Lucille's. He had arrived at her home up at the head of Steam Hollow in Rockfish Gap around twelve forty-five.

The Sheriff called in at ten minutes after one to report with a laugh he had run off the culprits: two thieving raccoons. He also told the dispatcher his aunt was in bed asleep.

Ten minutes later dispatch received the 911 call from Mrs. Breeden. There were no other deputies within half an hour's drive of the remote area so the Sheriff responded solo. All indications were he had merely gotten out of his cruiser and as he stepped up on the porch Breeden ambushed him. Major Thompson stated that the investigation was continuing. As second in command he would effectively be in charge of the Sheriff's department's operations for the time being and assured the citizens there would be no lapse in service. Commonwealth's Attorney Grimes stated he would be handling the prosecution of Mr. Breeden and he would be seeking the death penalty.

When John and Davy came in for lunch they heard it all on the twelve o'clock "News at Noon" program. John snorted and said scornfully, "Told you the Sheriff'll be an immortal hero around here forever now. We'll have to listen to them sing praises to him every frosty morning. Maybe we ought to get Ben Dean to write a song honoring him. Call it something catchy like 'Watson's Worries' or 'Banana Seat Spandex Blues' or something like that."

Davy just shook his head as he smeared mayonnaise on a piece of bread, getting it ready for cheese and deer bologna. Saturday lunch was cold fare. "Ain't you ashamed of yourself for saying the Sheriff was up in Rockfish Gap snaking some old gal when he was really up there looking after his old Aunt Lucille?"

John snorted and went into the bathroom and shut the door.

# Chapter 41

Connie Pencilschwietzer called Saturday evening and asked John and Davy to come to their home for lunch the next day to discuss the upcoming trip to Finland. She invited them to come to Sunday services with her also. Davy promised her they would be there at eleven and thanked her. John flatly refused to go to church and was furious Davy had told the preacher's wife he would attend. Davy told him it would be good for him to go and he should get over his aversion for churches.

"A man who has been through all the war you been through shouldn't be afraid a little religion might rub off on you. You know, if we go on this trip, we're going to be expected to go in a bunch of old churches over there. That's what Ms. Pencilschwietzer told me. So you might as well get on with it. Besides, you ate enough food at the Judge's funeral. Didn't seem to bother your stomach too much then! You went in the church for the Judge's funeral too. I don't understand why you can't go on a Sunday morning. Are you afraid of having to put some money in the offering plate or something?"

"Funerals are different! And besides it wasn't in a church. It was at the VFW!" the old warrior shouted.

"What's the difference? Pencilschwietzer preached in there. Same difference. The Good Book says if two or more of you are gathered in his name it's church," Davy roared back.

"Fine, I'll go and sit in the truck if it makes you feel better! And I'll find a truck to sit in over in Finland too! It's none of your business why I will or won't go to church!" John said as he stormed out the door, knuckles white, his locust walking cane gripped tight in his hand. "I'm going for a walk!"

"Grampap, you need to think about going in the church and looking for life instead of focusing on the dead in the graveyards outside!"

"Yes, and you need to pull your head out of your ass and get out and see some young ladies before you die of CSR!" the old man shouted.

"What is CSR?"

"Chronic sperm retention!" John shot back over his shoulder as he stormed out the door, his walking stick clanging on the metal storm door. "If you don't quit bulling over Miss Spilt Milk Lizzy and find yourself a new girlfriend that stuff is gonna back up on you and kill you."

When John got home from his walk an hour later Davy was gone in the pickup. After watching four innings of a lopsided Braves baseball game on TBS John turned out the lights in the living room, flipped on the pole light in the yard, and peeked out the door window at the empty driveway.

In the early morning hours John woke up sweating and shaking. He'd been having the gut-wrenching old nightmare again about the German sniper. In his dream, the trapped man stretched his fingers to reach his pistol, knew he was doomed, turned, and looked up at John with a look of pure hate on his face. This time, though, John recognized the trapped man. It was Sheriff Mark Watson. In his dream, as he had in real life with the sniper, John picked up the gun, aimed it carefully at the white ear, and pulled the trigger anyway. A feeling of panic woke him up panting and heaving, the sheets soaked with cold sweat. He had to pee. He went to the bathroom and then looked out the front window and was relieved to see the pickup parked under the pole light. It took two hours of reading Mark Twain until he was able to calm down and fall back into a fitful sleep.

Sunday morning broke bright and clear. John was drinking a cup of coffee on the porch steps when Davy came out yawning and rubbing his eyes and sat down on the old metal glider. Neither of them said anything for a while until John broke the ice.

"What time did you get in?"

"Around one o'clock or so. I went to the bowling alley and ran into the Trumbo boys. We went over to Skunktown and they raced their old Dodge Challenger in the quarter against some boy from Lovingston who had a '65 Chevy Malibu with a hopped up 327 in it," Davy answered. "Lost their butts too. That boy's Chevy is the real deal. He's put a lot of money in it and has it set up right. That thing smoked the famous Trumbo Dodge good! Tim and Tom were some kind of mad all the way home."

"Did Tom get his deer head back from the taxidermist yet?" John inquired.

"No, not yet. Old man Bowers said it would be July or August before he had it done," Davy said with another yawn. "You going along with me to church this morning?"

"I'll go and sit in the truck as long as I don't have to go inside and sit through Pencilschwietzer's bullshit sermon," John answered softly.

"Well, you best get ready. We need to be getting gone."

The great country music poet and songwriter Tom T. Hall wrote in a simple but beautiful song entitled "I Love" that one of the things he loves best in this world is "Sunday school in May and hay." It was just such a wonderful late spring morning with bees buzzing around irises and dandelions and the earthen smells of springtime and cow manure in the air. A dairy farmer who owned the twenty-acre field adjacent to the church had mowed the orchard grass and clover hay on Friday. It had dried well on Saturday and would certainly be baled on Monday afternoon if no showers sprung up. The damp, sweet, musty smell of the hay mingled with the pungent sensual odor of the blooming Chinese chestnut trees lining the west border of the churchyard.

Davy pulled the truck up to the shady side of the old brick spiritual fortress and rolled the windows down for John. Cool air moved off the side of the red brick building and caressed the sun-bleached hair on John's forearm as he leaned back in the reclining seat of the big Dodge. A man and a woman in their late thirties with two little identical twin girls dressed in matching white dresses and wearing pink and white cowgirl boots walked past them. With big smiles they said, "Good morning," in sing-song voices. The lady was wearing heels and large gold looped earrings. She was carrying a maroon Bible with a gold bookmark in it. She smiled and gave him an adoring look as her husband held the door open for them.

"Sure you won't go in with me, Grampap?" Davy tried.

"No, son. I'll do my praying out here. You go on," John answered quietly with a gesture of his hand. "Me and God will have us a talk right out here."

Davy closed his truck door and went in the church. John leaned back in his seat and realized the windows in the chapel were open. He could hear people stirring around and talking in there. Suddenly, organ music swelled out of the windows and floated across the newly mown hay. A dairy farmer over in the next field was walking with a big German shepherd dog toward a Holstein cow with a newborn calf beside her. John recognized him as one of the Stein boys. They were Seventh Day Adventists and would have gone to church in New Market on Saturday. The organist was playing a song John had heard before but couldn't think of the name. They'd sung it in the church on the mountain when he was a boy. He remembered standing barefoot beside his stoic father in the old house near Sand Springs that had served as a general store, a U.S. Post Office, a residence, and a church on Sunday. He could remember his mother singing loud and his father not singing at all.

The organist here was very good. When she finished, Pencilschwietzer's voice boomed out a welcome and the congregation responded back. John guessed there must be a hundred and fifty people in there from the way it sounded and the number of vehicles in the parking lot. A new Chevrolet Blazer pulled in under the trees behind the truck and the Commonwealth's Attorney, Mr. Grimes, hustled out of the driver's seat and slipped in the back door late. John heard Pencilschwietzer announce the first song as Hymn number 137. John heard a rustling of hymnals and people standing as the organist played the introduction. They certainly have some good singers in there, he thought as the words broke over the organs droning.

Pass me not, oh Gentle Savior,
Hear my humble cry.
While on others Thou art calling.
Do not pass me by.

John loved to hear the singing so he leaned his head back against the headrest and shut his eyes listening. Despite himself he was humming along. By the third verse he had the chorus down and sang softly along with them.

"Pass me not, Oh Gentle Savior," he whispered to himself. That would be nice. Not being passed over for heaven. He tried hard not to, but a tear formed in the corner of his left eye.

After the song was over Pencilschwietzer welcomed everyone again and talked for a while about the church schedule for the coming week. The major concern was the upcoming summer Bible school for the children. Then he asked if anyone had any prayer requests. There were various requests for people who were having cancer treatments and one lady suggested they pray for the soul and the family of the slain Sheriff. One old woman who asked for prayers went on for several minutes expounding on what John thought was open bragging about all the terrible maladies and afflictions her family was suffering. Finally Pencilschwietzer broke into a prayer. John thought he would never finish. He even prayed for his neighbor's cat that had been hit by a car. Next came the offering and John was wondering how much Davy was going to drop in the plate. Looking across the mowed hay, the farmer in the field and the German shepherd had the cow and calf up to the barn. Pencilschwietzer prayed over the money and gave thanks for it and everybody sang "Praise God from Whom All Blessings Flow."

Pencilschwietzer asked everybody to turn their Bibles to Matthew 18 verses 21 and 22, a passage where the disciples asked Jesus how many times they were supposed to forgive someone. Peter asked Jesus if they were supposed to forgive their Brother seven times and Jesus said it should be seventy times seven. Pencilschwietzer announced he would be talking on "seeking God's forgiveness" and he started with a question.

"What are we, every one of us? The answer is nothing more than wretched sinners one and all. Many of us feel like our lives are failures, a seemingly never ending succession of mistakes and shortcomings to show for our days. Some of us in here are eating ourselves up inside with regrets and guilt that is in effect ruining our lives. We have all fallen short of the glory of God. Jesus says to forgive your neighbor seventy times seven. Let's see. That works out to 490 times. Wow! The neighbor's dog likes to pull my trash out all over my yard. Does this mean I have to ignore it 476 times yet?"

The congregation laughed.

"If God wants us to be forgiving with one another over and over, how forgiving does he want us to be with ourselves? I once counseled with a man we will call Stan who was lying on his death bed dying of cancer. This was years ago in another place far from here. He told me he had something in his heart cutting away at his insides for over thirty years, effectively ruining the latter part of his life. When he was a much younger man he had driven to a poker game one night with some of his friends and consumed a large amount of whiskey to the point where he was drunk. He hadn't gone there with the intention of getting drunk but he did. One of his pals had a bottle of white lightning and you know the devil was laughing and celebrating with every sip Stan took!

"When Stan went to leave, one of his concerned friends took his keys away from him to prevent him from driving and offered to take him home. Stan laughed at them and pulled another key from his wallet. Laughing and cursing, living the "high life," he sped down the road in his sports car. He ran through a yield sign he didn't even see and hit a young couple head on who was on the way to the hospital to deliver their first son. The entire young family died in the wreck but Stan lived with nothing more than a broken leg.

"He was then rightfully convicted of manslaughter by the courts and then spent eighteen months in jail. Years later, as he lay in his bed dying, he was consumed with the guilt and misery associated with the frivolous actions and decisions he had made on one night thirty years previous. I thought to myself as I sat beside him in the last hours of his life, "What would Jesus tell this man if he were here with him?"

"For a long time I could only sit and hold Stan's hand. I prayed for Jesus to guide my tongue and heart to be able to say the right thing to this man who was lying there in tremendous physical pain and—worse, much worse—spiritual agony. I asked God to assist me in helping this tortured man to attain the forgiveness of Christ Jesus and the Grace of the Holy Spirit. All that would come to my mind was to tell him over and over, Jesus loves you, Stan. Trust Jesus. Jesus loves you, man! Trust him, Stan. Trust Jesus!"

"Stan died right there with me holding his hand. For years I struggled with my own feelings of guilt and inadequacy for not being able to do right by this tormented lonely man, not being able to tell him what I felt like I wanted to and thought I needed to. I knew I had failed Stan and worse yet I had failed God as a minister of his faith. What I didn't do was trust Jesus myself. I researched all of the scriptures related remotely to forgiveness in a feeble attempt to prepare myself for such an occasion in the future. When I had done so I realized that what I had told Stan was what Jesus wanted me to. He had answered my prayers. I came to the realization that the essence of being able to accept God's forgiveness is knowing that Jesus knows you! He knows your failure but he still loves you. He loves you!"

"When all else is said and done in this world, if you can just know that Jesus loves you what else matters? What else matters? If he loves you then you must be forgiven! He says, 'If I am for you who can be against you?' You *are* forgiven! He bought your forgiveness with his blood on the cross. He purchased your forgiveness with his pain and suffering. What does the number one message of the New Testament say?"

"'For God so loved the world that he gave his only begotten son....'"

"In the faith world of our Catholic brothers you can go into a confession booth and tell the priest your troubles and be forgiven right there on the spot. Or so they believe. In our Protestant world we're much more stiff and secretive. We've evolved a sense that *real men* bear their sorrows alone. You don't let others, even your pastor, know that something is bothering you. Until you're on your death bed like Stan was. We aspire to be our *own men and our own women,* private and indifferent. Great American islands of misery. Our society expects our men to be like a John Wayne or Clint Eastwood, standing alone, tough, remote. It's not "cool" to come forward and confess our weaknesses and ask for His divine grace and the forgiveness that only He can grant. We simply need to Trust JESUS!"

Pencilschwietzer went on for a while with his sermon and John sat in the truck listening. He felt like his soul was going to explode. Suddenly he got out of the truck and walked to the back door of the church. Stepping into the musty smelling coolness of the church basement, he went up the steps and entered the back lobby of the sanctuary. The ushers gazed at him with looks somewhere between questioning and surprise. One of them even looked alarmed and tentatively walked toward him.

John swallowed hard, nodded to them, and began walking up the aisle toward the pulpit, his stride long and his shoulders pulled back his huge feet booming against the tile floor and his cane tapping along. All eyes turned to him as if he were a bride walking down the aisle and Pencilschwietzer stared at him and stopping his oration in mid-sentence. Heads kept turning aisle by aisle to look up in alarmed surprise at the old grizzled giant striding toward the front of the church. Davy took one glance at his Grandfather and reflexively bent forward and put his face in his hands, suddenly embarrassed; shocked beyond belief.

When John got to the steps in front of the altar he stopped and nervously looked around. It was one of those moments described by the people who witnessed it saying, "You could have heard a pin drop!" The mooing of a cow wafted through the window.

Pencilschwietzer broke the silence and said, "Do you have something to say, Mr. Dean?"

John twisted his hands around the handle of his cane with his head leaned back addressing the image of Jesus in the stained glass behind the pulpit he blurted out, "I need forgiveness. My God, I need your forgiveness. I don't want to be like that there Stan fellow this preacher just spoke about! I've done so many terrible things in this messed up world. And I want to see my Fern. I know she is in heaven and I have so much to make up to her."

Pencilschwietzer came down from the pulpit and took the old giant by the hands. The Pastor nodded to the organist who began playing and the congregation joined in singing, "What a Friend We Have in Jesus." John wept. His massive shoulders bent from war and a life of toil over stone and mortar shook in spastic grief, relief, and submission. Davy sat on the pew with his head down. Connie Pencilschwietzer sitting next to him took him by the hand and squeezed it. Then she put her arm around him and patted him on the shoulder. Davy never felt so confused in his entire life.

The Sunday mornings of the following weeks found the old man getting ready for church early in the morning. He got Davy to show him how to knot his tie properly, something Fern had done for him on the few occasions he had put on a suit over the years. He took his reading glasses to church with him so he could read the words to the hymns that he didn't know and follow along in the Bible when the preacher quoted scriptures. The little children liked to listen to him sing in his twangy way, reminiscent of his mountain heritage.

John made a resolution to read the Bible from front to back and his Mark Twain books got dusty lying by his bed unread. John couldn't believe how relieved he felt and how much better the world looked as he continued to take his long walks. Davy was simply amazed. What in the world would his crazy grandfather do next?

# Chapter 42

July 27th finally rolled around and Davy was apprehensive to say the least. He had fastened his seatbelt and was sitting snug in the aisle seat of an Iceland Air jet. Connie Pencilschwietzer was next to him in the middle seat with Pastor Bob at the window. Davy was actually feeling a little drowsy from the Dramamine tablets Connie had given him an hour earlier in the airport, even though his heart was beating fast and tiny rivulets of perspiration were gathering under his arms. Pastor Bob had taken some too and Davy noticed it hadn't taken long for the usually exuberant chatterbox of a man to act like all the life had drained out of him. John declined the drugs and said he was fine and ready to go. Neither flying or sailing ever bothered him he claimed.

John was flying first-class in the more spacious section up ahead of them. He was just too large for the regular seats and Connie had talked him into spending the extra money, convincing him it would be worth every penny. She was worried about blood-clot problems if John was cramped up too long in the coach seats and the fact of the matter was that the old giant wouldn't fit in them. When John had ducked down entering the airplane and saw how tight the regular fare seats were, he was glad he had listened to the preacher's wife and spent the extra money, even though he had done so after considerable grumbling. Pencilschwietzer had reclined his seat and appeared to be ready to take a nap.

Davy thought the one stewardess in first class was the prettiest girl he had ever seen. She had to be over six feet tall with blonde hair and the most sparkling blue eyes he had ever seen. She made eye contact with him and smiled, melting his heart in a way he had not felt for some time. He tried to read her nametag when she slid past him inadvertently rubbing his elbow with her thigh. Her name was Dagbjort and Davy wondered if that was her first name or her last one. The other busy stewardesses had similar names with lots of J's, B's and T's. Connie noticed Davy looking the girls over and said, "They must have had quite a time in kindergarten learning to spell their names, don't you think?"

Davy chuckled and was a little embarrassed he had been so obvious in his ogling that Connie would notice. They were flying out of New York with a scheduled stopover in Iceland where they would switch planes and then fly on to Helsinki. Having never flown before, with the exception of flying down the back roads of West Virginia in the back seat of the Trumbo boys' Dodge, Davy was nervous. They were departing New York and its oppressive temperature of 101 degrees Fahrenheit at 8 P.M. scheduled to land in Reykjavik at 1:30 A.M. Eastern Daylight Time.

Connie had taken care of getting their passports and plane tickets purchased. She had helped them decide what kind of clothing they would need to pack and had all the arrangements for their stay worked out. Since John had joined the church he had been like a different person. He truly was a changed man and Davy marveled at the way the old man seemed to have had a tremendous weight lifted from him. He smiled a lot now and didn't even cuss anymore or make crude comments about women. Davy noticed John turn his head to watch as Dagbjort walked by him. Hard for an old dog to break all of his bad habits! She was a looker, that was for sure, and had all the working parts accentuated in her stewardess uniform. Pastor Bob had put on a set of earphones he took out of the little seat pouch in front of him and was resuming his sleepy pose, leaning way back in his seat.

A voice came over the speaker system and the stewardesses showed everybody how to put on their seatbelts and what to do in case of an emergency. Davy double checked his lap belt and was surprised when the plane jolted a little and suddenly they were under way. As they accelerated down the runway and the engines roared to life he felt the nose of the plane go up and then they were up in the air, climbing. Davy broke out in a cold sweat. Connie reached over and squeezed his hand. "We'll level out soon, Davy, and it won't be so bad. Just relax and take deep breaths, honey."

They were soon leveled out and cruising at 32,000 feet and the stewardesses were hustling around like busy bees. All the seats were full and Davy felt much better. They were getting a big stainless steel food cart moving down the aisle and were serving drinks. Connie and Davy both had Cokes and Pastor Bob started snoring until Connie elbowed him in the ribs and he rolled on his side toward the window. An hour later they served a fish dinner that Davy thought was very good. As the plane sped over Newfoundland and the North Atlantic they watched a movie called *Dances with Wolves* that Davy thought was one of the best movies he had ever seen. When the movie went off, Connie dozed and Davy felt sleepy until he had visions of crashing into the icy waters. To relieve his anxiety he forced himself to imagine floating on a raft with Dagbjort. It wasn't long until he slipped off into a light sleep.

It seemed like he had only been napping for a few minutes when Connie patted him on the arm and told him he should get his seatbelt on. "Wake up, Sleepyhead. We're landing in Iceland and time to switch planes." Pastor Bob was hooking his belt up. Davy looked at his watch and it was 1:04 A.M. The sky outside the window of the airplane looked like twilight. The plane made a smooth landing on the runway and Davy could see out the window a landscape that looked like a gloomy, rocky desert. The landing was so smooth the passengers applauded as the plane taxied up to the terminal. They exited the plane into an airport that looked like a modern bus terminal. Passengers were looking for their connecting flights. It was clean and orderly. John came lumbering over to them smiling. Connie herded the group through customs where a very fit-looking middle aged blond man scanned over their passports, carefully stamping the back pages of each. Connie led them through the building and found the gate they would be departing from in twenty minutes. John went to the bathroom and Pastor Bob went to a duty-free liquor store to check the prices of his favorite scotch.

"He sure likes that scotch liquor, doesn't he?" Davy said to Connie.

"Yes, he does. But he never abuses it and I don't fault him," she responded casually. "Everybody needs a little spice in their lives sometimes. You don't have to be a saint to be a Christian. Besides it is part of the Finnish culture. Finns love their alcohol and coffee for sure."

"I didn't think Pastor Bob was a Finn," Davy said.

"He isn't but he would have made a good one!" she answered with a laugh.

They lugged their carry-on bags with them to some empty seats in the hallway next to a line that was forming for the Helsinki flight. John and Pastor Bob soon joined them and they didn't have to wait long. When the door was opened and the flight announced they exited the building and had to walk about one hundred yards to the loading stairs of their next flight. It was a cool and brisk fifty-two degrees Fahrenheit. John remarked how nice it felt.

"They ought to drag some of this air down to New York when they go back. Bet they could sell a lot of it down there!" John exclaimed.

It took only a few minutes to get settled on the plane and stow their bags in the compartments above the seats. Connie asked a stewardess for a blanket, saying she was cold and promptly snuggled up with a soft blue cotton blanket over her. Pastor Bob popped another Dramamine and rolled over toward his window yawning mightily. Davy looked around and noticed with no little dissapointment that Dagbjort was not on board. Reading his mind Connie chuckled and said, "You certainly didn't think she was going to go along to Finland with you, now did you Davy?"

He could feel his face getting red as he said, "Well, I am a single man in a foreign land, Mrs. Pencilschwietzer."

"Yes, and a very handsome and beautiful young man you are and don't you forget it, Master Davy Dean. Don't worry," she said with a twinkle in her eye. "There will be a lot of fine-looking Suomi girls for you to meet in the next few days to keep your blood rising. Suomi is what we Finns call ourselves. We couldn't stand losing you to an Icelandic girl, now could we?"

Davy was totally unaccustomed to talking to a woman in this manner. The only woman, with the exception of Lizzy, he had ever been around casually for any period of time was his grandmother, Fern, and the only girl he had ever really dated was Lizzy. Gramma had been so conservative and old-fashioned she would never pick and tease about things of this nature. It was confusing and in no little way exhilarating to him. "Well, you don't have to worry on this flight. All the stewardesses are older gals," he blurted.

"Older like me?" Connie said batting her long eyelashes and looking him directly in the eyes.

"No! Not like you at all!" he stammered, falling directly into her trap.

"Older, but not as old as me?" she grilled him.

"Not nearly as young or pretty as you, Ms. Connie," he mumbled.

"I think you had better take a nap before you trip over your tongue, young man!" she said with a laugh.

Connie leaned her head over on Pastor Bob's shoulder and snuggled up to him. After a few minutes Davy glanced at her and she had her eyes closed and her lips were parted. He could smell her perfume and the musky sweet smell of her breath. Davy leaned back in his seat and tried to go to sleep. He was getting tired. A stewardess came through the curtains separating the first class section from the economy seats. John was lying back and sprawled out like a 300-pound sack of mill feed. He had taken his shoes off and stretched a sock-covered foot out in the aisle. Davy smiled when he thought how much his grandfather's foot resembled the discarded seat of a four-wheeler. As he rested with his eyes closed he wondered what Lizzy would think when she found out he was in Europe. Perhaps the Morris boy wouldn't seem so exotic and daring to her even if she was probably naked and asleep with him at that very moment. Sleeping in her favorite position with her leg thrown over Morris.

"Forget her!" Davy thought. "She ain't no Dagbjort! I reckon I been like the fly in the vinegar jug Gramma Fern always talked about. The fly who thought the vinegar jug was the sweetest place on earth only because it was the only place he had ever been. Well, this fly is going to buzz a little!" Davy thought as he dozed off.

Vaguely conscious, at first, of Connie Pencilschwietzer's hand falling on his thigh, Davy got up and went to the bathroom in the back and washed his face. Returning to his seat Connie was curled up with her arms around Pastor Bob, both of them snoring softly. Davy eased into his seat, looked at his watch, finding it was three in the morning at home. No wonder he was so sleepy. He fell asleep and dreamed about the baby Hereford calves his tenant Mr. Mongold had on the mountain pasture that he could always go home to.

Connie was shaking him gently and he felt like he was coming out of a coal mine. Passengers were getting their seatbelts back on and the pilot said over the intercom they would land in roughly ten minutes at Helsinki International Airport where the temperature was twenty-two degrees Celsius and the wind was gentle out of the south. The local time was 11:04 A. M. under partly cloudy skies. The landing was rougher than the one in Iceland and they bounced hard a couple of times.

Taxiing up to the unloading ramp everyone began the usual dragging of their belongings out of the overhead compartments. Then they were off the plane and going through customs again. Connie let out a laugh and yelled, "There's Aunt Terttu and Uncle Heikki!" She went running to an elderly couple who were smiling and waving. Aunt Terttu was a tall handsome lady with a serious look to her. Heikki was talking in Finnish a mile a minute and shaking hands with everyone. He was shorter than his wife and squarely built with a firm jaw, piercing blue eyes, and silver hair combed straight back.

"Very handsome people," Davy said to John. When they shook hands, Davy knew immediately this man had worked hard in his life and had been prosperous.

"Welcome to Finland!" he said.

Terttu smiled and hugged Connie. "Let's get your luggage and go to the car." Terttu looked up at John and said to Connie in Finnish, "Big American Yankee. Looks like a hell raiser. I don't think we have a bed big enough for that one."

"Gentle as a lamb, Auntie!" Connie replied. "Gentle as a lamb, unless you are at war with the Yanks, and then, I understand, he would make a good Finnish soldier. Stories I have heard say he wiped out a couple hundred Germans in the war and then a bunch of North Koreans too, just for good measure."

# Chapter 43

They were northbound in two cars headed up Route 2 from Helsinki toward Forrsa. Davy was riding in the front seat next to Terttu who was driving her Volvo. Pastor Bob and Connie were in the back seat. Heikki was driving John in his Mercedes wagon and hauling the luggage. John had the seat reclined and was enjoying the scenery. All the travelers except Pencilschwietzer and John were suffering from jet lag and very tired. Pastor Bob's Dramamine that had enabled him to sleep nearly the entire flight had worn off and he resumed his usual chatterbox ways. Davy was having a hard time keeping his eyes open.

The highway was a well-maintained four-lane road, much like good old Interstate 64 that ran through Cambridge County. The first thing he noticed were the graceful white birch and fir trees growing along the highway. There was a high chain-link fence along the sides of the road that he asked Terttu about. Pastor Bob interrupted and explained the fence was designed to keep Mr. Moose off the highway.

"It's not like hitting a one-hundred-pound whitetail deer!" the pastor said. "Running into a 1,100-pound moose going seventy miles per hour makes an awful mess."

Davy glanced at Terttu who just smiled and said, "Yes, Heikki likes to hunt the moose. He gets one every year when they migrate through our old farm. The meat is very good! Almost as good as reindeer."

Despite his interest, Davy fell asleep and woke up an hour and a half later as they were driving down a two-lane highway that ran adjacent to beautiful mile-long field of short grain interspersed with small creeks and dark evergreen woods. Picturesque farmhouses and barns dotted the vista. Connie exclaimed, "Oh, look! There are some Finnish land race horses!"

"I didn't know you knew your horses so well, Connie," Terttu stated in her beautifully heavy-accented English.

Soon they made a left and drove a short ways until they came into a little town. There wasn't much there other than a convenience store, a bank, and a few shops. "Welcome to Humppila, Davy!" Pastor Bob exclaimed. "Take the courthouse and the jail out of Cambridge and it wouldn't be much larger."

Terttu smiled and turned left. There was a little lake on the right with a pier sporting a diving board and a long dock on the other side. Children were jumping and diving into the dark blue water.

"I didn't think you all would go swimming this far north," Davy drawled.

"Is good to jump in the water after sauna all year round," Terttu answered. "Cut hole in ice and jump in even in winter. You like sauna?" she asked.

"Never been in one, ma'am, and ain't sure I want to either," he replied. "It gets hot enough for me laying stone in Virginia in July and August to suit me."

"Oh, you must go to sauna to know about Finland!" she exclaimed. "Heikki wants to take you to visit his smoke sauna at his cabin."

"I reckon I could try it then if it's something that's important," Davy offered.

"Oh, it's important all right, Davy!" Connie laughed. "We Scandinavians all get naked and crawl into a steamy place together and then jump in cold water. Our ancestors invented it in the old days as a way to combat the boredom of being crowded inside small airtight cabins in the dark snow and ice all winter!"

Davy turned around and looked at her inquisitively. Pastor Bob spoke up and said, "Yes, you heard her right. Everybody does it like that, naked and all, and nothing is thought of it."

Terttu made a left down a street lined with very nice, well-maintained houses. Pulling into the driveway of one of the homes on the right she said, "We are home. You are welcome!"

Heikki and John soon pulled in behind them and they got out of the car laughing and joking like they had known each other all their lives. After unloading their suitcases and bags, the Dean boys were shown to a small cabin behind the house that served as a guesthouse. There was a couch that doubled as a bed on the first floor and a loft with mattresses on the floor. Davy took the loft and John claimed the downstairs bed. Connie soon came knocking on the door and made sure they had everything worked out and gave them orders to come to supper. Terttu was expecting them to be hungry. John assured her he wouldn't let them down.

"Grampap, don't you go embarrassing me eating like a hog the first evening we are here!" Davy ordered.

"Loosen up, young pup! We're half way around the world and on a stone mason's holiday. You tend to your plate and I'll tend to mine," John said jokingly to his grandson.

Terttu served a meatloaf made of rainbow trout and pikeperch along with boiled potatoes and some steamed kale. John and Davy both were suspicious of the fish meatloaf at first until they tasted it. Then they couldn't get enough. It was John who finally asked Davy if he should have been the one who warned his grandson about being a pig at the table instead of vice versa. The meal was topped off with a dessert of a flat rhubarb and strawberry pie. Davy ate one piece and liked it fine but John went wild over it and ate three pieces. Terttu smiled and kept piling it on. After dinner Connie and Pastor Bob excused themselves and said they were going to bed.

"It's still afternoon, isn't it?" John said looking at his watch.

"It is ten thirty at night," Pastor Bob answered looking at his watch. "It won't get dark here until around midnight."

Davy and John bade everyone a good night and walked the path out the back door to their little cabin. "I don't know if I can sleep with this much daylight left," Davy commented, but he was soon falling asleep in the loft as he listened to the rhythmic breathing of his grandfather downstairs.

About one thirty he woke up when John rolled over on his back and began snoring like a lion with a bone stuck in his throat. Davy climbed down out of the loft and went outside. It was dark but a different kind of dark than he had ever known at home in western Virginia. The stars looked different too but he couldn't say why. Finally locating the North Star, he marveled that it was almost overhead. Connie and Terttu were sitting on the screened porch talking in Finnish. Davy listened to the melodic language for a while and urinated behind an apple tree. Before he climbed back into the loft he gouged John in the ribs until he snorted twice, rolled over, and quit his snoring.

Lying down in his bed he prayed for a while asking God to protect them on their travels. Davy gave thanks that his grandfather had overcome his problems with going to church and had been saved. John had gone all the way after his first trip to the altar. Pencilschwietzer had baptized the old man in front of a crowd of people among whom you could scarcely find a dry eye when John had looked up with baptismal water dripping off his forehead and said with his arms raised, looking up at the sky, "Thank you, Jesus! Thank you, God! Now I can be with you, Fern, when I come on down the road after you! It won't be long now."

He sure must have been carrying a big load, Davy thought. Worrying about not making it to Heaven with her must have been killing him. It was simply a miracle to the young man that his gruff old grandfather had come to the cross and found salvation. Davy's own faith was very deep but also very private. He disdained the TV evangelists and their constant begging for money. "What a disgrace they are!" he would say to himself. "I wish they could all be like Billy Graham! Now there is the real deal." Pencilschwietzer seemed sincere enough and he was friendly too. Davy had attended church with his grandmother Fern before she passed away and it was a special relationship they had shared. Lizzy had gone with him occasionally when the mood hit her, but for the last couple of years, before she left him, they seldom went and she opted instead to sleep in on Sunday mornings.

"Here I am clear around on the other side of the world with this crazy old man who is the only family I reckon I have," he thought. "Maybe tomorrow we can find this Kauko fellow's grave and let him pay his respects. He is a weird old man, but I sure do love the old rascal."

With the mountain land John and Fern had given him and now all this money he stood to inherit, Davy Dean was a fairly well-to-do young man. It made him nervous to think about what he was going to do if John lived a long time. Thoughts like that brought on confusing feelings of guilt. The last thing he wanted was for his grandfather to die but he couldn't imagine having to care for him in a way some of the folks in the Brethren Home needed. He had no idea how he was going to take care of his grandfather if John had a stroke or became bed ridden. Or worse yet, went clear crazy, which he had done before. It was obvious the old man expected him to take care of him until the end and that's what he had agreed to do. Davy had lately been having many anxious moments thinking about the probabilities of what was going to occur in the future in respect to the agreement he had made with the old giant. Somehow every time he had tried to talk to

John about it, John had acted like Davy shouldn't worry. He would just say over and over, "It will work itself out, son. Don't worry about it. I won't be around to be a ball and chain around your legs." Thinking about it made Davy shiver a little.

John began snoring again and Davy put his pillow over his head and went back to sleep as daylight started breaking around two thirty. He could still hear the women talking quietly from the porch.

The next morning at eight Connie knocked on the door of their cabin, yelling it was time for breakfast. After eating bacon and eggs John asked Terttu if she had any of that fish meatloaf left over. She set the remains of the serving dish on the table. John asked for mayonnaise and spooned half a quart-sized jar on top of the fish and commenced to clean the bowl out. Terttu and Heikki looked at him in astonishment as he took a piece of bread and sopped out the remains. Heikki let out a little whistle and said, "Perkele!"

Heikki took John and Davy around the yard to show them all the plants and shrubs. There was a bush that had grape-sized berries on it. John thought they were gooseberries. Heikki didn't know what they were called in English but in Finnish they are called *karviaismarja*. He had a little garden with beautiful potatoes and peas growing. On the south side of a small barn he had planted several stalks of sweet corn right up against the wall in the sun. Heikki explained that corn did not grow well this far north but peas and the like did very well. John told him he should come see the corn growing in Virginia. "You come over some time in the middle to end of summer and we will have a big roasting ear party. You happen to catch a good rain when the ears are coming on in the milk and you can stand in the garden and almost hear them growing! That's one of my favorite times of the year," John said.

"Yeah, Grampap, most people don't eat the cob too, like you do sometimes," Davy added.

"That's where a lot of the flavor is, boy! And besides, I don't eat them. I just suck the juice out of them."

Heikki looked a little confused, not exactly understanding what they had just talked about.

"Let's get in the cars and go to the church," Connie called from the porch.

They loaded up in the two cars and headed through the central intersection of the hamlet to the Lutheran church on the western border of Humppila. John was sitting in the front seat of Heikki's Mercedes and he couldn't help wishing Fern was along. A short way farther the church appeared on the left. John noticed the graveyard was on both sides of the road and they pulled into a parking lot adjacent to the large stone church on the left. Heikki led the way toward the front of the church through rows of small neat tombstones all alike and very neat.

"This is the cemetery for our men who died in the era of World War II," Heikki explained. "Most of them died in the terrible fight most historians refer to as the Winter War of 1939. Stalin had long coveted our land and resources. He thought he would have an easy time taking us. He was wrong. Our valiant men met them in a line between Lake Ladoga on the east and the Gulf of Finland on the west. Our men were outnumbered four to one but we have a belief that is very true. We believe that one Finnish soldier is worth ten Russians. We spit on the Russians. The worst thing that ever happened is that your President Reagan helped them out of their cage. All these fine men lying here died in the war. Two of Terttu's brothers are here." Heikki showed John and Davy the graves of Terttu's family and then led them down to a stone closer to the church. "Here lies your Kauko Tuomola. See. He has a plaque showing he was awarded the Mannerheim Award for bravery. They say he took out seven Russian tanks himself."

Davy looked at his grandfather's face and saw his cold blue eyes taking in every detail. John said nothing and stood with his hat in his hand, staring at the stone. Finally, Davy asked, "Did you lose anyone in that war, sir?"

"Yes, three uncles and two older brothers. I was only eight years old. My home was in a little town just north of the battle lines. I could hear the cannon and the fighting. The Russians finally broke through in 1940 as the whole world watched. At the battle of Suomussalmi we lost 900 men but we eliminated 30,000 of the Slav horde. Ironically, the Russians' poor performance against us was one of the reasons Hitler decided to attack them when he launched his Operation Barbarossa. Many historians blame the purge Stalin had made against his military officers in the years prior to 1939 for their performance against us. Others say it was because their soldiers were poorly equipped and depressed from living under the lunacy of Bolshevism. Stalin found out a lesson that Hitler was to learn later at Leningrad. The same thing your American forces found out in the Battle of the Bulge when they had to fight in what we would consider as mild winter conditions. It is not fun to fight in our winters. Kauko Tuomola distinguished himself as one of the fiercest soldiers of the time but he did nothing that many others did not also do!"

"Well, did them Russians take over your whole country?" Davy asked.

"No. If they had you would not see the prosperity you see here! They never did defeat us militarily. We forced them to make a treaty with us! We had to give them the land around Lake Ladoga and the Karelian Isthmus. When the Russians took over, my family, along with any others that wished to evacuate to Finland, were allowed to move out of the ceded territory. The Finnish farmers and landowners were required to give the refugees parts of their land to make farms for themselves. That is how I came to meet my beautiful Terttu. Part of her father's farm was given to my family to work."

John looked up at the church and said, "I was in England before we went to Normandy. We were just a bunch of young kids, really. We were scared to death about what we were fixing to do but we knew we were all there to kick Hitler's ass for him. At least I was. Some British guy traded me some old magazines for a bottle of beer and I read an article about the Winter Wars in which they praised this man lying here. They talked about how brave and fierce he was. I decided I would do my best to do the same. I wish I still had that article. It may sound silly after all these years since those terrible days that I can remember reading how Kauko was so cool under fire and could think when under attack and used cover so well. Courage ain't nothing but an idea. The ability to think under extreme pressure, along with God's grace, of course, are all that saved me. Bullets whizzed by my head so many times I don't know why they didn't find me. There have been sad and confusing times in my life when I wished they had. I'm glad now they didn't and I understand it was God's will. This brave man from this beautiful town gave me something precious that I'm convinced helped me do my duty and survive. He gave me an example. If you'll leave me be for a while I would like to spend a few minutes alone here. Would you all mind?" John asked. "I know. I am a crazy old man but I've come a long way in my travels."

The group left John and headed around to the west side of the church where Connie wanted to visit the graves of her grandparents.

When they were out of sight around the church John knelt down by the grave. He reached into his watch pocket and pulled out a match box. He carefully slid it open and pulled out a small white flint Indian arrowhead wrapped in cotton. "Kauko, I want to leave something here for you as a gift. It's precious to me and I think you'll understand. This arrowhead was passed down to me from my grandfather from several generations ago. They called him Kill Buck. He was a Shawnee Indian who was a great warrior too. He lost his land to my other ancestors but he fought like the wild man he was. I got a lot of him in me, I reckon. You died protecting your family and you'd understand that. I am grateful for your actions in combat and salute you as a great warrior. I don't know if the stories I read about you were true but I tend to believe they were. I'm going to leave you something I hope you'll like."

John took the small flint point and pushed it into the dirt next to the headstone, down far enough it wouldn't be noticed. Then he smoothed out the soil and grass so the mark he had made would go unseen. Standing up John bowed his head and said, "Dear Lord in heaven take care of this fine man's soul and thank you for the inspiration and courage he gave me." Walking away to join the others, John looked back and whispered, "I'll see you in heaven, Kauko. I'll introduce you to Fern when I get there if you ain't never met her yet. And if you have.... well, don't you charm her!"

The rest of the group was making their way back to the front of the church where they met the Lutheran pastor at the front door. He seemed happy to take them on a tour of the Humppila Lutheran Church and explained it had been rebuilt after a fire destroyed the original building shortly after the turn of the century. It was simply beautiful and John sat in one of the benches while the others walked around. Davy walked over to him and said, "Well, Grampap. You finally got to visit your hero's grave."

"Sure did, Davy. Sure did," the old man answered and Davy suddenly noticed how tired and gray the old warrior looked.

Heikki got things rolling again when he said, "Let's go home and take a nap. This evening we go to Forrsa to see a hockey game. My grandson Rami Jokinen is playing."

As John walked past Kauko's grave on the way out he saluted. Heikki noticed and thought, "Who can ever understand the crazy Americans? He seems like a good man, though, and he did storm the gates of hell in Normandy. Americans and Finns. A lot alike, yet vastly different. One just trying to survive in his homeland while the other thinks he must save the entire world by sticking his nose into everything. Of course, most Finns were angry the US didn't come to their aid in our hour of need! A lot of Finns would have liked them to send help in 1939! Hard to know what an American is exactly. I thought they were all black with kinky hair when I was a little boy, like Africans. I didn't know they were any different from

Africans and Indians. Eisenhower and Nixon looked half black too! And this Bill Clinton, what a rascal!" Heikki chuckled.

"Mrs. Terttu, you got any of that fish meatloaf left over?" John asked. "I could eat a big sandwich of that when we get back if you do."

"Don't you remember? You ate it all for breakfast," she answered.

An almost boyish sad look crossed his face that made her say in a consoling tone, "Don't worry, John, I will make you a whole pan of it if you like. That is, if I can get Heikki to go catch some fresh fish. All he ever catches is tough old pike."

That evening they drove the short drive to the ice rink in Forrsa. A large crowd had already gathered. The two teams were out on the ice gliding around in their pregame routines. Heikki pointed to the tallest player on the Forssa team and said, "That is my grandson, Rami!"

John and Davy listened closely as Pencilschwietzer provided an almost constant tutorial on the game rules and strategy. When there was a particularly violent collision immediately in front of them and Rami was driven into the glass John got excited, jumped up and yelled, "By jingos! Go after him, son!"

The hometown team won 3-1, scoring their third goal on an empty net. Davy saw more pretty girls than he thought existed in the entire world. On the way home John spotted several small animals in a field that caused him to exclaim, "What're those things? Some kind of kangaroos?"

"Those are the Finnish rabbits! We call them "pupu." Aren't they something?" Heikki responded.

"I bet those things go thirty pounds!" John speculated. "They're half as big as a lot of deer in Virginia. Old Floyd Hawk would have a ball with his beagles chasing those things. Heck! They're bigger than his beagle dogs! We'd need some of Dewayne Hensley's bear dogs to run those things."

Heikki laughed and told John how he made snares and traps for the rabbits as a boy. The sun was almost on the horizon as they pulled into the driveway. John looked at his watch and it was 10:44 P.M. He shook his head and realized there was no wonder he was as tired as he was. "These Finnish summer days are long ones," he said to Heikki.

"In a few months the nights will be just as long," the old farmer noted. "We need to get a good rest tonight. The festival in Tammela tomorrow should be entertaining for you."

# Chapter 44

The next morning they loaded up into the two cars and drove east about forty kilometers to the town of Tammela. Heikki explained they were going to a festival and witness a reenactment of an event that took place in 1632 when the Swedish King Gustav II, who ruled Finland at the time, conscripted nineteen young Finnish men and their horses to fight in his war against the Germans. These men eventually proved themselves to be the fiercest warriors in the entire Swedish army and distinguished themselves for their ferocity and fighting ability. They were eventually given the honor of fighting next to the King himself. The papists all over northern Europe prayed to God to protect their armies from the *Hakkapeliitta*. Translated literally, *Hakkapeliitta* means something similar to "hack on the head." It had been a sad day in the town of Tammela when the Swedish soldiers snatched up the heartiest young men and forced them into their army. Before taking them away, the Swedish commander had allowed the boys to attend a last church service at the same church standing in the town now.

As part of the reenactment the soldiers marched into town square in period costumes. Actresses and actors dressed in traditional Finnish outfits mixed in around the edges of the square. John and Davy were wide-eyed even though they couldn't understand a single word the crier was reading from his scroll. One old woman stepped out of the crowd and started yelling what had to be, from the tone of her voice and its inflection, insults at the Swedes. The soldier barked a sharp response back at her, eliciting a laugh from the crowd.

"What was that all about?" John asked and Connie Pencilschwietzer translated, "She was cursing the Swedes and the soldier told her, 'Shut up, you old hag!'"

The soldiers then came walking around in pairs, pulling healthy-looking young men out of the crowd. When they passed the group from Humppila Heikki was standing behind Davy and gave him a strong shove out into the path of the recruiters who promptly manhandled the surprised and embarrassed Virginian by his elbows and lined him up to march off with the rest of the conscripts. John and Heikki whooped and laughed as the soldiers marched Davy with the rest of their prisoner warriors off around the far side of the church.

"Don't worry, John!" Pastor Bob explained. "They're marching them about two kilometers away to the site of their camp. We'll catch up with them later. That's where the festival and all the food and exhibits are. We'll go in and attend the same service they held here 400 years ago."

They entered the church past several ladies in beautiful colorful Finnish traditional dresses who were handing out bulletins. The first thing John noticed when taking a seat on the hard wooden pew on the right hand side of the chapel was the simple beauty of the place. The lofty ceiling, a good twenty-five feet high, was covered with rows of boards of various widths end to end from back to front. It reminded John of stories his father had told him about helping to float logs down the Shenandoah to the saw mills in northern Virginia when he was a child. On the left side of the chapel was a raised pulpit where the pastor would speak. The organ music was impressive as was the singing in the melodic Finnish language. "Such a strong, beautiful people are these Finns!" John thought. "No wonder they're so tough on the battlefield."

"Oh, Fern. I wish you were here to see this," he caught himself whispering to the wind. Then he smiled and thought, "I'll be along soon."

The service stretched longer than John would have liked and he couldn't understand one word the Finnish Lutheran preacher was saying but he amused himself with looking at the stone construction of the building. In his mind he could see how they had laid off the foundations and raised the massive walls. What a chore that had to have been!

After the service was over and everyone filed out, the group from Humppila followed the crowd at a brisk pace. John was glad he had been walking so much at home and it made him feel good knowing he could keep up with the others with his ever present old locust cane tapping down the sidewalk beside him. The festival covered a whole hillside and there must have been close to one hundred booths set up: everything from jewelry stands to old-time blacksmiths who were making swords and lance tips. Eventually they found Davy at the soldiers' camp and he was having a good time with the re-enactors who were providing him with copious amounts of enlistment beer. Pictures were taken by Terttu and Connie as the soldiers gave Davy a certified parchment, written in Swedish, stating he was now a soldier of the Swedish King. Much laughing and backslapping ensued.

Having rejoined the group Davy announced the Swedish army drank a lot but didn't feed too well and he was hungry so the group began looking for lunch. Pastor Bob said, "Let's go find some *neulamuikku!*"

"What is that?" John asked.

"Best fried fish you ever ate. Swimming in the lake they call them *vendace* but when it's fried they call it white fish or as some say, 'needle fish.' Either way it's like eating a whole fried sardine. I know it doesn't sound good but I think you'll enjoy trying some. It's excellent with beer," Pencilschwietzer replied.

When they got to the booth John was intrigued. Several men and women were working around a cast-iron skillet that was a good five feet across. The women were flouring up the finger-sized fish and when the oil was the right temperature in the center of the pan they dumped a pile in the middle. One of the men used a long-handled metal spatula to turn and flip the frying fish. As they became golden brown he would work them up on the sides of the giant pan where they would continue getting crisp as the oil cooked out of them and made its way back to the center of the pan. Pencilschwietzer bought a paper tray full and offered one to John and Davy. After eating one John broke out into a smile and promptly ordered a bowl for himself. Davy managed to swallow his down but said he would much rather look for a cheeseburger and some fries.

Connie Pencilschwietzer laughed and said, "My dear boy! You won't find anything remotely similar to a cheeseburger around here. Come with me and we will go find some pocket sandwiches I'm sure you can make do with."

"I'm gonna bring some Turner ham sandwiches like the Fulks Run Ruritans sell over here and make a fortune!" Davy stated.

"I doubt they would have much of a taste for Virginia sugar-cured ham but you might have something there. If it caught on, it would be something entirely different for the Finnish palate," Connie mused. Everywhere he looked there were some of the most beautiful girls Davy had ever laid eyes on. Connie noticed more than one of them glancing at the tall, slender American with the dark suntanned look of a stone mason.

"Seen any girls you would like to meet?" she asked Davy.

"About a hundred or so!" he replied with a grin. "Don't reckon they would want anything to do with a Yankee mountain man like me though."

"I doubt that's true, Mr. Tarzan of Cambridge County!" Connie responded. "I have been watching them checking you out. Been looking at you myself!" Her flirting made his face redden. "For a man, you really are a beautiful specimen, Mr. Dean."

Changing the subject to avoid her surprising remarks he asked, "How come so many of them have their hair dyed brown or black? I can tell they are natural blondes."

"Just about everybody here is blonde, so, women being women wherever you go dark hair is exotic to them, I suppose," Connie mused.

"They ought to stay natural. Looks better. Besides, most American girls would kill to have the complexion and hair of these girls," Davy remarked.

Mrs. Pencilschwietzer glanced sideways at Davy and said, "So now you're an expert on the ladies, are you Mr. Dean?"

Of course the young man blushed red again at the flirtatious remark by the pastor's wife. "I swear, Mrs. Pencilschwietzer. Sometimes you're so forward you perplex me."

Connie smiled.


Back at the fish fry Heikki and Terttu each ordered a round of the *neulamuikku* and John had seconds. Everyone bought large paper cups of dark-brown foaming beer to drink along with their fish.

"I wish I could show the guys in the Cambridge Ruritan Club how they fix these little fish. They could sell a ton of them on the Fourth of July," John said enthusiastically.

The afternoon slid by too soon and as the group made their way back to their cars John looked up to notice Heikki holding hands with Terttu as they walked ahead of him. Heikki was talking a mile a minute and the matronly Terttu smiled at him and nodded occasionally. It caused a pang of loneliness and jealousy in John that he was all too acquainted with.

The next day Heikki took John and Davy fishing while the Pencilschwietzers went to visit some friends in Forssa. They drove about an hour north of Humppila via narrow dirt roads and finally arrived at a cabin on a lake with its own dock. The cabin was a jewel of construction, made of logs that looked like they grew together. Heikki showed them his old-fashioned smoke sauna. John thought it would be a good place to hang hams and side meat and Heikki told him that in the old days they did just that. Heikki said they would come back for a picnic in a few days and they could all share the sauna experience.

When they rode the boat out into blue waters of the lake Davy and John both agreed it was the most beautiful water they had ever seen. Heikki told them if they got thirsty to just dip their cups in the water. "The water in this lake is quite drinkable. A small village on the other side of the lake several miles away put in a water treatment plant when they incorporated two years ago only to find the water was less pure after it had been filtered than it was right out of the lake," the stocky Finnish man stated with a smile.

Heikki got the rods and lures out of a utility building and loaded them into the boat. Soon the party was trolling around the edges of the lake. They caught several nice-sized fish the Dean boys thought looked like big small-mouth bass. Heikki said Terttu would be pleased with them. He called them "pikeperch" and said they were the best eating fish in Finland. The sun shone on the lake and as they rounded a point several moose were swimming toward an island.

"Pull closer to them, Heikki. I want to see them better!" John yelled.

Heikki did the opposite and steered away from the huge animals. "Those moose would smash this boat like it was a toy if we get too close! They can surprise you how fast they can go in the water." The moose climbed the rocky shore of the island with water running off their gangly sides.

For lunch they had sandwiches washed down with Karhu beer. The can had a picture of a big bear on it. Davy looked at his grandfather and was pleasantly surprised at how happy he looked. John was singing "Going to Georgia," one of Ralph Stanley's classics.

*Wish I had me a big white horse*
*Corn to feed him on,*
*Pretty little girl to stay at home*
*Just to feed him when I'm gone.*

"I sure wish my dad could be here with us," Davy suddenly said, interrupting the old man's singing.

"Me too, Davy. Me too. I never could talk to that boy. Or maybe I talked to him too much and said all the wrong things at the wrong times. Sometimes I think I got over worrying about him a long time ago except when it catches you off guard. When you least expect it. It slugs you in the gut. In a given moment I can shut my eyes and see him as a little boy standing there in his overalls and bare feet, drawing a picture in the dust with his toe just friendly as a robin in the spring. He wasn't always the dark horse he is now, Davy. He was a fine boy. My drinking and craziness back then and that damned Vietnam mess done it to him! Scarred him it did, just like Korea and Germany did to me for a while. Some people can let go of it and some can't. Worrying about failures in life will ruin a fine day like this one if you let it. I think I'm awful lucky to be fishing on the prettiest lake God ever made, with a fine Finnish friend here and the best grandson an old dog like me could ever hope to have. I mean that, boy," the old giant said looking directly into his grandson's milky-blue Scotch-Irish eyes. "And, now I done been baptized and forgiven of a life full of horrible sins and long as I behave and believe in Him I know for certain Jesus will let me in heaven. I hope heaven is like this place and I hope you'll be saved too, Davy! I can't imagine being there without you coming along some day too."

Davy was saved from having to respond over the lump in his throat by Heikki hollering about the pole on the right bending nearly double from its mooring in its holder. He grabbed the rod and launched into a tremendous fight with a very big fish. When he finally got it in beside the boat, Heikki saw it was a large pike. He expertly extracted his lure from the side of the ferocious teeth and to the Dean boys' surprise and disappointment, unceremoniously let the big fish drop back into the water. "Terttu wouldn't like us bringing a tough and nasty old pike home to her. Let's catch a few more pikeperch and make her happy."

"I wish I just had a picture of that one to show the Trumbo boys!" Davy exclaimed.

That evening Terttu and Connie prepared the most delicious broiled fish and potatoes imaginable. John said he never thought he would eat so much fish from one day to the next. "When I get back to the States I won't know how to eat a hot dog no more. I'll just hang out around the dumpster behind old man Simpson's fish market with the other stray cats," he said with a laugh.

"Eat it all so I don't have to put it away!" Terttu exclaimed. "Tomorrow we go to see the old castle in Hämeenlinna. You will enjoy the museum there. Here, John. Have some more potatoes."

"I doubt if you'll ever lose your ability to eat a hot dog. One time he ate thirty chilidogs in one setting. Drank a six-pack of Dr. Peppers too," Davy bragged.

Heikki and Terttu looked at John, thinking the young man was exaggerating, but John nodded his head in agreement. "I done slipped off a good bit in my eating. I don't think I could get past twenty-five of those little dogs anymore."

# Chapter 45

Hämeenlinna was another clean, well-managed city with an ancient castle located on yet another beautiful lake. The castle had been used as a prison until the 1970s and recently been renovated to make it a tourist attraction and to protect its historical value. John and Davy were both intrigued with the unbelievable amount of stone work in the place, some crude and some sophisticated. The guide spoke good English and was very friendly. On one of the upper levels there was a museum of archeological and historical Finnish artifacts.

Connie took them to a display from the Humppila area featuring a wooden canoe and paddles that were surprisingly well preserved in an exhibit that was one of the oldest displayed and explained to them, "These old relics were dug up out of the bog behind my grandmother Syrjala's home. You must remember that the entire Finnish land mass is rising every day. The sheer weight of the tremendous glaciers that covered our country during the last ice age actually pushed the land down and it's in the process of slowly springing back up. There were many more swamps and bogs back in those days and the constant lifting of the land also serves to drain it. They did an archeological dig in the back fields of the Syrjala farm a few years ago and dug that boat right out of the ground almost perfectly preserved in peat moss type of turf."

"Just think!" Pencilschwietzer said. "Connie's ancestors back 800 years ago could have built and used these things."

"Maybe someday they will dig up all our old junk at the old Dean home site up on the Blue Ridge where that rascal Roosevelt run my family off their 5,000 acres," John said with no little amount of disgust.

"Your family was from up on the Blue Ridge? I thought they were from the Shenandoah Mountain," Pencilschwietzer asked.

"My daddy moved to Richlands after his family got run off Dean Mountain up above Elkton. Just go east out of Harrisonburg to the top of the Blue Ridge above Elkton. Take a left on the Skyline Drive and you'll run into the Dean family cemetery. The old home place was a mile or so down over the side at a good strong spring. Most of the people that were run off were relocated into the towns or surrounding areas but my daddy couldn't stay off mountains where he felt at home. I guess the old Scotch-Irish blood was too strong in him. He needed his Highlands. So, they agreed to relocate him up on the Alleghenies. Now my rightful home is a playground for hordes of jerks from New Jersey to come and toss their chewing gum and cigarette butts on and admire the fall leaves while they ride your bumper pushing you down the road no matter how fast you drive. Then they ride their bicycles drinking out of them squirt-bottles wearing those spandex britches and stupid looking helmets in big old herds. A couple of those idiots get hit and run over every year and then the paper makes it sound like it's everybody's fault but the poor, poor victim's. Makes me sick on the stomach to think about it sometimes," the old man said.

"Most of us Finns ride bicycles regularly!" Heikki protested. "Why are you opposed to riding bicycles? You Yanks would rather ride in your huge Cadillacs and SUVs burning up most of the world's gas, I suppose!"

"I got nothin' against riding a bicycle and I've seen lots of people riding around here but they're going somewhere dressed regular. In America we have a lot of idiots riding in those stupid-looking skintight bloomers who don't know how to ride to the side of the road like your folks do. You all have those little bike and walking paths around your towns that are great!" John snorted. "And as far as your statement, Heikki, about us Yanks burning up most of the world's gas, I reckon we stand guilty as charged. Too many folks standing in line to sell it to us, I suppose."

The tour guide led them on through the rest of the old castle and Davy couldn't help to wonder how miserable life had been living in this drafty old maze of stone during the long frosty winters. How rough it would have been to be trapped in a place like this under siege. He and John were both very surprised to hear the tour guide inform them the giant castle

271

was never attacked. "In fact," he said, "It was never defended. Each time invading armies approached the area the castle was rapidly abandoned prior to the invaders' arrival and its inhabitants fled the area."

"That bunch must have moved down and settled France," John said. "Sounds like how a bunch of French folks would likely act. Old Daniel Boone would have loved to have had a place this good to defend when he was under attack by the French and Indians down in Kentucky. I can't imagine taking the time and effort to build something so big and not staying in it to fight."

"You're no longer on your Blue Ridge Mountain, are you sir?" Pencilschwietzer retorted.

John's face got red and he noted that he wasn't and it was a point well made. "I reckon I ain't. My pappy used to tell me that they would've fought old Roosevelt if the chestnut blight hadn't made life so different and hard. When that blight hit it killed over 70 percent of the trees in the forest. All the chestnuts they used for food and feed for their hogs were gone. The chestnut tree was the sustenance of their lives. Just like I suppose these white birch trees I see the woods are full of here. What would you think if they all died within a couple of seasons, Heikki?"

"It would be devastating, no doubt!" he exclaimed thoughtfully. "Let's go find the cars. I have a real treat for you. I hear from Connie you love baseball?"

"Yes, I do," John replied.

"We are going to go to a Finnish baseball game but it will be different from anything you have ever seen, I assure you!" Heikki smiled

They arrived in a small town John could not pronounce the name of and parked amid a large number of vehicles. A walk up a long gentle hill took the group out on a flat playing field partly encircled by a ridge that made a natural arena around three sides. Hundreds of people were lining the playing field in bleachers and on blankets stretched on the grass, enjoying the warm late afternoon sun shining from a crystal-clear blue sky. The sun's rays were slanted, making Davy think of late September in Virginia. "Difference in latitude," he mused. Two teams of around fifteen players were warming up on the field, throwing baseballs.

Finally the game was ready to begin between two highly competitive towns: Hyvinkaa and Riihimaki.

"Where does the pitcher throw from? I don't see a mound," Davy asked.

"The pitcher stands next to the batter and tosses the baseball straight up in the air," Pensilschwietzer said.

"We call it *pesapallo*. The game was started by a man named Lauri Pihkala who invented the game by combining baseball with some local games back around 1920 after having gone to America and witnessed the success of American baseball. The actual structure of the game is almost identical to baseball and the rules have changed little since its conception. There is a governing federation known as the Pesapalloliitto that has been organizing and confederating recently. Pesapallo has three out-bases and a home base. Players use a bat to hit the ball out to catchers and then move from base to base trying their best to get to them before the ball does," Heikki explained.

The game started and the first batter hit the ball and ran down the third base line. John and Davy looked at each other totally confused. The pitcher stood right across a three-foot circle from the batter and tossed the ball high up in the air, making it land in the cylinder of the home base circle. The next batter hit the first pitch out into the outfield and one of the fielders caught the lazy fly ball. The batter stepped up to the box to swing again and Davy said, "Wait a minute. He just hit a fly ball that the outfielder caught so why isn't he out? Why's he coming back to bat?"

"Catching a ball in flight is not an out but forces all runners not tagging up and standing on their base to return to home base. Also, the line at the back of the outfield is not a home run. Any ball hit over it is similar to a foul ball in the American game. And to make things more confusing for an American, the strike zone is different and walking requires fewer invalid pitches," Pensilschwietzer tried to explain.

"We have a league that somewhat corresponds to your Major League Baseball," Heikki said. "We have a league called the Superpesis. In the men's league there are fourteen teams who play twenty-six games each against one another. The best eight teams make the playoffs and continue playing until we have a Finnish champion. Superpesis is the most popular summer league sport in Finland, second only to ice hockey as our most popular team sport. Soccer is a distant third. The women have a Superpesis of their own and it attracts more spectators than all other women's sports put together. In some towns it is more popular than the boys' game!"

"I'm not so sure I could ever understand this game!" John exclaimed after a couple of innings. "The runner runs to third base, then straight across where our first base is, then second base and then way back there to the third base behind your first base! This is too confusing for me, although it is kind of fun to watch them. They're really into the game. Where'd they ever come up with such colorful uniforms? I haven't seen anything like them since the '70s in the US when the Pirates and the A's used to wear those crazy-looking uniforms."

The game moved on and the Dean boys kept trying to understand what was going on and finally settled back just enjoying the sights and sounds of summertime in Finland. It was a beautiful evening. The team from Riihimaki finally put together a big scoring inning and went ahead 6-1. Davy went to the concession stand and bought a couple of hot dogs that were served on a stick with no bun and two sodas.

As the game wound down John got up and walked to the restrooms. When the game ended and John had not returned, Davy and the troops began looking for him. Heikki spotted him up in the woods on the ridge and they yelled for him to come on to the cars. When John sheepishly approached the group he showed them the blue stains on his fingers.

"Darnedest crop of blueberries I ever seen growing in those woods. I bet I done eat a quart! Some of them is big as marbles!" the old giant exclaimed.

"Tomorrow we will go pick some if you like. Terttu sends me out into the forest to pick them all the time but I think she just does that so a bear might eat me and she won't have to cook so much!" Heikki joked as Terttu looked at him in amusement.

"Ahhgh!" she said. "No bear would eat a tough old badger like you when there are so many sweet berries to munch on."

The ride back to Humppila was made exciting by a moose that almost ran over Heikki's Mercedes. John swore later on they were so close he could see the car's reflection in the moose's eye.

Heikki laughed as he responded, "You should have grabbed him by the beard with that big hand of yours and taught him not to eat the grass so close to the highway!"

# Chapter 46

The vacation days in Finland sped by and one day the group took a bus trip down to Helsinki. They boarded a huge cruise boat to cross the Suomenlahti, better known as the Bay of Finland, for a day trip of sightseeing and shopping in the ancient Estonian seaport of Tallinn. The day was clear and cool, perfect for sightseeing in one of the most beautiful cities in the world. Another day they spent in Helsinki. John particularly enjoyed the Uspenski Cathedral, a Russian Orthodox Church, with its ornate beauty.

Davy's favorite stop was the statue of Field Marshal Mannerheim on his horse. He said, "Look at the way he sets that horse. He would've made a good Confederate general." Davy had Connie take a picture of him with John and Pastor Bob standing under the neck of the great horse.

Later in the day they took a tour of the monument to the world-famous Finnish composer Jean Sibelius. John was once again very glad he had been walking at home so much and could keep up with everyone. On a tour of the imposing fortress Suomenlinna that juts out into the sea, he actually left the group behind as he walked ahead to see the striking views from the castle walls that once defended the gates to Helsinki.

Another day was spent on a trip to the forest to pick blueberries and gather mushrooms. Heikki showed them the various edible mushrooms and within a short while they had a large basket full of the succulent fungi. "Terttu will make a fine supper with these!" Heikki bragged. The rest of the day was spent picking blueberries and by early afternoon they had close to two gallons. "Now she will make us blueberry pie too!"

On the last full day of their visit Heikki and Terttu informed the Dean boys that no trip to Finland could be complete without properly going to sauna. Heikki had made all the arrangements ahead of time and they rode once again back out to his cabin in the woods. One of the local farm boys had been employed to start the fires early that morning in the smoke sauna and everything was in order. A large number of people had been invited for a picnic later in the evening. John was largely amused about going to the sauna but Davy was apprehensive and obviously did not like the prospects of getting naked in front of other people. "I don't think I would like going in a smoky old place just to get good and sweaty. I can get hot as hell and sweat enough at home. All I have to do is to volunteer to work up in old man Burkholder's barn putting up hay. He stacks her to the roof and I like to died up there in his barn a few times."

"You just don't want to get naked is your problem," John said. "Who's going to tell anybody anyway? Haven't you ever heard the old saying about 'When in Rome, do as the Romans do'?" Relax, old son!"

"I don't know, Grampap!" he responded.

Heikki put Davy at ease when he graciously announced they would all wear bathing suits to avoid their Yankee guests any undue discomfort. The smoke sauna was built on the banks of a small pond, dug out of the bog, with dark, brackish water. When they ducked down and crawled up into the log structure to sit on the burlap-covered benches, the aromatic smoky steam encompassed them and John laughed out loud. "What do you think of this, Davy boy? This here's the real thing, ain't it?"

The earthy smell of the dark, smoky log structure was intoxicating. Heikki reverently poured water with a dipper from an old wooden bucket onto the super-heated stones causing clouds of hissing steam to well up and raise the temperature considerably but not yet uncomfortably. Heikki never stopped talking in Finnish to Terttu and Connie, who broke out laughing and giggling.

After about ten minutes sweat was flowing like water off everyone and Heikki motioned for them to exit the low door. Davy walked into the dark waters of the pond and splashed its cool water over him. John walked out farther into the black, murky bog and turning toward the shore fell over on his back like a felled oak, laughing, splashing and kicking like a big baby. His great belly, his knees, and his face were all that were out of the water and Connie began splashing him and Davy.

After cooling in the pond Heikki directed them back into the warm sauna. This process was repeated several times until Heikki announced they would go to the "clean" sauna in the cabin to cleanse the soot and pond water off themselves. The sauna in the cabin was electric-heated and the ladies went in first. Davy was dripping water on the porch and was shocked when Connie Pencilschwietzer walked out of the sauna buck naked to towel off behind a curtain. He stood staring with his mouth open and couldn't believe how beautiful she was with the firm body of a much younger woman. She glanced up and made no effort to cover herself and even smiled at him before she pulled the curtain closed. He grabbed a towel lying on the porch bench and wrapped it around his midsection as John and Heikki came around the corner of the cabin and stepped up on the porch.

After the men took their turn in the showers and got dressed, the ladies put together a picnic on the kitchen table. The food was exceptional with smoked ham and smoked fish. Terttu asked John if he would like to try an old-fashioned Finnish dish called *mämmi* made from malt. She told him it was a traditional Easter dish that they always saved for foreigners. Davy looked at the brown foul-looking goo and made a face, but John scooped up a piece and popped it into his mouth. The women all watched him expectantly like they were sure he would throw up but John chewed it up, nodded, smiled, swallowed, and grabbed another hunk of the *mämmi*. "Reckon I could have a glass of that butter milk or *piimä* as you all call it," he said. "I think that would go good together with this stuff."

"Aagh!" Connie exclaimed. "Damn Yankees have cast-iron guts and no taste buds!"

Davy took a taste of the *mämmi* and swallowed, barely managing to get it down. "Stuff don't taste too hateful but the looks of it are enough to gag you," the truthful young man said.

Heikki laughed and said, "This is a true story. Right after the second World War, an Englishman was sent to Finland to report back to their government about the state of welfare in the country. He was invited into a home at Easter and they were eating *mämmi*. He quickly reported to his superiors, 'Send food! They're eating the same food twice here!' "

The long Finnish evening hung on the best it could but nothing lasts forever, especially good times on golden evenings.

Their flight was scheduled to leave the Helsinki airport at nine the next evening, flying nonstop back to New York. At the airport the Dean boys shook hands with Heikki and hugged Terttu as they expressed their gratitude for their Finnish friends' hospitality. Pencilschwietzer was already swallowing his Dramamine tablets and Connie was her usual exuberant self bouncing all around with the luggage. Davy avoided eye contact with her as much as he could since the incident from the sauna when she had caught him looking at her. Connie took delight in his discomfort and pushed her advantage to the limit.

In the airport John bought a little iron bell with "Suomi" written across the top. He told Davy he thought it would make a good Christmas tree ornament.

Soon they were in the plane and watching the ground pull away from them. John looked out his window and said to the wind, "My good friend Kauko. Your land is a strong and beautiful one. I'm sorry you had to make the supreme sacrifice for her but if it makes you feel any better Finland is worth your having died for it. Soon I'll join you and it won't really matter in eternity, will it? And Fern, I'm sorry I never brought you here with me. I should have when I had the chance. Good-bye, Finland, you beautiful Lady. I'll never see you again and thank you, Jesus, for letting me come here. This is the first time I ever went to a foreign country where the purpose of my trip was not to fight and kill people."

A tear rolled down the old man's cheek and a few moments after he wiped it away the lovely Icelandic stewardess Dagbjort popped out of the cockpit and asked him if he would like a drink. He said he would and ordered a Scotch and water which she served with a smile. John stretched out in his first-class seat and watched the lovely tall Viking glide among the other passengers as she served them and soon found himself wishing he were much younger.

Back in the coach section Pencilschwietzer was already virtually passed out from the Dramamine, slobbering on the window. Connie had her blanket over her and curled up leaning against Davy pretending to nap as the plane leveled off. Davy got up and went to the bathroom for as long as he could make it last to get away from her. When he returned to his seat she turned toward him, pulled the corner of her blanket up over him and placed her hand on his chest. When he finally turned his face toward her he whispered, "What're you doing?"

She whispered, "I have a question for you, Davy. Did you enjoy what you saw of me yesterday?"

"You were absolutely beautiful and quite frankly, Mrs. Pencilschwietzer, you scare the hell out of me!" he whispered as he turned and looked straight ahead.

But he did not move other than an involuntary stiffening of his muscles as she loosened one of the buttons on his shirt and slid her hand inside to make small circles in the hair on his chest. Bob snored against the window as her circles and pink fingernails went down over his flat belly to continue their explorations.

"Bob is incapable of fathering any children, Davy. He's been to the doctor many times and it is hopeless. I desperately want to have a child, naturally, and Bob and I have talked it over. We both want you to help us to have one. Discreetly, of course."

# Chapter 47

John was dreaming. He was a boy again, following a white mule his sick mother was riding and his grim, stoic father was leading up the old mountain trail, pulling and hurrying the bony-backed nag up the steep trail. John was struggling to keep up in the muddy cold days of March with a bitter wind blowing across the sweat on his neck. His poor-fitting shoes had rubbed a blister on his right heel that was raw and fiercely burning. He dared not complain or mention it to his father who had bought the used boots for a few cents at a rummage sale the day before at a church in town. They had already been worn out and discarded by some other boy or small man in Cambridge town. His father had taken his mother to old Dr. Watson whose words had crushed the boy, taking his breath when he overheard him talking with his father. It caused John to nearly pass out in fright when he heard the doctor tell his father that his mother was slowly dying.

"There's nothing anyone but God can do for her," he said. "She has consumption. Take her back up on the mountain where the air is cleaner. That's the only hope I can give her. I don't think she will last long. I'm not one to give false hope, Mr. Dean. Fact is she is dying and it probably won't be long coming."

They left his six-year-old sister, Mary Alice, with his aunt and uncle in town but John's father had made the boy come back up the mountain with them. He needed his help on the farm. In John's dream he struggled up the slippery trail after the mule, just as he had a lifetime ago. In his dream, as he looked up at his mother's wasted form she transformed into

Fern, turning, smiling down at him. John was so taken back by the vision of his wife that his feet would not gain purchase on the slippery slope of the Shenandoah mountain trail no matter how hard he tried to catch up to the mule. Finally, as his father was leading her higher up into the mist away from him, she turned and held her hand out to him in a terribly sad way. John woke up and Dagbjort was gently shaking him.

"Sir, sir. Please fasten your seatbelt. We are landing in Baltimore in a few minutes," she said in her Icelandic accent.

The long drive home down around Washington, west on I-66 and south on I-81 was exhausting after eleven hours in the jet. Pencilschwietzer drove his Oldsmobile with the flow of heavy truck traffic keeping a steady pace. He said he had slept like a log on the plane ride and was in fine shape to drive as the rest of them dozed. John was sprawled out in the front while Davy and Connie were in the back. Gliding across western Maryland and then through the eastern panhandle country of West Virginia they soon were back in Virginia passing Winchester, Woodstock, Harrisonburg, Staunton, and finally home in Cambridge County. The Pencilschwietzers helped John and Davy carry their bags into Davy's house. The yard was freshly mowed. John noted that the Trumbo boys were good to their word and had taken care of the place for them. Connie hugged John and Davy and Pastor Bob shook John's hand. Then he locked eyes with Davy and suddenly, with a strained smile, awkwardly gave the much younger man a hug.

"You are fine travel companions," the pastor said. "Please come see us when you can. I am planning to take up fishing again. I usually take off on Thursdays and drive up to the lake and fish until dark. I would be honored if you would go along, Mr. John. That'll give us time to talk about your spiritual life. Davy, I'm sure you wouldn't mind if I stole your grandfather away for a day or two, would you?"

"Maybe I could get Davy to fix some of the rock walls and flower garden borders while you two get away for a while," Connie volunteered. "I'd be glad to pay you, of course. Bob hates to do that kind of stuff."

And so it was arranged for the following Thursday. John and Davy arrived at the Pencilschwietzer's house early and Connie was already in the flower garden on her hands and knees pulling weeds and thinning flowers. She was wearing gardening gloves and a baseball cap with her hair pulled out the back in a ponytail, making her look like a teenager. She rocked back on her knees and wiped the sweat from her brow with the back of her hand. The top three buttons of her shirt were open and before they exited the truck John said, "Maybe you ought to go fishing and I'll stay here with her!"

"Shut up, Grampap!" Davy hissed at the old man. "You're a Christian now and aren't supposed to think about things like that."

"Just because I gave my soul to Jesus don't mean I had to get castrated at the same time."

"You beat all! You just beat all!" Davy said in disgust as they exited the truck. Pencilschwietzer came around the corner of the house carrying a cooler in one hand and a fly-fishing pole and tackle box in the other. "What's that you were saying?" he asked.

"Nothing, Pastor Bob," Davy answered. "My grandfather needs your counseling is all."

"Well, let's get on the road, Mr. Dean. There are fish to catch. Sure glad I don't have to spend the day working in the flower gardens. Mighty glad you're willing to help out, Davy. The Good Book tells us there is a time to plant and a time to sow. Unfortunately, I am afraid I'm not one to get it done. My talents and abilities lie elsewhere. You two make some progress around here today and have fun."

Davy was unloading his wheelbarrow and tools off the back of the truck as Pencilschwietzer gave Connie a brief hug and kissed her on the forehead almost like a father sending his daughter off to Senior Prom. John and Pastor Bob were soon headed off down the driveway.

"We won't be back until after dark so don't worry about us!" Pencilschwietzer shouted from the truck window.

Connie looked at Davy and said, "We have all day. Would you like a cup of coffee?"

"That would be real nice," he said.

Stopping at the door he took her by the hand and turned her toward him. "Connie, I'm sick nervous about this whole thing. Are you sure this is what you and Pastor Bob want? Somehow it seems totally sinful."

"Bob and I have prayed about it and thought it all through. It's nothing different than when Sarah offered Hagar to her husband Abraham. After all, it is the most natural function in the world. Neither Bob nor I were virgins when we met. Products of the '60s and '70s you know. I could go to the doctors and have it done artificially but Bob and I both think it would be better naturally with someone we know and trust. Plant my garden, Davy. I want a child so badly, and you can give us one." She wiped the sweat and dirt from her brow. Davy leaned against the door frame looking down the road where the truck had disappeared.

"I've been monitoring and watching my temperature and am sure I'm ovulating. The garden is ready for your seed and the only sin involved is how much I'm going to enjoy this. It's been so long. Poor Bob has his problems."

She took him by the hand and led him into the kitchen where she turned to him and kissed him. "You have a cup of coffee and I'm going to take a shower." Davy sipped on his coffee and listened to the water running in the bathroom down the hall. He realized she had left the bathroom door open. He set his coffee down on the counter, pulled the T-shirt over his head, slid his boots off on the rug beside the door and to her delight, he joined her in the shower.

Late that evening Bob and John pulled into the driveway. Much to Davy's surprise John was driving. Pastor Bob was drunk and leaning back in the seat. Getting out of the truck he staggered around in a circle looking at the yard and said, "You two bees have been busy as birds around here. Your patch looks well tended, Little Lady." The pastor abruptly took his pole off the back of the truck and headed into the garage with Connie right behind him holding him up by the elbow. He put his arm around her and smacked her on the rump. "Were you a good girl today little Connie? "

"I am so sorry, Mr. Dean. I don't know what would have gotten into him! I'll get him inside," she said as she led him into the garage.

"What in the world were you doing driving?" Davy asked his grandfather.

"It was either that or wreck with him driving. I never seen nobody for a long time so dead set on getting drunk. He had a flask in his fishing box and a pint in his vest. We didn't do too much fishing. He was pretty well drunk by mid morning. I wanted to come home long ago but he said we had to stay away from here until dark."

"Let's get home, Grampap," Davy said as John got out of the driver's seat and Davy hopped in.

Before they made it out of the driveway John turned to his grandson and asked, "Maybe we ought to head to Alaska in the morning. Don't you think screwing the preacher's wife is dangerous business, Davy?"

"It ain't like what you think, Grampap. Told me she and the pastor want a baby and old Bob can't get her done. At least you don't have to worry about me dying of that CSR disease no more."

"I swear, boy! I swear! There ain't no denying that hateful Dean blood. For crying out loud! I would have never in this world thought you might ruin my reputation in this one-horse town." Despite himself the old man began a deep belly laugh that lasted most of the way home. "I think I've heard it all now! You're as big a sinner as David was messing with that Bathsheba!"

"I haven't had old Pastor Bob killed, have I? Like David did Uriah?" the young man roared defensively.

"Not yet you ain't, son. Not yet but I expect you might without trying. I gotta do some praying about this one. For sure about one thing: I can't confide in the preacher about it. Funny. Last year I would have laughed my head off for a week. But now, after thinking about it, I'm afraid of how I feel."

# Chapter 48

Before daylight they had the Dodge pickup loaded with a couple of duffle bags and shaving kits. A shovel and some wheel chucks were thrown in the back along with an extra spare tire, a big blue cooler and a come-a-long winch. They had put a fiberglass topper on the truck the night before and threw an old double mattress in the bed of the truck with two old comforts, sleeping bags, and a couple of pillows. Davy changed the oil and oil filter along with the air filter and checked the air pressure in the tires. As an afterthought he put a small charcoal grill, a bag of charcoal, and some starter fluid in a small wooden crate and stuck that in the back too. On the way to the bypass along the access road they stopped at the Trumbos' trailer and Tim was already in the yard drinking a cup of coffee. John gave him $200 cash to look after the place while they were gone and told him he would settle up with him when they got back, whenever that may be. Tim assured him that would be enough and his credit was good.

"Seen your ex-woman last Saturday night," Tim said to Davy.

"Didn't see much then, did'ya?" John answered over Davy's shoulders.

"Her and that Morris boy split up. She said the biggest mistake she ever made was leaving you, Davy. Said to tell you that."

"You tell her I'm sorry some folks is so set on being miserable in this messed up world," Davy said. "You tell her that next time you see her! Tell her I done met a dozen girls in Finland that want to marry me that got blonde hair, blue eyes, and big knockers and I'm in love with all of them and they're all in love with me. Then you tell her I'm taking my grampap

285

to Alaska to see my daddy and I just might fall in love with an Eskimo girl and wear my nose off rubbing it on hers! Then tell her to go to hell and I'd be afraid to mess with her after one of them damn Morris boys done slimed her up!"

With that the Dean boys spun their wheels out of the Trumbo driveway and pointed their Dodge Ram west.

"You know how to get there, Grampap?" Davy asked suddenly.

"I figure we go west on Interstate 64 and sooner or later we ought to find our way to Montana. I want to look up an old buddy of mine that's a hunting guide somewheres around a town called Ennis. Swedish fellow named Svenson I served with in Korea. He owes me and I figure he can put us up for a night or two before we tackle that Alaska highway. I hear that road is nasty but it ain't too rough for us, is it boy?"

"I don't imagine," Davy answered as he loaded his lip up with Copenhagen snuff. "Fetch me that empty 7-Eleven coffee cup out from under the seat. I need a spit cup. Stuff a couple of those old napkins in it for me too, please. I want to put some miles behind us today. I wanna get as far away from Lizzy and far away as possible from Connie Pencilschwietzer too!"

John wisely didn't comment. His grandson was obviously and uncharacteristically angry.

They worked their way across West Virginia and then half of Kentucky. It was their plan to stay on I-64 west but when they were going around Lexington they missed the exit to Louisville and found themselves on the beltway around Lexington. John saw a sign that said West 60 and hollered, "Go that away." Soon they were headed west on the Wendell H. Ford Highway, rolling past little towns like Bardstown, Elizabethtown, and Leitchfeild. Davy kept it on sixty-five miles an hour and they listened to a new Ralph Stanley CD Davy had bought back at a little truck stop in St. Albans, West Virginia, just west of Charleston when they had stopped for gas. The words to one song—"Dear, What About You?"—in particular seemed like an omen to Davy.

The verses set him up but it was the chorus that reached down into Davy's soul and made him know Carter Stanley had lived feelings exactly like his own before Carter drank himself into oblivion. Ralph's tormenting banjo and scalding tenor set off Carter's lead perfectly.

*Every day, your memory grows dimmer*
*The clouds drift away the sunshine peeks through*
*Every night, no longer you'll haunt me.*
*My conscience is clear, Dear, what about you?*

About six o'clock that evening they rolled into a little town called Central City, Kentucky. There was a sign that said, "Central City—Home of the Everly Brothers." There was another sign that advertised Kentucky Fried Chicken along with yet another sign that said "Everly Brothers Monument" with an arrow pointing north.

"We might as well eat some Kentucky Fried Chicken in Kentucky, Grampap. It might taste better here," Davy said and John acknowledged he was hungry. They pulled into the KFC and went in through the side door as the August heat bore down on the glass structure. A little dried-up looking woman was working the register and a couple of greasy-looking girls about twenty were working the back. They all looked hot, tired and not in a customer-service notion. There was a despondent teenage black boy sweeping the floor and picking up errant napkins and ketchup packets in the dining area working in first gear, low range. His movements were as slow as the coming of Christmas to a six year old rich kid.

They ordered a couple of three-piece dinners, Original Recipe, and John asked the cashier, "Them Everly Brothers live around here? I used to listen to them when I was in Korea. They was really good."

"Those big-feeling jerks come around here once in a while to make all us poor folks see how rich and famous they are. I hope they never come back again!" she growled as she slid their trays to them. "You can get your drinks over there," she said, slamming two large paper cups on the counter and pointing to a fountain at the side.

"Pardon me, madam. Obviously we hit a sore spot. Which one was it, Phil or Don that robbed you of your prize a hundred years ago then left town singing and getting famous while you got old?" Davy shot back at her, obviously piqued at the old gal's bad manners.

They sat at a little table and ate their suppers as the old crone glared at them from her stool in the corner. When they finished eating they drove down Main Street looking for the monument. They found it, such as it was, planted in front of the fire department and almost on the sidewalk.

"You would have thought they could have done better than that," John said, looking at the marble tombstone that read "Home of the Everly

287

Brothers." "Looks like them Everly boys died and the fire department cremated them for sport at a practice session, or something."

"Sure don't rank with the statue of that Mannerheim fellow back there in Helsinki, does it, Grampap?"

"We been there and seen that, ain't we son? That Mannerheim was about fifty times as much a man as these two Kentucky crooners was. Of course, I expect Mannerheim would have sounded like crap singing 'Dream, Dream, Dream' what with a Finnish accent and all."

"We been there and got the T-shirt too, Grampap. Let's head west a couple more hours this evening. You know, I wish old Heikki coulda come along with us. He would appreciate this country."

"I'd like to have a big pan of Terttu's fish meatloaf," John said. "That and a jar of mayonnaise and a loaf of white bread. Wouldn't that be good?"

"The colonel still has my gut pinched pretty tight. I bet I'll be able to knock over a Coke bottle at fifteen yards around midnight after eating that greasy chicken back there. Did we bring any toilet paper?"

John reached under the seat and pulled out a roll of paper towels and laid it on the seat in the middle of the truck. Just before dark they drove into a little campground with a road sign pointing south that said, "Pennyrile Forest State Park." The area they drove into was deserted and they had the place to themselves. It started to rain as they crawled into the back of the truck, pushing aside all the things they had thrown in there so early that morning. Squirming around and fussing, they finally were able to get somewhat comfortable.

"We ain't doing this every night, Grampap," Davy said, but John was already asleep. The words of the Stanley Brothers' song kept floating in and out of the young man's head along with the passionate wet heat and sensuousness of Connie Pencilschwietzer. Davy hoped she and the Pastor Bob were doing okay. "What a mess I been led into," he thought. But he knew if he ever got the chance he would do it again. She was better than Lizzy had ever been and she was the only other girl Davy had had. His head felt light and he had a natural sense of apprehension about the road ahead of them trying to find his father in Alaska. What in the world would happen along the way? Whatever is gonna happen if we do find him?

He said his prayers and slid off to the rhythm of John's heavy breathing and rain on the roof of the topper. Davy fell asleep hoping John would stay on his side all night and not roll on him. John crawled out around two o'clock and Davy could hear him urinate beside the truck tire.

# Chapter 49

The next morning Davy got John up at around four thirty and pushed on westward until they merged with Route 24 and rolled past Mayfield, Kentucky, at daylight. They crossed into Tennessee following Highway 51 where that road ran into Interstate 155 at Dyersburg. Very soon they were on the bridge over the Mississippi and Davy was in awe, stunned by the power and might of the big river. John saw a sign pointing to St. Louis so they took that road and were soon heading north past Cape Girardeau.

"Ain't that the town that there Rush Limbaugh feller is from?" John asked.

"Believe it is, Grampap," Davy said. "You want to stop and see his home place? Think they got it marked like they did that composer in Finland, that Sibelius feller?"

"Probably have some tombstone set in front of the fire hall like those people put up for the Everly Brothers back there in Central City, Kentucky. I'm not interested in stopping to see nothing about Rush. He's about as big of an idiot as I ever listened to even if I do agree with a lot of what he says. I want to spend the night in St. Louis and see that big arch they got there."

"We can't stop everywhere and see everything if you want to make it to Alaska before the snow gets us," Davy said.

"I doubt if you'll ever pass this way again and I know very well I'm not. I'm paying for the gas so why are you worried if we don't get there until next summer? It ain't like your Daddy is waiting on us anyway. Heck, he don't even know we're coming. I tried to call him time and again but it's like he disappeared off the face of the earth."

Davy didn't respond for a while and John realized he had probably upset the boy with his remarks about John, Jr. when Davy said, "I tried a dozen times to get a'hold of him since Christmas. I even called the Sheriff's Department up there and they said they hadn't seen Dad come into town for a long time. Said he had took up with an Indian woman and has kids. He ever say anything to you about that?"

"First I ever heard it. Wouldn't surprise me much though. Your Daddy's a different sort since that damned Vietnam stuff. He went through hell over there and it rocked his soul. Reckon we'll just go and see. That wouldn't be so bad, would it? Having some Injun brothers and sisters? Cross that Kill Buck blood with some of that Alaskan Injun blood might make a fine warrior, wouldn't you think?"

Davy didn't say anything for a couple of miles and as they rode along the DJ on the classic country radio was playing Roger Miller's old song "Dang Me." Davy finally broke the silence and blurted out, "Grampap, maybe it's a bad idea to go up there and bother them. I mean, if Dad wanted us to know about him and his little family he would've told us about it and sent us pictures and names and stuff."

"Who knows? I'd like to see him before I kick off. If I got some grandkids I don't know I'd like to see 'em. Hey! Let's stop in St. Louis and eat a big steak and baked potato this evening. We'll get a motel room and maybe go to the Cardinals game tonight. They play the Cubs at seven o'clock. I heard it on the sports report while ago."

So, that's what they did. Davy rode the elevator up in the arch but John stayed on the ground. When he got down he confessed to his grandfather it had scared him to death. "It's a hell of a lot higher looking down from up there!" he said looking up where he had been.

After checking into a Best Western hotel they took showers and went to a steak house where the restaurant had a deal that if someone could eat seventy-two ounces of steak in seventy-two minutes he or she would get it free. John asked the waiter if he had a magazine to read during the extra forty-two minutes he would have left over when he downed the steak in a half hour. The waiter laughed but Davy told John he wouldn't be able to go to the ballgame if he did that, so John told the waiter he'd settle with four of their hamburgers and a big bowl of mashed potatoes with gravy instead. Davy had a twenty-ounce porterhouse steak cooked medium rare.

After supper they found their way to the ballpark. The weather was perfect and their seats were right behind third base. It was a beautiful summer evening and the Cardinals won 3-2 in ten innings.

The next morning they left early checking out at eight thirty heading west on Interstate 70. Around noon time they passed Kansas City and headed north on Interstate 29 and soon left Missouri behind crossing over into Iowa. They followed the Missouri River northward through some of the most beautiful river bottom land in the world. The farmland they saw mile after mile made a huge impression on Davy and was something he could hardly believe.

"These fields stretch on forever, Grampap!" he exclaimed. "I thought the big fields along the James River at Buchanan was huge. They ain't a drop in the bucket compared to this place. All the fields I ever seen in Virginia put together wouldn't make a drop in the bucket out here."

"No wonder this country is so strong. There's enough corn in the fields to the right of us to feed a billion people and half of the Chinese too!" the old man said.

Evening saw them passing Sioux City, Iowa, where they bought a bucket of Kentucky Fried Chicken that was a lot better than the same stuff they had bought in Kentucky. Flinging the bones out the window into the hot summer air, they polished off the twelve-piece box in short order. About an hour later they took a break on the banks of the Missouri River at a pull-off near a little place called Elk Point, South Dakota. They stretched their legs and took a walk down by the river and tried skipping some flat rocks in the swirling muddy water. John couldn't flick his wrist hard enough to make the rocks skip anymore but he tried.

As it grew dark they walked back up to their truck. A car load of boys in their late teens pulled in and got out of their old 78 Chevrolet. One of them threw a beer can into the weeds and mumbled something about out-of-state assholes parked at their spot. It was obvious they were drunk and in a dark mood. There were five of them and the biggest one opened his fly and started pissing on the wheel of the Deans' truck. Davy bristled up, yelled at him, and started toward them but John caught him by the shoulder and said in an icy tone that made Davy stop in his tracks, "I'll handle this!"

"Jesus Christ, look what a big old bastard we got here boys!" the leader of the group sneered as he whipped out a switchblade knife. As he flicked it open it gleamed in the low light of evening.

John reached in his pocket and pulled out a Smith and Wesson Model 649 and with no hesitation whatsoever blew a hole through the car's driver window and the bullet exited the roof. "When you quit pissing on my truck I'll quit shooting your car. Now, the rest of you get in this rust bucket! You lay your knife on the ground or I'll shoot you in the crotch!" he growled menacingly with the mean-looking little pistol that, in his huge hand, looked like a ridiculous child's toy pointing the way for them. "I mean *now, y*ou idiots! Before I start shooting again!"

The four would-be heroes dived into the car with their hands up saying, "Don't shoot us, mister." John walked up to the leader who was still standing beside the truck with the knife lying on the ground at his feet. The drunk yelled, "You old bastard! Look what you did to my car!" In one quick motion John backhanded the young man across the face and knocked him flat.

"Get in the truck and get her started," John ordered Davy.

Standing over to the young man who was lying on the ground cursing, John put the pistol behind his ear and said, "Get your sorry ass up and get in that car before I forget I done give my soul to Jesus and send you straight to hell."

As the big fellow got to his knees John kicked him in the rear and launched him toward the Chevrolet as Davy got the truck turned around and headed toward the highway. John crawled in the truck seat and didn't say a word as Davy spun off into the darkening night.

About ten miles down the road John said, "If you don't feel too tired I figure we ought to cross over into Nebraska and go on the back roads for a while in case those fellers start telling wild tales about two Virginia boys shooting up their car."

Davy shook his head and said, "You beat everything I ever seen or heard of, Grampap. You beat all I ever seen! I thought you was going to kill those boys!"

"So did they and that's why we ain't headed to the hospital with noses broke and our guts cut out of us."

They got off the interstate and headed west on Route 50 and then took Route 15 south back across the Missouri River at a little town named Vermillion. Then they took Route 12 west until a road sign for Route 81 south appeared. "Take that road, Davy. Just like being home. Route 81 south!"

About a half an hour south they took Route 59 west a few miles and near a place called Magnet, Davy spotted a lonely dirt road between rows of corn taller than the truck. A quarter of a mile back in the field, hidden safely in a sea of corn, the two climbed into the back of the truck in their crude bed. Davy asked John, "Why didn't you tell me you had that pistol?"

"I got all kinds of surprises up my sleeve, son. That's how I've lived to such a ripe old age."

"What're we gonna do when you get arrested for shooting holes in a vehicle and smacking that feller across the snoot? What you going to do then?" Davy asked. "Don't you ever learn? You're still on probation at home."

"They ain't going to the law. First reason is they're all drunk and, second, they won't want to admit that an old man with a pea shooter made them crap in their pants," John said. "At the same time I'm glad we got some distance and a state line between us for the night. We get out of here in the morning before daylight and we can be in Wyoming before dinner time tomorrow. Then we'll cross over into Montana. Them Montana fellers shouldn't care much about a little scuffle that happened in Vermillion, South Dakota."

As they tossed around in their blankets Davy said, "Well, Grampa, you're gonna have to get rebaptized when we get back. You done slid down in sin again."

"Pencilschwietzer says Jesus will forgive me if'n I just ask him to. That's all I got to do, is ask. But I guess that may change since you been breeding his wife for him. What's all that about? The more I think about it, it seems to me like Pencilschwietzer probably knew you was gonna shag her that day and went along with it?"

"Connie told me the pastor couldn't get her done and they both want a baby real bad. Said Bob wanted to adopt one but she told him she always dreamed of giving birth herself. They ain't into that scientific test-tube stuff so she said they talked it over and thought I would be a good feller to make them one. My only problem is I think I've started liken' her too much. That's why I wanted to get out of Cambridge so quick."

"You gotta be kidding me, son," John said in amazement. "My heavens. I don't know what to think about that. She's a beautiful woman. I bet that was something else!"

"No comment. I wouldn't want to kiss and tell and make your cleansed soul fall deeper in sin. I reckon we'll find out when we get back if you're going to be a great-granddaddy in Cambridge County. I mean, if we get back and her belly is all swelled up. I reckon they'll name it Pencilschwietzer," Davy said. "Hell, I don't think I want to go back! What a mess!"

"Odds is against knocking her up in one session. What if she isn't pregnant? What's she gonna do then? I just can't believe she would do something like this, being the preacher's wife and all. I mean she's a fine girl and so good looking."

"I thought about that but she told me she had been taking her temperature and counting her cycle for a couple of months and she figured she was ovulating right on time when we done it. She even said she would have me back next month if it didn't take this time. I told her I wanted to do it every chance I could and she told me that would be sinful to do it just for pleasure. I don't understand women any better that I understand old men like you who beat up Sheriffs and get saved in church and then shoot holes in peckerheads' cars! Go to sleep, Grampap! I'm tired and have a lot of driving the back roads tomorrow thanks to you. Here we lay in a sea of corn in the middle of America worrying about the law getting us, preachers' wives, and how to get to Alaska."

"Just goes to prove you can't deny that hot Dean blood!" the old man exclaimed.

"Shut up and go to sleep," the young man said with a laugh. "I bet them boys back there along that river did shit in their pants. Did anybody ever tell you that without a doubt you are one scary old man?"

"Even Jesus whipped the money lenders! Says so in the Bible. Don't figure those boys was any different and got what they deserved. I been reading about Saint Peter. He was a rounder too. Big guy like me. Cut that feller's ear off in the garden when Judas led them soldiers come to get Jesus. I figure me and him have a lot of the same qualities."

A few minutes later John was already breathing deeply in pre-snore mode thinking about Connie Pencilschwietzer carrying his great-grandbaby in her belly and her piercing, dancing green eyes and auburn hair. As he faded off to sleep he remembered an Irish girl he had spent the night with at the docks in San Francisco. What he remembered mostly about her were those killer green eyes, her red hair, and her loud throaty laugh. She had seemed to enjoy their night as much as John had long ago and so far away.

# Chapter 50

Before daylight Davy slipped out of the back of the truck, shut the back window, and after backing out of the cornfield headed west on Route 59 toward the town of O'Neill. They stopped at a convenience store in the middle of nowhere for gas. When he opened the back of the truck John lumbered out like a bear emerging from his cave after hibernating all winter. His hair was matted and his clothes looked like those of a homeless person who hadn't changed them for a month. He stumbled a little as he turned around once, got his bearing, and spotted a Porta-John that served as the restroom for the establishment standing alone in an adjacent vacant lot.

Davy went into the store looking for a hot cup of coffee. After a few minutes a ten-year-old redheaded boy rode his bicycle into the parking lot. He looked around to make sure nobody was looking and picked up a baseball-sized rock and arched it over the weeds striking the side of the Porta-John and making a loud bang. John let out a growl that sounded like a wounded grizzly bear and the kid scrambled back on his bike and fled around the other side of the garage. John exited the door like an angry hornet leaving a nest someone had whacked with a broom just as Davy came out the front of the store.

"What in the world is wrong with you?" he demanded of his grandson. "Why you flinging rocks up against the outhouse while I was in there? Ain't you outgrowed those kind of things?"

"Never done such a thing!" the younger man replied laughing. "If I'd thought of it I might have!"

"Well, there ain't nobody else around," John snapped. "I thought a mortar had gone off!"

An old woman came around the side of the garage with the culprit by the ear. The boy was kicking and squirming. She yelled, "Now you tell that man you're sorry, you little knucklehead!"

"I'm sorry, I'm sorry!" he yelled. "Don't, Ma! You're tearing my ear off!"

The woman let the boy go and he promptly ran back around the building. "I sure am sorry, sir. He pulls that trick and others when he sees out-of-state tags on vehicles and he thinks he can get away with it. I suppose he don't have much to do around here and the nearest kid close his age lives fifteen miles away."

"Little peckerhead about to cause me to have a heart attack!" John exclaimed. "Reckon I done worse from time to time when I was little. I will say one thing: it sure did clean me out good."

Davy shook his head laughing and got in the truck.

The old woman laughed too. "Well, at least something good come out of it! If you come by this way again and feel bound up just let me know and I'll fetch the little feller for you." She was laughing and slapping her knees as they pulled off heading west.

Taking Route 20 west they pushed on all day through monotonous field after field of giant sunflowers and tall corn until they finally crossed the state line into Wyoming at a tiny town named Van Tassell. John, who had been dozing all day, wanted to stop but Davy demanded they push on. Near Casper, Wyoming, a state police car slid in behind them and followed them for a few miles until Davy was beside himself with fear. John merely sat there and looked out the window. The trooper turned off at Evansville and Davy decided to head north on Interstate 25. At Buffalo, Wyoming, they picked up Interstate 90 and around supper time crossed over into Montana. The Big Horn Mountains were a sight to behold after driving across so many miles of prairie. Evening found them thinking about camping at a campground near the Little Bighorn Battlefield National Monument.

John was surprised at the posted signs warning to watch out for rattlesnakes. He kept a sharp eye out for them but didn't see any as they walked up the trail to the markers where Custer had died in all his pompous glory. Looking down toward the Little Bighorn River and reading the trail markers Davy and John felt like they could understand how the battle had developed.

"Darn dummies!" John exclaimed. "Anybody can see how the Sioux outsmarted them. No cover-up here. Using cover saved my hide too many times to count when the Germans was shooting at me."

"Custer didn't have the firepower you had either, Grampap," Davy said.

"He wasn't being shot at by Germans with rifles and throwing hand grenades hiding behind Rommel's tanks either. If the Injuns would've had the arms superiority that the Germans had they would still own this property," the old man retorted.

"I suppose they own the place now, Grampap. This whole place is in the Crow Indian Reservation. What if they decide we're trespassing tonight? They might sneak up on the truck and scalp us," Davy teased.

"I want to move on anyway. I don't want to try to sleep here. Too many ghosts hanging around haunting this valley. Too spooky for me," the old man said as he suddenly turned on his heel and headed back down the path. "My spirit will be wailing with the rest of them soon enough. Except, of course, I'm going to Heaven since I been saved. I doubt very seriously if George Armstrong Custer made it through the Pearly Gates. I expect he is riding in the Devil's cavalry, having been one of the Yanks that burnt the Valley."

As the sun sank in the west behind the Big Horn Mountains, the Dodge truck made its way north to the town of Hardin where the Deans got a room at a motel. They slept in the next morning and woke up to the brightest and clearest day they had seen in a while thanks to a cold front that had passed through in the night. The humidity was noticeably much lower too. The local radio station said it had gotten down to fifty-two degrees that night and would even be cooler the next night. After a big breakfast at a Shoney's all-you-can-eat bar they drove up to Billings and then due west on Interstate 90.

"When we get to Livingston we need to find a road that runs south to a little place called Virginia City, Montana," John said. "I want to find Carl Svenson, an old army buddy of mine, if he's still alive. That's where he was born and raised. He's been a hunting and fishing guide since he got out of the army. I got a letter from him a couple of years ago. It's just outside Yellowstone National Park. I want to see that old rascal if he's still breathing."

"Grampap, I was ten years old when you got that letter. It was way more than a couple of years ago. Did you ever write back to him or call him?"

"He'll still be there. Bullet fragments, big mouth, and all, I suppose. Let's go see anyway. We won't be coming this way again."

The vistas to the south and the west were phenomenal and a thing of wonder to the two Virginia boys. Some of the peaks still had snow on them which simply amazed Davy. It was the most exciting part of their trip thus far for him, give or take a pistol shot or two and the Mississippi River.

Winding ever westward through the big city of Butte they turned south at a place called Three Forks on Route 287 and finally entered a small town named Ennis.

"Holy mackerel!" Davy whistled. "Would you look at that pile of horns!" He had spied a pile of antlers some of the locals had accumulated and piled up that was as big as a small school bus stacked beside a sporting goods store. They stopped and walked in the front door.

"Looking for an old friend of mine, Carl Svenson," John stated to a man who was obviously the proprietor. "You know him?"

The old man looked at John funny and said, "Well, good luck if you're going to spend some time with him. Crankiest old SOB west of the Mississippi!"

"Then I feel relieved!" John exclaimed. "He hasn't changed a bit since 1953. Can you tell me how to find him?"

An hour later on a winding narrow highway they finally came upon the town of Virginia City. Passing the little campground and trailer park on the right they made a left up a drainage that bore a sign that read "Rudy Range Reservoir." For several miles they passed some fine ranches with huge stacks of giant square bales of hay stacked out on the ground with no cover. The winding dirt road followed the picturesque little river farther and farther up into the mountains. Coming around a turn they saw two cinderblock cabins ahead, one on each side of the road. A sign that looked like a forest service sign in front of the cabin on the right side of the road said, "Warning! Quinane Crossing."

"What is a Quinane?" Davy asked John.

"Don't know, maybe a bird or something, but this ought to be the place on the left."

They pulled into the yard and stopped the truck. There was the sound of wood being split in the backyard. John and Davy got out and walked around the house. Beside a large pile of wood a man almost as tall as John, wearing a pair of coveralls and no shirt, was setting a chunk of wood on a massive chopping block. His long arms were well-muscled as was his chest. A white flowing beard dropped from his ruddy face halfway down his chest. Turning around and looking at the Deans, the old man said in a Scandinavian accent, "Can I help you fellers?"

"Wouldn't think you would have forgot me so quick, Svenson. It's only been forty-couple years since we tore up a bar fighting at that there Fisherman's Wharf in San Francisco. You stabbed me in the ass if I remember and the scar don't lie. We was fighting over a little ole redheaded Irish girl named Rosemary Nicole," the elder Dean said.

Svenson looked around at John and in his appealing accent said, "Well, Mr. Dean. I didn't think I would have to tolerate you and your gluttonous behavior in this world again. But good to see you old comrade! Did you bring my guitar back to me? The one you stole?" The big Swede offered his hand and John shook it enthusiastically.

"No, I bought that guitar fair and square and it's safe back in Virginia."

"Who is the young pup backing your play today? He must be a patient young man to put up with your company long."

"His name is Davy Dean and he's my grandson," John responded. Svenson just kept on splitting wood.

"Dandy!" he said. "Pleased to make your acquaintance, young man. I hope you grow to be a better man than your hateful old grandfather. What in the world are you doing here at the end of the earth, John? Did you finally get run out of Virginia?"

"We're headed to Alaska to see if we can find my son, John Jr. On the way I wanted to see if you were still alive. By the way, what's a Quinane?" John asked, pointing toward the sign across the narrow gravel road.

"That's the old fart that owns the cabin across the road. He's an accountant from California and he comes up here all the time and bothers the hell out of the neighborhood. Gets drunk on Johnnie Walker Blue at a couple of hundred dollars a bottle and rolls around in the road. Couldn't drink no regular-priced liquor if he had to. Says one of his clients gives it to him. A whole case of it at Christmas. I had the sign made to keep him from being run over so quick when he gets drunk and crawls around in the road. I think he might be part Jewish. Fancies himself a Mountain Man. I used to keep his wife satisfied for him until she died seven years ago from cancer. She was something else—a lot younger than him and a hot blooded little thing. They found a lump in her breast one day in July and she died in November. Messed up a good hunting season. Soon as the funeral was over he drove up here and stayed the whole winter. He gets drunk and walks around yelling for her sometime in the middle of the night, slobbering and bawling and I have to go kick his ass and put him in bed. I live thirty miles from the nearest grocery store in the mountains of Montana and I have to put up with neighbors like that."

"You still do any guide work, Carl?" John asked shaking his head and wanting to change the subject.

"Not very often. I got plenty of wood. Kill an elk or a moose every year to make jerky and keep the freezer full. Social Security and the army pension pay for the electricity and the taxes. don't have anything to drain me dry like grandkids, illnesses, or paying divorce lawyers. I can live cheap up here. I got a couple of horses and like to ride out on a jaunt sometimes for a week or two. I help my neighbors the Andersons on their ranch when they need an extra hand. There always seems like there's something to do. I hope I go quick when my time comes. I wouldn't be no good at laying in a bed with someone wiping my backside for me," the old man said as he brought the axe down on another chunk of wood, sending the halves flying.

"I feel the same way," John said. "I was in one of them homes for a while. Some folks like it just fine but I didn't. Davy here rescued me and by golly, here we are."

"Mr. Svenson, did you ever guide any famous people?" Davy asked. "Grampap used to show me your advertisements in Field & Stream magazine. Looked like you catered to some high-class folks."

"Yeah. I took out a lot of movie stars and politicians over the years. I met that Hemingway feller once while we was fly fishing. The most famous one I ever guided was Babe Ruth," the Swede stated. "That one almost ruined me too, it did."

"What do you mean?" Davy asked with a puzzled look on his face.

"I never cheated in the guide game. Never. Most of my competition did, with baits and whatnot. The Babe was a first-class guy. I don't give a damn about what anyone said or wrote about him. I spent two weeks just me and him camping and hunting and he was all right. He hired me to take him on a grizzly hunt. I took him to every likely place I knew of and he hunted hard but it was just one of those times when nothing seems to work right. It was the last day of the hunt and I just had to get him a grizzly. Hell, son. He was Babe Ruth! So I cheated. I took him over the line into Yellowstone and got the Babe a damn grizzly. But you gotta understand, son. He was Babe Ruth!" the Swede said with a pained look in his eye. "Why in the world am I telling you this musty old story? I have no idea. It's been on my mind bothering me all day. Please don't tell anyone. He's dead and gone but I wouldn't want anyone to know he cheated on killing a bear even if he didn't know he did. By God, he was proud of that bear. It was a big one too! Made a good shot on the nasty feller!"

"You didn't tell him you was in Yellowstone did you?" John asked.

"Hell no. He wouldn't have gone if I had."

"Well, then, he didn't cheat if he didn't know. You cheated though. Just like when we used to fight. You'd pull out that fish-skinner knife of yours. I still got scars on my ass where you carved me. And we was supposed to be friends!" John exclaimed.

"Let's go in the cabin and get a bowl of beans. You boys can stay the night if you wish. Davy, you can even stay in the cabin if you like. I got an extra bunk. Old man, if you still snore like you used to you can sleep in the back of your truck. I don't care to hear you suck on your swollen tonsils ever again like you did in Korea."

The evening was filled with stories of wars, whores, and other times long gone. Davy lay in a bed beside an open window and listened to the two old giants fill in each other on forty years of living after their army days. He learned many new things about his grandfather, some of which startled him. Even though he was bone tired his efforts at falling asleep were unsuccessful. Memories and visions of Connie Pencilschwietzer's love making and her naked, hot body tormented him. Rising from the bed he walked out on the porch and asked Svenson if he could make a long distance call on his telephone. Svenson told him to help himself and they could settle up later on the bill. John asked who he was calling and didn't get an answer. Davy took a folded piece of paper out of his wallet and dialed the number. His hands were sweating and he was praying Bob didn't answer the phone. It rang seven times and just as he was getting ready to hang up he heard Connie's voice on the other end.

Much to his relief, she said she was glad he had called. Bob was asleep. Davy had forgotten to take into account the difference in time. Small talk ensued about where they were and where they had been. Davy heard the screech of the screen door as she went outside on the porch and shut the door behind her.

"Why didn't you tell me you were leaving so quickly? I have worried myself to death wondering if you were upset with me."

"We just needed to go. Grampap wants to make it to Alaska before the bad weather catches us. I want you to know something, Connie," he whispered into the receiver. "I can't hardly think about nothing but you."

"I feel the same way, Davy, but those feelings have to be controlled. Poor Bob has not handled this thing like I thought he would. He drinks far too much now and asks me embarrassing things about what happened between you and me. Details, if you know what I mean. I didn't think he would do that."

"What'd you tell him?" Davy asked in an alarmed tone.

"I only tell him you were gentle and kind. I refuse to tell him you were like an incredible young stallion. And a most effective one too. I'm sure I am pregnant."

Her words rocked him. "Connie, you don't know that yet, it's only been a week! I have to tell you something though."

"Well, say it then."

"I think I'm in love with you!" he blurted out. "You're the most beautiful and wonderful woman I have ever known."

"I have feelings for you too but that can never be, you dear, dear young prince. That can never be. It would kill Bob and he's my husband and it's sinful to dwell on it. Good night, Davy. I pray for you constantly and hope you'll remain our friend." She hung up the phone before he could even say good-bye.

# Chapter 51

They stayed another night at Svenson's and he took them up into the high country to check a herd of cattle the Andersons had on a government lease plot. A glacier had torn the top of a mountain off eons ago, creating a rounded, gentle and passable top that lay among the jagged peaks of its neighbors in all directions. Svenson pointed out bull elk and literally hundreds of mule deer. Both John and Davy were amused at the mule deers' distinctive pogo stick type of bounding. When the Swede drove them back down into the flat bottoms of the Anderson ranch, Svenson suggested that John get out and ride on the back.

"You can hang onto the roll bar and really get a good view from back there," he said. "I have a surprise for you that I'm sure you'll never forget. Trust me."

"I get uneasy every time you tell me to trust you," John said as he struggled up on the bed. Standing up, he spread his feet and grabbed hold of the roll bar directly behind the cab. Svenson took off, gradually going faster and faster across the flat river bottom pasture toward a herd of antelope in the distance. When they drew near, the startled animals began running and Svenson chased them, staying right on their tails. Davy looked at the speedometer and saw they were going nearly seventy miles per hour across the flat river bottom. Something started hitting the windshield that looked like wet M&Ms and within a minute the window was covered with brown freckles. Svenson was laughing like a fool and Davy was suddenly worried his grandfather might fall off.

"Stop this truck right now!" he cried out in alarm. To his relief Svenson brought the truck to a halt.

Jumping out, Davy looked up on the back of the truck and was relieved to see his white-knuckled grandfather standing in the same spot, holding onto the roll bar with white knuckles clinched tight. His face and shirt were covered with large brown freckles. Svenson took one look at John and began laughing uncontrollably and finally rolled on the ground holding his sides. John pulled out his handkerchief and began wiping his face.

"Darn things started shitting when you got close to them, didn't they?" John said. "And you knew they would!"

Svenson only laughed harder. Davy wanted to kick the old Swede in the pants, thought better of it and a smile sneaked onto his face too. John climbed down off the truck and motioned for Davy to get back in the passenger side. He walked past his old comrade and rolled behind the wheel of the still running truck. Davy was already in the passenger seat and John jerked the truck in gear spinning dirt and gravel all over the prostrate Swede who was still on the ground laughing.

"You gonna leave him there?" Davy asked.

"Yes, I am. At least until we drive over to that little river and I wash up some," John said with a smile. "That old Swedish meatball loves a good joke. We'll let him think we're really mad and he has to walk ten miles home. That'll turn it around on him. It was a pretty good joke. I sure didn't know antelopes start crapping when they get scared. I thought I was going to fall off when he was going that fast. He could have killed me, the old fool! He always would do any crazy thing for a good laugh. Imagine. Acting like a kid in his mid-seventies. No wonder no woman would ever tolerate him for more than one night."

To make up for his prank Svenson fixed elk steaks over wood coals along with baked potatoes and a bowl of steamed spinach that evening. John and Davy ate their fill and relished the elk meat. Davy asked the Swede if he had ever been up to Fairbanks, Alaska, and he said he hadn't. "Would have liked to whack one of those really big grizzlies they grow up there but maybe in my next life. Reckon if I was to drive up there I'd go due north of here and catch Highway 15 north to Calgary and then take the Alcan Highway northwest to Fairbanks. It's a long, long drive they say. That little woodpecker head Guinane went a couple of years ago after his woman died. Said them people up there don't like laws and such. I reckon they're even more independent than we are here in Montana."

The next morning the two old-timers said their good-byes and shook hands. Svenson invited them to come back but John told him, "That boy there may come back sometime but I won't make it no more. I expect this will be our last time on this earth face to face." John looked Svenson in the eye and said, "I have to ask you, Carl. Do you know Jesus?"

"Yeah, I know him. That is if you are talking about the Mexican feller that works for the Andersons. His name is Jesus. If you are talking about that other Jesus that toted a cross, I don't feel like I need him much."

"You need to reconsider. I brought you something to remember me by," John said. He went to the truck and pulled out a box containing a Good News Bible from under the front seat. "I want to leave this with you and hope you'll read it. I got baptized by a preacher back in Virginia and it's been the biggest relief to me. I want you to consider it, Carl. You're a good man even if you are quick to carve a little on your buddy with a knife and pull childish jokes with antelope turds."

Svenson took the Bible, thanked him sincerely, and gave John what Davy thought was the most awkward hug he had ever seen any human being give another. "Thank you, my friend." Svenson said. "Never owned one of these before. My own daddy was a devout atheist and my mother died when I was born. I'll read it every word. But I expect the other Mexican Jesus is more dependable." With that said, the big Swede turned on his heel and carried his gifted Bible over and laid it on the pile of wood. He picked up his axe and as they drove away they heard it fall on a big chunk of wood that would find the fire that winter when the snows came.

The Deans drove all day north, passing through Butte and then Helena where they crossed the Missouri River seven times before pushing on to Great Falls where they spent the night in a little town called Shelby. The next morning was cool and clear. Approaching the Canadian border at a little town called Sweetgrass, Davy exclaimed, "Look there, Grampap! Look at that Indian on a horse. Looks like old Kill Buck himself!"

"Well I declare!" the old warrior said. "Ain't that a fine statue! Old Great-Granddaddy Kill Buck would have been proud. I wish them Whetzel boys that murdered him and a lot of other Indians could see it."

At the border there were several Canadian Agents wandering around. They looked at Davy's driver's license and asked to see John's identification. "Where you men heading?" asked the tallest one.

"Driving up to Fairbanks, Alaska, to see my father," Davy responded.

"You fellows don't need a passport but you do need to show us you have means to travel. Do you have any credit cards or cash on you?" asked the big man.

John pulled out his wallet and displayed a stack of one-hundred-dollar bills an inch thick. "Is that enough for you, son, or do I need to get in the back of the truck?"

"Drive carefully and have a good trip," the man said with a smile. "Don't lose all that money gambling at Whitecourt."

As the Deans pulled away to the north Davy asked John, "What's Whitecourt?" John responded that he didn't know.

They saw a sign that said, "Speed Limit 110." It took them a few miles to figure out that meant kilometers and not miles per hour.

Passing through Lethridge and then on to Calgary they started noticing a few oil wells and refueled at a Husky Gas Station. Moving on north to Edmonton by Highway 39, west to Highway 22, and then Route 43 to Valley View, they finally found "Whitecourt." The tired travelers spotted a sign boasting "Off Track Horse Race Betting, Big Screen TV, Pool Table At Gina's Lounge." Under the sign in bright orange letters it said, "A Friendly Place to Stop."

"I believe we should stop here!" John said. "Looks like our kind of people."

Gina's Lounge was filled with tough-looking oil rig workers and farmers. Since they had been on the road so long Davy and John booked a room, ate a hearty supper at the diner, and went straight to bed. Along about midnight Davy woke up to the sound of men yelling and a woman screaming in the parking lot. He peeked out the window in time to see a policeman hit a big farm boy over the head with a baton. The farm boy wilted under the blow and was unceremoniously dumped in the back of a van that had a star on the side of it. Davy checked the locks on the door and went back to sleep listening to John's snoring, wondering what happened to the woman who had screamed and woke him up.

The next afternoon found them pulling into Dawson Creek and they got out of the truck at Mile Post 0 of the Alcan Highway. Davy asked a truck driver who was stopped there if he would take a picture of him and his grandfather at the sign. They posed handsomely as the picture was snapped on their five-dollar disposable Kodak camera. Back on the road again they headed northwest through a lot of empty country and spent the next night in the back of their truck in a little place called Watson Lake, where they crossed over into the Yukon Territory. The next day found them traveling through Kluane Lake at Kluane National Park and Preserve, passing a sign that read, "Cross Border At Beaver Creek" and other signs with warnings saying, "Road Construction Ahead- Blasting." The road changed from hardtop to gravel and then to dirt. They passed the south side of the lake on narrow roads carved out of sheer rock cliffs and squeezed past tractor trailers that looked like they were jackknifed coming around some of the sharp corners.

"I'll be darn glad to get off this cliff!" Davy exclaimed, his knuckles white around the steering wheel.

Late that afternoon they stopped at a little town named Beaver Creek at the border finally crossing into Alaska. Pushing on that evening along Route 2, the Alaska Highway, they spent an uneventful night in a little motel at a place called Tok where Route 1 forked off to the southwest toward Anchorage. The next morning bright and early they resumed their trek, passing Eielson Air Force Base before reaching the city of Fairbanks.

"Look for signs for Route 3 headed south toward the town of Nenana. It shouldn't be far," John said. "We get to Nenana, then we need to find the Sheriff there and see if he can tell us where to find your dad."

Davy was in fact starting to get extremely nervous about meeting up with his father. Perhaps they would find out he had died or simply disappeared like he supposed a lot of men did in Alaska. Or even worse, maybe if they did find him he might run them off. That would be the hardest thing to deal with. Just thinking about his father took his breath away a little bit and made his palms sweat. He looked over at his grampap who glanced up and looked him in the eye, seeming to know what the younger Dean was thinking.

"Every man has to do what he has to do in this world, Davy. I failed at being a good daddy to your father. I've failed at darn near everything I've ever done in this world except soldiering. I was good at that and setting stone. Let's see if we can find your pappy and see what he's up to. Maybe we can patch things up a little."

"I hope he don't run us off, Grampap. I don't think I could stand that."

# Chapter 52

Sheriff Glen Weatherholtz of Nenana, Alaska, noticed a Dodge pick-up truck with Virginia tags pull into the grocery store parking lot where he was sitting in his truck writing a report in his vehicle. He watched as the two men slowly stopped and got out studying the police markings on his GMC Jimmy. The driver was a good-looking young man who appeared unsure of himself but the old man that exited the passenger side looked like he was on a mission. The Sheriff noted his extraordinary size immediately. Few men passed through town who were physically bigger than the Sheriff himself, who was a very large man. "Bigfoot Weatherholtz" everyone called him and he didn't mind at all. It wasn't unusual for him to stick his big foot up hardheaded people's asses when they needed it. Knife scars on his arms and a healed-over bullet hole or two were proof that Bigfoot Weatherholtz was the rightful "Bull of the Woods" in the Nenana area. He was a fair man who never backed down in any circumstance but was smart enough to retreat to a better position from where he could launch a successful fight. Bigfoot was a fair, well liked, and respected law man in a place where rough, tough, and fiercely independent people live.

"What can I do for you men? If you're looking to fish in the Ohio River you came a little too far north and west," he said with a smile.

"My name is John Dean, Sr., and this here is my grandson Davy Dean. We crossed the Ohio a couple of weeks ago and made a wrong turn at St. Louis. Ended up here," the old man said with a smile as he shook hands with Bigfoot. "You can help us, sir. We're looking for my son, John Dean,

Jr. The last we knew of his whereabouts we got a Christmas card that was post marked here in this town. You know of him?

"Well, sir. I do know him. He was around here for a couple of months about two or three years ago. He and I didn't see eye to eye on a few issues. He moved on. Somebody called my office a while back asking about him. Was that you?" the Sheriff asked.

"Yes sir. I called about a year ago," John replied. "I think I may have talked to your secretary. She said she didn't know him."

"That's not surprising. You probably talked to Mary and she wouldn't have known him. As a matter of fact she isn't here anymore either. A lot of people come through here and head somewhere else. He wasn't here long. Ran a bulldozer for Elmer Bentley until they fell out. Your son ain't no stranger to 'Ole John Barleycorn'. He was here long enough to make a few dollars and buy some provisions. Then him and his wife and kids got on a track vehicle and went over to Crowfoot. Haven't heard anything about him since," the Sheriff drawled.

Davy looked at John with wide eyes and blurted out, "Wife and kids?"

"Yeah, he's married to an Athabascan Indian girl they call Roxey. I believe he has three or four kids. Couple of little nips. Two boys and she was pregnant with another one when they took off from here. The oldest one might be six or seven now. A pretty big kid he was and stout looking for a youngster. Reckon he takes after his grandfather. You're a right good-sized fellow, sir," the Sheriff stated looking at John. Turning his head to Davy he said, "I take it you didn't know you got some half brothers, did you young man?"

Davy didn't answer immediately but a perplexed look on his face confirmed the Sheriff's supposition.

"Can you tell us where we might stay tonight and then give us directions to this Crowfoot place so we can go there tomorrow and look him up? It's getting late today and we could use something to eat," John inquired.

"You can't drive to Crowfoot. Most of the time a track vehicle can't get there and you have to fly. I have a friend that will take you in his bush plane for a hundred dollars or so. I have a couple of bunks and a shower in my garage that you're welcome to use tonight. You can leave your truck at my place while you're gone and I'll watch it for you. There is a little diner on the other side of the village that serves some good grub. You can buy me a steak to pay for your keep, if you don't mind my company for supper," the Sheriff offered with a smile.

"Can't beat a deal like that," John replied. "Yes, sir! That would do just fine."

"Follow me up to my house then," Bigfoot said.

Heading south along the Tanana River, the spectacular vista to the left was backed by a majestic mountain range looming behind the wide, swirling, slate-colored water. On the right, standing in stark contrast to the raw power and beauty of nature on the left were rows of doublewides set up in the air on cinderblock piers. Pulling into one of the houses the Sheriff stopped and parked his vehicle and the Deans pulled in beside him.

"Looks like you folks might be irritated with high water every once and a while," John drawled.

"Why yes, sir, we are. Back in 1967 we were darn near wiped out by a flood," the Sheriff answered. "You fellows can take whatever gear you got into the building out back and make yourselves at home. There's clean wash cloths and towels on the shelf beside the shower. Knock on my door when you're ready to go eat. I might take a little power nap myself."

The garage was a Spartan affair with a couple of old army bunks lined against the wall beside a sink, a toilet, and a shower stall. A snowmobile, a Honda four-wheeler, and a portable climbing tree-stand took up most of the building. A cluttered work bench and large assortment of tools hung from the ceiling and walls.

"What do you think about Dad being married to an Indian girl with three kids?" Davy asked his grandfather.

John chuckled. "Your daddy was always difficult. Reckon maybe he ain't changed in that respect. Davy, you just got to resign yourself to the fact that you can't control anybody in this wicked world but yourself and sometimes that is a chore too great for a simple human. Let's just see what happens and roll with the punches. Look on the bright side! You got three half-brothers to get to know. Maybe they'll be interesting. I ain't going to live forever and having somebody you're blood related to ain't the worst thing that can happen. They're far away enough that they likely won't bother you in Cambridge County if'n you don't want them too."

"I don't know, Grampap! I almost fell down when that Sheriff told us about Dad. I couldn't hardly breathe. I expect he might be pissed we're here."

"Well, we tried to contact him, didn't we? The wind don't have an address and that's what John Jr. is, the wind that blew to the north land. This is some powerful country, ain't it? Never thought I'd get to see it. Finland was this far north but fairly flat what we saw of it. This place is still wild yet. I hope we see a grizzly bear or two. I'd like to shoot one and show those red-headed Trumbo boys the claws. I bet it would scare the crap out of them," the old man said with a grin.

"You're still pissed about that buck you missed and they got!" the young man teased.

"Get your skinny little butt into that shower while I check out this bottom bunk," the old man snorted.

The dinner at the diner was excellent and also very expensive. The Sheriff wasn't embarrassed to run up the tab for John. He ate until Davy was certain his grandfather had been bested at the table.

That night as he lay in the top bunk trying to sleep, Davy's thoughts were deep in the womb of Connie Pencilschwietzer as he wondered about the little Dean who might be forming there in his cradle of warm amniotic fluid with no clue of his origins. Davy fell asleep with the memory of the musky, erotic smell of her body.

# Chapter 53

John Dean, Jr., was going fishing. His wife, Roxey, and the kids were taking a nap. The long summer days that almost didn't end made it necessary for the little ones and their mother to take a siesta around one in the afternoon even though the shadows of the first of August were lengthening. The little family lived in an abandoned shack they had taken over in the wildness of Alaska. For almost two years his little clan had survived pretty much on their own by hunting, trapping, and keeping a large garden. Roxey was good at canning, drying, salting, and smoking meat, fish, and vegetables. Their large root cellar was on its way to being filled with enough potatoes and cabbage to see them through the looming, long winter.

John Jr.'s head was clear and his color better than it had been in years even though he was rotting on the inside. Living isolated with his family alone and staying away from alcohol of all kinds was the difference. Roxey and the kids were the real beneficiaries of his abstinence. Gone were most of the depression and drunken rages that had so often resulted in violence and bad times. He did grow his own pot and enjoyed smoking a little bowl every evening. It helped to calm him down and mellow him out. Roxey liked to smoke it with him. He grabbed his poles and gear and started to walk down the path to the water when he looked up and saw his father and another young man walking up the path toward the house. The old man had a big silly grin on his face and suddenly he realized the other man was his son, Davy.

John Jr. stood still in his tracks as the old man walked right up to him and gave him an awkward hug. "You look good, Junior! Look good. I believe you're slimmer than you ever been!"

"Well, I expect I couldn't be more surprised if Jesus Christ and John the Baptist themselves come up that path riding bicycles," John Jr. said.

"We've improved ourselves quite a bit but we're a far cry from Jesus and the saints. Just your old Pappy and your son Davy," the old warrior exclaimed.

John Jr. stepped toward his son and offered his hand which Davy shook firm. Then they too exchanged a crude, stiff hug that men are inclined to share when words are not available to say what they are feeling.

"My God! You have turned into a fine-looking man, Davy. Fine-looking young man! Why didn't you send word you was comin'?"

"Tried to," Davy said. "Would be easier for you to tell us why you haven't written or called for the last couple of years. We thought you might be dead. The Sheriff back in Nenana helped us get here or we never would have figured out how to find you. Our truck is at his house."

"He ain't my favorite feller in the whole world but I was drinking a lot when me and him had dealings. I don't drink no more and won't allow no alcohol anywhere around here. I owe the Sheriff one for steering you right, getting you here, I guess," Junior said. "Let me go get Roxey and the kids up. You got three brothers you ain't never have met." He glanced back over his shoulder at his son's face, noted and understood the surprise, and said, "Things happen in Alaska that seem sort of natural here that ain't thought of in the same severe light back in Virginia. Kind of like Vietnam in some ways. It ain't the lower forty-eight. I got me a little woman that probably ain't much older than you, boy. Indian gal named Roxey. Come on in and meet her and the kids."

The cabin was neat but very small and poorly lighted. Low ceilings caused John Sr. to have to bow his head as he entered. A stocky, square faced Indian girl with black eyes and long hair sat up holding a baby to her naked breast in a wide bed along the back wall. Another child lay sleeping by her side. Curled up on a braided bench an older boy, probably six or seven years old with huge feet for his size sticking out from under his covers, awoke with an alarmed start and quickly lept to his mother's side.

"Roxey, we got family from the Old World come to visit. This here is my pappy, John Sr., and this is my growed-up son, Davy. Get us some coffee going, woman," Junior ordered. The young woman shyly got up and started a pot of coffee. "That big one is John Dean the third and I call him 'Sass'. That's short for Sasquatch. The middle one is Jake, and the little tit-sucker is Garnett, better known as Badger. You little fellers, meet your big brother Davy and your grand-pappy John."

The two older boys crawled back to the corner of the bed out of shyness and then Badger pointed his finger at his grandfather and said, "Big! Big! Man!" Roxey yelled something in her native language at the kids and started rattling pans while making coffee.

Junior plopped down in a rude chair and said in a matter of fact manner, "Probably a good thing you fellers showed up. The old doc that comes around every once in a while told me last week all these gut aches and chest pains I been having are going to kill me any time. Says I got something called pancreatic cancer and I won't make it another month. Says there ain't a damn thing anybody can do for me. I probably got it in my liver and lungs and God knows where else. That's why I've lost all this weight."

John Sr. let out a loud feral grunt and Davy looked at his father in shock. The look on Junior's face was cold and the corner of his mouth twitched slightly. It spoke volumes about a man hard as steel and resigned to his fate .

"Well, I don't know what to say," John Sr. blurted out. "Is this here doctor sure about his diagnosis? How can he tell all that out here in the bush?"

"Says he's sure as he can be without taking me to a Fairbanks hospital. I'm not going there. We kind of live off the land and don't even own this place here. It don't mean nothing anyway. We all gonna go sooner or later. Before we go any farther in this discussion let me make something perfectly clear. I won't set foot in no VA Hospital ever again and I won't accept no orders from *nobody* to make me leave here for no damn reason. That's settled and this here is where I'm gonna die. Right here!"

"Well son, I'm sorry to hear such shocking news but I'm glad we're here," the old giant muttered. Roxey brought them mugs of bitter, black coffee. She didn't offer sugar or cream. John Jr. looked at her and winked. "Ain't she a peach? Her family all died in a boat accident eight years ago. Damn submerged log had big roots that hooked 'em and turned the boat over in bad swirling waters. I took her in and we just kind of fell in together. One thing led to another, you know. Maybe you can take them all back to Virginia when you go. After I'm in the ground, that is."
No amount of talking could budge him on going for medical treatment.

John Sr. finally gave up trying but over the days that followed he would not give up on trying to save his son's soul. John Sr. explained his new faith in Jesus and would read the Bible to his son every chance he got as Junior weakened and finally there was a chapter John read that seemed to register on the dying man. John Sr. had opened the Bible at random one afternoon to Isaiah 35 starting at verse 8.

*There will be a highway there*
*And it shall be called the Highway of Holiness.*
*The unclean shall not pass over it.*
*But it shall be for others.*
*Whoever walks the road, although a fool,*
*Shall not go astray.*
*No lion shall be there, Nor shall any ravenous beast go up on it,*
*It shall not be found there.*
*But the redeemed shall walk there,*
*And the ransomed of the Lord shall return,*
*And come to Zion with singing,*
*With everlasting joy on their heads,*
*They shall obtain joy and gladness,*
*And sorrow and sighing shall flee away.*

John Jr. had his father read those verses over and over. They discussed what they thought it meant. Sass who was playing in the corner walked over to his dad and whispered in his ear. John Jr. smiled and said softly to the boy, "Tell your grampappy what you think. I believe you have it."

The boy who looked like he was cloned from his grandfather said quietly, "It means that if Daddy believes in God he'll be clean of all his bad things and can walk on a special highway through the shadows of the night world without worrying about the bears and wolves. It means your God will protect him."

"You reckon those lions and ravenous beasts they're talking about there could be the ones you and I faced in war? You reckon they could be all the terrible things we been part of?" Junior asked his father.

"I expect they are, son. For the life of me if I could go back to the days you were my little boy and read this book with you, maybe things would have been different. Sometimes I feel like I was a monster to you and your momma. Can you forgive me?"

"Mom took me to church every Sunday so part of the blame is mine. Let's just forget all that, Pappy. Let's just remember the good times. You did take me fishing a lot. I used to love that. Do you remember?"

"Yeah, I remember taking you fishing!" the old man smiled. "That other stuff, the drinkin' and stupid stuff were during my crazy days before they got me on the medicine. Sometimes I don't really remember a whole lot. I remember one time I got a lure caught in my back and had you cut it out with my pocketknife. You never even flinched when you was cutting. I was impressed with that."

"I was scared to death you was going to beat my ass if I hurt you."

"I know, son. I know."

"Promise me something, Pappy. Don't never whip my boys after I'm gone. You can spank them if they need it, but don't whip them like you did me. Not like you done me. I can understand a butt smackin' but a kid don't deserve what you dished out to me!" Junior said.

"I ain't like that anymore and I'm sorry, son. The craziness is gone now, thank the Lord! I try my best to be a good Christian but I fall short every day. That's the great thing. Once you give yourself over to His love you're forgiven. I was baptized and you wouldn't believe how it made my heart feel different," the old man whispered. "I read this book every day and learn more and more how to act and how to think. I am grateful for every day God gives me to learn more. I want you to walk down the Highway of Holiness with me, son."

"Keep reading to me, Daddy. Keep reading to me."

The kids were all like a bunch of friendly puppies with their new-found brother and grandfather. They went fishing and caught all they could eat and much more. Roxey smoked the rest and labored every day preserving food for the winter. John Jr. faded fast and more weight fell off him. One evening Davy asked him how he felt and he responded with a soft laugh, "If I was back in Virginia at the Piggly Wiggly in Cambridge I sure wouldn't invest in any green bananas!"

Then one morning he woke up from a troubled sleep, as if from a nightmare and said in a panic, "Baptize me, Daddy! Baptize me, please."

"I ain't a preacher, son!" the old man blurted out, a confused look on his face.

"You believe in that book. You come in here reading and testifying to me! Well, you've convinced me! If everyone lived by those ideas you've read to me this world would be a much better place. It said in that passage you read last night, something about '*If two or more of you are gathered in My name then I am there with you.*' I know He is here right now, Pappy. Baptize me! Wash away my sins unless you don't think there is enough melted water in Alaska to get the job done!"

John nodded to Davy who carried a bucket of drinking water over to him. John took the ladle and poured it over his dying son's head and said, "In the name of the Father." Another ladle poured over Junior's soaked head and John said in a choked voice, "In the name of the Son." And then the third he roared in great confidence, "And in the name of the Holy Ghost, your sins are washed away, son!"

Junior smiled a sad but happy smile and his father and his son placed their hands on his head. John prayed as three faces unaccustomed to tears were laced with them. "Lord, please accept us pitiful sinners into Your kingdom. Forgive us, Lord God, of our silly sins. Thank you for this blessing of John Jr.'s baptism!"

Roxey brought towels and dried off Junior's head and he promptly went into a deep sleep. Davy took the boys out to the water to fish while Roxey and the old man sat with his dying son.

Around ten that morning while Davy had the little ones down at the water, John Jr. let out a long sigh and quit breathing. Roxey never even shed a tear. She gave the old man instruction to help her carry her man out behind the cabin and they buried him in a deep hole she and the boys had already dug. Roxey went to find Davy and the boys and they all spent the rest of the morning covering the grave with a large pile of rocks. Sass cried a lot but Jake and Badger thought it was fun making the rock pile. The fun ended when Badger threw a small rock and cut Jake's lips and set him to bawling.

When they were finished John Sr. made a crude cross and beat it into the ground at the head of the grave. Roxey sang a long, repetitive song in her native tongue as John the third knelt beside her crying. Davy and John sat on a log and listened, keeping an eye on the two little ones.

When she was finished she took her oldest son's hand and led him to his grandfather. "You go back to Virginia. Take this boy. He look just like you, Old Man. Me and the little boys will have plenty to eat this winter if I don't have to feed you three any longer. I was your son's woman but I never loved him. Cruel circumstances brought us together and he was mostly good to me once he quit the bottle, although he would never buy me some of the things I needed or wanted. He was useful and after he quit drinking easy to live with but now he is gone. Take the one with your name and go."

# Chapter 54

A cold late September wind whipped the U.S. and Alaskan flags on the flag pole in front of the Post Office in Nenana as Davy talked to Sheriff Weatherholtz about the matter of taking John the third, or Sass as they called him, back to Virginia with them. The Sheriff said that was family business he had no desire getting involved in. John made arrangements to forward money to an account in a Fairbanks bank for Roxey and the boys. The Sheriff expressed his sympathies over the sudden loss of John Jr. and agreed to make sure regular deliveries of food and supplies would be sent to Roxey and the two little ones. The Sheriff said, "Roxey is a good gal and she knows how to take care of herself and the boys. I expect next spring she'll move back here around Nenana. Probably take up with some of her cousins. There's a lot of fellows around here that will eventually be courting her, that's for certain. After she's done grieving, of course. Them Indians are serious about their grieving and such."

The Sheriff took Davy aside and handed him an index card he had wadded in his shirt pocket. His office had received a phone call from a Connie Pensilschwietzer asking him to have Davy call her as soon as possible at her residence. The Sheriff said she instructed to have him call collect and sounded urgent. Davy went to a phone booth at the grocery store and dialed the number. On the tenth ring Connie answered the phone.

"You wanted me to call?"

"Davy! Thank God you got my message!" Her voice broke and she began crying until she blurted out, "Ten days ago Bob had too much to drink and took off in his car. He ran off the road and hit a tree. He died on Tuesday and the funeral was last Friday."

Davy couldn't respond for a while. She asked him if he had heard her. He finally got out a whisper and said, "Yeah, I heard you." After an uncomfortable thirty seconds that seemed like a year he was able to fill her in on the details concerning his father and his half brothers. She was astonished. Connie told him she had been having morning sickness and a pregnancy test kit from Rite Aid indicated positive. She was sure she was pregnant. Finally she broke down and begged, "Davy, please come home to me. I need you to see you!"

"I have a six-year-old brother and an old grandfather I got to take care of. There ain't no way out of it! I want you to know that I scarcely think of nothing else but you. I know it's been sinful. We'll be back in Virginia in a week or so. I'll try to call you in a couple of days when we hit Montana. Connie, I feel so guilty about Bob. I feel so damned guilty!"

"Don't even think about that! He and I planned what happened. It was our doing, not yours! There's no changing any of that now. It was his idea to start with, really! He was a good, good man and I loved him dearly but he had his weaknesses. Please come home to me, Davy Dean. I need you! You have no idea what a scandal this has caused! Bob having preached about the sins of excessive drinking and all."

"I'll be back in probably two weeks or so and we'll talk it out then," Davy said. "Things will work out somehow and I'll stand by you with this child you're carrying."

Retracing their route was easy and if Sass was missing his home he didn't show it at first. He sat in the middle of the front seat and took a keen interest in the scenery as they traveled. Davy drove fourteen hours the first day and kept up the grueling pace. Little Sass was amazed at the first motel they stayed in. He had never seen much television before and had never eaten in a big restaurant. The first night John and Davy took the beds and put the boy on the couch with a blanket and pillow. After the lights went out Davy heard him crying softly. Davy cut the light on and asked him what was wrong. Sass cried softly and said he wanted his mommy and daddy. Davy sat on the end of the couch, held his little brother's head on his lap, and patted him on the back. Soon the boy slept. Even though he was extremely tired Davy didn't move back to his bed until well after midnight and fell asleep to the rhythmic snoring of his grandfather.

The next morning four inches of snow was on the ground and Davy drove another fourteen hours. John and the boy had a big time counting animals they saw along the highway and playing I Spy.

In a little over ten days they crossed the Virginia state line on I-64 and within an hour pulled into their driveway. Home again.

Every night before he went to sleep, John prayed for Roxey and the boys. He prayed for the soul of his only son and he prayed for God's grace to forgive him of his sins. "Lord, please let John Jr.'s sins go against me. I was a piss-poor father. Please, let him be with his mother in heaven. Help me to be a good influence on this new grandson you have given me. Forgive me of my sins, Father God, for I know they're too many to count. And thank you for my grandson Davy who is the best of us all in this family. Amen."

The old man rolled over and fell asleep, ignoring the pains in his chest.

# Chapter 55

Things in the small community of Cambridge happened much too rapidly for the enjoyment of the local gossips. They would have preferred events to have happened with more time in between so they could savor each juicy detail by keeping the phone lines hot and the whispers going over a longer period of time. That way they could have collectively reviewed the scandals both real and perceived under the microscopic eyes of the community in a clearer light. They should have been able to enjoy the whole scenario at a slower pace, savoring every detail.

Davy and Connie got married at Christmas, practically before Pastor Bob was cold in the grave according to some. In an agreement McNally supervised, Davy sold his house and bought Ben Dean's cabin for a song, then turned around and gave Ben lifetime rights to live there. Davy, Connie, John, and Little Big Foot along with John's sister, Mary Alice, built a large log addition onto Ben's cabin and then a small barn and a few well-planned outbuildings. It was John's dream come true. He was back on his sacred mountain and the head of his clan.

Connie home-schooled Sass and in April she gave birth to a beautiful little girl they named Paivi, a good Finnish name. Paivi Pencilschwietzer-Dean. Davy bought a couple of milk cows and a few beef cattle, three sows and a boar hog, two dozen laying hens and a big red rooster. The mountain home was a happy place and the collective effort rendered the clan largely self-sufficient. Aunt Mary Alice taught Connie how to can and preserve the food they grew in a big garden. Sass loved to help plant and tend the vegetables. Aunt Mary Alice called him her weed-pulling machine and mothered the boy every chance she got. He was quick to help Davy milk the cows and do the farm chores too.

In the evenings Sass sat on the floor in total concentration, fascinated with "Uncle Ben", as he called him, and the tunes he played on the fiddle. It was inevitable. Soon he became Uncle Ben's student and the boy took to the fiddle like a duck to water. Within a year he was sawing along nearly as well as the old master. On an impulse Ben bought the boy a banjo at a pawnshop in Lexington and the young protégé was even faster solving its mysteries than he had the fiddle's. Ben grew so attached to the boy he made arrangements through Mac to leave everything he had to the boy in his will. Sass was the son Ben had never got to know and the boy worshiped him along with his giant grandfather John.

One evening at dark Davy and Sass were walking in from the barn and Sass was carrying a bucket of fresh milk. John was sitting on a log rolled up against the side of the barn. "Why don't you take that milk in to the women so they can strain it and get it into the cooler, boy. I want to talk to your Uncle Davy a minute." Davy sat down beside his grandfather and the boy trudged on to the house. Someone in the kitchen turned on a light.

"That boy's goin' to be just fine," the old man drawled watching his grandson enter the back door of the house.

"Believe he is, Grampap. He's the spitting image of you and he worships you and Ben. I swear that kid can do just about anything he tries to."

"Davy, I got something to tell you. I been thinking a lot about my long and crazy life. I want you to know you and your grandma Fern was the brightest and finest lights in it." Davy started tracing in the dirt with the toe of his boot. It always made him nervous when his grandfather started talking in a sentimental mode. "You know, when they put us out on that beach in Normandy we didn't have anywhere to hide or run. I recognized what had to be done and I was fortunate enough to lead myself and my buddies through it. That's why we succeeded. With no place to hide, it was do or die. Course lots of fellers did die. Lots of good fellers. I guess when your grandma died and I went to live in that Brethren Home, it was the same thing for me. You saved me from myself there. You led me out of it. You and God. That place was really kind of nice. I wasn't. God threw me out on the beach I called "Jesus' Launching Pad" and you were there to lead me out of it. I know you don't really believe me sometimes when I tell you I'm a full-fledged Christian. It's taken me a lifetime to get where I am now but I am so grateful He allowed me to find salvation. I feel so different than I used to. I want you to make sure that boy gets a good Christian upbringing after I'm gone. I see so much promise in him. I wish we could have brung the other two with us. I worry about them sometimes but I know the Lord will look after them. That Roxey is practical and tough."

Davy jumped up and two steps toward the house, stopped and said back over his shoulder, "Of course I'll look after him. It's my sworn duty and sole purpose in life to babysit the entire Dean clan. And you know what, Grampap? With God's help I just might turn a few of you out to a good ending. Let's go get some supper. My wife and Aunt Mary Alice have tenderloin, mashed potatoes and gravy, and collard greens for supper this evening. I'm starved."

John lived three more years and the family prospered. He died suddenly on a cold, frosty but sunny morning in February. He had taken to walking up on the hill to the edge of the woods every morning at first light and they could see him standing in the long rays of the morning sun in his old brown winter coat in the corner of the pasture leaning on a fence post looking up toward Reddish Knob. He would go up there to talk to Fern and say his prayers. Those watching could occasionally see him fling his arms around, talking animatedly with his maker and the oak trees. Sass and Connie were carrying a bale of hay to the calves when he looked up the hill and saw his grandfather lying on the ground with one leg bent the wrong way. He yelled for his Uncle Davy and they ran up the hill to John while Connie went to the house to call 911. He was still conscious when they reached him. Davy lifted his massive head and checked to make sure his mouth was clear. Sass knelt beside him, tears running down his cheeks, and held the big hand that had slain so many and had worked so hard. John smiled a crooked smile, the left side of his face hanging useless, and whispered, "I can see her, Davy. I can see her!" The old man coughed, gasped, and then sighed a long contented sigh and whispered, "Take me home with them Jesus!" Grabbing the hand of his great-grandson, he looked the boy in the eye. "Promise me you will trust Jesus! Just like in the song." Sass hugged his dying grandfather around the neck and said, "I promise, Grampap!"

His last words were, "Sass, take care of my guitar and deer rifle. They're yours."

That spring they planted irises and primroses on his grave where he lay next to his sweet, sweet Fern while the children came to play in the shade of the tree he so grudgingly helped to plant on that afternoon so long ago.

Some evenings in the quiet hour before dark, especially after listening to James Alan Shelton's CD playing his guitar to the Carter Family's "Old

Gospel Ship" Davy and Sass can still feel Johns presence and listening closely to the wind in the ridges it brings to mind the beautiful words of the bluegrass gospel song Vernon and Kelley Hughes wrote, "Trust Jesus" that John loved so well and alluded to on his death bed.

*Trust Jesus He'll guide you, no he won't deny you*
*Trust in the Savior everyday*
*Trust Jesus He'll feed you and He'll always lead you*
*Get saved and you'll live a better way*
*Oh I was a sinner, I thought I was a winner*
*I never ever took the time to pray*
*From those who believed him*
*They said one day I'd need him*
*I couldn't understand what made them say*
*Trust Jesus He'll guide you, no he won't deny you*
*Trust in the Savior everyday*
*Trust Jesus He'll feed you and He'll always lead you*
*Get saved and you'll live a better way*
*Then I realized without Him my life would be so dim*
*I asked Him to guide my life one day*
*He came into my heart and gave me a new start*
*Now I'm telling others on my way.*

A month later Mary Ann Bartley, Helen McNally, and Anna Crawford were in Anna's backyard planting flowers. Ellen Shifflett, the nosy next door neighbor and biggest gossip in Cambridge, came over to the yard fence and struck up a conversation. She eventually got around to pumping the ladies for information about the Deans and the "Mountain Clan" as the gossips of the town called them. "I'll tell you one thing. I don't miss that nasty old John Dean. Why he tried more than once to get me alone."

Mary Ann Bartley stood up straight and looked Mrs. Shifflett in the eye and said, "He was the noblest man I ever met and it would have been the best day of your life if he ever paid you any attention!"

Mrs. Shifflett turned and stormed toward her house and yelled over her shoulder, "My, my, Mary Ann! You have come a long way with assertiveness! I liked you better before!"

"John Dean was the hardest fighting, hardest loving, most noble man in the world. He was ... He was ... He was ... one hell of an American man and I'll never forget him!" she screamed and Helen took her by the hand in a calming gesture.

"No, Mary Ann, I expect none of us will forget him," Anna murmured with a smile. "Let's take a couple of these primroses over and plant them on his grave. He would like that."

Six weeks later Davy went to the post office and found a postcard from Montana addressed to his grandfather. Tears filled his eyes as he read the gnarly cursive script.

*Dear John,*

*Bet you are used to getting Dear John letters! Ha! Ha! This is the first letter I have written in years. Just a note to tell you your gift of the Bible was the greatest gift anyone ever gave me. Thank you! I have read the whole thing through twice and have been attending a little church in Virginia City. It is like I got adopted into a family and that is a new experience for me. The preacher is a good boy and I go to Bible study every Wednesday night. I got in a big argument when we was reading in the book of Jonah about a man living in a whales guts for a couple of days. Hogwash! The preacher said some of those stories are to be taken as examples so I guess I need to keep my ears open and my brain working. However, I found a verse in there that shook me up in Isaiah 35. Read it! It makes sense. It talks about a Road of Holiness. I want to walk that road too but I have not been baptized yet and for some reason it scares me. I know I need to do that, for sure. You and I faced North Korean snipers and tanks and here I am afraid of a preacher with a little water sprinkler! Ha! Hope God don't mind a jokester. If he does then I'll never make it. I figure he likes a little laugh now and then. If I keep trying maybe I'll put aside my rough and tough self image and get brave enough to take the plunge.*
*Trust Jesus and write back if you can,*

*Your friend,*
*Svenson*

*PS- And I ain't talking about that Jesus that works on the Andersons' farm. I'm talking about the one that toted the cross. The one you introduced me to. Ha! Ha! Besides the one that worked for the Andersons went back to Mexico and broke Anderson's daughters heart. Also, I want my guitar back!*

CPSIA information can be obtained at www.ICGtesting.com
265022BV00001B/3/P